The
TELEGRAPH
PROPOSAL

Books by Gina Welborn and Becca Whitham

The Montana Brides Inspirational Romance Series

Come Fly With Me (eBook novella)

The Promise Bride

To Catch a Bride (eBook novella)

The Kitchen Marriage

Anywhere With You (eBook novella)

The Telegraph Proposal

The
TELEGRAPH
PROPOSAL

Gina Welborn
and
Becca Whitham

ZEBRA BOOKS
KENSINGTON PUBLISHING CORP.
www.kensingtonbooks.com

ZEBRA BOOKS are published by

Kensington Publishing Corp.
119 West 40th Street
New York, NY 10018

All Kensington titles, imprints, and distributed lines are available at special quantity discounts for bulk purchases for sales promotion, premiums, fund-raising, educational, or institutional use.

Special book excerpts or customized printings can also be created to fit specific needs. For details, write or phone the office of the Kensington Sales Manager: Attn.: Sales Department. Kensington Publishing Corp., 119 West 40th Street, New York, NY 10018. Phone: 1-800-221-2647.

Zebra and the Z logo Reg. U.S. Pat. & TM Off.
BOUQUET Reg. U.S. Pat. & TM Off.

First Printing: November 2019
ISBN-13: 978-1-4201-4401-7
ISBN-10: 1-4201-4401-4

ISBN-13: 978-1-4201-4402-4 (eBook)
ISBN-10: 1-4201-4402-2 (eBook)

10 9 8 7 6 5 4 3 2 1

Printed in the United States of America

For our fathers.
You loved us well,
you loved our mothers well,
and you taught us what to look for in men
so we married well.

ACKNOWLEDGMENTS

After six stories and five years of our lives revolving around this series, it's time to say goodbye. We are so grateful for all the people who've contributed their professionalism, prayers, and loving support as we brought this cast of characters to life. As always, we are grateful to our agents, Tamela Hancock Murray and Bob Hostetler of the Steve Laube Agency, but we also want to include Karen Ball, who was Becca's agent when this series originally sold. A huge thanks to the entire Kensington Publishing family, most especially our editor, Selena James, who has been a delight to work with, and to Dr. Ellen Baumler of the Montana Historical Society in Helena, who sent us dozens of articles and pointed us in the right direction to help with historical accuracy.

But on this story, there's one person whose contributions went above and beyond: Kimberley Woodhouse. She is just flat-out amazing. Along with her professional assistance and personal friendship, she prayed over this story as though it was her own.

Thank you to our readers, who have shared their hearts with us, allowing us to hear how these stories touched or challenged them. Our prayer is always that we bring you joy and a little something to think about as you read.

Our families—our husbands, in particular—have put up with a lot so we could write. Life doesn't stop just because you are on deadline. How many conversations have been interrupted with, "Hold that thought. I just got a great idea and need to write it down before I forget it"? How many times did they have to make us dinner and bring it to our writing caves so we could keep typing? Only God knows, and He will reward them for their sacrifices. But here . . . on this page . . . we want to say that Matthew, Jerah, Jadan, Rhyinn, Niley, Steven, and Lyndell are the best cast of characters we've ever created, and that Jeremy Welborn and Nathan Whitham are men worthy of being the heroes of every story.

Finally, thank you to our triune God, who is the author and finisher of our faith. We pray we have brought honor to Your name by using the talent You gave us in a worthy manner. Amen.

"A man is lucky if he is the first love of a woman. A woman is lucky if she is the last love of a man."

—CHARLES DICKENS

"Friendship is certainly the finest balm for the pangs of disappointed love."

—JANE AUSTEN

"Do not remember the sins of my youth and my rebellious ways; according to Your love remember me, for You, LORD, are good."

—PSALM 25:7

Prologue

Thursday, January 5, 1888
Denver, Colorado

Marriage did not make women experts on men. Nor did owning or being the namesake of the Archer Matrimonial Company. Mother was wrong about how to handle their most difficult client. To prove it, Antonia invited a new friend to tea to glean insight on the man who continually rejected candidates for a correspondence courtship even though they perfectly matched his detailed description of suitable qualities.

"That's the fifth time you've mentioned this Hale Adams person." Antonia set her teacup on its matching bone-china saucer. "Is he important to you?"

Across the linen-draped table, Yancey Palmer traced her finger along the delicate pattern of yellow roses nestled in twining vines and deep green leaves rimming her china cup. Her blond hair was piled into a loose bun. She reached up and pulled out a tendril, wrapping it around her index finger. "It's a long, rather convoluted story."

But Antonia needed to hear it. His rejections of the nine

candidates previously sent to him made her despair of ever finding the perfect *Mrs*. Adams.

And she desperately needed to find the woman.

Antonia wanted to open a second matrimonial company location—maybe in Helena, Montana, as they seemed to be gaining clients there—but Mother felt Antonia was too young and lacking in wisdom.

Hardly. Twenty-four was plenty old enough, and *she* opened all the mail, read the biographies and required characteristics, and did the initial pairing of candidates. Mother rarely disagreed with the matches. Until Mr. Adams. Then their differing philosophies were severely tested. Mother said the agency's job was to give clients what they wanted. Antonia believed their job was to give clients what they *needed*.

The two weren't always the same thing.

Proving Mother wrong about Hale Adams was Antonia's route to greater autonomy now and—with a pinch of luck—running her own office in the future.

But she could never let Yancey Palmer know any of this because Hale Adams was a client of the agency. Antonia set her teacup on its matching bone-china saucer and stretched her hand across the table to touch Yancey's forearm. "Please. Tell me all about Mr. Adams."

Tears welled in Yancey's dark blue eyes. She let go of the curl to cover her lips with her fingers.

Surprised, Antonia sat back. "I'm sorry. I didn't mean to bring up a painful memory."

"It's not bad. At least, not entirely." Yancey picked up her teacup. It seemed she always needed her hands occupied. "I fell in love with Hale Adams when I was ten years old."

"Goodness. That's awfully young."

Yancey chuckled, though the sound was more bitter than humorous. "I can't tell you how many people have said the same thing, but I knew—I *knew*—he was the man I'd marry as soon as he punched Bruno Carson in the nose for trying to steal my plate of food."

Antonia leaned closer to the table in her eagerness. "Go on."

"He was as tall as the Gunderson twins, although my ten-year-old mind didn't quite comprehend that Hale was full-grown at eighteen while Isaak and Jakob were only eleven. All I knew was that this handsome stranger had come to my defense. Why wouldn't I fall in love with him?" Yancey stared into her cup for a long moment before she took a sip of her tea.

"What does Mr. Adams look like?" Antonia had met him back in October, but if she didn't ask about his appearance, Yancey might find it suspicious.

"He's about six feet tall, with blond hair and brown eyes. He wears glasses that constantly require adjusting." Yancey looked out the window, the teacup still in her hands. "He was my ideal for ten years, but . . ."

When she didn't go on, Antonia prompted, "But what?"

Yancey set down her cup before returning her attention to Antonia. "Are you sure you want to hear this?"

More than Yancey Palmer could know.

Antonia sat back, drawing her hands into her lap. "Why don't you continue with what happened after Mr. Adams rescued you."

"Hale was only in town for a few weeks visiting his aunt and uncle before leaving to attend law school. I didn't see him again for five years, but he was the man I compared every other boy to, and they all came up lacking. When he came back to Helena, I was fifteen and so sure of my love for him, I assumed he would return my affection instantaneously. But the first thing he did was begin courting my sister."

Antonia pressed the fingertips of her left hand over her lips. "You mean Luanne?" The lady had become a dear friend, but she'd never said a word about her younger sister ruining a promising relationship. "So what did you do?"

Yancey lifted one shoulder. "I went to Luanne and told her that Hale was mine."

"And she let him go?" Antonia asked more loudly than she intended. Several people sitting at tables nearby turned their heads to stare at her. She ignored them and lowered her voice. "Just like that?"

"Which means she didn't love him." Yancey's pronouncement was filled with conviction. "A truth that bore itself out when Luanne met Roy a year and a half ago."

Mr. Roy Bennett was a man who could take a girl's breath away, that was for sure. Luanne had fallen irrevocably in love with him in a matter of weeks. Antonia held back a sigh. If only she could make everyone as happy as Mr. and Mrs. Bennett . . . and find that kind of love for herself one day.

A tall, lanky waiter approached their table. He refilled cups and brought a tower of tea-time delicacies before slipping away as silently as he'd come.

Antonia selected a crustless cucumber sandwich. "What happened when your sister called off the courtship with Mr. Adams?"

"Nothing." Yancey shook her head, the curl dangling against her neck swaying in and out of the sunlight streaking through the restaurant window. "Absolutely nothing. At least, not on his part. I tried everything from coming up with excuses about why I needed to walk past his law office to dancing with other men at weddings to make him jealous. Nothing worked."

"So then what did you do?" Antonia took a bite of her sandwich, the crunchy cucumber a perfect complement to the smooth creamed cheese.

"After four years of fruitless pursuit, I gave up and got engaged to Joseph Hendry." Yancey selected a scone from the second tier and set it on her plate. "I was trying to prove that I was over Hale. I'm not sure if I was trying to convince *him* or me, but it didn't work."

Which was why the agency strictly forbade anyone from entering into an arranged correspondence courtship through them if they admitted to having been in love with someone within a year of signing up as either a prospective bride or groom.

"But that's not the worst of it. I . . . I think . . ." Yancey bent her head, her words soft. "I'm responsible for Joseph's death."

A gasp escaped before Antonia could stop it. "I was told only that you'd come to Denver to recover from the loss of your fiancé." She lowered her gaze to her cucumber sandwich. "I didn't realize he . . . he . . ."

"Was murdered?"

The sandwich fell from her nerveless fingers. She snatched it back up and placed it on her luncheon plate. "As you aren't in jail, I assume you weren't the one who killed him, so why do you feel responsible for his death?"

"I should have fought harder for him to stay in Helena." Yancey's voice was filled with regret. "Joseph said he was going to Dawson County to chase down a story linking a high-ranking government official to counterfeiting. I had a bad feeling about it, but . . . I wanted him out of town so I could think straight."

"About?" Antonia brushed breadcrumbs from the white linen tablecloth.

Yancey drew the cup of strawberry-infused butter closer to her plate but didn't make use of it. Instead, she stared into it for a long moment. "I was coming to realize that—although I'd irrevocably damaged my chances of ever being with Hale—I needed a husband of similar character."

"I take it Mr. Hendry was not such a man." Antonia picked up her sandwich again and took a small bite.

"Don't get me wrong." Yancey sliced into the pink butter, pulled out the knife, and sliced into it again. "Joseph was wonderful in his own way. We were simply too much alike. I told my parents my misgivings, but that I felt compelled to marry him because I'd accepted his proposal. My father said, 'Two wrongs don't make a right, darling.' It was his way of saying he didn't think I should marry Joseph."

Antonia agreed. "What did your mother say?"

"She never contradicted him or pushed me to set a wedding date." Yancey pulled the knife back out, laying it on the side of her plate without ever procuring any butter. "Of course, three days later—the day Joseph came back and I'd decided to end our engagement—he was murdered. He never would have gone away if—"

"Nonsense. It sounds like Mr. Hendry was a newspaper man." Antonia waited for Yancey to nod before continuing. "And I'll bet he was a good one."

A hopeful look—one filled with a heartbreaking desire for absolution—flooded Yancey's face. "That's . . . that's true. He was rather single-minded while pursuing a story."

With some single-mindedness of her own, Antonia steered the conversation until Yancey admitted she might not be responsible for her fiancé's death after all. Seeing the relief on her friend's face—and that she'd finally started to eat—was quite satisfying, but Antonia felt a new exhilaration. An idea had popped into her head and it refused to budge, despite every mental argument against it.

The way to heal a broken heart was often with a new romance. And not only would Antonia be assisting her new friend, she might be making her most difficult client happy regardless of his stated wishes. Hale Adams said he wanted a serious-minded woman, someone to share his passion for reading and who enjoyed staying at home rather than needing to be entertained every night of the week. In other words, a mirror image of himself.

Based on his rejection of all nine previous candidates, Mr. Adams recognized his need for someone to balance him on an instinctual level.

However, before Antonia took the audacious step of putting her plan into motion—pretending to be Yancey Palmer in a letter to gauge whether Mr. Adams would be interested in her—a few questions needed answering. "Tell me why you've been in love with Hale Adams all these years. There has to be more than him rescuing you from a bully ten years ago."

A soft glow filled Yancey's face. "He's a man of his word. If Hale Adams says he's going to do something, he does it and does it well. He's the most upstanding, moral man you could ever hope to meet. He writes a list of things he needs to accomplish during the day and always gets them done. His office is a mess, but he knows the contents of every pile. He's not as handsome or as impressively built as men like Isaak and Jakob Gunderson, but Hale commands respect simply by walking into a room. Everyone in Helena listens when Hale Adams speaks. You don't need to see his diploma from Harvard School of Law to know the man is brilliant. He's simply . . . perfect."

Antonia gripped her fingers together, excitement building. "Then what are his flaws?"

"If it were up to him, he'd stay inside his messy law office with its upstairs apartment all the time." The reply came without hesitation or repudiation. It was a simple statement of fact. "He's a faithful church member, but outside of Sundays, he has very few social engagements on his calendar."

"While you enjoy an active social life?" Antonia guessed.

Yancey smiled her answer. "And, I dare say, am often the life of the party. I would have been good for him, but that's water under the bridge now. No, more like cinders of the bridge I burned. It would be useless to try to reach him now, even if I wanted to. Which I don't. Not anymore." The regret lacing each word made it clear that Yancey still cared about Mr. Adams.

Deeply.

Antonia rubbed her bottom lip. In the past, when she'd felt this tingle of excitement racing along her spine, it meant she'd found a perfect match for one of her clients. Hale Adams and Yancey Palmer would never agree to a correspondence courtship with each other, but Antonia wasn't going to let a little thing like that stop her. She could set up a post office box independent of the agency, provide it to both Yancey and Mr. Adams as the mailing address of whatever pseudonyms Antonia chose for them, and recopy their incoming letters to omit any information that was too specific before mailing them to the recipient.

It just might work.

The tingle of excitement grew.

Shakespeare said a rose by any other name would smell as sweet. His beautiful words were, of course, describing two people who *couldn't* love each other based on their names alone. But the same reasoning applied for two people who *could* love each other if they didn't know the other's name.

If it was good enough for the brilliant William Shakespeare, it was good enough for Antonia Archer.

Chapter One

Friday, April 27, 1888
Helena, Montana

Yancey pressed the latest letter from Nathan St. John against her chest and sighed. The wait had been worth it. She'd picked up his letter on her way to the train depot but hadn't wished to read his precious words with people around. She'd brought it to work, where it seemed every person in Helena had come to visit the telegraph office. Each tick of the clock, blast of a train whistle, or call of the conductor had her itching to yank the pages from her pocket. But she'd waited for the moment the depot cleared of customers so she could rip open the envelope and devour Nathan's typewritten words. Four months ago, she'd been skeptical about Antonia Archer's declaration that she had a client who would be Yancey's perfect match.

Then Nathan's first letter arrived.

He'd described himself as blond, average in looks, of average height, and with an acceptable amount of ambition. Yancey could almost hear Hale Adams describing himself in the same way. The next two months of correspondence proved Antonia hadn't lied. She *had* found another Hale—only better because, with Nathan, there were no past mistakes or burned bridges for Yancey to overcome.

And her parents agreed.

After erring by accepting Joseph's marriage proposal without thinking it all the way through, Yancey consulted her parents before signing up with the matrimonial company. Then she showed them Nathan's biography and discussed her growing affection for him. So far, they all agreed that Nathan St. John seemed to be a wonderful match.

Yancey sighed and pulled the letter away from her chest to reread the last line.

I pray it isn't too forward of me to say that I am beginning to grow impatient with the constraints of a correspondence courtship.

Nope. Not too forward.

Not at *all*.

The sound of the office door opening set her heart to pounding. She didn't want anyone intruding on this moment, but she dared not ignore whoever it was.

Yancey turned her back to the customer, folded the letter along the crease marks, and stuffed it back into the envelope. Smiling because at least she'd had a few moments of quiet to read the letter in its entirety, she turned around to greet the intruder. "Isaak?" Surprise made her voice squeak. "What are you doing here?"

"Hiding. If you'll let me." He pointed at the wall behind the counter between the office and the depot.

It was ridiculous that a man of Isaak's size thought he could hide by keeping his back against the wall. The only people who'd be unable to see him were those who didn't come inside or who didn't glance through the office windows overlooking the platform. He was six feet, five inches tall, with broad shoulders topped by the second-handsomest face in all of Helena, Montana. Only his twin, Jakob, was better-looking. Yancey had always been partial to the younger-by-five-minutes Gunderson brother, which was why she hadn't quite forgiven Isaak for upstaging Jakob's dramatic marriage proposal to Miss Zoe de Fleur yesterday morning.

In front of the family's burning business, no less.

Yancey stuffed Nathan's letter inside her skirt pocket. "Be my guest. May I ask from whom you are hiding?"

A blush filled Isaak's cheeks as he scuttled through the narrow opening at the end of the wooden counter into the employees-only area of the telegraph office.

Her mouth fell open as realization struck her. "You're going after Zoe, aren't you? And you don't want her to see you until she's on the train."

He nodded. "I have Jakob's blessing, just so you know."

She wasn't completely surprised. Jakob's attentions to Zoe were like Fourth of July fireworks—a big, showy blaze that quickly faded into wisps of smoke. As a mail-order bride herself, Yancey had taken Jakob to task for his inattention, but she'd somehow missed that Isaak had quietly fallen in love with the dark-haired Frenchwoman. As Yancey was forming the words to ask if Isaak thought Zoe would welcome his attentions after she'd publicly rejected his marriage proposal—and Jakob's—a very different concern usurped her train of thought. "What about your mayoral campaign?"

Isaak scratched his jaw. "That was the other reason I wanted to get here early. We need to talk." He slid to the edge of the wall and craned his neck to peek around the corner through the glass-windowed doors into the depot. He then looked at the three large windows on the adjacent wall overlooking the train platform, a frown drawing his lips into a tight line.

"Would you like me to lower the blinds so no one can see us in here?" Yancey kept a tight rein on the humor attempting to bubble over at the high-and-mighty Isaak Gunderson skulking around like a schoolboy. He'd never skulked even when he *was* a schoolboy.

"That would be great." He scooted along the wall until Yancey could pass him.

She lowered each shade, the yellowed canvas casting a golden light onto the hardwood floors. Only the luggage porters observed her. She smiled and waved at them as she pulled down the last blind. "I'll stand here"—she pointed to a spot where she could observe the doors leading to the depot—"and let you know if anyone is approaching."

"Great." But after that pronouncement, he remained silent. He took off his black bowler and stared down at it.

Yancey had never seen Isaak Gunderson at a loss for words. And she'd known him her whole life. They'd practically grown up as siblings. At any other time, she would have teased him, but something inside warned her to keep silent. To wait until he was ready to speak.

"I . . . uh . . ." Hesitating? She barely recognized this Isaak. "I need you to do something for me."

"Of course."

He looked up, his unique eyes—a combination of moss green with brown flecks near the iris—boring into her. "Don't be too quick to agree. This isn't going to be easy for you, Yance."

"You only use my nickname when you're trying to butter me up, but I have to tell you"—she shook her index finger at him—"I'm immune to your charms."

His lips twitched into something resembling a grin. "This is about Hale."

Her chest constricted. It had been almost an entire year

since she decided to put aside her infatuation with the man, but—whenever his name came up unexpectedly—she still reacted. Bothersome yet true. She cleared her throat and kept her face impassive. "What about him?"

Isaak tossed his bowler on the countertop. "Before I tell you, I need your word that you'll keep this quiet."

"Of course." If she had a dime for all the secrets she'd kept over the years, she'd be as wealthy as Mrs. Hollenbeck.

"I've talked Hale into running for mayor."

Her natural enthusiasm that someone of Hale's caliber would agree to run vied with her misgivings about his ability to campaign. The man hated crowds. "How on earth did you manage that?"

"Told him he was the only man who could defeat Harold Kendrick. Helena deserves better than that crook, and Hale knows it." Isaak shifted his weight from his left foot to his right. "Winning is going to be an uphill battle for him, even with Uncle Jonas in his corner."

"Hale's not good with people."

Isaak shook his head. "I disagree. He's great with people as long as there aren't more than four or five of them to deal with at a time."

Yancey chuckled her agreement. "Do you remember last year at the Independence Day picnic? He arrived at noon sharp, stayed only long enough to eat and hear Mayor Kendrick speak, then took off the moment the official festivities were over. He probably spoke to a grand total of five people the whole time."

Isaak gave her another of his piercing glares. "No. I can't say I follow Hale's every movement with such . . . enthusiasm."

"It's not like I was watching him the entire time." Just forty-five out of the sixty minutes. How embarrassing.

"I need you to promise me"—Isaak pointed his index finger at her, then curled it into his fist, pulling his hand close to his chest—"I'd *like* you to promise me that you'll continue to help with the campaign launch a week from tomorrow and the July fourth barbecue—"

"—which I still think needs to be . . . something grander." She ducked her head so he wouldn't see the heat climbing into her cheeks. She'd entreated him to ask Zoe to cater a full-scale dinner, but with the future between him and the French chef so uncertain, she didn't want to rub salt into his wounded heart by mentioning it again. "Kendrick does a barbecue. Hale needs to set himself apart."

"I don't disagree." Isaak spread his hands, palms up. "But I have no more say in this campaign. You'll need to talk Hale into it." He took a deep breath. "Can you promise me that you'll continue to help with the campaign without being *enthusiastic* about working with Hale?"

Yancey placed her hands on her hips. "In case you haven't noticed, I've not chased after Hale Adams since last July."

"But you did admit to me back in March that you intended to break your engagement to Joseph Hendry because he wasn't Hale." Isaak lowered his chin and raised his eyebrows. "And that no other man has ever made you feel the way he does."

Yes, but that was early in her correspondence with Nathan. Soon after, their letters lengthened, deepened in substance, and made her heart soar. Hale may have been the first to make her feel like her feet left the ground at the mere mention of his name, but he was no longer the only one.

How grateful she was that falling for Nathan had gotten her over Hale.

Mostly.

But she was determined to transfer every bit of her hopes and dreams to Nathan St. John as soon as possible. It was difficult to fall hopelessly in love with a man without ever having met him face-to-face, but it sounded like he might send for her soon so they could begin the sixty-day courtship in Denver.

She hoped so. Oh, how she hoped so.

Isaak tugged at his shirt collar. "So? Will you promise to help Hale get elected until I get back? If I get back, that is."

Yancey dropped her hands to her sides and took a step closer to her friend. "What do you mean, 'if you get back'?"

He looked at the floor, but he was so tall, Yancey could still see his face. He sniffed and swiped his right hand under his nose. "I don't know if she'll have me."

Sympathy replaced every bit of ire she retained on Jakob's behalf over losing Zoe de Fleur. "You really love her? Don't you?"

Isaak nodded before raising his eyes. "I never understood it, Yance. How you could pursue Hale with such single-mindedness. Not until now."

Having someone as no-nonsense as Isaak Gunderson validate her devotion to Hale was too little, too late, but tears of gratitude stung her eyes. "Thank you."

"And now that I get it, I understand how difficult it will be for you to work with Hale without pursuing him. I'm not asking you to stop for always. I'm just asking you to stop from now until November. No tricks, no trying to make him jealous, and no stratagems until the election is over. After that"—Isaak raised his hands as though surrendering—"you can be as enthusiastic as you want."

The train whistle blew, announcing its imminent departure.

"Look, Yance." Isaak picked up his bowler. "I know I'm doing the right thing going after Zoe."

Yancey shot a glance at the shades she'd lowered. "Even though you're trying to sneak out of town without anyone noticing?" Her lips twitched. "You're hard to miss, Isaak."

He put his hat on his head. "My parents and Jakob have

agreed to say I'm taking a trip to replace what was lost when the store burned."

"A rather clever way to make people think you mean inventory instead of Zoe."

Isaak pressed his hat lower with the palm of his hand. "I don't want anyone knowing Hale has taken my place until he announces it himself tomorrow."

The train whistle blew its second warning.

Isaak inched closer to the corner of the wall. "I hate tossing the campaign to Hale then leaving town for who knows how long." He snuck a peek through the doors leading to the depot before returning his attention to her. "Please help with the kickoff next week and the Independence Day picnic. After that—if it's too hard—stop working on the campaign. Can you at least promise me that much?"

She reached inside her skirt to touch Nathan's letter. "I promise."

Later that day, across town

Hale Adams checked his pocket watch again. Four in the afternoon. After three hours of heated debate, the votes between Anaconda and Helena—the two cities vying to be Montana's capitol if it ever became a state—were still tied. None of the arguments, finger pointing, or pleas had swayed a single person to break rank and vote for a rival city.

At this rate, Montana would never become a state because they couldn't decide on a capitol city. Everyone crammed inside the sweltering room knew it.

Time to make his motion.

Hale stood and walked down the center aisle of the courtroom. City Hall only had offices and two courtrooms, one of which had been converted into a makeshift meeting room today. He reached the bar, pushing open the polished wooden gate to stand in front. "Gentlemen!" He had to shout his greeting three more times before the room quieted enough for him to speak in a normal tone of voice. "Can we all agree that statehood is our goal?"

Several nods and a few shouts of assent.

"Excellent." Hale turned his head left and right to make sure he had the attention of Harold Kendrick, Marcus Daly, and William Clark, the three men whose opinions every other man followed. They were seated behind the plaintiff's and defendant's tables, their chairs facing the bench seats filled with delegates.

Hale looked down at his notes, not because he needed to remember what he'd written but to draw everyone's attention. Uncle Jonas—who was sitting in the back row as an observer because his duties as territorial judge made his attendance too sporadic for him to be a delegate—had taught Hale the power of a dramatic pause when he was a young lawyer. He'd used the technique multiple times with great success.

The room quieted.

He lifted his head to find every eye on him. Kendrick and Clark glared like jealous schoolgirls watching a prettier girl flirt with a boy. Neither of them had been able to command so much attention. Daly looked like he always did—respectful and respectable—as he waited for Hale to speak.

He pushed his glasses back in place with a finger. "As we delegates are deadlocked, I move that we defer the selection of Montana's capitol. I have researched the legality of a delay, and it's entirely lawful. Once we achieve statehood, we can hold an election, and the good people of Montana can vote for whichever city *they* prefer to be their capitol."

Silence. Then the room erupted with applause.

"Hear, hear!" The shouts echoed around the room.

"I second the motion," was heard from different corners of the crowd as several men raised their hands.

Harold Kendrick pounded his gavel on the plaintiff's table. As mayor of Helena—for the time being anyway—he was hosting this latest round of debates. Kendrick scowled at William Clark, the foremost advocate of Anaconda for state capitol and the only occupant of the room more corrupt than Kendrick. "Well, Clark? Do you second?"

William Clark scratched his salt-and-pepper beard as he swept his gaze over the men—likely gauging their interest in the motion—before he said, "I second."

After the secretary nodded to show he'd recorded who'd moved and who'd seconded the motion, Kendrick called for a vote by show of hands. When a slew of hands went up, he changed his wording. "Looks like we have a majority, but let's be sure. All those opposed, show of hands."

Five hands went up.

Kendrick counted them out loud. "Of our thirty delegates, we have twenty-five for delaying selection of the capitol city until after statehood and five against. Anyone dispute my numbers?"

No one voiced any objection.

"Then"—Kendrick pounded his gavel with shattering force—"motion passed. Our thanks to Mr. Hale Adams for the brilliant suggestion. You should be a politician, Son. You'd make an excellent one." The last was a barb intended for Uncle Jonas, who had lost the mayoral election to Kendrick four years ago.

Hale thanked the mayor for his endorsement anyway. Too bad he couldn't announce his candidacy for mayor on the heels of it, but there was an order to things. He needed to talk to several people—not the least of whom were his aunt and uncle—before the general populace knew he was running. However, Kendrick's demeaning use of *son* needed to be countered. Hale gave the mayor a polite smile. "I'm glad you think so, *Harold*."

Kendrick's skin turned pink, then red.

Satisfied he'd made the impression he'd intended, Hale tucked his notes under his arm and returned to his seat. The meeting adjourned a few minutes later. He searched for his uncle while making his way through the delegates but didn't see him. He headed straight for Uncle Jonas and Aunt Lily's house, where his uncle—who had badgered Hale for almost four years about running for mayor—would gloat and say, *I told you so*, a number of times.

Couldn't be helped.

Hale stuffed his notes inside his leather satchel as he walked outside. Even though City Hall was a good mile away from the charred remains of The Resale Co., the scent of burned wood carried on the breeze. Thin clouds stretched across the sky like cotton pulled into wisps. No rain in the near future, unfortunately. The city could use a good dousing to get the smoky smell out of the air.

Hale lowered his gaze to the boardwalk a few feet in front of him so people wanting to chatter wouldn't interrupt him. He reached his aunt and uncle's house quickly.

He loved this house . . . or had come to love it in the last five years. Aunt Lily always had cookies or cake on hand for whoever dropped by, and Uncle Jonas—when he was in town—dispensed wise, fatherly advice. Ten years ago, when Hale's world fell apart, he barely knew his mother's elder brother and wife. Now they were dearer to him than his own parents.

After a couple of knocks, he opened the door. The scent of baking bread greeted him. "Hello? Anyone home?"

Aunt Lily's voice came from the back of the house. "Is that you, Hale? I'm in the kitchen."

Hale closed the front door behind him. He took off his hat and coat and hung them on the stand before strolling through the dining room toward the kitchen. This was the type of house he was looking to buy. Big enough to hold a family but not ostentatious. Tastefully decorated with comfortable, quality furniture. And filled with memories of holidays, meals shared with friends, and good conversation.

Uncle Jonas once said that while it was the husband's job to provide a house, a wise one allowed his wife to make it her home. Hale had plenty of money saved so his future wife could determine which house within his budget she wanted to turn into her home.

A decision that seemed to be drawing closer.

Smiling, he pushed open the door to the kitchen. The delicious bread smell was strong. "Mm. What are you baking?"

Aunt Lily held up a crescent-shaped roll. "It's a croissant. Zoe taught me how to make them when she . . ." Aunt Lily turned her head and wiped at her cheeks. "I'm sorry. I don't mean to be a watering pot, but I'm still upset about Zoe leaving town this morning after yesterday's . . . events."

Hale changed the subject to give her something else to think about. "Are these the rolls Mrs. Hollenbeck can't stop raving about? The ones you served at her welcome-home breakfast?" He picked up a still-warm croissant and took a bite. "Mm. Heavenly."

The compliment worked as he hoped it would. Aunt Lily turned back toward him with a tentative smile and nodded. "I'm glad you like them."

"Hale?" Uncle Jonas walked into the kitchen. "I was just about to tell your aunt about the meeting. Why don't you go ahead."

Mouth filled with flaky, buttery goodness, Hale turned to his aunt for help.

"Give the boy a moment to finish his bite, darling." She picked up another croissant and handed it to her husband. "Here. Now go on out to the dining room. I'll bring coffee in a few minutes."

Uncle Jonas winked at her. "You are a ruby beyond price, my dear."

"And don't you forget it." She placed two more croissants on a china plate and held it out. When Uncle Jonas took it from her, she waggled her hands at him and Halc. "Now run along, boys."

Laughter and loneliness vied for the same space inside Hale's chest at the loving banter. This was the kind of marriage he wanted, one in which a husband and wife teased and laughed and enjoyed each other. He hated that he might have to put his own happy ending on hold—yet again— because of someone else's actions. Isaak, however, had a much better reason than Yancey Palmer ever had. Hale swallowed down his bitterness. Why, after all these years, did her interference in his courtship of her sister still bother him? Luanne was now married to a fine man, and—in retrospect—Hale understood that his pursuit of her was more about wanting a home than wanting Luanne. He liked to think he would have come to the conclusion they weren't suited before he proposed marriage, but he never got the chance.

Because of Yancey Palmer.

Had that been the end of her meddling, he'd have forgiven her. But no. She made it clear to every eligible woman in Helena under the age of thirty that Hale was *hers*. No woman would have him for fear of going against her.

Well, he'd figured out a way around that.

News for later in the conversation. Hale swung open the door between the kitchen and dining room. "Actually, if you don't mind, there's something else I need to discuss with both of you."

Uncle Jonas's smile faded. "That sounds serious."

"It is, but it's a good serious." Hale glanced at his aunt to gauge her reaction. She held both hands to her chest. Hale reached out to touch her shoulder. "I promise. It's . . . it's about my future plans." He tipped his head toward the dining room. "Shall we?"

Aunt Lily lowered her hands and smoothed her apron. She eyed him as she passed by. "You're sure everything is all right?"

"Yes."

After piling three more croissants on the plate he held, Uncle Jonas winked at Hale on his way past. "A bit of sustenance while we talk."

Grinning because he was about to suggest the same thing, Hale followed his uncle into the dining room. He waited for his aunt to set out three china plates and then for her and Uncle Jonas to sit before beginning. "I have three things to tell you. Which would you like to hear first—personal, professional, or political?"

The older couple stared at each other for a full second—a silent conversation passing between them—before Uncle Jonas leaned against the back of his chair. "As it appears you've already thought about what you want to tell us enough to apply alliteration, why don't you go in the order that makes the most sense to you."

Hale's lips twitched. "As I was planning to do that anyway, I agree to your request."

Aunt Lily huffed. "You two and your humor. Just tell me already. Are they all about the meeting today?"

"The political one is." Hale sat down. "I researched the legality of putting off the selection of a capitol city and still being able to apply for statehood."

"And?" Aunt Lily reached for a croissant and set it on her plate.

"It's legal."

"I take it that because both of you are here"—she looked between her husband and Hale—"instead of in another five-hour delegates' meeting that accomplishes nothing, you proposed a motion to that effect and it passed?"

"Yes. Twenty-five to five." A proud smile softened what were the otherwise stark features of his uncle. "I had to refrain from standing and applauding, Son."

The praise and endearment warmed Hale's chest. "I'm glad you approve. Harold Kendrick—"

Aunt Lily *harrumphed*. "Don't tell me. He was one of the five dissenting. That man would oppose peace on earth and goodwill toward men if an Adams or Forsythe proposed it."

Hale took a croissant from the plate centered on the table. "Actually, he was so outnumbered, he not only voted for the motion but also said it was a brilliant solution."

The look of shock on Aunt Lily's face was as readable as the glee on Uncle Jonas's.

"Which brings me to my professional news." Hale took a steadying breath. Now for the I-told-you-so part of the discussion. "Isaak came to see me yesterday."

"Before or after the fire?" Uncle Jonas took a croissant and tore it in two.

"After." Hale added butter to his croissant, took a bite, and lost his ability to think about anything except the flavor filling his mouth. But the news he'd come to share could only be put off so long. Hale swallowed . . . and swallowed again. "Isaak talked me into running in his place."

Aunt Lily clapped her hands. "Oh, that's wonderful, Hale."

"It certainly is." Uncle Jonas had an I-told-you-I'd-make-a-politician-out-of-you gleam in his eye. "And as soon as you tell us your personal bit of news, you and I are going to have a long talk about what you need to do to defeat Harold Kendrick."

"Oh, yes." Aunt Lily turned to Hale. "But first, what's your personal news?"

Chapter Two

Hale felt his cheeks warming. He lowered his eyes, staring at the half-eaten croissant on his plate until he regained his composure.

"You've met a girl, haven't you?" Aunt Lily's voice was full of excitement.

Hale cut a look at her. "How did you know?"

She smiled with matronly warmth. "A woman can tell. What's her name?"

He couldn't help but smile. "Miss Portia York."

"I don't recognize the name. Do you, darling?" she addressed her husband.

"No." Uncle Jonas's forehead creased. "Is the York family new in town?"

Hale shook his head. Now for the part they might not like—although they liked Zoe well enough. So there was no need to be nervous. Yet he was. He wanted them to like Portia. To welcome her. Which was more likely to happen if he didn't surprise them with her sudden appearance.

Hale pushed his glasses higher on his nose and lifted his chin a bit. "Miss York and I were connected through the Archer Matrimonial Company."

Aunt Lily's eyes widened. "The same ones who brought Zoe to Helena?" She didn't sound upset.

Hale breathed a little easier. "Yes. Jakob asked me to research the agency when I was in Denver last October for that legal convention regarding new bankruptcy laws. I was impressed by their vetting process and decided to sign up as a client."

"How long have you been corresponding with Miss York?" Uncle Jonas sliced butter out of a clay crock and began slathering it onto one half of his croissant. His tone was noncommittal, a lawyer getting all the facts.

"Since mid-February." Hale cleared his throat. "And I very much wish to bring her to Helena for a sixty-day courtship period as a precursor to marriage."

Aunt Lily clapped her hands again. "Oh, Hale. I can't tell you how happy that makes me. Jonas, why are you frowning?"

"Because there's something the boy isn't telling us." Uncle Jonas took a bite of his roll, closed his eyes, and sighed.

"Well"—Aunt Lily leaned forward in her chair, her attention solely on Hale—"don't leave me in suspense."

"It's nothing bad, I assure you." Hale picked up his croissant. "I simply need your advice about whether now is the time to bring Miss York to Helena. It will come as no surprise to either of you that campaigning will be difficult for me."

Uncle Jonas *harrumphed*. "I am more than happy to help, as I've told you several times."

More like a thousand and one times.

"We can discuss that in more detail later." Hale added butter to the warm roll. "Right now, I'm concerned about Miss York. I might be rather busy"—and rather grouchy, given how much he anticipated hating campaigning—"and I don't wish to give her the wrong impression of me."

He'd finally found a woman he thought he could build a

life around. He didn't want anything to ruin his chances of success with her.

Aunt Lily reached over and put her hand on his arm. "I know this isn't going to be easy for you, but your uncle isn't the only one who will rally to your cause. I can think of at least a dozen women who will work tirelessly for you. Women might not be able to vote—"

"Yes they do." Jonas grinned at his wife before turning to Hale. "Indirectly, of course, but never underestimate the power of the woman behind the man."

A snicker came from Aunt Lily. "Now, Jonas dear, don't give Hale the wrong impression of marriage just when he's about to bring his girl to town."

"The boy is twenty-eight, darling." Uncle Jonas wiped the corners of his mouth. "And he's seen his fair share of both marital bliss and misery."

True. Too true. Hale set down his croissant, wiped his fingers on the napkin in his lap, then placed his hand over his aunt's. "So you think I should bring Miss York to Helena despite the campaign?"

Aunt Lily nodded. "As your uncle has said repeatedly, married men get more votes. We don't wish to rush you into marriage—at least not until you've had a chance to meet this young lady—so the next best thing is a serious courtship."

"I agree." Uncle Jonas buttered the other half of his croissant. "And now, I'm going to forgo further questions and advice—although only for the next few minutes—so this little piece of heaven doesn't grow stale in my hand."

Directly after leaving his aunt and uncle's house, Hale headed to his office where he wrote, edited, and revised a letter to Miss York in pencil before recopying it in ink. It took almost an hour, so it was after six by the time he was finished telling her his latest news. He ended with:

Miss York, we have shared our hearts and lives through paper and pen. These poor tools are no longer up to the task. If you are not put off by my decision to run for mayor and all the public scrutiny it will bring, I humbly request that you come to Helena. I earnestly desire to see your face and hear your voice as we commence the next stage of our courtship.

Your devoted servant,
Hale Adams, Esq.

His heart pounded at the addition of "devoted" in the closing, but it was truth. He felt devoted to her even though they had yet to meet.

He looked over his desk into the waiting area. The Persian carpet and tufted sofa were leftovers from his aunt's redecoration of her parlor five years ago. He accepted them because his clients needed someplace to sit while waiting. He'd meant for a wife to finish decorating his office, but then came Yancey Palmer. Tired of hearing he'd eventually get around to purchasing curtains, Aunt Lily bought the blue-and-white ones hanging in the waiting room and in his office as a Christmas present eighteen months ago.

When Miss Portia York arrived, he'd give her the freedom to redecorate his office, his apartment upstairs where they could live until children came along, and anything else in his life she found too boring.

Including him.

When he'd first arrived in Helena, his excuse for sticking to nothing but work and church had been the demands of setting up his practice. After he established himself, he set about the business of making the city his home by the usual route: a wife and family. Ever since Yancey Palmer had ruined that plan, he found it too exhausting—and too lonely—to make significant changes to the patterns of his life.

Then he'd met Mrs. Archer, agreed to become a client, and was introduced to Miss Portia York. Now he was eager to get on with the life he'd always wanted.

He wrote a letter to the matrimonial company, telling them he'd asked Portia to join him in Helena. There were some procedural things the agency needed to handle in order to satisfy the contractual obligations to both parties.

He checked the time. The post office would be closed, but he could slip the letters into the overnight box. And, with any luck, there might be another letter from Portia. She usually wrote twice a week, as did he.

He hurried out the door, smiling as he walked. He'd begun to think of her as Portia rather than Miss York. If she agreed to come to Helena, he'd forgo using her Christian name until she gave him permission to do so because that was right and proper, but he would allow himself the privilege of that intimacy in the privacy of his thoughts.

When he entered the post office, he stopped on the threshold. Yancey Palmer was there with her best friend, Carline Pope. Both blond and blue-eyed, they looked like sisters. They certainly acted like it. But then, Miss Palmer adopted everyone as family . . . whether a person wanted it or not.

She smiled with cool civility. "Good afternoon, Mr. Adams."

How very odd. She usually greeted him as Hale. It was her way of claiming a closer connection between them. To hear her use the more formal, proper Mr. Adams was . . . unsettling, though he couldn't figure out why. He took off his hat and dipped his chin in polite acknowledgment. "Miss Palmer. Miss Pope."

Miss Pope smiled. "Mr. Adams, very nice to see you. We were just leaving." She wrapped her arm around Miss Palmer as the two of them approached the exit.

He stepped back to let them pass through the door, hiding his letters behind his back until they were safely past. Not once did Miss Palmer turn her head to give him that look he hated, the one declaring he would be hers one day and everyone knew it.

What was different about her today?

Vexed at himself for giving her a second thought, he entered the post office and closed the door behind him. He slipped his letters to Portia and the agency through the slot, then went to check his box. There was a stack of mail waiting for him. Most was business correspondence, but two were personal. One was from Portia and the other from Isaak Gunderson. Wanting to read Portia's letter in private, he slid it to the bottom of the stack and ripped open Isaak's. Inside was a page torn from the notebook he always carried with him and a typewritten list. The note read:

Hale~

    I'm going after Zoe. I'm not sure when—or even if—I'll be back. In the meantime, here's the schedule of all the planned campaign events. Before I leave town, I'll make sure Yancey will continue helping with the campaign—she really is the best *at planning events—on the condition that her days of chasing after you are over. If she can't make that promise, I'll tell her to drop out of helping. She's also great at keeping secrets. Even if she can't promise to help with your campaign, I know she'll agree to say*

*nothing about you taking my place until you
announce it yourself on Saturday. So there's
nothing for you to worry about. Just run the
best campaign you can and WIN!*

> *Best of luck to you,*
> *Isaak*

In the margin of the typed schedule, he had scrawled,
Starred items planned by Yancey.

Hale glanced out the post office window. Miss Palmer
and her friend were gone. Was the promise not to chase after
him the reason for her coldness? Or was she dropping out
and upset by that?

Did it matter? He didn't want Yancey Palmer anywhere
near his campaign.

He checked the list. Only two of the seven events were
starred. One of them was the joint grand opening of The
Import Co. and official campaign announcement; the other
was the Independence Day picnic.

Not too terrible.

He checked the list again. The first item on Isaak's list
was the general meeting at Mrs. Hollenbeck's house tomorrow afternoon for everyone who'd agreed to help with the
campaign. Hale had asked to remain a behind-the-scenes
adviser, so he'd not known about it until yesterday when
he'd agreed to run for mayor. His chest constricted at the
thought of so many people in one place, all of them wanting
something from him. Miss Palmer would certainly be attending, unless she was dropping out.

Which he hoped she would. Except that meant she
couldn't promise not to chase him again.

Oh . . . that girl was such a thorn in his side.

The sooner Portia came to town, the better. Too bad he
hadn't asked her to come by May the fifth, the day of the

grand opening and campaign kickoff. It was possible she'd rush to come to him. If she did, it would certainly indicate that her desire for them to meet and progress their courtship was as strong as his.

But what if Portia didn't want to come at all? Then what would he do?

He shook his head. He was putting the cart before the horse. No sense getting worked up about mere possibilities when he had enough actual realities to keep him occupied.

He left the post office and headed home. His stomach rumbled on his way past Gibbon's Steak House. He ducked inside to ask Malachi if he could have his usual table at seven. Assured that the restaurant would do everything they could to accommodate his request, Hale hurried home to read Portia's latest letter.

He went upstairs to his apartment. Hm. Perhaps he should accept Aunt Lily's offer to make it homier. The only color relieving the white walls was a painting of Niagara Falls. Growing up in Buffalo, New York, the Falls were a favorite outing for his family. Hale threw out almost every reminder of those days when he came to Helena but couldn't bear to part with the painting. It hung above the small clock on his fireplace mantel. To the right of his fire iron set was a cast-iron safe. A woman would likely want it somewhere less noticeable, but it was convenient for now—and secure. No one came up here except him.

What would Portia think if she came? His leather wing-back chair was brown, his wood floors were brown, his table was brown, and the curtains hanging over the windows to his balcony were brown. Even the bedspread in the next room was brown.

Yes. If Portia agreed to come, he was absolutely asking Aunt Lily for help. He didn't want his prospective bride taking one look at the temporary home he was offering and board the next train back to Denver.

After opening the curtains to allow light—and some red and green from the flower box outside—into the drab room, Hale sat down and tore open the sealed envelope. The letter was addressed to *My Dear Hale*. His chest burned at the sight of it because the closeness growing between them wasn't only on his end. He read each paragraph, fighting between wanting to savor every word and eagerness to hear all she had to say.

On the third page, one bit of news leaped out at him. *I have begun helping a family friend run for political office. I hope you aren't put off by a woman eager to do her part to ensure her community is represented by the best man possible.*

No. Not even in the slightest.

Hale ran his fingertips over the sentences, savoring her beautiful handwriting. He was more certain now than even ten minutes ago that Miss Portia York of Denver was his match.

Saturday, April 28, 1888

Hale stepped into the foyer of Mrs. Hollenbeck's spacious home, his shoes squeaking on the polished black-and-white-checkerboard marble floor. He handed his hat and coat to the butler who'd opened the door for him. "Thank you, Simmons."

"My pleasure, sir." He glanced outside as he draped Hale's coat over his arm. "If I might be so bold, do you know where Mr. Gunderson is?"

"What have you heard?"

"Only rumors, sir, but troubling ones." Simmons closed the door.

"I assure you, Mr. Gunderson is . . ." Hale stopped the word *perfectly* from leaving his throat. It was yet unclear if Isaak had convinced Miss de Fleur to marry him. "He's fine."

Simmons bowed. "Very good to hear, sir."

Hale turned to his right. The carved mahogany archway between the foyer and parlor was filled with people. Mrs. Hollenbeck had hosted Luanne and Roy Bennett's wedding over a year ago, and people were able to spread out on her lawn, into the ballroom, and into several other rooms. Now, it seemed like the same number of people were crammed into her parlor.

His mouth went dry. Why had he agreed to this?

Because now that his family name was ruined in Buffalo, New York, Helena was home.

Because two days ago, he'd considered all the other possible candidates while Isaak sat across the desk listing why none of them were suitable replacements.

Because the town deserved better than someone like Harold Kendrick, a man who used his power to promote his own interests.

There were more items on the list, but Hale repeated the three main ones in his head until his heartrate slowed.

Mrs. Hollenbeck weaved through the crowd, stopping to greet everyone until she made it to Hale. "Good to see you, Mr. Adams."

He took her hand and bowed over it. "A great pleasure, ma'am."

Like her butler, she looked over Hale's shoulder. "Have you seen Isaak? He apparently left town for a shopping trip, but no one has seen him since. Everyone is talking about his dramatic marriage proposal to Miss de Fleur and whether it means he should drop out of the race."

"Might I have a private word with you about that?" Hale tilted his head toward the empty foyer.

The wealthy widow frowned. "Of course."

They stepped away from the crowded parlor, and Hale bent his head to whisper, "Isaak has dropped out. I'm taking his place."

"Did he go after Miss de Fleur?"

"It's not my place to say, ma'am."

Mrs. Hollenbeck's immediate smile and the conspiratorial gleam in her eye said she understood what he hadn't said. "I can think of no one better suited to take over for him than you, Mr. Adams."

She couldn't? Equal measures of gratification and trepidation snaked down his spine.

"We shouldn't delay telling everyone else." Mrs. Hollenbeck took his arm and tugged him toward the parlor. She touched a shoulder here, spoke an *excuse me* there, and soon she and Hale were in the center of the room.

Too soon.

He eyed the archway but kept his feet rooted to the floor.

Because Helena was home. Because it deserved better than Kendrick.

"Ladies and gentlemen"—Mrs. Hollenbeck clapped her hands five times—"may I have your attention, please."

Conversation stilled. Every eye turned to her and then to him as well. Hale held his facial muscles in what he hoped was a pleasant expression. Around the room, brows lowered, eyes squinted, and gazes flitted between him and Mrs. Hollenbeck. Everyone's except Yancey Palmer's. She stared at their hostess, never once looking at Hale.

As with their encounter at the post office, her lack of attention felt odd. Not unwelcome, though. Not at all.

"Thank you for your attention." Mrs. Hollenbeck smiled, turning her head to include everyone in the room. "Mr. Adams has some important news regarding our mayoral candidate." She looked at Hale with an expectant gleam in her brown eyes.

He stepped into the small circle of space at the center of the crowd. It was no different from being in a courtroom. No different. He could do this. He'd trained at Harvard, for heaven's sake. He took a deep breath—or as deep as his still-tight lungs allowed—and worked up enough spit to speak. "Ladies and gentlemen. As I'm sure all of you are aware, Isaak Gunderson and his family have quite a bit on their plates in light of the fire this past Thursday."

A few grumbles greeted this statement of the obvious.

Hale ignored them. "Isaak came to visit me on Thursday night, and we discussed his ability to continue as a mayoral candidate."

The sound of a collective intake of breath filled the parlor.

Hale turned his head left and right to gauge their reactions—just as he did when he was forced to argue before a jury. Which he did as infrequently as possible.

A few people were still squinting at him, while others had a wary look in their eyes.

Time to make his point. "I hope you won't be too disappointed, but Isaak and I agreed that it was best if he stepped down."

"Who's going to replace him?" The question came from a man Hale couldn't see.

Mrs. Hollenbeck stepped forward. "Give Mr. Adams a moment to finish explaining, Mr. Cannon."

Hale stretched his six-foot frame and lifted his chin a bit so he could look the grocer in the eye. "It's a good question, sir. I hope you—and everyone else here—will approve of the answer."

A few brows cleared. Some people began to smile at Hale.

He glanced at Yancey, not sure why her reaction mattered to him, but her expression gave away none of her feelings. *Bland pleasant* was the best description he could come up with, which was uncharacteristic. She usually appeared as if she was waiting for a reason to laugh—and it almost always seemed like it was at him.

"Go on, Mr. Adams." Mrs. Hollenbeck's words accentuated a poke to his arm.

"Right." He turned his head so Yancey Palmer wasn't in his line of sight. "Isaak asked me to take his place."

Sighs—of relief or disappointment?—filled the room before they were overtaken by applause. The band constricting his chest loosened. Hands extended toward him. He began shaking them, greeting people by name.

Which was imprudent, because it didn't take long for someone he didn't recognize to come along. What now?

As though she read his mind, Mrs. Hollenbeck stepped up and introduced him to every unfamiliar person until his head swam with new names and his hand ached. The line finally dwindled, but the worst was yet to come.

Cries of, "Speech! Speech!" couldn't be ignored.

But Hale didn't make spontaneous speeches. Too much could go wrong. Words were powerful things. They needed to be crafted. Finessed. Massaged until their meaning was clear. He lifted his hand, asking for quiet. "Instead of a speech, how about I answer your questions? I'm sure you have many."

Charles Cannon went first. "Where do you stand on banning either the steam car or horses on Helena Avenue?"

"There are pros and cons to both." Hale explained the various problems and solutions he and Isaak had discussed.

"In other words"—Mrs. Hollenbeck inserted as he was winding down—"Mr. Adams believes he can address the concerns of people on both sides without making this an all-or-nothing issue."

He frowned. Wasn't that what he'd just said?

More questions followed, and Hale had an answer for every one of them. The ease he felt was almost exhilarating.

Until Yancey Palmer raised her hand. "It seems like you and Isaak have talked over strategy, but I would like to know your campaign slogan."

His mind went blank. "My slogan?"

Her look transported him back to third grade, which was the last time someone stared at him like he was an idiot for being unable to answer a simple question. "Isaak's was going to be 'Go with Gunderson.' How do you feel about 'Helena Needs Hale'?"

He hated it, but was that because it was an inherently bad slogan or because Yancey Palmer was the person who suggested it? The question—and the nods and grins on the faces of the people surrounding her—made him think harder. "What about 'Vote Hale Adams for Mayor'?" Specific. Straightforward. Simple.

And yet smiles turned to frowns.

Miss Palmer's eyes began to sparkle with laughter. Why? He'd said nothing humorous. "How about 'No Helena without Hale,' or even better . . ." She paused and raised her eyebrows. "'Hale—the best for Helena'?"

He was about to suggest his first, perfect slogan again, but her enthusiasm was contagious. Everywhere he looked, people were smiling and nodding.

Mrs. Hollenbeck stepped closer and put a hand on his arm. "How about a compromise? 'Adams for Helena.'"

Hale smiled at the widow, although—really—what was wrong with *his* slogan? "A good solution, ma'am."

"I don't think so." Hale didn't recognize the feminine voice, so it wasn't Yancey Palmer's. "I like 'Helena Needs Hale' better."

"Me, too."

"So do I."

Applause erupted.

Mrs. Hollenbeck waited for it to fade before saying, "I

believe a vote is in order. All those in favor of 'Helena Needs Hale,' please raise your hands." So many went up, there was no reason to vote on any of the other suggested slogans. "'Helena Needs Hale' it is."

There was another round of applause, after which Simmons appeared in the parlor to announce that lunch was ready.

Mrs. Hollenbeck patted Hale's arm. "Well done."

"Thank you, madam." Except for the slogan, he *had* done well. There wasn't a question he felt ill prepared to answer, and he'd explained his positions without stammering through them.

Mrs. Hollenbeck leaned close, her voice low. "Would you mind staying behind for anyone who has more questions while I take the rest to the dining room?"

"I'll be fine."

She smiled, then turned to the rest of her guests. "If you will follow me . . ."

No one had questions, so the room was soon empty except for him and Miss Palmer.

She extended her hand. "Congratulations, Mr. Adams. It seems you have successfully transferred Isaak's supporters to your cause."

Hale shook her hand briefly. "Thank you for your support, Miss Palmer."

She tilted her head to one side. "I'm assuming Isaak told you of our agreement regarding my participation in your campaign?"

Surprised by the lack of emotion in her voice, Hale nodded. "He did."

She smiled with that same *bland pleasant* expression on her face. "I promised Isaak, and now I'm promising you, that I have no intention of embarrassing either you or myself during next week's grand opening or the Independence Day event."

He wanted to clarify by adding, *Or at any time before, between, or after*, but it seemed ungentlemanly. "Then I expect we can work together successfully."

Her smile remained placid. "Excellent. Until next week then, Mr. Adams?"

"Until next week."

She dipped her chin, then turned and exited the parlor.

Hale stared after her. That was easier than expected. And if she kept her promise, he didn't foresee any problems.

Except, perhaps, her reaction to Portia's arrival.

Chapter Three

Yancey tucked a strand of hair back into her topknot. Her back and feet ached after staying to the end of Mrs. Hollenbeck's party and then the additional time it took to help clean up. The walk home now accentuated that pain with every step.

At least she wasn't alone. Carline—who had stayed with her and helped with the cleanup—didn't seem to mind their slow and steady steps. She lived only two blocks away from Yancey, and they'd shared thousands of stories over the years as they walked back and forth from school, parties, work, and everywhere in between.

"You're awfully quiet." Carline bumped her shoulder against Yancey.

She shrugged. "Probably because my feet hurt."

"Like that has ever stopped you before." Her friend's light laugh filled the late-afternoon air. "Do you want to tell me what's on your mind?"

They stopped at the corner of Ewing and Fifth and waited for several horse carts to pass before stepping into the street.

"Well . . ." Yancey thought through what she *wanted* to say but wasn't sure she *could* say.

Conversation stalled while they navigated around manure piles and mud puddles.

The rebellious strand of hair that refused to stay in her bun fell in front of Yancey's eyes again. This time she tucked it behind her left ear. As soon as they reached the other side of the street, she took a deep breath and decided to plunge in and answer her friend's question. "I think you're right."

"I usually am." Carline stepped onto the boardwalk and let go of her blue and white, cotton-print skirt. "What am I right about this time?"

Yancey grinned. "My Hale treasures."

She'd started her collection the moment she had returned from the Independence Day picnic almost ten years ago. Her world had fundamentally shifted that afternoon. One minute she was struggling to pull her right arm out of Bruno Carson's painful grasp while keeping the plate of food in her left hand away from him, the next she was staring into a stranger's face, knowing in the core of her heart that she'd just met her future. Somewhere in between, Bruno Carson got a bloody lip, let go of her arm, and ran away.

Because Hale Adams had rescued her like a knight in shining armor.

He was tall and handsome in a bookish way with his clear brown eyes behind those wire-rimmed glasses. He kept pushing them back into place with his index finger while asking if she was all right or if she needed his assistance getting back to her parents.

She didn't need his assistance, but she asked for it anyway. Anything to remain in his company for a moment longer.

The first thing she did when she returned home that day was to pull the ribbon from her hair and place it in a small box, keeping it for the "something blue" she'd need at her wedding. Over the years, she'd collected more treasures and added them to increasingly larger boxes.

"You're ready to get rid of them?" Carline's question brought Yancey out of her memories.

They'd walked another block without Yancey realizing it. "I think it only fair to Nathan."

Carline stopped, forcing Yancey to do the same. "You're really going to leave Helena if he asks you to come to Denver?" Carline's face and words were filled with a combination of awe and dismay.

Knowing full well how difficult it would be, Yancey nodded. "I will."

"But Helena is your home."

Not if Nathan asked her to make a home with him, although Yancey didn't say the words aloud. She and Carline had talked many times about how much they'd be willing to sacrifice for the man they would marry. Of course, Yancey had always pictured Hale during those conversations . . . at least until recently.

The picture of Nathan St. John was hazy, like some of the photos her brother-in-law, Roy, developed and then discarded. But just because the picture was blurry didn't make the subject itself bad. Once she met Nathan and had a clear image of him to treasure, she'd be able to replace Hale in every way.

In the meantime, all of her treasures—none of them things Hale had even given her—needed to be discarded.

Yancey started walking again. "Even if Nathan never asks me to go to Denver, I still think that as part of the promise I made to Isaak, now is the time to get rid of my Hale treasures. Are you going to help me or not?"

Carline sighed. "Well . . . I think one doesn't necessarily have to go with the other, but of course I'll help. It *was* my idea in the first place."

They reached Yancey's home in five minutes more. The scent of baking bread greeted them as soon as they opened the kitchen door.

Mother stood by the stove with a dozen golden-brown dinner rolls.

"Mm." Yancey sniffed the air. "Those smell delicious. Might Carline and I have one to share?"

Mother glanced at the clock over the sink. Not a single blond hair fell out of place. If she removed her yellow apron, she'd be ready to host the Ladies' Aid Society. Yancey hoped to learn the trick of looking presentable while cooking one day. Preferably before Nathan asked her to Denver.

"I suppose half a roll won't spoil your appetites." Mother turned her gaze on Carline. "Are you joining us for dinner tonight?"

Carline shook her head. "I would love to, but Uncle Eugene is here from Butte. He's trying to talk my parents into sending me to a finishing school somewhere in Boston or Philadelphia. I can't remember which."

Yancey pressed her lips together to keep from commenting on Mr. Eugene Nordstrom and his overbearing plans for Carline. The time to discuss it wasn't now.

Mother lifted two dinner rolls from the baking sheet and held them out. "You look like you could both use a whole one. Enjoy, my dears."

Taking the rolls and calling their thanks over their shoulders, Carline and Yancey hurried to her bedroom and closed the door.

The moment the latch clicked behind her, Yancey gave into the desire to share her opinion of Mr. High-and-Mighty Nordstrom. "Just because your uncle has made you his heir doesn't give him the right to dictate your life while he lives. He either trusts you with his millions or he doesn't."

Carline bit into her roll, an exasperated look on her face.

"I know you don't like discussing this, but honestly." Yancey ripped her roll in half, a puff of steam escaping into the air. "Do you *want* to attend a finishing school?"

Carline swallowed. "I might."

The admission shocked Yancey so much, she almost dropped the warm bread. "But why?"

Carline sat on the floral quilt of Yancey's mostly made bed. "If you are going to leave me for Denver to marry Nathan, why wouldn't I want to see a bit more of the country?"

"But . . ." *I want you here so I can always come visit you.* The sentiment was so selfish, Yancey winced even though she'd stopped herself from saying the words aloud. She placed the torn roll on her desk—she wasn't hungry anymore—and sat on the bed next to her friend. "If seeing the country is your goal, is attending a school the best way to do it?"

Carline sniffed. "What I want is to love, be loved in return, and to start a family of my own. I've never really wanted anything else."

Yancey sensed a *but* coming. She kept silent, waiting for Carline to speak again.

"But Uncle Eugene isn't wrong. As his heir, I'll attract certain men." Carline pinched off a piece of bread and popped it into her mouth. Her cheeks turned pink as she chewed. A sure sign she was about to mention the man she secretly loved. "We both know Windsor Buchanan will never propose to a girl who spit tea all over him the first time they met. Like you, I need to move on from my infatuation with a man who hasn't noticed me in years. Who knows, maybe I'll find my own Nathan St. John in Boston . . . or Philadelphia."

Yancey wrapped her right arm around Carline's shoulders. They'd endured a lot together, none more difficult than the men they'd loved so long but maybe not so well. "What if you send a letter to Antonia Archer telling her what kind of man you want? She found Nathan for me. I'm sure she can find another Windsor Buchanan for you."

An unladylike snort came from Carline. "I doubt it. That

man is one-of-a-kind." She popped the rest of her bread into her mouth.

Yancey chuckled. Windsor was almost as tall yet more muscular than the Gunderson twins, wore his dark brown hair hanging to his shoulder blades and his beard to the middle of his chest, and if he ever trimmed either to a fashionable length, he would be the handsomest man in all of Helena . . . maybe in the entire territory. He ran his own bladesmithy and was so precise when sharpening knives, axes, and other cutting tools that his customers waited as much as a month for his skill rather than going across town for the same services. He lived in what amounted to a shed behind his business, dressed like a rough mountain man except on Sundays, when he greeted congregants at the church door in a full suit and tie, and ate only what he'd hunted or grown himself. He was the epitome of manliness, yet he'd attended *Romeo and Juliet* three nights ago after Yancey begged him to make the sixth in their party. He hadn't agreed until he heard Carline was part of the group. Yancey had taken it as a sign he wasn't as immune to romance as he appeared, leading her to impetuously say, "Tonight is a night for falling in love," as soon as the whole party arrived at Ming's Opera House.

The comment earned her a swift kick from Carline and several desperate glances after the entire party was seated in the box.

Yancey gave her friend's shoulders a squeeze. "I thought Hale Adams was one-of-a-kind. Nathan is proof I was wrong."

"Speaking of which"—Carline stood and brushed crumbs from her skirt—"we're here to formally dispose of your Hale treasures. I need to be home in half an hour, so we'd best get to work."

Yancey stood, too. "You're right. Let's get this over with."

Carline lifted the bottom edge of the quilt while Yancey

pulled on the leather handle of the rectangular oak box hidden under her bed. The pine floorboards were scratched from the hundreds of times she'd pulled or pushed the box across them.

Knowing she was doing the right thing didn't stop Yancey's chest from aching. She'd loved Hale for so long. So very long. And in truth—he was a good man. He just didn't care two beans or a pickle for her.

She opened the lid. On top were a deep pink dried rose and a blue satin ribbon. The rose was important because Hale had brought a dozen of them to her mother the first time he'd come to the house for lunch. Ever since then, pink roses had been Yancey's favorite flower. She lifted the rose from the box, held it over the waste bin, and crushed the crisp petals inside her fist.

"Goodbye, Hale," she whispered as she sprinkled the crumbled rose over lint, hair cleaned from her brush, and other bits of refuse.

She nudged the ribbon aside to take out a yellowed newsprint advertisement for Hale's law firm. She ripped it in quarters and let the pieces flutter into the waste bin. Next came an article about a case he'd won. She ripped and released it. As the pieces fell, the heaviness in her chest lifted.

Not much, but enough to keep going until nothing was left but the blue ribbon.

She held it up, her hand shaking.

"Are you sure?" Carline knelt beside Yancey.

She laid the satin across her thigh, smoothing it with her hand. Every other treasure was adjacent to Hale— something he'd done that had nothing to do with her. "This is my one true memory with him."

"I know." Carline wrapped her arm around Yancey's waist.

"How many times have we planned ways for me to wear this in my hair or sew it into my dress or wrap it around my bridal bouquet?"

Carline answered by hugging Yancey closer.

"He didn't give it to me." Yancey wrapped the ribbon around her index and middle fingers, savoring the silky feel against her skin. "Would it be so bad to keep it?"

"I can take it for you." Carline's offer was made out of deep friendship. She knew what letting go would cost.

Would that be cheating? The ribbon would be gone. Mostly. Yancey sighed and shook her head. "The entire purpose is to leave Hale Adams behind. It has to go."

She wriggled the ribbon off her fingers, held it over the waste bin, and let it fall.

Across town

Mary Lester swung her props—a mop and bucket—while hobbling across Lawrence Street toward The Import Co. Water sloshed from the tin pail, dampening the hem of her drab brown cape. Dressed as a peasant woman, she doubted her own son, Mac, would recognize her. Even so, she scattered glances left and right. No one gave her a second look. Perfect. Her disguise was working.

As she passed one of the store's gleaming windowpanes, she caught her reflection. Hard to say which was ugliest: her cape, the dirt-colored cotton dress beneath it, or her wig of lanky brown hair covered by a frayed mobcap.

Movement behind the glass shifted her focus to Jakob Gunderson. He held a pen, a small jar of ink, and tags— presumably to add prices to the luxury items displayed in the store set to open in two days. The Gunderson brothers and their stepfather, David Pawlikowski, ran two stores in Helena, this new one and another across town that sold second-hand items—at least they *had* run both until two days ago, when The Resale Co. burned to ashes.

Mary knew who'd set the fire and would soon make him pay. But first, she needed Jakob Gunderson.

She placed the mop and bucket next to the door. Praying to a god she no longer believed in that it was unlocked, she twisted the knob. It turned. She let out a grateful sigh, opened the door, and stepped inside. The scents of lemon oil and beeswax mingled with the piney undertone of freshly milled wood. She kept her head down to hide her face with the brim of the mobcap. If Jakob declined her offer, she couldn't risk him knowing her true identity. Too many lives were at stake.

"Excuse me, ma'am, but we aren't open for business yet." Jakob's tone of voice held none of the derision she usually encountered when dressed like a wretch.

It strengthened her conviction that he was the man she needed.

"I come to see if you need a cleaning lady." She used her hag voice and spoke loud enough for the group of ladies crossing behind her to hear before she shut the door.

Jakob set the pricing tools on the nearest table. "We don't need any help, but—"

Click. She locked the door behind her.

The audacity of her action ostensibly stopped his words.

Now that she was safe inside, she used her normal voice. "I'm not here about cleaning." She trudged past him, commanding him to follow with the crook of her finger. "We will talk in the back where no prying eyes can see through all these windows."

No answering footsteps followed. She looked over her shoulder to see him standing in the same spot.

"You are in no danger from me, Jakob, I assure you." The man was six feet, five inches and would tower over her even if she weren't hunching her shoulders as part of her disguise.

"How do we know each other, ma'am?" Again, no trace of disgust in his words, although they were stiff with formality.

She wasn't revealing herself to him until they were away

from the windows filling the beautiful store with dusky light. She crooked her finger again. "Please. In back." She watched him out of the corner of her eye, her breaths becoming short. What if this didn't work?

He frowned but followed.

She kept her face averted even after they'd crossed into the back room and she'd closed the forest-green brocade curtain between the retail space and stockroom area in back. "I need your word as a gentleman that you won't repeat a word of what I'm about to tell you to *anyone*." Her tone sounded like steel even to her own ears, but she needed him to understand the weight of what she was about to say. "You are a man of many friends and come from a close family. If you cannot keep a secret, we are done here."

He was quiet for a long moment. She resisted the urge to look at him so he could see she was in earnest. Jakob Gunderson was her first—and only—choice to replace Finn Collins, whom she'd lost last April. After a year of observing Jakob closely, she knew him to be both an honest man and one who was quick-witted enough to come up with convincing lies when necessary. The icing on the proverbial cake was that his job required him to make deliveries of furniture and goods all over town. He could go anywhere and no one would find his presence the least bit odd. Familiarity made him as invisible as she was in her disguise.

Jakob took a long, slow breath. "Before I make that promise, I need some assurance that whatever you wish to tell me is neither illegal nor immoral."

She chortled at the irony. "I can give you no such assurance because it is both. However, I *can* promise you that, should you agree, your part in it will be as a rescuer." He had no reason to trust a stranger, but he'd trust her even less if he knew who she really was. That was why she needed his promise *before* revealing her identity.

She snuck a glance at him. The Gunderson twins were

almost identical in appearance. Tall, blond, well-muscled, good-looking boys with beautiful eyes—Isaak's green, Jakob's blue—both with distinctive brown flecks near the iris. But they differed sharply in personality. Isaak—the elder by five minutes—planned every inch of his route before taking a step forward. Jakob jumped first and looked later If he went over a cliff, he learned how to fly on the way down, a skill she desperately needed.

Mary held her breath, waiting for him to jump.

"Why me? Why not Isaak?"

Poor boy. He was so used to judging himself against his twin, he failed to see his own strengths. "Because, my dear Jakob, you are better suited for the task than anyone else in Helena, and because you need a purpose."

And because the sting of Miss Zoe de Fleur's public rejection of his marriage proposal made him vulnerable. He'd want to be a hero in someone's eyes.

After a long moment, during which Mary took up praying again, Jakob sighed. "All right. I promise."

Mary pulled the mobcap and wig from her head and turned toward him.

He gasped. "Madame Lestraude?"

"As you see." Although it bothered her that he used the name she'd adopted when she became a brothel owner. As a friend of her son, he knew her real name. Yet he'd chosen to call her by her alter ego. Madame Lestraude wore burgundy silk dresses, painted her face, and coiffed her hair. *She* was a role. A disguise. Someone the real Mary Lester had created to survive. Had she come so far she couldn't go back to being Mary now even if she wanted?

"I hardly recognized you, ma'am."

"Which was the point."

Jakob tipped his head to acknowledge her statement. "How can I be of service?"

"You can help me rescue young girls from prostitution."

His eyes went wide and he coughed into his hand several times. "But . . . but you're a . . . I mean, you . . ."

"Run a brothel where women sell themselves every day?"

His neck and cheeks filled with splotches of red. Oh, to be so innocent again.

"Because you don't frequent my establishment"—or any of them, making him one of only a handful of men in Helena who refrained from visiting even the cheap crib houses—"I will forgive your ignorance of my business practices. I only accept women over the age of seventeen who come to me of their own free will. I cannot abide young girls being abducted into prostitution. These are the ones I seek to rescue."

Jakob ran his fingers through his blond hair. "But . . . last year. Emilia and Luci?"

Mary understood his confusion. As far as he knew, she and Finn Collins had almost abducted Emilia Collins McCall and her sister, Luci Stanek, into prostitution. Mary looked Jakob in the eye. "I am prepared to tell you the truth, but I will remind you that you promised not to repeat any part of this evening's conversation." She waited for Jakob to nod before continuing. "My son made a nuisance of himself investigating Finn Collins's death last April."

Jakob huffed. "What did you expect?"

Exactly what happened. Mac couldn't take off his county sheriff's badge long enough to stop investigating his best friend's death. So she'd smeared Finn's good name. It would have worked except for three things: Emilia refused to believe that her husband—a man she'd never met and had married by proxy—would sell her and her sister into prostitution, Mac fell in love with Emilia and therefore kept investigating even when the evidence against Finn should have been overwhelming, and Mary's own mistake.

"I'm sure you heard that I took Luci Stanek into *Maison de Joie* with me." Saying precious Luci's name and her brothel's name so close together brought back memories. Mary ducked her head to hide the heat creeping into her cheeks, although after all these years, she wasn't sure if she was more angry or embarrassed that she'd been so easily abducted into the life she now led. "I was protecting Luci "

"Because Edgar Dunfree was touching her hair and telling her how pretty she was."

Mary snapped her attention back to Jakob. "I was unaware you knew about that."

His nostrils flared. "I was there when Luci told us about it."

"Then you can understand why it was a mistake to rescue a twelve-year-old girl from a man's caresses so soon after another twelve-year-old girl was stolen from a brothel."

Jakob's eyes suddenly widened and his jaw fell an inch. "Finn was helping you rescue girls, wasn't he? He never intended to sell Emilia or her sister to you, did he?"

"No. He did not."

"Is that what got him killed?"

It was the logical conclusion. And wrong. Finn had been killed by a man Jakob loved and trusted—the same man who'd set fire to The Resale Co. She wasn't ready to expose those truths yet, but she wouldn't lie about the risks of her smuggling operation. Brothel owners who'd lost business had killed Sheriff Simpson fourteen months ago while he was attempting to transport a girl to the train line. Mary shivered. If those same brothel owners ever discovered she'd masterminded over thirty rescues in the past twelve years, they'd glory in torturing her to death. "This is dangerous work, Jakob. More than one person has given his life to help me."

Jakob rubbed his earlobe and stared across the space between them.

"I will think no less of you should you decline to join us." Although it would mean she'd have to put off plans to punish the man responsible for Finn's death. She needed leverage and—this early in the game—she couldn't bluff. She'd already planned out a rescue for Tuesday in which Jakob could take a small part. She didn't need much from him. Just enough that her threat had teeth.

Jakob lowered his hand. A slow grin lifted his lips. "Madam, I'm your man."

Chapter Four

Saturday, May 5, 1888
The Import Co. Grand Opening

*H*e was admiring a set of silver candlesticks imported
from Spain when Madame Lestraude strolled up, a
primal smile on her rouged lips. She held out a folded piece
of parchment sealed with burgundy wax imprinted with
a solitary rose.

Furious at her bold approach, he took the letter. "I hope
you're enjoying the grand opening."

"Immensely. Everyone is abuzz with the grandeur of the
store and Mr. Gunderson's withdrawal from the mayoral
race. I can only imagine your feelings on the matter."

"It came as something of a shock."

"Ah." The puff of air conveyed nothing. "As for me, the
announcement was . . . enlightening. A pleasure to see you
as always. I trust we will meet again very soon." With that,
she bid him adieu and slipped back into the crush of people
eager to touch, smell, and own pieces of the world outside
Helena.

He snapped the wax seal while checking to see how
many people noticed their exchange. No one was looking at

him with shock or censure—why would they, when Big Jane, Chicago Joe, and several other wealthy brothel owners were shopping and exchanging pleasantries in their midst?—but his chest remained tight. He glanced down and read:

C'est la guerre!
ML

Why declare war? He'd done nothing to her family. Emilia McCall had escaped the fire with no damage save a bit of ash falling on her hair and shoulders.

He crumpled the parchment between his fingers. The madam and her enigmatic message would have to wait. He weaved his way closer to the door. His lungs needed air untainted by scented candles, quarreling perfumes, and hair pomade. As he stepped into the sunshine, he saw Madame Lestraude step into her carriage. Her driver closed the door and mounted the box.

Madame turned, her eyes on him as deliberate as her slow pull drawing down the shade.

Did she think he would come to her now? No, their next meeting would be the time and place of his choosing.

Only . . .

He craned his neck to look over his left shoulder and then his right. No one would think twice if he crossed the street to join husbands biding their time with cigars and conversation while their wives spent money on things they didn't need but could afford. From there, he could stroll to the shuttered bank as if he was returning to his office and duck into the carriage when no one was looking.

Fisk lifted a hand in greeting.

He waved back and stepped into the street, careful to avoid the dense piles of manure testifying to the success of today's grand opening.

He took his time chatting with Fisk, Cannon, Watson, and

several other important men of Helena, relishing the way it kept Madame Lestraude waiting. Her carriage remained motionless except for an occasional horse's stamp of impatience. Anyone who had noticed her ascent was gone, and everyone else would think it empty.

He excused himself from the men after sparking a debate sure to consume their full attention. As he drew even with the door of her carriage, he stopped, pulled out his pocket watch, and pretended to check the time while skittering his gaze left and right to see if anyone was watching him.

No one.

He opened the carriage door and climbed inside. "I am not your lackey to command."

"Yet here you are." Madame Lestraude knocked on the wall of her carriage and it sprang to life. "Don't worry, we shall set you down somewhere close enough for you to walk back to the grand opening, but far enough away that no one will observe your descent."

"What if someone had seen me?"

"Then you should have taken even more care in your circuitous route." She inclined her head toward the curtains. "I find it quite useful to observe without being observed myself."

He picked up the cane he'd tossed inside before his hasty ascent to cover his embarrassment. "What is so important it couldn't wait until a more opportune time?"

"Ah." The syllable scraped across his nerve endings. "I shall enlighten you, because Helena has grown too large for one man to know all that goes on within it."

His pride pricked, as she'd meant it to. Once upon a time he had known everyone and everything that happened inside of Helena. Had campaigned on it, as a matter of fact. The city was too large now. He was no longer at the center of every social circle as he once had been.

"Alfred and Martha Deal, in addition to running a

second-rate boardinghouse, sell women who will not be missed into prostitution."

He jerked backward against the padded seat. "How long have you known this?"

"It doesn't matter. As long as people stay out of my business, I return the courtesy." She paused for a moment. "Sometimes the Deals ride the trains, offering their card and a shoulder to cry on to naïve young women who, when their rosy dreams are shattered, want to disappear to wallow in self-pity. They approached Emilia on her way into town last year."

"I assume they did the same for Miss de Fleur."

She nodded.

"Excuse my cynicism, but why do you care?"

"Were it just Miss de Fleur, I wouldn't. She made her bed, so she can lie in it."

Her callous answer didn't surprise him, but he was hard-pressed not to reach across the seat and throw her from her own carriage. "So why the dramatic declaration of war?"

"Because she dragged my Nico along with her."

"Your Nico?"

"He's a good boy. I'm thinking of adopting him when he gets back from his grand adventure."

He choked on a laugh. "Replacing Mac?"

"Nico loves me as the mother he's never known. Mac keeps telling me love can redeem any soul. Who knows, maybe it will." She pierced him with her brown eyes. "Nico is family."

"Fine, but I've not hurt the boy."

"Oh, but this was not our agreement. You were not to even threaten my family."

He gritted his teeth. He didn't see the connection and he didn't want to ask.

"Your fire at The Resale Company resulted in a breach of our . . . understanding. This was not your intention, but

the consequences will be meted out just the same." She cocked her head. *"I'm curious. Did you set it yourself or hire an underling?"*

He'd used one of his best employees, a man who had followed instructions to the letter before slipping out of town unnoticed. Unlike Edgar Dunfree who, against orders, used his own name to purchase the printing press, a sale recorded and preserved in a cloth-bound ledger now burned to cinders. If anyone else made the connection between a man who used to boast of their once-close working relationship, the leveling foot found in Collins's barn, and a printing press, there was no longer any proof.

"Are you afraid your Nico will be accused of arson given his . . . other activity?"

Her patronizing smile mocked his mimicry of her dramatic pauses. *"You refer to his vandalism at The Import Company, of course. I have chastised him and acknowledge that he played some part in the threat against him for which I blame you."*

"Speak plainly, woman. I tire of your games."

"Very well. In plain terms, you pitted Isaak and Jakob Gunderson against each other by using Miss de Fleur to fuel their long-standing rivalry as a means to force Isaak from the mayoral race. As a result, in the literal heat of the moment, they humiliated the girl with dual proposals. She turned to the Deals for a solution. Nico, although he loves me, is more attached to his sister. He planned to flee with her and would have met with her same fate. My disgust for children conscripted into prostitution is well-known to you. It is for this that I will destroy you."

"How could I have foreseen such a convoluted turn of events?"

"Ignorantia juris non excusat. I laid down the law, and now I will not excuse you."

He tapped the gold-plated top of his cane. *"You've gone*

*to great lengths to keep your little rescuing ring hidden from
the other brothel owners, and with good cause. How do you
propose to destroy me when I have the means to destroy you
as I did Hendry by stirring up hatred against you?"*

*Her countenance held no fear. "When one side has all
the weapons, it is a slaughter. That is why, my dear Jonas,
this is war."*

After peering through both windows of Madame
Lestraude's private carriage to confirm that the street was
vacant, Jonas yanked open the door and descended before
anyone could see him. Everyone knew he'd helped the
woman set up her business years ago, before prostitution
became illegal. If anyone questioned why he was speaking
with her, he could always use their prior connection to say
he was now helping her diversify her businesses with completely legal ventures. She wasn't the only madam in town
doing the same.

People would believe him. That was one benefit of being
a judge. However—if he told his lie too often—someone
might check his veracity, and that would never do.

The coachman wasted no time cracking his whip over
the horses' heads, setting them in motion. They clattered
down the dusty street in the direction of the red-light district
where, presumably, the madam would begin preparations for
the evening entertainments at her brothel, Maison de Joie.

If only he could set fire to her business the way he had
The Resale Co.

Jonas tucked his cane under his arm—it was just for
show anyway—and hurried toward City Hall. For the sake
of his finances, he needed to give up his office there, but it
had taken him years to procure the space. He wouldn't give
it up easily.

City Hall was nearly empty. Jonas greeted a few people

with his most genial smile, but once inside his office, he let his mask fall away. He locked the door behind him and pulled out Madame Lestraude's declaration of war. He ripped the note in half, then in quarters, and kept ripping until it was shredded. He tossed the pieces in the waste bin to be burned later.

Madame Lestraude's convoluted story about why she'd declared war between them was a sham. She didn't care about that street urchin, Nico. No, she was angry about Finn Collins. She'd blamed herself for his death, thinking it was because he'd been caught smuggling one of the young girls she rescued from prostitution. But ever since she found out Finn died because he'd repaired Jonas's printing press—the one churning out pages of near-perfect counterfeit money to finance his eventual bid for U.S. Senator when Montana became a state—she'd been looking for revenge.

Jonas paced the small confines of his office. He'd once seen a caged lion, frustration seeping from every muscle of the great animal at his impotence. He felt the same way.

His bid for senator would be costly, and his counterfeiting operation—even running nonstop—wasn't enough. His house was still heavily mortgaged from borrowing against it to finance his mayoral bid four years ago. Lily didn't know they'd almost gone bankrupt, and he'd do everything in his power to keep her from finding out. Nor was he putting her in danger of losing her home ever again. He'd promised her a mansion as large as Pauline Hollenbeck's. Lily said she didn't need more than what they had now—she was truly a ruby beyond price—but Jonas was determined to see her in the home she deserved.

Although there was a limit to the number of people who could be eliminated while he went about fulfilling his promise.

Joseph Hendry, the nosy reporter from the *Daily Independent*, had uncovered the counterfeiting operation last

December. Jonas had rectified the problem, but it was only a matter of time before his lucrative scheme was exposed again.

Madame Lestraude knew about it, and her son was the sheriff for Lewis and Clark County. Jonas had specifically warned his men to keep the counterfeit bills out of Helena and the surrounding county, but they were trickling in. It was inevitable. Sheriff McCall and Marshal Valentine weren't fools and, unlike other law officers around the territory, were impervious to bribery.

Which reminded Jonas of another frustration. Harold Kendrick was interceding on behalf of too many criminals, interrupting the flow of convicts Jonas was using as free labor in his copper mine. Using convicts was illegal, but it wasn't hurting anyone. Only now Kendrick was drying up the supply.

Fred Drum—the warden of Deer Lodge Penitentiary— was part owner of the mine because he could deliver plenty of convict labor. He was a portly man inclined to do as little as possible for the greatest amount of gain. He was worried that Kendrick knew too much, worried the mining operation would be uncovered, and worried his heart couldn't take the strain. Jonas doubted Kendrick knew about the mine. Most likely the mayor was drying up the supply of convicts for some nefarious reason.

But what about Madame Lestraude? Did she know about the mine? Jonas wasn't sure. She'd threatened to shut down "every one" of his illicit businesses. He only had two: counterfeiting and the mine. Clearly, she knew about the first. She was probably just guessing he had more than the one, but he couldn't afford to underestimate her.

She needed to go, but she had countered his best move against her before he'd known they were playing a game. After restating her declaration of war, Jonas had countered by saying he'd tell Big Jane and Chicago Joe—the two brothel owners who'd most recently lost girls to Madame Lestraude's smuggling operation—that she was to blame. The woman laughed in his face. "No you won't. Not when Jakob Gunderson participated in a rescue last Tuesday night."

Jonas pounded his fist on his desk, the stacks of books and papers jumping in response.

He loved his "boys." He and Lily had never been blessed with children. Their dear friends, the Pawlikowskis, taught their twins to call him uncle and his wife aunt. Jonas and Lily had even made the boys their heirs. Years later, when Hale left home for Helena, he had truly become a son. They changed their will, making their once-distant nephew their sole heir. Though Isaak and Jakob were no longer his heirs, Jonas still loved them. If he exposed Madame Lestraude while Jakob worked for her, he might be killed along with her. Jonas wasn't willing to take that risk.

No. He had to come up with a different plan.

For now, he had to make sure Hale was elected mayor so he could become a judge as soon as Montana became a state. Of Jonas's two illicit businesses, the mining operation was the most sustainable. He needed sheriffs and marshals to arrest criminals. He didn't care if the men were honest—like McCall and Valentine—or corrupt, as long as they kept a steady flow of convicts heading to jail. The important cog in the process was the judges. Jonas needed men with a pronounced sense of justice who would impose maximum sentences. Hale Adams was just such a man and would be impervious to bribery by someone like Kendrick.

But first Hale needed to win an election to prove he could do it—to himself and to the people who would vote for the first judges in the newly formed state. The same people who would vote for the first senators. Jonas needed them to see that he still had enough political clout to defeat Kendrick without going up against the man directly. Besides, if statehood came as soon as Jonas was hearing it would, he didn't want to be stuck in the mayor's position when he was unmistakably the best man in the territory for the job of U.S. Senator.

Jonas inhaled and exhaled with a *whoosh*. He needed to collect himself and return to The Import Co.'s grand opening. Hale had announced his candidacy, but the boy was at a loss when it came to campaigning. He'd need all the help he could get. Especially from the Honorable Jonas Forsythe.

Chapter Five

Mrs. Hollenbeck shook Hale's hand. "I'm delighted you're running for mayor, Mr. Adams. You can expect my full support." She spoke loud enough for the next five people in line to hear.

"Thank you, ma'am. That means a great deal to me." Hale squeezed her hand gently, his face aching from smiling and his shoulders hot from the sun.

He moved to the next person in line. They weren't here for him. None of the people in line were. They were waiting their turn to enter The Import Co.—the newest store in town. Emilia McCall was posted at the door, allowing a handful of people in as others left to keep the new store from overcrowding. Hale's job was to take advantage of their wait by shaking hands and making sure everyone received "Helena Needs Hale" buttons. He'd run out of them half an hour ago, giving the basket to Miss Palmer when she stopped by to see how many were left.

After greeting the Watsons, Hale leaned a bit to the left to see how many people were still in line. The two women at the end looked very much like—no, were—Mrs. Archer and her daughter, Antonia.

What were they doing in Helena?

Perhaps they were here to check on Jakob Gunderson.

The agency provided a full refund if either of the parties involved in a correspondence courtship falsified information regarding their appearance or situation.

From what Jakob said, Miss de Fleur was everything he'd requested, she just fell in love with someone else. Which didn't constitute a breach of contract. Not that Hale was an expert in . . .

What kind of law did matchmaking services fall under? And Mrs. Archer was looking at *him*, not Jakob.

Hale worked his way down the line, grateful there were only five people between him and the Archers. No one in Helena knew he'd engaged the services of a matrimonial company, and he wanted to keep it that way—especially if the reason the ladies were in town was to tell him that Portia wasn't coming. Enough people were going to be prying into his privacy now that he'd declared for mayor. He didn't need them prying into his romantic failures.

If it was a failure. Until he spoke with the ladies, he was indulging in speculation.

He kept his greetings short but respectful as he worked his way toward them. "Mrs. Archer, Miss Archer. To what do I owe the pleasure of your company?"

"Mr. Adams." Mrs. Archer held out her hand in greeting. As Hale shook it, she whispered, "Is there somewhere private we can talk?"

His pulse picked up its tempo. "Is something wrong?"

Mrs. Archer cut a censorious glance at her daughter. "No, but we do need to talk about . . . our mutual business."

Curious.

His office was too far away for ladies to walk on a hot day. "Please come with me. I'll ask the owner of The Import Company"—Hale pointed at the black-and-white-painted sign on the side of the brick building—"if we can borrow his private office."

"Of course." Mrs. Archer smiled but it didn't reach her

eyes. "It looks like quite a nice gathering. May I ask what it's for?"

Hale explained about the combination grand opening and candidacy announcement as he ushered the ladies around the back of the store to the alley entrance. They weren't there to shop, so it wasn't improper to enter via the back door and avoid the line. When they entered the stockroom, Hale excused himself to find David Pawlikowski. He was hanging a "SOLD" tag on a tall grandfather clock while assuring a large woman with makeup as heavy as her jowls that he could order her an identical one.

After receiving permission to borrow the man's office, Hale led the ladies up the back stairs, opened the door, and allowed them to precede him.

There were two desks in the spacious room. One was on the right, the surface piled high with papers, cans of paint, and tin ceiling tiles. That one had to be Jakob's as he'd been in charge of the store's construction. The desk directly in front of them held nothing but a wrought-iron picture frame. Some rolls of wallpaper and a ladder were propped against the wall on the left, the space in front of them large enough for another desk.

Hale grabbed the two chairs and set them side by side in front of the clean desk. "Please have a seat."

"Thank you," the women replied in unison—Miss Archer with a look of defiance on her face.

The two ladies were both tall, lean, and had square jaws. They had dark hair under their hats—the elder's a sensible bonnet tied in a bow under her chin, while the younger wore a concoction with a long, red feather and an enormous bow tied to the side.

He leaned his hip against the edge of the desk and faced the women. "Now, what brings you all this way?"

Instead of answering, Mrs. Archer turned her head to glare at her daughter.

Miss Archer glared right back.

Mrs. Archer shook her head. "You got us into this mess, so you will get us out of it."

That sounded ominous.

Miss Archer raised a gloved hand to grip the gold locket hanging around her neck. "I didn't get us into any mess. It will all work out just fine."

"A matter of opinion—one which I highly doubt." The older woman huffed. "Get on with it."

Hale might as well have been somewhere else for all the attention they were paying him.

With a heavy sigh and a stinging glance at her mother, Miss Archer finally looked him in the eye. Lifting her chin, she squared her shoulders. "Did you or did you not request that Miss Portia York come to Helena to commence a sixty-day courtship?"

"I did."

"Then it's safe to say you are happy with her?" There was both a challenge and a question in her words.

"I am."

The younger woman turned her head to give her mother a triumphant smile. "Even though she wasn't the kind of woman you said you *wanted*."

She wasn't? Hale tried to remember the qualities he'd listed on his original application for the agency's services.

Mrs. Archer bent her head, tipping it so her face was hidden from his view by the brim of her bonnet. She whispered, "Our philosophical difference is the least of our problems here."

What on earth did that mean?

"He can hear you, Mother."

The women stared across the two feet of space between them, the veins above Mrs. Archer's high collar visible. Whatever was going on, it appeared it had the woman strained to her last nerve.

"Go on," he encouraged in his best lawyerly voice.

Miss Archer shifted her attention back to him. "Well . . . as you know, you rejected the first nine women we sent to you."

"Yes, I recall that I did." Where was she going with this?

"But then I sent you Miss York's biography and you've been writing to her ever since."

He waited for her to continue.

She lifted her chin a bit higher.

". . . And?"

"So it's safe to say you're happy with her." Miss Archer was working him the way he did clients who needed to be talked into something they didn't want to do even though it was for their own good.

"Go on." This time his patience had reached its limit and the words came out as a command.

There was a little less defiance on her face. Maybe even a bit of concern. "Well . . . you see . . . I went a little outside the agency's normal practices to procure Miss York for a correspondence courtship."

His neck heated. "Define 'outside normal practices' for me."

She waved her hands like she was warding off a bee. "Oh, it's nothing bad, I assure you."

Hale lowered his chin. "In my experience, Miss Archer, whenever someone must assure another person that what they're about to say is nothing bad, it's usually something bad."

Miss Archer's smile wilted. "Not if you want Miss York to join you in Helena for a sixty-day courtship."

"Which we've already established." Hale attempted to keep his exasperation at bay. But this woman was pushing his limits of gentlemanly behavior. "I'm still waiting to hear how far outside normal agency practice you went with regards to Miss York."

Miss Archer shot a look at her mother, who was now the one looking triumphant. "It's nothing bad."

"You've already assured me on that point, Miss Archer." And he was even less inclined to believe her now than the first time.

"It goes back to your rejection of the first nine candidates we sent you."

"They weren't compatible." Which was rather obvious.

"Although they were exactly what you asked for." She raised her head, a challenge in her brown eyes. "So instead of giving you the woman you *asked* for, I sent you the woman you *needed*."

He narrowed his eyes, trying once again to picture the qualifications he'd listed eight months ago on his application. But—honestly—did it even matter? Portia was who he wanted. However, the lawyer in him wasn't about to say as much. "Are you saying she came to your agency in an unusual way?"

Miss Archer shook her head, the dark red feather tucked into the ribbon of her hat waving from side to side. "Miss York filled out an application and was vetted just as you were, Mr. Adams. I only changed her name and some of her specifics so you wouldn't guess her identity."

He heard the words and understood their meaning, but he couldn't quite comprehend what she was implying. Unless . . . "Did you read the letters she wrote to me?"

This time the feather waved up and down.

He crossed his arms over his chest as though they could shield him from feeling undressed. And she thought this was *nothing bad*? He'd like to hear precisely what she thought qualified for that.

Then again, he really didn't.

She was talking again. He shoved the arguments and accusations shouting inside his head to one side in order to hear her. ". . . knew she was the perfect match for you, but in case you rejected her, as you had the others, I didn't want there to be any awkwardness between you."

He frowned. "Are you saying I know Miss York?"

Another nod, this one less vigorous so the feather barely waved.

He squinted, trying to picture the women he'd met in Denver. "Who is she?"

Miss Archer shot another glance at her mother, took a shallow breath, and looked him in the eye. "Yancey Palmer."

The name exploded inside his skull. He stood so fast, the picture frame toppled. Yancey had lied. Out and out *lied*! He'd opened his heart in those letters, which was hard enough when they were written to a woman he trusted—the woman he thought was his perfect match.

But to Yancey Palmer?

His skin burned with mortification. "I ask you to leave this office, Miss Archer. And I expect a full refund for allowing Miss Palmer to use your agency to pull off this scheme."

"But . . ." Miss Archer looked at him like he was confused or was the one who'd done something wrong. "She didn't—"

"Not another word." He held up his hand, his palm facing her. "I don't care what Miss Palmer said to manipulate you into deceiving me, there is no justification for what you've done. None. Now please leave before I do something we'll both regret." He stomped to the door and opened it. Given what he wanted to do—and say—it was far and away the most gentlemanly option.

Miss Archer stood, her eyes blazing. "If you would just listen—"

"Leave. Now!" The bellow from his throat must've scared the girl because—after a huff—she stormed out.

Mrs. Archer stood. She snapped open her purse and withdrew a piece of paper. "The magnitude of this offense required that I come to you in person to offer both my apologies and a full refund." She laid a banknote on the desk. "I've added additional funds to cover your expenses in corresponding with Miss Palmer and the letter you sent to us requesting her to join you in Helena."

Hale was tempted to march across the room, pick up her feeble attempt to repair the irreparable, and tear it in half right in front of her.

"It also comes with an offer to continue working with you free of charge should you desire." Mrs. Archer touched her hat as though to assure it was still in place. "I completely understand if you are unable to place your trust in me after this. In which case—if you wish—I will refer you to another agency and pay their fee."

If he couldn't trust her again? *If* he wanted to contract with another mail order agency? No and never. He worked his jaw open enough to say, "Not at this time, madam." He gestured to the exit for her as well—also something a gentleman shouldn't do. But he needed the woman out of this office before the rage racing through his veins exploded in a tirade.

Mrs. Archer didn't take the hint. "I think it important that you understand, Miss Palmer—"

"I think we've said all there is to say at this point." Hale barely recognized his own voice. The only other time he'd been this infuriated was on his eighteenth birthday, when he'd found out about another person living a lie.

Mrs. Archer dipped her chin. "Nevertheless, you need to listen to—"

Hale spun around and left.

Yancey was checking the price tag on a set of pillowcases trimmed with Brussels lace when a touch on her elbow turned her around.

Judge Forsythe stood there with a frown on his face. "Have you seen my nephew anywhere?"

"I haven't been keeping track of him since we ran out of buttons." Yancey looked around the store. "Did he make it inside?"

"There's no line outside, so I assume so."

Yancey swung her gaze past the open archway leading into the stockroom. Her eye caught a particularly stylish hat with a tall maroon feather poking out of the brim. Antonia Archer owned a hat exactly like it. Was she here? If so, was something wrong with Nathan? Yancey's breath hitched.

"Are you all right, Miss Palmer?" The judge's question sounded like it came from another room.

"I'm fine, but please excuse me." Without waiting for his reply, she strode toward the back of the store. "Antonia? Is that you?"

The woman spun around. It *was* Antonia. "I'm sorry, Yancey. I'm so sorry."

"About what?" Yancey pressed her palm against her pounding chest. Heat spread up her neck and down her arms. Nathan didn't want her. Or had been injured. Or was lying in a hospital somewhere. Or . . . "Is Nathan dead?"

Antonia jerked backward. "Good heavens, no."

Yancey exhaled with a *whoosh*. "Oh, thank goodness. I was—" The look on Antonia's face stopped Yancey's words. "Something else is wrong. What is it?"

"I don't know where to begin. I never . . . I mean, he was so *happy* with you. I never imagined it would end like this."

Nathan didn't want her. After all their tender words—after he hinted that he wanted to bring her to Denver—he didn't want her. What had changed?

"Let's go somewhere private." The suggestion came from Judge Forsythe.

Before Yancey could tell him—politely, of course—that

this was none of his business, the sound of heavy footsteps drew her attention.

Hale Adams was stomping down the stairs, his face red. He stopped on the third step from the bottom and pointed a finger at her nose. "You lying, scheming, manipulative—"

"Hale!" Judge Forsythe cut into his nephew's tirade. "Calm down."

"Not this time, Uncle. She's gone too far."

Yancey stared at him. "Gone too far? What are you talking about?" The only thing she'd done wrong as far as Hale Adams was concerned was running out of campaign buttons. Yes, she'd underestimated the number of people who would want them, but she hadn't *lied* about it. Or manipulated anyone into wearing one.

"Mr. Adams," Mrs. Archer's voice came from the top of the stairs. "Please. Miss Palmer is as innocent as you are."

"Ha!"

Yancey turned her head away from Hale's scorn. Store patrons gawked and craned their necks for a better view of the drama unfolding in the stockroom.

Lovely. She was being berated for some unknown reason and everyone in Helena—enough of them, at any rate— were watching like the forest-green brocade curtain tied to the door between them made her an actress on a stage.

"Let's take this upstairs, shall we?" Judge Forsythe whispered.

"Sir, under any other circumstance I would follow your advice most heartily." Hale's voice was loud enough to be heard by the back row of their audience. "But I refuse to be in the same room with this . . ."

Yancey returned her attention to Hale.

"This . . ." He repeated as he waved his hand in her direction.

The inexplicable insult was as confusing as it was uncharacteristic. Hale—the man who prided himself on always being a gentleman—had refused to call her a lady or a woman or even a person. Tears stung her eyes—not of grief or remorse—but of rage. "Nor do I wish to be in the same room with you, Mr. Adams." She kept her voice as low as possible and swooped her hand toward the door to the alley. "Please. By all means. *Leave.*"

He stared down at her, unmoving.

"Go to your office." Judge Forsythe's command brooked no argument. "I'll meet you there in half an hour."

Hale slid his eyes from her to his uncle. Some kind of communication passed between them, because after a long moment, Hale clomped down the last two steps and out the door.

Yancey picked up her skirts and ran up the stairs. Hale's scent—a combination of cedar cologne and typewriter ink—lingered in the air. For years, she'd breathed in the fragrance like life. Now she choked on it.

Mrs. Archer met her at the top, swinging her hand toward the open door to her left. As Yancey passed, she heard the matchmaker say, "Sir, what Miss Palmer and I need to discuss is of a confidential nature."

"I am that young man's uncle," he responded, as though that gave him the right to know everything about his nephew's life.

"Then speak to him." Mrs. Archer's tone was polite but firm.

Yancey gripped the back of a chair, her mind jumping from one thought to another.

She'd never seen Hale so livid. Not even at Bruno Carson. She'd done nothing to engender such rage.

Nathan didn't want her. What had she done?

Hale shouting accusations she couldn't begin to unravel and Mrs. Archer calling down—

Wait. Why was Hale talking to Mrs. Archer?

"No, Antonia." Mrs. Archer's voice cut into Yancey's wonderings. "I will speak to Miss Palmer. You go to the hotel and wait for me there."

"But—"

"Antonia Elinor Archer, you turn yourself around and go before I fire you from the agency."

After a slight pause, a swish of fabric announced Antonia had done her mother's bidding.

"Sir," Mrs. Archer continued, "I must ask you to leave."

There was an even longer pause before Judge Forsythe said, "Of course, madam."

When she heard the door click, Yancey let go of the chair and looked around. She had so many questions—all of them equally important and unfathomable—that she didn't know which to ask first.

Mrs. Archer held out both hands as she walked closer. "I'm so sorry, my dear." She drew Yancey into a hug.

"I don't understand what's happening." Yancey pulled away.

"I think you'd better sit down for this."

Yancey obeyed, her stomach hard with dread.

Mrs. Archer looked at the floor, drawing a deep breath before raising her eyes to Yancey. "While you and my daughter were having tea last January, Antonia decided you and Mr. Adams would be a perfect match as long as you didn't realize you were being set up together. She began a correspondence courtship between you as Portia York and Mr. Adams as Nathan St. John."

Yancey slapped a hand over her mouth. She had no breath to form words, even if she could think of something to say. Nathan—her dear Nathan—was gone. Had never existed except as a figment of someone else's imagination. It was like hearing about Joseph Hendry's murder all over again. She closed her eyes and concentrated on forcing air into and out of her lungs.

"To maintain your confidentiality, Antonia opened your letters to him, rewrote them in her own hand, and then sent them to Mr. Adams. She did the same in reverse, typing his letters to you."

Yancey swayed. She let go of the hold over her mouth to grip the edges of the chair. She'd once asked why he typed his letters. He replied that his handwriting was illegible. She'd thought it odd because he was an educated man. A college graduate. Someone with that level of schooling wouldn't have illegible handwriting.

It wasn't odd. It was a deliberate lie from a woman she'd considered a friend.

She pressed one hand to her nauseous stomach. Her private letters—her intimate communications—had been read by Antonia. Even worse, by Hale.

Yancey tasted bile and opened her eyes to look for a waste bin in case her breakfast came back up.

"Mr. Adams would not let Antonia or me explain that you were as innocent as he." Mrs. Archer placed her hand over her heart. "I'm terribly sorry, Miss Palmer. I would offer you a refund, as I did to Mr. Adams, but—as Antonia set up your correspondence outside of the agency—you didn't pay for our services. I don't know what to do to make this up to you."

There was nothing to do. Nathan was gone and—in his place—was a man who loathed her. Who had berated her in public for something she hadn't even done. Who waved his hand at her with insulting dismissal.

"I hope you believe that I knew nothing of this." Mrs. Archer gripped both hands in front of her heart as though praying. "As soon as I found out, I bought the first train tickets available so Antonia could offer a personal apology."

Yancey nodded, unable to form words.

"What can I do?" Mrs. Archer placed her hand on Yancey's knee.

She flinched, unable to stop the instinctive recoil from a woman who—through no fault of her own—had just delivered a crushing blow.

"Is there someone I can get for you?"

There were at least a dozen people Yancey wanted. None of whom the matchmaker knew, so she shook her head.

"Would you like to be alone?"

No, but she had little choice unless she wanted to face the stares and whispers of all the people who had witnessed her humiliation and all the other people who'd heard the story by now. Her stomach lurched. Afraid she'd be unable to control her nausea much longer—and unwilling to subject herself to another embarrassment—Yancey summoned up enough breath to whisper, "I'd like to be alone."

Mrs. Archer patted Yancey's knee before she stood. "Again, I'm terribly sorry. The only comfort I can offer is that Antonia will never do anything like this again."

Which was no comfort at all. Yancey closed her eyes again, concentrating on keeping her breakfast down.

"Are you sure I can't get someone for you? Mr. Jakob Gunderson, perhaps?" Mrs. Archer named the client they both knew had engaged her agency's services.

Yancey shook her head. *Please leave. Please, please, please leave.*

"All right." A slight breeze and a scrape of wood on wood accompanied the words. Soft footsteps soon followed. Stopped. "Antonia and I are at the Grand Hotel if you think of anything we can do to make this better. Again, I'm very sorry." The door clicked open, more footsteps, and another click.

Yancey's control broke. She stood and raced to the metal waste bucket sitting on the floor beside the desk, leaning over it with barely enough time before vomiting.

Heave after heave emptied her stomach of breakfast and her soul of every dream she'd transferred to Nathan St. John.

Chapter Six

"What are you doing in here?"

Yancey turned her head enough to see Jakob, one hand on the door, the other holding a wooden crate with straw hanging over the top edge. She wiped the corners of her mouth with the back of her wrist. If only she had some lemonade or tea to wash down the acidic bile coating her tongue and throat.

"Hey. Are you all right?" He set the crate on the floor and closed the office door before hurrying to her side.

With Mrs. Archer, pretense was possible. Not with Jakob. They'd been friends too long. Yancey shook her head, her chin trembling.

Jakob wrapped her in a comforting hug. "What's wrong?"

In broken sentences interrupted by sobs, she told him her tale of woe as briefly as possible. She ended with, "And Hale had the gall to believe I instigated the whole, miserable thing."

Expecting to hear his shocked gasp or a promise of retribution against the man who'd wronged her so deeply, she was surprised by Jakob's silence. She pulled back to look him in the face. He appeared more resigned than outraged. "I'm really sorry about that, Yance, but . . ."

She stepped away from him, swiping at her cheeks even though most of her tears had been absorbed into his white shirt. "But what?"

"What Hale did was wrong. No question. But . . . I can see his side of it."

Her mouth fell open.

Jakob shrugged. "Take it from someone who recently discovered that the woman he'd offered his heart to was in love with someone else. You aren't thinking straight when it happens."

Oh.

"And Hale will always see you as the girl who broke his heart by ruining his courtship of your sister." Jakob spread his large hands in a helpless gesture, as though there was nothing she or anyone else could do about it.

"Hale never loved Luanne."

"Does he know that?" Jakob tipped his head to one side. "Or did you decide it for him?"

Yancey stared.

"Look"—Jakob dropped his hands to his sides—"I'm not defending what he did, I'm simply saying he has some good reasons for mistrusting you when it comes to his heart."

"But I've not said or done anything in the last year . . . almost."

"I know." Jakob nodded. "But two years ago you decided to ignore him for six months to make him realize how much he secretly missed you."

Yancey hung her head. "I forgot about that."

"And there's the time you pretended to be someone else in need of legal advice, then showed up in his office."

She'd forgotten about that, too. "He still shouldn't have yelled at me."

"Do you want me to pummel him?"

Yancey looked into Jakob's face. He seemed serious.

But then he smiled. "I'm on your side, Yance. Just tell me what you want me to do . . . within reason, of course."

Hale pummeled into the dirt suited her just fine.

She sighed. Might be worth it if Hale wasn't a lawyer and his uncle a judge. Sure as sure, she and Jakob would both end up in jail. Short of disappearing or going back in time, there wasn't much he or anyone else could do.

Yancey eyed the door. "I don't suppose you could take half an hour off to walk me home?"

Jakob glanced at the crate he'd set on the floor. "I can if you need me to."

Did she need him? Really? She'd survived worse than being called a lying, scheming, manipulative whatever Hale was going to add before his uncle cut him off. She'd once been linked to a scam bringing innocent women and girls to Helena to be sold into prostitution. Her name was left out of the article, but everyone knew she'd stood in as proxy bride for Finn Collins—the man accused of the heinous crime.

She reached out and put a hand on Jakob's arm. "Thank you, but I can manage. Your family needs you here today of all days."

He lowered his chin. "Are you sure?"

No, but she needed to be. "I'll manage."

He glanced at the door again. "Do you want me to escort you down the stairs?"

Oh, someone was going to be a lucky woman when Jakob Gunderson offered his heart again. Too bad they loved each other as siblings, making anything more between them impossible. She could use a true knight in shining armor right about now.

She squeezed his arm. "I'd prefer a moment alone."

He laid his hand over hers. "I'll be running between downstairs and the third floor if you need me."

"Thank you."

After he left, Yancey took a few minutes to think over what Jakob had said . . . and to prepare herself for what awaited her once she left the safety of the office. She took several deep breaths, checked her hair in the window's reflection, and smoothed the front of her skirt.

She paused at the door. People were bound to talk. She didn't have to listen. She was innocent, regardless of what anyone else thought. But . . . oh, how she hated it.

She straightened her posture, opened the door, and put one foot in front of the other.

Sure enough, the first thing she heard when she reached the bottom of the staircase was Mrs. Watson's voice. "If you ask me, it's about time he gave that Palmer girl a come-uppance."

"What do you think she did this time?" This voice was unfamiliar.

"Whatever it was, I've never seen Mr. Adams so furious." Mrs. Watson's voice began to fade. "Did I tell you about the time . . . ?"

Yancey ducked her chin and hurried out the back door to the alley behind The Import Co. She should go down to the telegraph office at the train depot to relieve her father so he could enjoy the grand opening, but she turned her feet toward home. There was chocolate cake left over from last night's supper, and she intended to finish every last slice.

Once she cleared the alley, she kept her head down and weaved through the lingering crowd. But not fast enough to avoid hearing their words. While some people were nicer than others, everyone assumed she had once again thrown herself at Hale Adams. Someone called her laughable and pathetic.

Laughable and pathetic.

The words chased her down the street and into her house, where there wasn't enough chocolate cake to drown them out.

Jonas tapped his cane along the ground as he strode to Hale's office. He wrenched the door open, not caring that it banged against the inside wall so hard it left a small dent in the wood paneling of the foyer. He marched through the waiting area and—the moment he cleared the double doors—pointed his cane at his nephew. "Your behavior to Miss Palmer was unconscionable."

"False." Hale jumped to his feet, slapping the file he'd been reading atop the atrocious pile of papers and books strewn across his desk. "My behavior was civilized given what she deserves."

"And what is that? To be locked in the stocks where people can throw rotting vegetables at her or be burned at the stake?" Jonas named medieval punishments to shock Hale out of his unjustified rage.

"Something like that." Hale raked his fingers through his hair. "That woman has interfered in my life for the last time."

"She didn't interfere in your life."

"With all due respect, sir, you're wrong."

Jonas raised his eyebrows. "Are you going to ignore me as you did both the Archer ladies?"

The mention of the matchmakers' names brought Hale around the front side of his desk. "How did you know they were the Archers?"

"It wasn't hard to figure out." Because that bossy woman who all but slammed the door in Jonas's face had called her daughter by all three of her names. "Do you wish to remain in ignorance, or would you like to hear the facts of the case?" He gripped his cane, waiting for a response.

Hale crossed his arms over his chest, his lips pressed flat.

Given that he failed to say no, Jonas continued. "I've

heard the entire story from Miss Archer." Whom he tracked down after she ran down the stairs at The Import Co. He caught up with her just outside the alley door and—after stating his theories as though they were facts—the girl spilled out the entire story. "*She's* the one who pretended to be Portia York, not Miss Palmer."

"After being talked into it." Hale pulled his arms tighter.

"No!" Jonas pounded his cane into the floorboards. "Miss Archer came up with the plan of pretending to be both Miss Portia York and a Mr. Nathan St. John—pseudonyms inspired by Miss Palmer's initials, Shakespeare characters, the Revolutionary war hero Nathan Hale, and our second president, John Adams, respectively."

Hale groaned.

Jonas had also groaned when he heard the *noms de plume* because they were as trite as the Archer girl was silly. "She said she tried to tell you several times but you wouldn't listen. Rather ungentlemanly of you, Hale." Jonas watched his nephew's face, waiting for the moment Hale understood how unfairly he'd treated Yancey Palmer by assuming she'd engineered the whole affair.

Hale looked out the window. "Given Miss Palmer's past machinations, it was entirely reasonable for me to conclude she was the one who instigated a fraudulent correspondence." He launched into a detailed account of Miss Palmer's schemes, beginning five years ago when he arrived in Helena.

The more he talked, the more of his father Jonas saw. Hale had disowned his father when he was eighteen, refusing to have anything more to do with the man who'd kept a second family hidden away for six years. Jonas had taken the long journey from Montana to New York to advise his sister on filing for divorce. When he'd confronted Lawrence Adams, the man had gone on and on about how he'd never intended to fall in love with another woman and how she'd kept him at arm's length after their initial tryst, but their feelings for each other couldn't be denied.

It had struck Jonas then—as it was striking him now—that the way to reel in an Adams was to give him a taste of heaven and then withdraw it.

Jonas mentally kicked himself for failing to see the father-and-son resemblance until this moment. How could he take advantage of Hale's weakness? Yancey Palmer had captured his heart as the fictitious Portia York. It was possible she could do it again. Hale needed a champion, someone who could charm money out of a turnip.

Miss Palmer fit the bill perfectly.

And given her past history with Hale, she'd fall back in love with him, thereby absolving him of today's debacle—something the public needed to see before they cast their votes in November.

Jonas waited until Hale finished his story to begin his subtle campaign. "I know you're angry at the girl, but that's no excuse for you to be less than the gentleman you were raised to be."

Hale set his jaw. "I refuse to have anything to do with her ever again."

"Don't be stupid, Son." Jonas used the endearment to soften his verbal blow. "Helena may be big but it's not *that* big. Yancey Palmer and her family are fixtures in this town. They—and she, in particular—are well-liked. To snub her would alienate the very people we're trying to woo."

"I don't plan to *woo* anyone." The inflection in Hale's voice told Jonas that his word choice had hit home.

"Then you might as well go back out there"—Jonas pointed in the direction of The Import Co. with his cane—"and announce that you're withdrawing your name from the campaign."

Hale's mouth fell open.

Taking advantage of his silence, Jonas repeated advice

he'd given Hale in the past—advice the boy couldn't keep ignoring. "You cannot continue to cut people out of your life whom you judge unworthy. You did it to your father and my sister. You cannot afford to do it to Miss Palmer, not while you are running for mayor and not when she is innocent."

Hale held himself rigid. "You're sure Yancey had nothing to do with this?"

"As sure as I am that you are innocent of any wrong-doing . . . at least regarding this mail-order bride business." Jonas watched as his words eased the hostility in his nephew's face.

Hale took a deep breath, holding it for several seconds before letting it out in a *whoosh*. "I was so sure . . . I mean, why wouldn't I jump to that conclusion? It was logical, given her past history with me."

"Then if your logic was correct, what was your mistake?" When Hale first talked about becoming a lawyer, Jonas often quizzed him this way, stretching him to think beyond the easy assumptions and conclusions in order to see the opposing argument. Since then, Hale had learned how to debate, which was nothing more than finding valid points on both sides of an issue and presenting each with equal dedication. "Come, Hale. Work it through from beginning to end and tell me where you went wrong."

After a long moment, Hale said, "I failed to listen to Miss Archer's full explanation."

"Meaning you jumped to your conclusion without hearing all the facts."

Hale nodded.

"And then you compounded your error by accusing Miss Palmer—in a very crowded store, I must remind you."

Hale looked down. "Quite unforgivable of me. I will apologize to Miss Palmer the next chance I get."

"Which you will make sure is in a very public place."

Hale's head snapped up. "I'm no longer a child, Uncle Jonas. I know what's right."

Jonas smiled. "Excellent. Your chances of beating Harold Kendrick just went up by fifty percent. Speaking of our illustrious mayor . . ." Jonas paused for effect, turning Hale's attention to more important matters. "I'm going to tell you the same thing I told Isaak. Kendrick will fight dirty. Do not sink to his level."

Hale's eyes narrowed. "Any chance he set that fire last week to scare Isaak out of the race?"

Jonas feigned shock. He'd been prepared for this question.

Hale waved his hand back and forth as if he was erasing the comment. "Forget I asked. Even Kendrick isn't that reprehensible."

The revulsion in his nephew's voice made Jonas blink. Had he sunk lower than his arch rival? Was he, in fact, *reprehensible*? Jonas stood before his uncertainty showed on his face. "Now we must get back to the grand opening. You've a great deal of campaigning to do."

Chapter Seven

Sunday, May 6, 1888

"Yancey? It's almost time for church." Mother's voice came from the hallway.

Yancey rolled onto her side and folded the pillow over her head. She wasn't going anywhere today. She was staying in bed until she figured out a few things. Did she want Jakob to pummel Hale Adams after all? Did she bear a smidgeon of responsibility for his misunderstanding? And how long would it take before all the people in Helena who'd witnessed her humiliation—or heard about it from Mrs. Watson—either moved away or were too old to remember it?

A knock was followed by the click of the door opening.

"Yancey? Why aren't you ready?" Mother's voice was full of gentle concern. The bed dipped and Yancey felt a hand on her arm. "Are you unwell?"

"I feel awful." Yancey enunciated clearly so her words would penetrate the pillow hiding her face. And it was the truth. She might not know how she felt about Hale or Mrs. Watson or the anonymous person who called her laughable and pathetic, but she knew one thing for certain. She felt awful.

Mother *tsked*. "I thought something was wrong yesterday when you left the grand opening so early." She tugged at the edge of the pillow. "Let me feel your forehead for a fever."

Knowing she wasn't going to get away with saying no, Yancey let go of the pillow and allowed it to fall open. "I'm not sick, but I'm not going to church today either."

"Why not?" Mother placed a cool hand on Yancey's forehead. Did all mothers check for illness anyway, or was it just hers? "You don't feel feverish."

"I'm not sick." Just laughable and pathetic. Yancey pulled the pillow back over her head. "Am I really nothing but a manipulative schemer?" She hadn't been able to get Hale's accusation out of her head since he'd leveled it.

"What did you say, dear?"

Yancey let the pillow flop flat and repeated her question.

A sad smile lifted Mother's lips. "Who said that about you?"

"Hale." Yancey blinked back tears, wishing she knew if they were of anger or sorrow.

"Oh, dear." There was no comfort in her mother's voice, which could only mean one thing.

"You agree with him, don't you?"

Mother shook her head. "Don't go putting words into my mouth. I didn't say that, nor do I believe it."

Afraid of the truth but needing to hear it anyway, Yancey asked, "Then what do you believe?"

This smile was full of matronly love. "You are a treasure, Yancey dear. There is no one else I know who can brighten up a room the way you do simply by walking into it." She stroked Yancey's hair. "There's a reason your father and I call you our joy."

The endearment struck her in the heart.

"And we"—Mother placed a hand on her chest—"aren't

the only ones who know it. People flock to you because you make them feel good. And because of that, they will follow you wherever you lead. It's a gift, really."

A "but" was coming.

"But"—Mother fulfilled Yancey's expectation— "it's a gift you must treat with care."

After wriggling out from under the bedcovers, Yancey leaned her shoulder blades against the headboard. "What do you mean?"

Mother shifted on the bed so the two of them were facing each other. "When you use your great enthusiasm to motivate people to good works, as you have with the Ladies' Aid Society, you honor how God created you."

"But"—Yancey beat her mother to the next thought— "sometimes I'm a little too enthusiastic about winning people to my side. I need to honor a person's no."

Mother nodded. "As you should have with Hale for all these years."

Yancey toyed with a loose thread atop a pink rose quilted into her bedspread. "Why didn't you stop me?"

A soft huff left her mother's lips. "My dear girl, what more could I or your father have said or done?"

"Probably nothing." The truth stung. "But I wish you had tried harder."

"As I wish you had listened the first time."

Ouch.

Mother put her hand on Yancey's foot. "I hope you will listen to my advice regarding what to do about Hale now."

She didn't want advice. She wanted to ignore yesterday as though it had never happened. Regardless of who was right or wrong, her hopes and dreams had been torn out of her chest.

But she couldn't hide in her bedroom forever. She'd

promised to help with both the kickoff *and* the Independence Day picnic.

She pulled the covers tight against her waist. "I guess I could use some advice."

Mother smiled her approval of the decision. "Helena needs a good mayor, and Hale Adams is the best candidate for the job. Do you agree with that?"

"Yes." But only because Harold Kendrick was the other option. No, that wasn't fair. Hale was a good candidate. Yancey just didn't know how to act the next time she saw him.

"Then keep your promise to Isaak and help Hale get elected. Not because it will impress him or make him like you or any of the other emotions you've tried to elicit from him over the years. Help him because it's the right thing to do and because you have the skills he lacks."

After her mother left, Yancey pondered the advice. She'd *been* helping Hale without chasing him regardless of what anyone else thought. And going forward, she would continue helping him. Not because she'd promised Isaak, but because she—Yancey Marilyn Palmer—was so over her infatuation with Hale Adams that nothing would ever make her the laughable, pathetic girl she'd been until now.

She flung back the covers. She'd go to church, hold her head high, and make sure she smiled at Mrs. Watson and her little group of gossiping biddies.

Resolve in place, Yancey rushed to dress in her blue calico. She pulled her hair over her shoulder, braiding it as she ran down the hall. She made it to the carriage room in back of the house just as she secured the end in a band. Her father was lifting the reins to set the surrey in motion. She slowed her pace to keep the horses from spooking.

As soon as she was settled in the back seat, Mother looked over her shoulder. "Good girl."

The praise sustained Yancey until they arrived at church. Hale Adams was among the congregants who were milling around in the open lot waiting for the doors to open. The moment he saw her, he made a beeline for the surrey.

Every head turned.

Mother shot another glance over her shoulder, this one a mix of surprise and confusion.

Yancey lifted both shoulders. She had no idea why Hale Adams—who regularly attended Carline's church across town—was marching straight toward them.

When he reached the surrey, he held out his hand. Yancey wanted to slap it away and tell him she was quite capable of climbing out of a carriage—and living her life—without him. But the rude gesture went against her resolve. She placed her hand in his and allowed him to help her down.

The instant her feet touched the ground, he dropped her hand. "Miss Palmer"—he bent his neck in a stiff bow—"allow me to apologize for my behavior yesterday. I wasn't in possession of all the facts and accused you unjustly."

She snuck a glance over his shoulder to see the reaction of those close enough to hear. Mrs. Watson was wide-eyed, a gloved hand cupped around her mouth, the tall ostrich feather poking out of her hat intertwined with a nearly identical feather in Mrs. Hess's hat because their heads were so close together.

Yancey curled her fingers into fists. Knowing she'd be whispered about and seeing it happen in front of her eyes were two different things.

She would not cry. She would not even sniff.

She lifted her chin and returned her attention to Hale. With a regal head tilt—at least she hoped it was regal—she acknowledged his apology. "Thank you, Mr. Adams. I hope we can both put this entire incident behind us."

For the good of the campaign.

He bowed again, this one a fraction deeper. "You are too good, Miss Palmer."

She was. Too bad he'd not figured that out before yesterday.

Or five years ago.

May 7, 1888

Monday, after a quiet day at work, Hale went to his favorite restaurant for dinner. Gibbon's Steak House was a mere two blocks from his home and office, and they served their own beef from cattle specially bred and fed. The restaurant was usually busy, but the headwaiter knew Hale's routine and always saved him a table at seven in the evening.

Hale entered the restaurant at precisely five minutes to seven. "Good evening, Malachi. It smells delicious in here, as always."

Instead of answering with his usual, *And as always, we've saved a special cut of meat just for you, Mr. Adams*, Malachi smiled with cool civility. "Good evening, Mr. Adams. How may I help you?"

Taken aback by the coldness in his tone, Hale cleared his throat to give himself a moment to think of a suitable response. "I'm here for dinner." He felt foolish stating the obvious.

Malachi looked down at the reservations list. "What time would you like to eat? My earliest opening is eight thirty."

"But—"

"On Wednesday."

Hale felt his cheeks fill with heat. Why was Malachi being so inhospitable?

"Did you know my wife has been ill of late?" The maître d' lifted his chin as though he expected Hale to dispute the statement of fact.

"No."

"Miss Palmer has come every week with a basket of fresh-baked goods." Malachi eyed Hale up and down. "She's a gem of a girl, that Yancey."

Someone behind Hale snickered. He scratched the back of his itching neck. As usual, Uncle Jonas was right. People were choosing sides in what would have been a private matter if Hale had handled himself with more circumspection. Galling, to be the center of attention for something so trivial.

No . . . not trivial. Personal. Embarrassing. And unnecessary.

If only Mrs. Archer had done as she promised and vetted every female candidate *herself.* Or if she'd exercised more control over her daughter. Or if he'd spoken calmly to Miss Palmer in front of witnesses. Or if his very public apology at church yesterday had sounded more sincere—but it was all he could do to force the words out of his mouth with her standing there looking at him like he was a slug she wanted to crush beneath her boot.

Too many regrets, none of which helped him now.

He smiled at the *maître d'.* "Please put me down for eight-thirty on Wednesday."

Malachi bent over his reservations list, the pencil in his hand scraping against the paper. "Until then, Mr. Adams."

"Until then." Hale placed his hat on his head and left the restaurant. What now? Would he receive the same cold shoulder at other restaurants? His icebox was empty at home, so he had no choice but to try a different restaurant. He ended up at Last Chance Café. He'd never eaten anything but lunch at that establishment. He was surprised to find they served the same menu for dinner.

He ordered his usual ham and cheese sandwich with black coffee. His food was delivered at the same time Jakob Gunderson walked through the café doors.

Hale braced himself for a lecture.

Jakob stopped at the table and dropped a look at the empty chair. "May I join you?"

There were plenty of open spaces where he could sit, but to be polite, Hale pointed his open palm at the chair. "Of course."

Jakob sank into it with a sigh. "I think this is the first I've been off my feet all day." He waved at someone across the room. "I've never seen you here for dinner. I thought you usually went to Gibbon's."

"They were"—Hale searched for a suitably ambiguous yet still honest explanation—"unable to accommodate me."

Jakob smirked. "The Yancey effect?"

Before Hale could ask what that meant, Jakob turned his attention to the pretty young waitress who'd rushed to the table. She smiled at him like he was the answer to whatever dreams she had for her future.

Ten minutes ago, she looked down on Hale like his presence was an affront.

Jakob waved off the menu she held out to him. "I'll take the meat loaf and the pot roast dinners with extra gravy. And I'll have both an apple pie and some chocolate cake for dessert."

The waitress didn't seem fazed by the huge order. "Coffee or tea, sir?"

"Coffee, please, and lots of it."

The girl giggled and hurried off to the kitchen.

"The *what* effect?" Hale asked as soon as she was out of earshot.

"You've never experienced it because you've never been on her bad side before." Jakob scratched his jaw. "When we were thirteen or fourteen, Yancey and I got into a public disagreement at school. I forget now why we were at odds, but within two days of hurting her feelings, everyone in school hated me. I do remember feeling justified in whatever it was

I said or did to make her angry, but that didn't stop me from being the villain at school." He paused and looked Hale in the eye. "Even after I apologized."

Hale bit into his ham and cheese. What Jakob was describing and what happened at Gibbon's Steak House were eerily similar.

"She told me about the debacle with Miss Archer." Jakob lowered his chin.

Hale swallowed. "I'll admit I jumped to a conclusion."

"It made her the subject of gossip. Do you realize how much that bothers Yancey?"

"I think I have an inkling."

Jakob shook his head. "Why? Because it bothers you some?"

Hale took another bite of his sandwich. The lecture from Uncle Jonas was bad enough, he didn't need another one.

"I'm going to let you in on a little secret." Jakob picked up his napkin and unrolled it to reveal the silverware. "Yancey loves people. *Loves* them. And when someone doesn't love her back—or is at least friends with her—it eats at her."

The waitress came back to the table and filled Jakob's coffee cup. She left without refilling Hale's.

Jakob's eyes crinkled with mirth.

Hale dropped his sandwich on his plate, the cheese falling out. "And you think *that*"—he jerked his chin toward the retreating waitress—"doesn't bother me?"

"I didn't say Yancey was *bothered* by gossip, I said it *eats* at her." Jakob placed his napkin in his lap. "You didn't stick around after you apologized yesterday—"

"I went to my own church." As was right and proper.

"—so you didn't see all the looks and whispers Yancey endured from the gossip biddies." Jakob picked up the red mug filled with coffee and held it close to his lips.

Hale sat back in his chair. "I'm sorry for that. Truly.

And I admit my behavior to Miss Palmer has been less than gentlemanly in the last forty-eight hours."

"I offered to pummel you for it." Jakob took a sip, his eyes never leaving Hale's face.

Hale looked down and brushed crumbs from the napkin in his lap. "As you have failed to accost me, I take it she declined your offer."

"She did, but she thought about it for a long time." There was a short pause before Jakob said, "I also told her your reaction wasn't all that surprising, given your past with her."

"That's what I told Uncle Jonas." Hale winced. He sounded like a child caught stealing candy but trying to justify it with hunger. "However"—he took a breath and looked Jakob in the eye—"I shouldn't have confronted her in front of your customers. I apologize, Jakob."

"Apology accepted." Jakob leaned back to allow the waitress to place a plate of steaming pot roast and an enormous mound of mashed potatoes covered with brown gravy in front of him. She'd brought a coffeepot with her and added a splash to Jakob's almost overflowing cup.

She eyed Hale's empty cup for a long moment before refilling it halfway.

Jakob's shoulders shook, but he managed to keep from laughing outright until the girl turned and left. "I should warn you, it will take several weeks for the Yancey effect to wear off. And that's only if she truly forgives you."

Meaning she hadn't yet. Hale picked up his sandwich and took a bite. To be fair, his apology had been rather stiff . . . and maybe just a touch forced.

He didn't want to talk about Yancey Palmer or his own shortcomings anymore. When he'd finished his bite of ham and cheese, he changed the subject. "Has the fire marshal determined the cause of the fire at The Resale Company?"

Jakob dipped his chin, an acknowledgment that the subject was now closed. "Not conclusively, but he said it was suspicious. Something about the smoke pattern on the walls and the charred edges on the floor being wrong." Jakob picked up his fork and poked it into the potatoes and gravy. "I confess I stopped paying attention when Ma grilled him on the technicalities." He took his bite of potatoes, closed his eyes, and sighed as he chewed.

Hale waited for Jakob to swallow. "Does he know where it started?"

"The back office, which doesn't make sense. If anything, the fire should have started on the other side of the building where we keep"—Jakob shook his head—"*kept* turpentine and varnish. I'm not sure if I feel better or worse that it wasn't Isaak's or my fault for improperly storing chemicals."

Hale glanced at his half-eaten meal, his appetite gone. "Do you think Harold Kendrick could have set it? To drive Isaak out of the race?"

"I don't know. Maybe. But it seems rather extreme." Jakob didn't seem surprised or offended by the suggestion, unlike Uncle Jonas.

The waitress delivered Jakob's second dinner, the meat loaf and mashed potatoes drowning in dark brown gravy. While he flirted with the girl, Hale took time to think.

He was trained to pay attention to clients, to judge whether they were telling the truth or trying to conceal information. When he'd suggested Kendrick was guilty of arson to Uncle Jonas, his reaction seemed rehearsed. The enmity between him and Harold Kendrick was no secret. The most logical explanation for the feigned surprise was that Uncle Jonas had thought through all the ramifications of the fire—including the possibility that Kendrick set it— but wanted to keep his suspicions to himself rather than outright accuse his rival without solid proof.

An explanation that didn't quite satisfy Hale. Keeping

suspicions from the general public was one thing, keeping them from family was another.

"Do you think Kendrick set it?" Jakob held a forkful of meat loaf over his plate, gravy dripping down the sides.

Hale wiped his mouth with the red cotton napkin and returned it to his lap. "If he did, I have underestimated my opponent."

And it was a good thing Miss Portia York was a myth. He didn't want someone he loved within reach of Harold Kendrick, a man who may have set fire to a building while women were inside it.

Chapter Eight

Friday, May 11, 1888

Yancey glimpsed the unmistakable form of Isaak Gunderson through the windows overlooking the train platform. Her heart bumped against her sternum. She laid Mrs. Abbott's message on the counter. "Will you excuse me? I'll just be a moment."

While Mrs. Abbott was still saying, "Of course, dear," Yancey raced out of the telegraph office.

Was Zoe back? Or had Isaak been unable to persuade her to come home with him?

Yancey had ached for both of them, wondering how their love story would end.

By the time she crossed through the depot waiting area and onto the wooden platform, Zoe was beside Isaak, both of them glowing with love for each other. They were a remarkably handsome couple. His muscular frame, blond hair, and rugged features were the perfect complement for her willowy frame, near-black curly hair, and delicate skin. How she managed such a fine figure when she made the most incredible food was a mystery.

"I'm so glad you're back." Yancey pulled Zoe into a hug,

then reached out with her right hand to grip Isaak's arm. "You simply must tell me everything that's happened since I saw you last."

Zoe held up her left hand. A plain gold band graced her ring finger. "Zis is what happened."

Squealing with delight, Yancey pulled Zoe back into another hug. "An elopement? How exciting."

Isaak shook his head, but the scowl on his face was ruined by the twinkle in his eyes. "Same old Yancey, I see."

She stiffened and took a step back. Had Isaak been in communication with Hale? Or heard about Antonia Archer's deception? Silly her. A man on his honeymoon spent all his time with his bride. He didn't leave her to send a telegram home to check on a campaign he'd given up. Did he?

Before Yancey could ask what he meant by his comment, Zoe wrapped an arm around her husband's waist and snuggled next to him. "Isaak is as happy to see you as I am."

Yancey relaxed. "And I'm glad you are both back home where you belong." She glanced through the windows on her left into the telegraph office. Two people were waiting. "I should get back to work."

A young man with dark hair and bright blue eyes stepped close to Zoe. He seemed familiar, but Yancey couldn't recall his name. He stuck out his right hand. "Hi. I'm Nico, Zoe's brother."

"Miss Yancey Palmer." She shook his hand. "Have we met before, Nico?"

Isaak tugged at his shirt collar. "I don't think you've been formally introduced."

She was missing something. Some connection or memory that tied Isaak, Zoe, and Nico together. But wasn't Zoe an only child?

"Nico is not my actual brother," Zoe answered Yancey's unspoken question. "But he is family in ze same way ze Forsythes are Uncle Jonas and Aunt Lily."

"Speaking of Mrs. Forsythe, she'll be thrilled to have you home." Yancey shot another look into the telegraph office. Three people were waiting. "I really must go, but I hope we can all get together very soon."

"Soon," Zoe echoed.

Isaak and Nico both dipped their chins in identical gentlemanly bows. They were as opposite in physical appearance as two men could be, but Nico apparently had decided to take Isaak as his model for gentlemanly behavior. An excellent choice.

Much better than Mr. Hale Adams.

Yancey offered a small wave, then hurried back into the telegraph office where Mrs. Abbott waited with a smile on her face. "Was that Isaak Gunderson and the Frenchwoman who rejected his marriage proposal?"

"And who was the boy with them?" Mr. Krenshaw asked before Yancey could answer the first question.

Mrs. Abbott turned around, taking the slip of paper she'd started to hand over the counter with her. "I know I've seen his face before."

Mr. Dickenson—who was the third in line—joined in the conversation. "He's the boy who punched the twins after they proposed to Miss de Fleur."

"It's Mrs. Gunderson now," Yancey announced, as gratified to share the good news as she was to figure out why Nico had seemed familiar. She held out her hand to Mrs. Abbott. "I can take your message now."

The remainder of the day passed in much the same way, with people coming in to send or receive messages. Those who were residents of Helena were full of news about Isaak and Zoe Gunderson's return.

When Yancey's shift ended, she rode Judith straight to Carline's house. Judith was a six-year-old bay mare with a gentle disposition and a penchant for cold cooked carrots. She plodded through easy trips from home to the telegraph office and back—never startled at the sound of the steam trolley or when children who didn't know better waved their hats in greeting—but would leap to a gallop whenever an urgent telegram needed delivering. She was a family horse, but she loved Yancey best.

Yancey waved to friends and acquaintances, stopping every few minutes to hear their latest news. Mr. Babcock's new plow was working better than he could have hoped for, Mrs. Lightman's latest grandchild was teething, the Snowes had just signed papers to purchase a ranch on the east side of Helena, and Miss Rigney was questioning whether or not to return to teaching in the fall.

As female teachers were forbidden to have any relationships with men—and Deputy Nick Alderson had begun paying particular attention to the attractive young teacher—Yancey expected Miss Rigney's decision to leave the classroom meant there would be another wedding at church soon. Wouldn't that be lovely? She *did* love a happy ending.

And everyone was bursting to tell Yancey that Isaak Gunderson had come back to Helena a married man. It took twice as long to reach the Popes' house as usual.

Carline opened the door and stepped onto the full-length front porch before Yancey finished tying Judith to the hitching post outside the white, two-story home. "Did you hear that Isaak's back?" Carline waved a dismissive hand. "Never mind. Of course you did. You probably were the first to know."

Yancey grinned and started to climb the five steps going up to the house. "Probably. I saw them when they got off the train. They are both glowing."

Carline sighed. "I love a happy ending."

"I was just thinking the same thing, but"—Yancey looked through the open door to see if Mrs. Pope was within earshot—"I have to say, it's nice that people are talking about someone other than Hale Adams and me."

Carline laughed. "I can understand that. Come on in."

Yancey unpinned her wide-brimmed straw hat from her hair and stepped into the house. The scent of roasting beef made her stomach gurgle.

"Hello, Yancey dear." Mrs. Pope walked into the living room. Her blond hair was coming loose from the bun at the base of her neck, the curling tendrils clinging to her damp skin—her appearance still better than how frazzled Yancey looked when she cooked. "Are you staying for dinner?"

"If it won't be too much trouble." With Carline's Uncle Eugene still in town and making life miserable for the entire Pope family with his overbearing demands, Yancey didn't want to assume she'd be welcome as usual.

"You're no trouble." Mrs. Pope added a slight emphasis to *you're*, although not so much as to be outright rude.

Carline gave Yancey a significant look and shook her head as if to say, *Don't ask*. To her mother, she said, "Do you need help with dinner, or may I take Yancey back to my room and show her the new dresses Uncle Eugene bought me?"

Mrs. Pope glanced at the cuckoo clock on the wall. "I could use some help, but not for another twenty minutes or so."

"Thank you, Mother." Carline took Yancey by the hand and pulled her toward her bedroom. Once inside, she flung open the door to her closet. Like most girls, Carline's wardrobe consisted of four dresses: two for everyday wear, one for church and special occasions, and one for gardening or other messy work. Four new dresses hung in the closet, the shiny fabric gleaming in the late-afternoon sun. Carline pulled out the pale peach one and held it against her chest. "Isn't this the most ridiculous lot of frills you've ever seen?"

Yancey pressed her palm against her cheek. "I'm so relieved you think so. I was trying to come up with something nice to say and couldn't think of a thing other than that the color is pretty."

"On someone with a different skin tone, maybe." Carline held the dress away to stare at it. "If it weren't for all the ruffles, I'd look like I wasn't wearing anything."

Yancey burst into laughter. "Show me the others."

Carline tossed the frilly peach thing on her patchwork bedspread and reached for a mint-green one. This one was also made of a shiny fabric, likely satin. She held it up to her chin. "Better, but still too many ruffles for my taste."

Yancey eyed the dress from top to bottom. "If you took off the one around the neck, it would be better."

Brightening, Carline looked down. "Yes. That's exactly what it needs." She tossed it on the bed on top of the peach dress, then reached for the yellow one.

The moment she held it near her face, Yancey let out a gasp. "Oh goodness. It makes you look ill."

Carline chuckled. "That was my exact thought. I hope Uncle Eugene never insists I wear it in public. People will think I have consumption." She tossed it on the growing pile. "But at least it's not frilly."

"Too bad you couldn't have the same style in the green fabric."

"Yes. Between the two, there's one good dress." Carline pulled out the pale blue one and held it up.

Yancey gasped. "Oh. Oh. It's beautiful."

The color complemented Carline's skin tone, brought out the blue in her eyes, and there wasn't a ruffle in sight. Instead, the bottom of the skirt had pleats that gave the dress interest without flounces.

"I saved the best for last, although"—Carline tucked her chin to look down—"I'd prefer to save it for my wedding. Not that I'm ever going to have one."

"Don't be silly." Yancey regretted the instinctive words the moment she saw her friend flinch. She wrapped her arm around Carline's waist. "What's wrong?"

She shook her head and sighed. "Uncle Eugene's visit

was supposed to last three days. He keeps extending. Pretty soon, he's going to wear down my parents so they'll convince me to go to a finishing school back East."

Which had nothing to do with getting married, but Yancey remained silent.

"With you *not* leaving for Denver"—Carline hugged the dress close, crushing the blue satin under her fingers—"I don't want to leave Helena. I never did. I just said so because I didn't want you to worry about me when you left. Can you imagine me at some hoity-toity school for millionaires' daughters? I'll be a laughingstock. The girls will all shun me, and even if I have the opportunity to meet any men, they will most likely find me stupid and provincial."

Yancey squeezed her friend's waist. "Then don't go."

Carline shook her head. "I don't know if I'll have a choice. Uncle Eugene is so insistent, and Mother's already starting to be swayed. Last night, she sat right there"—Carline pointed to her dress-covered bed—"and listed all the advantages of getting a broader view of the world."

Yancey turned and took the blue dress from Carline's fingers. After tossing it atop the others, Yancey held out both hands and waited for Carline to grip them. "As much as I hate to admit it, your mother might have a point."

"Not you, too," Carline whined.

"Don't misunderstand me, I think you should do whatever is best for you. I'm just not sure staying in Helena *is* what's best." Yancey pulled one hand free and used it to push aside the dresses so she and Carline could sit side by side. "My mother gave me some advice about Hale that I think applies to you. She told me I needed to help Hale win the mayoral election not because of what it will get me, but because he's the best candidate for the job. And that's precisely what I'm going to do. Not because I want to, but because I need to."

The look on Carline's face said she didn't understand the connection.

Yancey took a deep breath and tried again. "You are going to inherit ten million dollars. It might be next week or twenty years from now. Like me, you've grown up in a nice but not opulent home with ordinary parents and ordinary friends."

Carline huffed. "No one has ever called you ordinary, Yancey Palmer."

The compliment made her smile. "You know what I mean. You haven't grown up prepared to handle that kind of wealth. I'm no expert, but I imagine there's a trick to it. All you need to do is look at the difference between Mrs. Gibbon and Mrs. Hollenbeck." Yancey named the two wealthiest women in all of Helena. One was mean as a snake, the other as kind and generous as God ever made a woman.

"Then why can't I learn the trick of managing wealth from Mrs. Hollenbeck?" Carline reached out a hand to toy with a blue-satin pleat.

"You probably can." Yancey waited for Carline to turn so they were eye to eye. "But who knows? If you go to finishing school, you might meet a wonderful man who is tired of silly rich girls and wants one who was raised like an ordinary person."

Carline's smile was tenuous. "I'd rather Windsor Buchanan run after me so we can elope like Isaak did with Zoe."

"So would I."

Carline stood and hung the blue dress back in her closet. "I'll have to think about it. Whether I go or remain here, there's a lot I need to learn."

"Me, too." Yancey held up the yellow dress.

Carline took it and hung it next to the blue one. "Are you really going to help Hale Adams get elected for no other reason than because he's the best candidate for the job?"

Yancey huffed. Why was it that every topic always came back around to that man? Too much of her life centered on him.

And frankly, why did she care what he thought of her? She didn't!

A laugh bubbled up. "Do you know what I just realized?"

"What?"

"I no longer need Hale's smile or approval to tell me whether I'm worthwhile as a woman." Yancey looked around the room, seeing the yellow walls, white curtains, and cheerful rag rug as though for the first time. "My future no longer depends on him. I'm free. And in a very strange way, I have Nathan St. John to thank for it."

"But they're the same man."

"That's irrelevant." Yancey picked up the last dress and held it out. "The important thing was letting go of Hale and all the dreams I've foisted upon him over the years." A sudden idea made her heart pound. "What if I return Nathan's letters to Hale? I certainly don't need them anymore."

"Getting rid of your Hale treasures helped." Carline hung the frilly peach dress next to the green one. "Perhaps getting rid of your Nathan treasures will do the same."

And if Hale was inspired to return "Portia's" letters, so much the better. Unless he'd already burned them. That was fine by Yancey. She wanted them gone—either by his hand or hers.

The days of wasting her time over Hale Adams were over.

Across town

After work, Hale snapped the lock on his front door in place and fixed a smile on his face as he sauntered—not raced but *sauntered*—in the direction of the Palmers' house. The Yancey effect had invaded his private sanctuary, also known as his office. The two most galling visits had come from Mrs. Hollenbeck and his uncle. Mrs. Hollenbeck used her quarterly appointment not to discuss the current balance of her various investments and an accounting of her charitable giving but to lecture him about why Yancey Palmer was an asset to anyone running for office. Uncle Jonas, who was on his way out of town for another three weeks to fulfill his duties as territorial judge, only stayed for five minutes, but his words still rang in Hale's ears. *You will invite Yancey to help you plan an additional event—preferably one in the next two weeks—in which she will very publicly support your candidacy. You will saunter—not race but saunter— through town with a smile on your face and stop to greet people all the way from here to the Palmers' house. Your apology was not enough. You must make that girl like you. Have I made myself clear?*

If Hale had another home to go to, he'd have packed his bags and headed out within the hour. He was twenty-eight, yet in the last four hours he'd been made to feel ten years old more times than when he actually *was* that age.

The streets of Helena were bustling with people going home from work or hurrying from one store to another before the shops closed in an hour. Hale purposefully smiled at everyone whether he knew them or not, stopped to assist three different ladies with their parcels, and stood outside Babcock's Hardware Store chatting with Mr. Lombard, who was a fixture on that particular porch.

It wasn't as terrible as Hale imagined it would be. He usually avoided town until just before seven when most people were tucked inside their homes for their evening meal.

His routine was to work until five, lock his outside door, spend another ninety minutes working on things which required concentration, wash up, then head to Gibbon's Steak House or another restaurant for dinner before returning home to read for an hour before bed.

It was a boring life, but it suited him for now. When he was married, he'd head home at five, play with his children while his wife finished up dinner preparations, and then enjoy an evening by the fireside helping his children with their lessons while his wife knitted. They would put the children to bed, sit together reading their books, then walk hand in hand to their bedroom.

A nice dream he was smart enough to know would never fully come true, but that didn't keep him from thinking about it. People exhausted him. He needed hours of quiet before facing another day at work.

He thought back over the letters he'd written to Portia. Had he ever expressed his desire for a peaceful life? If so, Yancey wouldn't have answered him back. The girl flitted from one social engagement to another as though it were her occupation. Although—now that he thought about it— he didn't go out on the town enough to know if that was true or just his impression of her. Where had it come from?

Hale reached the Palmers' house at five thirty only to be informed that Yancey wasn't home. Mrs. Palmer's yellow apron was streaked with red. "I'm making a cherry pie. Would you like to have dinner with us?"

"No, thank you, ma'am. I appreciate the offer, but I very much need to find your daughter." The words felt sticky coming off his tongue.

"She's most likely at Carline's house. And if not, Carline will know where to find her." Mrs. Palmer swiped her fingers across her stomach, leaving another trail of red on her apron. "Do you need directions?"

"I do." Which was galling to admit. After five years of living in Helena, he ought to know where Mr. and Mrs. Pope lived, particularly because he'd shared a pew with them on many Sundays over the last five years.

If Mrs. Palmer was shocked by his admission, she hid it well—which was a relief after the many times he'd been raked over the coals today. She pointed him in the right direction, repeated her offer to host him for dinner, and when he declined again, closed the door.

Hale's stomach protested. The delicious smells emanating from Mrs. Palmer's kitchen were no less alluring because she'd shut the door. The walk to the Popes' house was a mere two blocks. A cool breeze blew across his cheeks. Last night's rain left the streets damp and a pervasive scent of wet earth in the air. Though he chose to make his living inside the walls of an office, he dreamed of one day having a garden of his own. For now, he made do with the small window box of flowers outside his upstairs apartment window.

The Popes' home was along the same lines as the Palmers', modest and well-kept, with a full-length front porch. Lilac bushes grew on either side of the stairs, their gracious scent perfuming the air well before he crossed between them to climb the steps. He inhaled their fragrance and prayed for strength to get through the unpleasant task ahead. As soon as he reached the door, the smell of roasting beef overpowered the lilacs. His stomach squeezed, reminding him that he'd eaten only an apple and some cheddar cheese for lunch.

He knocked three times and took one step back. The thud of footsteps increased in volume, then the door swung inward revealing a man Hale didn't recognize. His hair was thin on top of his rounded face, his cheeks were filled with weblike red veins, and the look in his blue eyes was a cross between hostile and suspicious. "Who are you?"

"My name is Hale Adams. I've come to speak with Miss Yancey Palmer. Is she available?"

Before he finished speaking, Miss Palmer appeared in the background. She came closer, a streak of flour on her chin. "Mr. Adams. What are you doing here?"

Hale stepped backward again. "Might I have a moment of your time?"

The stranger blocking the doorway didn't move until Miss Palmer said, "It's all right, Mr. Nordstrom. Mr. Adams and I are well-acquainted."

True and more tactful than Hale expected. Or deserved.

Mr. Nordstrom turned sideways, allowing Miss Palmer to pass him, then closed the door most of the way.

With a grin, she pulled the door closed. When she turned her attention to him, her smile faded. "What can I do for you, Mr. Adams?" Her tone was cordial and cold.

Hale removed his black hat and held it behind his back. "I was wondering if you might join me for a campaign meeting sometime in the next week or two."

A lopsided smile curved her lips. "A public show of support, Mr. Adams?"

"Quite so, Miss Palmer." His fingers ached from how tightly they were squeezed on the brim of his hat.

The curve of her lips evened out on both sides, yet it lacked warmth. "Let me make a few things clear, Mr. Adams."

Hale braced himself for a dressing down.

"I agree that we"—she pointed at her chest and then at his—"need to be seen together for the sake of the campaign. However, I have no desire to be alone with you on what could be misconstrued as a private social engagement."

"My apologies. I should have mentioned that I will, of course, be inviting Mr. and Mrs. Isaak Gunderson to join us."

Amusement flickered in her eyes. "Yes. You should have. It does no good, Mr. Adams, to keep vital information to yourself when you are trying to work with people." Her expression turned serious. "I would be more comfortable if you invited your aunt and Mrs. Hollenbeck as well. As our purpose is to show a united front for the sake of your campaign, I'd like to be one of several people who are known supporters."

A good point. One he should have thought of himself. "I will ask them to join us."

"Thank you." She wiped her fingers on the brown apron tied around her waist. "I'm free every night for the next two weeks save for Thursdays."

She was? Hale blinked to bring this unexpected view of her into focus. It couldn't be her normal activity. There must be a shortage of entertainments in town. "I will coordinate with the various parties to select a date and time."

"Again, thank you." She dipped her chin in a way that seemed too regal for a girl dressed in calico and wearing flour on her apron and face. "If you could send round a note letting me know when it's arranged, I'd appreciate it."

Hale loosened his grip on his hat. "I'll borrow a carriage and come for you, with Mr. and Mrs. Gunderson along, if that's amenable."

She rubbed her chin, as though just now aware of the flour. "That will be fine. Include the time you'll pick me up and I'll be ready."

He doubted it. Flighty women delighted in keeping men waiting in order to make a grand entrance.

But six nights later, when he knocked on her door precisely at a quarter to seven, Mr. Palmer opened it and invited Hale inside. Miss Palmer was in the parlor, which had been redecorated since the last time Hale visited. She rose from the settee, the shimmery blue dress she wore making a soft, shushing sound. Her matching reticule bulged, the drawstring unable to close over the top of the little bag. It looked like she was carrying a brick. To bash him in the head? "Mr. Adams."

He took off his hat and bowed. "Miss Palmer. You look lovely this evening." Which she did. She *really* did. Another layer went across the top of the wall he kept between himself and her. Beautiful women were not to be trusted. They lacked character, their way in the world and ability to make men lose their heads too easy. For proof, Hale need only look to his own father.

"What time may I expect my daughter home?" Mr. Palmer's calm voice cut into Hale's misgivings.

"Somewhere between eight thirty and nine."

"Very well, then." Mr. Palmer kissed his daughter on the cheek and whispered something that sounded like, "Be nice."

Miss Palmer nodded, her next breath shaky. "Good night, Papa. I'll see you when I get home."

Hale offered her his arm. She stared at it without placing her hand inside his elbow. Would she deny him the gentlemanly gesture? He was about to lower his arm when she took it, her touch so light he barely felt it through the black suit.

They crossed the threshold and down the steps in silence. Polite phrases tumbled inside his head, none of them feeling genuine or appropriate for the occasion. Due to his own lack of good judgment, he was escorting a woman he'd avoided for the past five years to dinner at his favorite restaurant. The place would never have the same appeal after tonight.

Miss Palmer, who was reputed to be a brilliant conversationalist, was equally silent.

What a delightful evening *this* was going to be. Hopefully, the presence of the newlyweds, his aunt, and Mrs. Hollenbeck would ease the awkwardness between them. Thank goodness Zoe and Isaak were already in the four-seater carriage. Hale opened his mouth to suggest that he and Isaak share the front bench while the women shared the back one. He pressed his lips together again. No man who looked at his wife the way Isaak did would agree to leave her side.

After assisting Miss Palmer into the borrowed carriage—where she immediately struck up an animated conversation with Zoe Gunderson—Hale crossed in front of the matched bay horses and climbed up beside her. He flicked the reins, calling a soft, "Move along."

"Is this Mr. Buchanan's carriage?" Miss Palmer's tone was congenial.

Not sure if the question was for him, Hale waited to see if someone else answered. No one did, so he replied, "It is."

The bladesmith wasn't a particular friend of Hale's, but he was of Isaak Gunderson's. After Hale and Isaak caught up on his elopement and "the great Yancey Palmer debacle," as Hale had mentally dubbed it, Isaak agreed to help smooth things over. Procuring the carriage was one of those ways.

A soft chuckle came from Miss Palmer.

"Something amuses you?" Hale flicked a glance her way before returning his attention to the team. He usually walked or took the steam car through town so, although he knew how to handle a carriage, he needed to concentrate so he didn't make a fool of himself.

Out of the corner of his eye, he saw Miss Palmer clasp her hands together in her lap. The satin ribbon of her reticule dug deep into her white lace gloves. "It's nothing." She then turned on the seat to engage Isaak's bride in conversation again.

Hale's grip on the reins tightened, but he managed to keep from transferring his tension to the horses. They clopped along at a steady pace. The women chattered for several blocks. Neither he nor Isaak said anything. Hale cleared his throat. Etiquette demanded that he at least engage in *some* conversation. He waited for a break in the conversation between the ladies. "Miss Palmer—"

"Please stop."

"But—"

She reached over and pulled on the reins. "Whoa."

Oh. She didn't mean stop talking, she meant stop the carriage. She turned away from him to address a middle-aged woman with a tight expression. "Mrs. Morrow. How is your daughter?"

The woman gave Hale a sidelong glance filled with disgust before turning her head to beam at Miss Palmer. "She's much better today, thank you for asking. The baby should be here any day now, so that'll make everything all right."

"Please give her my best and tell her that the Ladies' Aid Society—myself included—are keeping her in our prayers."

Miss Palmer kept talking, but Hale didn't hear another word. In his mind's eye, he saw the flowing script of Portia telling him about her charitable work with a local ladies' group. How similar were Portia and Yancey? He snuck a glance at his companion. He could only see the side of her face and how well the bodice of her shimmering blue dress fit her figure. A small blond curl resting against her neck caught the light.

Portia had described herself as blond.

Portia and Yancey. Yancey and Portia.

Was it possible they were more alike than dissimilar? His hands jerked, pulling the reins too hard and making the horses snort.

"Careful there," Isaak whispered from behind. "I'd hate to return the horses with sore mouths."

Cheeks warm at the rebuke, Hale relaxed his grip.

"—see you soon." The inflexion in Miss Palmer's voice said she was wrapping up her conversation with Mrs. Morrow. "Good evening."

Hale waited for Mrs. Morrow to repeat the farewell and step back before setting the horses in motion again. Mercifully, the restaurant was only another block away. Hale pulled the carriage to a stop. Isaak sprang out and jogged around the front of the horses to assist the ladies out. Mrs. Hollenbeck and Aunt Lily were visible through the large plate-glass window etched with Gibbon's Steak House. They waved, and Hale dipped his chin to acknowledge their greeting. As soon as Isaak and the ladies were safely on the boardwalk, Hale snapped the reins.

The carriage lurched into motion. He steered it behind the restaurant to a dirt-packed lot with several hitching rails. He found an empty one near the back, tied up the horses, and gave them each an apple, "I hope you enjoy your dinner, because I'm fairly certain I won't."

He shook his head. Now he was talking to horses. Look at what Yancey Palmer had driven him to. He marched toward the restaurant, defying his uncle's instructions to saunter with a pleasant expression on his face at all times. Hand on the door, he took a deep breath and pulled it open.

Chapter Nine

Wishing to avoid more awkwardness between her and Hale, Yancey took a seat between Mrs. Forsythe and Mrs. Hollenbeck. The latter smiled with a hint of amusement. "Very wise."

The simple comment made Yancey suppress a grin. Her days of making a fool of herself over Hale Adams were done. Let the era of the new-and-improved Yancey Palmer begin.

Conversation flowed among the five of them as they waited for Hale. In all her imaginings of sitting beside Hale in a carriage, never had she thought it would be so uncomfortable. He'd said barely two words.

Shy was one thing. Downright unsociable was another. The man graduated from Harvard, for crying out loud. Surely he should be able to manage a ten-minute conversation during a carriage ride.

When he arrived at the table—a smile fixed on his face as though someone had glued it there—Yancey held her breath, waiting for the same surly man who'd driven the carriage to reappear. He sat down and struck up a conversation with his aunt.

Yancey released her breath.

Her irritation with Hale faded over the next ten minutes as he slowly lost his phony smile while engaging in conversation with everyone around the table. The scrupulously polite smile only appeared when he spoke to her.

Mrs. Forsythe leaned close. "Thank you for coming tonight. I know continuing to support Hale's campaign can't be easy for you."

Yancey's throat tightened. "It isn't, but I'm determined to prove that I am no longer romantically interested in Ha—" She swallowed back the rest of his first name. Just because everyone else around the table was using it, she wasn't going to claim that intimacy. Not anymore. She'd done so in the past for all the wrong reasons. "In Mr. Adams."

Goodness. That was harder than expected. She'd called him by his formal name before. Why was it so hard this time?

She squared her shoulders and smiled at Mrs. Forsythe. "He's the best candidate for mayor. I'm here as a show of support for his campaign, nothing more."

Mrs. Forsythe reached over to squeeze Yancey's hand. "You are a treasure, Yancey dear."

Hearing her mother's words on Mrs. Forsythe's lips made Yancey's chest ache. She wanted to be a treasure to someone else. Someone who would vow to love and cherish her all her days. Someone to whom she could vow the same in return.

The letters inside her reticule suddenly weighed ten pounds. She eased the satin ribbon from around her wrist and set the purse in her lap. When she removed her gloves, her right wrist was ringed in red and imprinted with a lace pattern. She rubbed at it to relieve the pain.

"What do you think, Yancey?" Isaak's question held a note of exasperation.

She looked around the table. Every eye was on her. "About what?"

Isaak sliced a startled look at his wife. She must have

kicked him under the table—no, she was too gentle for that. Whatever she'd done, the scowl on Isaak's face eased when he addressed Yancey again. "Hale just said he thought it might be a good idea to differentiate himself from Kendrick by doing something other than a picnic on July Fourth."

"Oh, I agree wholeheartedly." She turned and smiled at Hale—Mr. Adams.

He blinked several times. "You do?"

"Yes." Yancey rattled off her idea to host a catered brunch for select people of large-scale influence, some who were already openly supporting his candidacy and others still on the fence. This would be followed by an evening potluck dinner and games which would last until the annual fireworks display.

"What time were you planning on having dinner?" Mr. Adams asked, something akin to horror in his tone of voice. "The fireworks won't start until nearly ten thirty in the evening."

His aversion to crowds was well-known, and everyone around the table chuckled at his display.

In the past, Yancey would have pitied him. Or come to his defense. Or made excuses for him.

Not anymore.

"Mr. Adams"—she smiled at him with scrupulous politeness—"I'm aware that three or four hours of mingling is not your cup of tea, but if you are going to run for mayor, you're going to have to buck up and do things which make you uncomfortable."

She certainly was.

Mrs. Hollenbeck snorted with laughter. "Well said, Yancey."

Mr. Adams flushed.

For a fleeting moment, Yancey felt sorry for him. But that was the reaction of the old her. The new her had told the truth. Mr. Adams would just have to squirm and get over it.

If he intended to respond to her challenge, he didn't get the chance. Isaak turned the conversation to the logistics of the brunch and extended dinner as though they were scheduled events rather than mere propositions. Yancey had thought through much of the planning already. She inserted her ideas, including Zoe catering the brunch at Mrs. Hollenbeck's house. Both women readily agreed to the suggestion, and soon everyone at the table was so engaged in conversation, the waiter had to come back twice before they were ready to order dinner.

Hale—*Mr. Adams*—was beginning to look at her with grudging respect.

It made Yancey feel a little giddy. Self-assured. Accomplished. Hale Adams might be the best candidate for mayor of their fine town, but Yancey Palmer was the best person to help him win.

The discussion veered from politics to a wide variety of subjects. At every naturally occurring opportunity, she made sure everyone around the table—and everyone else in the crowded restaurant—understood she was over her romantic infatuation with Mr. Hale Adams.

"I put away my romantic interest in Mr. Adams when Mr. Hendry started courting me"—in response to Zoe finding out that Yancey had once pretended to faint when he was nearby.

"I firmly believe Mr. Adams is the best candidate for mayor. Whatever our past difficulties, we've put them behind us for the sake of Helena"—to Mollie Fisk, who stopped by to announce that she and her fiancé, Jefferson Brady, had reconciled and were now planning a fall wedding.

"Thank you for your concern, Malachi, but Mr. Adams apologized for his misunderstanding. We are on friendly terms now"—to the maître d' during his check on the quality of their food and service.

But her assurances were as much for them as for herself.

It was all fine and good to declare she was over the man, but it was slightly more difficult to put into practice.

Especially when he was in his element.

Somewhere between the consommé and the perfectly cooked steak, Hale finally relaxed. He laughed easily, told several witty stories, lightly flirted with Mrs. Hollenbeck, and teased Isaak by telling Zoe what her husband was like at fifteen. He even asked Yancey to call him Hale because everyone else was.

The time flew by. The dessert plates were being cleared when Hale pulled out his pocket watch and clicked open the lid. "I told Mr. Palmer I'd have his daughter home by nine and it's a quarter until that time now."

"Trust Hale to always have his eye on the time," Mrs. Hollenbeck teased. Everyone laughed, his punctuality as well-known as his aversion to crowds. "As enchanting as this evening has been, I must get home myself. Perhaps we can arrange another meeting and finalize the details later."

Goodbyes were said in a hurry, and Yancey was back in the front seat of the carriage headed home in a matter of minutes. The ride was quiet, but not uncomfortably so. Birds and crickets chirped, wind rustled tree leaves, and the steady clip-clop of horse hooves and the crunch of rocks under the steel-rimmed carriage wheels were the only sounds. This was more like what she'd envisioned when she dreamed of coming home after a night with Hale. But she wasn't going to let her imagination run away with her.

She glanced behind her. Isaak and Zoe were sitting close together—his arm around her shoulders holding her close to his side.

They were such a lovely couple.

Yancey faced forward and sighed.

When they reached her home, Hale handed the reins to Isaak and said, "Be careful with their mouths."

For some reason, Isaak responded, "Very funny."

Hale grinned and hopped out of the carriage. He walked around the front and held out his hand to assist her down. This time she didn't hesitate to put her hand in his. Her reticule caught in a splinter of wood and she stumbled.

Hale caught her before she fell. "Are you all right?"

Yancey stepped away from him and stood tall "I'm fine. Thank you."

He looked pointedly at her reticule stuffed full with his letters. "Are you carrying a brick in there?" He grinned mischievously. "Because if you are going to hit me over the head with it, the time is now."

She ducked her head. The new Yancey was grateful he felt comfortable enough to tease her, while the old Yancey took several breaths to gather her composure.

Why did *not* loving him have to be so bewildering?

Yancey peeled the ribbon away from her wrist and opened the drawstring purse. "These"—she pulled out the packet of letters—"are what I received from Antonia Archer. I'm giving them to you for two reasons. First, I want to prove that I too was deceived by her, and second, I want you to know that I have given you up. For good."

He took the letters with his left hand, then turned and offered her his right arm to escort her to her door.

The word her father had whispered in her ear—*forgiveness*—came back to her. They'd had a long talk last night, and he'd encouraged her that part of forgiving Hale was owning up to how she'd contributed to his mistaken impression that she'd devised this trickery.

Even if he didn't accept it.

His apology at her church had been perfunctory, something any gentleman would offer a person he'd wronged. Tonight began as a necessary evil in order to get back in her good graces—or at least to keep her on his campaign. She wasn't ignorant of the Yancey effect, as Jakob had mockingly dubbed it years ago. People outright told her they wouldn't support Hale's campaign as a result of his insulting behavior toward her at the grand opening of The Import Co. At first, it felt good to rally people to her side—particularly as a balm for the other people who were still whispering about her. As the days wore on, she realized how detrimental her attitude was both to Hale and to the entire city.

Jakob, her mother, and her father had all encouraged her to own up to how she'd contributed to the misunderstanding between her and Hale. Perhaps the reason she was having such difficulty moving forward into her new "era" was because she hadn't owned up to her past.

They climbed the last step to the porch. Yancey took her hand from his arm and turned to face him. "For many years, I acted in ways both selfish and immature. I'm sorry for that. Truly sorry." Although she still believed he and Luanne would have been disastrous together. "From this day forward, you have nothing to fear from me. I will work on your campaign, I will support you for mayor, but I will never chase after you or make you the subject of my romantic silliness again."

Hale ducked his chin and ran his thumb across the edges of the letters. When he looked up at her, his face was as serious as she'd ever seen it. "I thank you for these"—he lifted the packet—"and for your apology. I was wrong to accuse you without hearing your side of the story."

He meant it. This was no perfunctory apology. It was as sincere as hers. Yancey pressed her lips together to keep them from trembling.

"I would very much like for us to move forward in a spirit of cooperation." He looked like he meant this, too. "Your ideas about the brunch and extended potluck dinner are excellent, even if I am dreading three hours of mingling." The last was said with self-deprecating humor.

She was proud of him—and grateful that he appreciated her ideas—but didn't know how to say it without sounding like the infatuated fool she'd sworn never to be again. She stuck out her hand. "Good night, Hale."

He stared down at her extended hand.

Was he going to refuse to shake it? Why had she put it out there in the first place? Men and women didn't shake hands like business partners. Oh, gracious. She'd been a fool again. This time in an effort to be an improved version of herself.

Just as she started to pull her hand back, he took it in his and squeezed. Warm tingles raced up her arm.

Relief. That's what it was. Because it couldn't be a reaction to his touch.

She withdrew her hand and curtsied, which was what she should have done in the first place. "Good night. I look forward to helping your campaign."

Not him. His campaign. The distinction was important to her, even if he didn't pick up on it.

He bowed. "Good night. I hope we can continue to be on friendly terms going forward."

Not to be friends, but to be on friendly terms.

So he *had* picked up on the distinction and was giving back his own.

It was what she wanted . . . which she told herself over and over as she walked into the house, relayed the evening's events to her parents, and prepared for bed.

But after blowing out the candle and pulling up the covers to her chin, the truth couldn't be denied.

She'd made peace with Hale Adams, turned him into a friendly acquaintance, and it hurt.

After dropping Isaak and Zoe at his parents' house and returning the borrowed carriage to Windsor Buchanan, Hale walked back to his upstairs apartment with the letters. He opened his safe and set them inside, next to his letters from "Portia York." He should burn both packets.

He should.

He should start a fire in his hearth, toss every page inside, and watch them burn as he sat in his reading chair.

But not tonight. Not when he still had so many unanswered questions spinning inside his mind.

Yancey Palmer puzzled him. At least this new one did. Before tonight, he knew exactly how to deal with her.

Stay as far away as possible.

Two things—no, three—told him his former approach was no longer possible.

First, avoiding her would give the appearance that he'd rejected her apology, something no gentleman would ever do. If he prided himself on anything, it was being a gentleman through and through. His father had been a gentleman in name only. He excused his behavior by saying he couldn't help falling in love with another woman and starting a second, illegitimate family. No true gentleman would even *look* at another woman. His father had gone one better—or worse—by becoming a bigamist. The betrayal cut too deep for words. Husbands were to love their wives and be loyal to them no matter what. Hale was determined to be everything his father was not—a faithful husband, a devoted father, and a true gentleman who not only spoke of things like integrity and fidelity but lived them.

Second, he needed Yancey Palmer on his side. Had the last ten days not impressed that truth on him, the reactions of several people at Gibbon's Steak House tonight would have. Malachi had bowed so low when he came to the table to ask if everything was to her satisfaction, his hair touched her hand. The woman was royalty in Helena, and more than just Malachi thought so. Six other couples had made a point to come to the table and speak with her, telling her all about their new kid goat or a baby's first tooth or some other meaningful event in their lives. Miss Palmer didn't just tolerate their interruptions, she shared their joy and participated in their story by peppering them with questions. Whatever sour looks they'd given him when they first approached the table were gone by the time she'd expressed her full support of his candidacy and dismissed their public argument as a misunderstanding between friends.

And third, she genuinely had good ideas. Where he'd only known what he didn't want—to be like Harold Kendrick with his Independence Day picnic—she'd offered a plan. He might not like all aspects of it, but he'd known at the outset that running for mayor was going to stretch his capacity to make small talk with strangers.

He placed the letters side by side and closed the door to his safe. No matter how puzzling she was, one thing remained clear.

He needed Yancey Palmer.

Friday, June 1, 1888

After a quick trip home to kiss his wife, take a bath, and change his dusty clothes from days on the road, Jonas headed straight to Hale's office for a full accounting of the last three weeks. As usual, piles of books and folders lined the walls and sat atop the chairs opposite his desk. "You really must make your office a more inviting place if you expect to win people to your side."

Honestly, what was the point of having a carved mahogany desk, a full wall of bookshelves, a telephone—something very few offices had, no less an ornate cast-iron model—and a brand-new typewriter, if no one could see them for all the paperwork and books stacked everywhere?

Hale peered over his wire-rimmed glasses. "I am willing to make many sacrifices for the sake of this campaign, but were I to change my habits altogether, people would become suspicious."

"Perhaps, but would it kill you"—Jonas hooked his cane over his arm, picked up the smaller stack on a chair, and set it atop the other—"to at least leave both chairs vacant for visitors?"

Hale took his time considering the option, which Jonas would have found irritating beyond his patience were it not for the glint in the boy's eye. "Try as I might, I can't conceive of a scenario in which it would. I suppose I *could* make that sacrifice."

"How magnanimous of you." Jonas attempted to match his nephew's teasing but fell short. Weeks on the road performing his rounds as territorial judge had taken a toll on both his health and his peace of mind. He needed to be in Helena from now until November to ensure Hale's election as mayor, but duty called. Jonas's only legitimate source of income was his judgeship, which paid less than half what he needed. The counterfeit money was for bribes. He wouldn't use it in town to pay his own bills, no matter how tempting. "I spoke briefly with Lily. She says Miss Palmer is firmly back in your camp. That you actually asked her to address you by your first name at dinner last week."

"It seemed prudent as everyone else was addressing me as Hale." He replaced his pencil in a clay mug holding several others. "You asked me to make that girl like me. I believe I have fulfilled your requirement satisfactorily."

"Excellent." Jonas paced across the small cleared space, tapping his cane along the floor with every other step. "I also hear there are plans for a special brunch and dinner for Independence Day, when you'll be giving a speech outlining your mayoral agenda."

Hale put a fist over his mouth, but not before Jonas heard a chuckle.

"Something amuses you?"

"In point of fact, yes." Hale directed a glance at the empty chair. "I fail to see why you cleared that seat if you are just going to pace back and forth. Also, it sounds like you've already had an accounting from Aunt Lily of what's gone on during your absence, so I fail to understand why you need one from me."

Another time, Jonas might have found the same humor in Hale's observation. Not today. "I'm worried about you. Kendrick is a snake. You know that better than anyone. I want to make sure you are taking him—and the threat he poses—seriously."

"What makes you think I am not?"

Jonas stopped pacing to jab his index finger on a clear space of the desk. "I know Kendrick is cheating. I just can't figure out how." And it was robbing him of sleep.

At least he was no longer worried about Madame Lestraude after her declaration of war. He had a plan for dealing with her. Her accountant—Mr. Green—had earned her trust over the years. Jonas knew a few of the woman's secrets, but Green knew them all. How difficult could it be to bribe, manipulate, or uncover some scandal about a man who continued working at a brothel after prostitution became illegal? Once Green was convinced it was in his best interests to work with Jonas, neutralizing Madame Lestraude would be easy.

"Uncle Jonas"—Hale's voice drew him back to the problem at hand—"please sit down before you wear a tread on my floorboards. They are only pine, not sturdy oak."

Unused to being told what to do by any man, let alone one half his age, Jonas collapsed into the chair with a mock harrumph. "Happy?"

"Quite so."

Jonas couldn't help but grin. "All right. I admit I'm fussing worse than an old woman. Now, tell me what my wife hasn't. Are you raising enough funds? Who has come out in support of you, and who is opposing? Have you scheduled any debates yet?"

"Yes, enough people, and July 24."

"I am in no mood for cheeky humor, Hale." Jonas glared over the messy desk.

"With respect, sir, I am running for mayor, not you."

Despite the deference in both his words and tone of voice, a severe response—including the words "ungrateful whipper-snapper" and "arrogant pup"—formed in Jonas's mind.

Hale took out his pocket watch and wound the stem. "Your schedule will keep you out of town for most of the time between now and the election. While I'm grateful for your wisdom and will act on any suggestions I deem sound, I do not need you to look over my shoulder at every turn."

Were it less important that he win, Jonas might have agreed, but the stakes were too high. He'd come to Montana Territory twenty-three years ago with the expressed intent of creating a name for himself on the national stage. He was now so close, his fingertips could brush those ambitions . . . but not close enough to grasp.

The difference was two inches.

One of those inches was getting Hale elected mayor. The other was unlimited funding. Jonas knew Montana politics. More votes were swayed with five-dollar bills than with five stellar ideas. For twenty years, he'd eschewed dirty politics, and look where it had gotten him. A political has-been who—were his clout too little to get his own nephew elected mayor—would be forgotten except by schoolchildren forced to research obscure facts about Montana before statehood.

He couldn't fail. Not again. He was fifty-six and didn't have time to waste.

Therefore, he would fight fire with fire. Kendrick had bribed his way into the mayor's office, and Jonas meant to match the scalawag dollar for dollar. He'd once heard William Clark say no man could be bought who wasn't first for sale. Jonas concurred. And men who could be bribed for five dollars deserved to get it in counterfeit money.

At only twenty-eight, Hale was too young and idealistic to understand that it was useless to fight against the way the world worked. But if Jonas played his cards wrong, he'd end up sidelined from the campaign he'd orchestrated into existence.

So he started again. "My apologies, Hale. I'm treating this as my campaign instead of yours. Tell me how I can help."

After his uncle left, Hale spent several hours buried in a complicated land dispute between Charles Cannon and J. P. Fisk. The two men had made a fortune buying land cheap, developing it, and then convincing the city council to expand Helena's borders so they could sell it for triple their investment. Cannon had purchased a foreclosed property more than a year ago and submitted plans for developing it. That was when Fisk provided a bill of sale proving he had purchased the same land. Both had legitimate claims and were unwilling to sell to the other.

Hired by Cannon, Hale was researching similar cases of dual claims filed under both territorial and state laws, looking for cases to support his client. His eyes were bleary by five in the evening. He checked his calendar. There were no client appointments on Monday until one in the afternoon. He penciled "Cannon v. Fisk" at the top of his list of things to accomplish.

He heard his front door open and shut.

He checked his watch and set his jaw. Why did people think two seconds before closing on a Friday evening was an appropriate time for an unscheduled appointment?

His jaw loosened when Madame Lestraude sailed through the open double doors between his lobby and office. He stood—as a gentleman should—but before he could say he refused to represent brothel owners, she held up her hand.

"Please hear me out, Mr. Adams. I promise I'm not here about my usual business." He hesitated, which she apparently took for his consent because she sat down in the chair his uncle had recently cleared of files. "I wish to adopt a young man currently in my employ and make him my heir."

He sat down and shifted until his back was pressed against the leather. "Are you speaking of Nico, the boy who calls himself Zoe Gunderson's brother?"

"I am." The pronouncement came with a regal nod more suitable to a queen than a brothel madam.

Isaak and Zoe would probably wish to adopt Nico themselves. If so, they might ask him to be their lawyer. It was logical enough reasoning for Hale to say, "I'm afraid I can't help you, ma'am."

"Why? Is adoption outside your normal practice? Are you incapable of growing beyond your current limits?"

"Of course not," he retorted, regretting the impulse to defend himself immediately.

A sly smile lifted her rouged lips. "Excellent. Then please draw up the papers." She stood. "I shall take up no more of your time."

Torn between relief and vexation at her abruptness—and feeling like a child's toy rolling up and down on a string as he stood again after having just sat down—Hale walked her toward the door while searching for a polite way to deny her request.

She paused at the junction of the waiting area and foyer. "Oh, and I may need your services to defend Nico against criminal charges." She disappeared from view. In the space between opening the front door and closing it, she called, "Give your uncle my best."

Not his aunt *and* uncle, just his uncle. What did she mean by *that*?

Hale flipped the lock behind her. No more intruders tonight, and he wasn't sauntering around town for the sake of seeing and being seen. The madam's visit put him in such a foul mood, he'd not be able to hold a smile without painting it on his face like a circus clown.

What now? Try to get more work done or go upstairs and read a good book? He'd neglected his reading of late, and his brain balked at returning to more case law regarding dual property claims.

And he certainly wasn't about to start drawing up papers for Madame Lestraude to adopt Nico—who didn't have a last name at the moment.

Reading it was.

Hale took off his glasses and climbed the stairs, rubbing the bridge of his nose to relieve the ache where the frame had dug into his skin. When he opened the door to his apartment, the first thing he saw—the blurry outline of it, at any rate—was his safe. He replaced his glasses and stared at the cast-iron box.

Portia and Yancey. Yancey and Portia. Were there similarities between the two women beyond blond hair and a weekly commitment to a charitable cause?

He needed to know the truth. He'd not rest until he researched the answer. He crossed to the safe, turned the dial to the proper numbers until the lock released, and swung open the heavy door. The two bundles of letters were on the top shelf. He pulled them out and sat down in his reading chair.

After arranging them in chronological order according to the post-marked date on the envelopes, he opened the first one.

A letter from him to her after reading the biographical information sent by the agency.

He should reread that first.

He leaned down to look inside his safe. The biography was folded in thirds and lying beneath a small velvet box holding a ring. The half-carat diamond was encircled by smaller diamonds set in platinum. He'd brought it with him from Buffalo, anticipating the day he'd slip it on the finger of his chosen wife. He pushed the box aside. How much longer would it languish on the shelf?

He withdrew the biography and shut the safe door without turning the lock. He'd tossed every other biography sent to him, this one alone catching his eye.

Why? After all the correspondence between them, he couldn't remember which details were shared in them as opposed to her biography.

He unfolded the paper and began to read.

Miss Portia York, age twenty. She has blond hair and blue eyes, is of medium height and build. She comes from a happy home with two older siblings and faithfully attends church.

"Comes from a happy home." The phrase wedged in his lungs, as it had when he'd first read it. He'd come from a happy home, too. Or so he'd thought until he was eighteen when his father announced he could no longer live a double life.

Hale wanted an honest-to-goodness happy home. Getting one increased dramatically if at least one of the partners in a marriage had experienced it. Because it wasn't going to be him, it needed to be his bride. In fact, the major reason he'd been drawn to Luanne Palmer was the genuine faith, generosity, and familial loyalty displayed by the entire Palmer clan. Including—he sucked in a breath and blew it out through rounded lips—Yancey.

One point of truth between her and the fictitious Portia. Hale continued reading the biography.

Miss York enjoys many activities, including reading, charitable work, and community events.

He'd been so thrilled by the happy family phrase, he'd jumped to the conclusion that Miss York shared his taste for poetry and serious literature. If Yancey Palmer enjoyed reading, she meant women's magazines filled with lace, buttons, and hats. Or was he jumping to another conclusion without knowing all the facts?

That seemed to be an issue between him and the lady.

He didn't have the same problem with anyone else—at least not that he was aware, although every man had his blind spots. He'd ask Mac. The county sheriff could be trusted to speak the truth.

Hale adjusted his glasses and continued reading.

Her desire to marry and have a family of her own stems from her own happy childhood. She believes love requires sacrifices, but that choosing someone who shares her goals, interests, and faith will mitigate the bumps and adjustments required when two people blend their hopes, dreams, and personalities.

Was that true? It seemed too mature for the flighty Yancey Palmer. Maybe he was jumping to another conclusion, but his interactions with her said this was false. To be fair, she'd admitted to acting with romantic silliness where he was concerned.

No point for or against the correlations between Portia and Yancey. He'd need to observe more before coming to a firm conclusion.

Finally, Miss York wants her prospective groom to know that once her heart is given, she is fiercely loyal.

Had the part about a happy family not sealed his interest, this last statement would have.

Hale refolded the paper. If anything was true about her, it was her tenacity. He'd given her no encouragement over the past five years, yet she'd held on to him with . . . well . . . fierce loyalty.

One point in favor of Miss Yancey Palmer.

Maybe two.

Chapter Ten

Yancey listened to Hale's speech outlining his mayoral agenda with increasing discomfort. As he droned on and on, she looked around Mrs. Hollenbeck's small parlor—so named because it was half the size of the large parlor. But what it lacked in size, it made up for in luxury. The honor of being included in this select group gathered in a room decorated with real gold leaf, mahogany-inlaid floors, and rich blue velvet to advise Hale was not lost on Yancey. What she *was* lost in was the legal jargon and myriad of details of his speech. Did anyone else realize he'd bore half the people to sleep and the other half to death?

It was worse than when he'd answered questions the day he announced he'd taken Isaak's place. At least then, Mrs. Hollenbeck had graciously cut him off at the earliest opportunity to summarize his points.

Yancey checked the gilded clock over the marble fireplace. Eight forty-seven. Hale had been talking for over half an hour. She glanced at each occupant. Isaak Gunderson was rubbing the back of his neck. Mrs. Forsythe and Mrs. Hollenbeck had their heads together whispering about something. Judge Forsythe was nodding his head as though he agreed with everything his nephew was saying.

"In conclusion," Hale finally said, and then kept talking through another page. When he was *actually* done, he looked at each person in turn. "Well? What do you think?"

Silence.

If no one else was going to tell him, it was up to her. "It's too long and too detailed."

Every eye turned to her. She thought she saw relief on Mrs. Hollenbeck's face.

"I agree," Isaak said. "People are more interested in the overall picture than they are the fine details."

"But the details are how we get to the overall picture." Hale slapped the back of his hand against the pages of his speech.

All twelve of them. Yancey had counted. "What's your vision for the future of Helena?"

"My vision?" Hale swung his gaze to her, confusion in his eyes.

"Yes. Your vision." When the look on his face didn't clear, she clarified, "Where do you see Helena four years from now?"

"At the same longitude and latitude it is right now."

Was he serious? She looked for the familiar glint of humor and didn't find it. "Not where as in *where*, but where as in how it's different than it is today."

"How it's better because of the policies you want to implement," Isaak explained further.

"But that's what I just said." Hale glanced at his speech. "Didn't I?"

"I think what Miss Palmer is saying"—Judge Forsythe was the only one in the room who still addressed her by her formal name—"is that perhaps you did it a little too well."

Bad choice of words. Over the course of the last few weeks working on Hale's campaign, Yancey had discovered aspects of his character she'd overlooked by making him her knight in shining armor. But she wasn't entirely wrong about him. If Hale prided himself on anything, it was doing things well. He wouldn't understand the idea of doing anything *too* well. "People aren't going to care as much about your competence as they will about your compassion."

Mrs. Forsythe nodded. "Yancey makes a good point. Everyone knows you're an intelligent man. But what they need to know is that you share their concerns."

Hale sat on the blue velvet settee and placed his speech in the empty space beside him. "It's no secret to anyone in this room that I have trouble connecting with people, particularly in large groups. Outside of this"—he tapped his index finger on the speech—"I have no idea how to share their concerns."

Yancey recalled Isaak's insight that Hale was good with people as long as there were only four or five of them. How could she break his discomfort? "Large crowds are made up of individuals and small groups of people. Stop looking at the whole and start looking at its parts."

"Excellent advice, Miss Palmer." Judge Forsythe wiped his palms together as though the matter was now closed and it was time to move the discussion along.

But Hale still looked lost.

Yancey stood. "Would you all come over here?" When everyone was gathered in a small circle, Yancey took Hale by the elbow and pulled him away from the group. "Tell me what you see."

"My family and friends."

"Good. Now imagine that the curtains are another group of people."

Hale tilted his head to stare down at her. "We have blue people in Helena now?"

Not sure if he was trying to be humorous or if he really

lacked the ability to imagine, Yancey chose to believe the former. "Very funny. Just play along for a moment. Do you care about those people—the blue ones—at this moment, or just about the four people in the group right in front of you?"

"I understand what you're demonstrating, but I don't see how it helps me overcome needing to eventually talk to the blue people—none of whom I know. Outside of asking them the state of their wills and property, I don't know what to say."

Yancey let go of his arm and took a step away. She tapped her bottom lip and thought through an idea. "I believe I have a solution, but it will take everyone's cooperation."

"What are you getting us in to, Yancey?" Isaak wasn't the only one with skepticism turning down the corners of his mouth. Judge Forsythe and Hale wore identical frowns.

"It's nothing bad, I promise you." Yancey placed a hand over her heart as part of her vow.

Hale let out a snort. "I've heard that before."

Something in his tone of voice made her think she'd been the one to promise such a thing, but she couldn't remember when. There was nothing she could do about the past now, so she might as well plow ahead. "I suggest that throughout the course of both the brunch and evening events, we"—she swirled her hand to indicate Isaak, Mrs. Hollenbeck, Judge and Mrs. Forsythe, and herself—"take turns escorting Hale. Among the five of us, I daresay we know everyone who will be at both events. That way Hale will know at least one person as he wanders from group to group. We can start discussing something we know concerns that particular group of people, then, once the conversational ball is rolling, Hale can participate." She turned her attention to him. "It wouldn't be any different than a new client coming to your office. You simply listen and respond to what concerns them."

Hale rubbed his index finger along the indentation above his chin. "That's not a bad idea."

Yancey chuckled. "Thank you for that ringing endorsement."

"But it doesn't fix the problem of my speech." Hale pointed his thumb over his shoulder. "I've spent the last five days working on it every night. I don't think I have the perspective to cut any of it."

"We can help with that." Isaak took four long strides and picked up the pages.

"Are you planning on tossing the entire thing in the waste bin?" Hale's question was a combination of teasing and dismay.

"The thought crossed my mind." It was hard to tell if Isaak was being funny or serious. "We can cut at least two or three pages."

"No." Yancey shook her head. "The entire speech needs to be no more than *three* pages."

Hale's mouth fell open. Isaak jerked his attention from the speech to her so fast, he winced. Mrs. Hollenbeck was covering her mouth, a distinct twinkle in her eyes. Mrs. Forsythe walked to Hale's side and patted his shoulder blade.

The look on Judge Forsythe's face was unreadable.

Yancey continued to gauge their reactions as she explained further. "I'm serious. Harold Kendrick has one good quality—he knows how to make a speech. They are funny and short. Emphasis on *short*."

Judge Forsythe continued staring. Then he smiled and nodded to her. "We may despise everything Harold Kendrick stands for, but we'd be foolish to underestimate how he captures a crowd."

Hale waved his hand. "I hate to be the bearer of bad news, but while I can keep my comments brief, I'm not funny. Not in a big crowd. I can be witty if I've taken time to think about a retort beforehand, but . . ." He shook his head. "I'm afraid funny is beyond my abilities."

"But what you *are* good at is clarity." Yancey turned her focus on Hale. "Last year, when Mayor Kendrick gave his speech, he was so vague no one understood what he intended to *do*."

"Because he's never actually done anything," Isaak called from across the room.

"Except line his own pockets," Judge Forsythe added.

"Which brings me back to my point." Yancey lifted three fingers in the air and wagged them at Hale. "You need to come up with three things—just three—you plan to do when you're elected mayor. Don't just state it. Paint a picture with words."

Hale stared at her, his gaze intense. A slow grin lifted his lips. "'Paint a picture with words.' I can do that."

Her stomach fluttered.

She pressed her hands against it to squash the butterflies. His smile meant nothing . . . or very little. He was simply complimenting her idea the same way he'd done at the restaurant.

And yet, her stomach fluttered again.

"New carriage?" Hale climbed into the front seat beside Isaak.

The meeting at Mrs. Hollenbeck's house had ended later than anticipated, most of it spent working on culling Hale's speech from twelve pages to three. In the end, he was happy with it, but he'd be home after ten if he walked rather than accept the offered ride.

"New horses, too." Isaak slapped the reins, setting the grays in motion. "Married men need carriages. Speaking of married, be careful or you're going to unravel Yancey's promise that she won't chase you."

Too tired to come up with a witty retort, Hale remained quiet. The subject of Yancey Palmer was not up for discussion.

But Isaak didn't take the hint. "You realize she's still in love with you, don't you?"

Hale drew his jacket closer together. The day had been warm, but the evening air had a bite to it. "No, she isn't."

"And"—Isaak continued as though Hale hadn't spoken— "if you keep smiling at her like you did tonight, you'll have only yourself to blame if she starts chasing after you again."

"Did you and Zoe know that Madame Lestraude wants to make Nico her heir before Mrs. Hollenbeck mentioned it tonight?" Hale turned the conversation to safer ground. His feelings toward Yancey were undergoing a shift. She'd been a thorn in his side for so long, he'd never considered her as anything else. After a month of working with her, he was beginning to understand why Uncle Jonas called her a natural campaigner. And her suggestions about viewing a crowd as nothing more than small groups of people who all just happened to be in close proximity and using words to paint a picture were nothing short of brilliant.

So he'd smiled at her to say, *Great idea*. Nothing improper in that.

"Don't want to talk about Yancey?" Isaak turned the team to the left. "Then I'll talk about Nico. Yes, we knew."

"And you aren't going to fight it?"

Isaak didn't answer. They rolled past mansions built by lucky miners, tradesmen who'd made a fortune buying and selling equipment to them and to less fortunate miners, and bankers who'd profited off all of them. Hale was about to repeat his question when Isaak finally spoke. "A few months ago, I would have fought it with everything I had in me. I thought it was my job to make sure everything was done right and done on time." He chuckled. "Yancey called me benevolently arrogant."

An apt description, though Hale wasn't about to add fuel to Isaak's fire by agreeing with anything Yancey Palmer had said.

"Nico is fifteen now," Isaak continued, "and has been living on the streets most of his life. For reasons known only to him, he's created his own family, with Zoe as his sister, me as his sister's husband—which is still a somewhat tenuous bond, given how badly Jakob and I embarrassed her—and Madame Lestraude as his mother. If I'm going to keep a relationship with him, I have to respect his choices."

Even if he thought them wrong was left unsaid, but Hale understood the logic—had argued the same with Mac over the years, in point of fact. However, he wanted no part of it if for no other reason than the high-handed way Madame Lestraude had twisted his words trying to manipulate him into helping her. "Does Mac know?"

"He does, and to answer your next question, he's relieved that he won't have to turn down his mother's money. He's more than happy to see every penny of it go to Nico." Isaak turned onto Sixth Street.

Hale turned his head to better view Isaak. "Do you know anything about Nico needing a criminal defense? Madame Lestraude mentioned it when she was in my office a month ago, but I've heard nothing since."

"That's all cleared up." Isaak steered around a particularly deep hole in the middle of the street. "Nico was responsible for the vandalism at The Import Company right before it opened."

He was? "Are you pressing charges?"

"No." Isaak shook his head. "As soon as we returned to Helena, he made a full confession. As a result, Pa decided against pressing charges."

"Seems strange she would ask me to defend him against something so trivial."

Isaak didn't say anything for a long moment. "Perhaps she was afraid he might be blamed for the fire at The Resale Company. He didn't set it, in case you were wondering."

"Are you sure?" Because it was better him than the other option.

"Nico and I grew quite close on our little elopement trip. I asked him about the fire, and he swore he had nothing to do with it. I believe him." The last was said with a hard look toward Hale.

"I was actually wishing he had."

Isaak shifted on the seat a bit to look Hale directly in the eye. "Kendrick?"

Hale nodded. "Which only makes sense if he thought he couldn't beat you."

"If Kendrick can beat Uncle Jonas, he wouldn't be intimidated by the likes of me." Isaak returned his attention to the horses.

"Or me."

Isaak shook his head. "I wouldn't be so sure of that. You have a degree from Harvard and have helped some very wealthy men with business deals that have made them even wealthier."

Hale took a slow breath in and blew it out through rounded lips. "All of which leads to one conclusion. Kendrick most likely didn't set the fire."

"Makes me wonder who did."

"And why."

Isaak slowed the team to let a wagon piled with crates, barrels, and burlap bags pass. "At least we have the insurance Uncle Jonas talked Pa into last year."

Madame Lestraude's farewell—*Give your uncle my best*—repeated inside Hale's mind. "Do you think there's something going on between Madame Lestraude and Uncle Jonas?"

Isaak jerked the reins, drawing the carriage to an abrupt stop. "What? No."

"I didn't mean that he's a . . . client." The word tasted like a green apple plucked too soon from the tree because—although he was ninety-eight percent sure his uncle wouldn't cheat on his wife—the remaining two percent was gnawing at him.

Isaak looked behind them, then down both sides of the street before focusing on Hale. "Then what did you mean?"

Hale recounted the madam's parting shot. "It's been bothering me ever since she said it. There's something behind it. I just can't figure out what."

Isaak checked the street again before setting the team in motion. "The woman has many mysteries surrounding her. Might be better to leave well enough alone."

Not advice Hale expected Isaak to give, but perhaps it was more evidence of change due to married life. As he appeared to want the subject dropped, Hale complied by asking if Zoe had settled on a menu for the brunch. The remainder of the ride home was filled with descriptions of food, which made Hale's stomach pinch with longing despite the healthy dinner he'd enjoyed.

They reached his office. Isaak pulled the team to a stop to let Hale out.

"Thank you for bringing me home." Hale retrieved his leather satchel from under the seat.

Isaak dipped his chin. "Before you go, I need to say something."

Hale's fingers tightened on the ivory handle.

"I'm serious about you being careful with Yancey."

"Miss Palmer is an asset to the campaign." Hale used her formal address on purpose. "Would you have me dismiss her ideas with scorn?"

"That's not what I meant."

"Then what did you mean?"

Isaak looked toward the sky as though waiting for the myriad of stars to tell him the answer. "Never mind. I'll see you on Wednesday morning at the brunch. Good night."

The carriage pulled away, so Hale's "Good night" was spoken over the crunch of wagon wheels. Isaak lifted a hand to acknowledge he'd heard it, so Hale didn't bother repeating himself. He fished the key from his vest pocket, slipped it into the lock, and opened the door.

Fatigue accompanied him up the stairs. Although he was pleased with the outcome of the meeting and his revised speech, the constant dissection of his failings both in public gatherings and in his writing had taken a toll on him.

Yet, when he set his glasses on the small table beside his bed and slipped under the covers, sleep eluded him.

If Yancey Palmer was confused, she wasn't alone. Tonight, when she'd taken him by the elbow and drawn him away from the rest of the people in the small parlor, he'd felt . . . comfortable. As if they were old friends instead of old combatants. He'd started to see her as Portia. The illusion was so strong, he'd smiled at her with genuine pleasure—and was taken to task over it.

Hale threw off the covers and grabbed his glasses on the way out the door. No embers burned in the fireplace because the weather was too hot, and the moon wasn't bright enough for him to sit in one of the rocking chairs on his balcony to read. He huffed and returned to his bedroom to light the hurricane lamp on the nightstand. If he were thinking straight, he'd have picked it up when he grabbed his glasses, but that was his whole problem. He couldn't think.

He marched back to the living room, muttering instructions to himself to stop acting like a fool. A minute later, he lifted the packet of letters from his safe. He needed this business of Portia vs. Yancey settled once and for all. If he found even the smallest lie in what Antonia Archer had done to obscure his identity, he could dismiss everything she'd written as Portia.

He placed the packet at his feet and lifted the first letter, the one he'd written to her after reading her biography. Other than the typewritten font, some misspelled words, and a few missing commas, everything was as he remembered writing it. He started a pile to the left of his chair and reached for the second letter, this one Portia's—Yancey's— answer. It was similar in content—a list of basic facts about her life. Everything was true, including that she worked in her father's business, although there were no specific names of people or places.

He set her letter atop his first one on his left and reached for the next letter on his right. The clock on his fireplace mantel was chiming two in the morning when he finished reading. Miss Archer had spoken the truth, at least with regard to his letters. He'd written that he owned his own law office in Helena, Montana. She'd written that he owned his own business in Denver, Colorado. Where Portia's letters spoke of working with a ladies' charitable group, Hale suspected Yancey had written the Ladies' Aid Society.

He closed his eyes, weariness so deep he felt it in his bones. His concern wasn't whether Miss Archer had changed names or proper nouns, it was whether she'd misrepresented Portia's personality and future hopes. Reading her letters again revived the longing—the one he thought he'd finally filled—for a home and family of his own.

He'd be a good husband and father. He'd make sure of it. He just needed someone he could trust with his heart.

He shuffled the letters into an orderly stack and replaced them in the safe. Tonight wasn't a good time to be adding more to his worries. He had a speech to make in three days in front of what was sure to be more people than he'd ever spoken to in one place at one time in his life.

He returned to his bedroom, where he knelt and prayed until he had poured out every concern at his Father's feet. When he climbed under the brown bedspread, he soon fell asleep, where he dreamed of an outdoor wedding attended by thousands. His bride wore a heavy veil, but he was sure it was the woman of his dreams. He said his vows, the preacher pronounced them man and wife, he lifted the veil, and a hag with black hair and rotting teeth cackled, "I fooled you!"

Chapter Eleven

Friday, June 29, 1888

"So?" Carline asked as she breezed through the doors to the telegraph office. "How did last night go?"

Yancey stood on her tiptoes, leaning across the counter to see if anyone was following behind her friend. Business followed a predictable pattern of crazy whenever a train was docked, with huge lulls in between. This was one of the slow times, but she wasn't taking any chances. "Close the doors behind you so we won't be interrupted."

Carline swung around, the skirt of her blue-check dress billowing in her self-made breeze. "That well, huh?"

Yancey waited until she heard the doors click shut before answering. "Yes. It went even better than I hoped." She stepped out from behind the counter so the two of them could sit on one of the three benches placed beneath the windows overlooking the platform. Once Carline was seated, Yancey launched into a detailed description of the previous evening. "At one point, Hale smiled at me, and it wasn't one of those"—she fisted her hands as if she was holding the lapels of a man's jacket and lowered the timbre of her voice—"'you annoy me, but I'm smiling to be polite' things or 'I guess you aren't quite as annoying as I previously thought' things. It was an honest-to-goodness, 'that was an excellent idea' without 'which I find so odd you should be insulted' added at the end."

Carline pressed her fingertips against her lips.

"I know," Yancey dropped her hands into her lap. "I couldn't believe it either and—I'm not going to lie—it made my stomach flutter."

"But . . ." Carline spoke through her fingers.

Yancey smiled so wide, her cheeks protested. "I didn't fall into a fit or throw myself at him. I was very calm and mature, if I do say so myself."

Carline clapped her hands. "I knew you could do it."

"I wasn't so sure because . . ." Yancey shifted on the seat to better see her friend. "I think a part of me will always love him, but I'm learning to keep his smiles and compliments in proper perspective."

"Good for you, Yancey."

She grinned at the praise. "What's happening with you? Has your uncle left town yet?"

"Finally."

"And?" Yancey prompted.

Carline's smile answered. "Papa told him that he wanted me to stay home for at least one more year because . . ." Her eyes began to twinkle.

"Well? Go on."

Carline's smile was full of good news. "Isaak Gunderson asked me to start working regularly at The Import Company because . . . Emilia McCall is with child."

Yancey clapped her hands with joy. "Oh, that's wonderful news. And I'm so glad you're staying. At least for now."

Carline sobered. "I want you to know that I thought long and hard about whether I'd be wise to go to finishing school back East. I decided to ask Mrs. Hollenbeck to teach me how to handle wealth."

"What did she say?"

"I haven't asked her yet. I was planning on approaching her at the Independence Day celebration." Carline plucked at the lace on her cuff. "Do you think she'll find me impertinent?"

"I sincerely doubt it." Yancey didn't mention that Mrs. Hollenbeck had asked after Carline last night. The widow had a matchmaking streak, and she was asking if Carline had a beau. The matter of Windsor Buchanan was a close secret between Carline and Yancey, so she'd kept silent, but she wondered how—and why—Mrs. Hollenbeck was asking. Which prompted Yancey to ask, "Did your decision to stay in Helena have anything to do with a certain bladesmith?"

Pink filled Carline's cheeks. "A little." She glanced down at her lap and cleared her throat. "I had a long talk with my mother last night after Uncle Eugene left. I finally told her I thought about Mr. Buchanan . . . a lot."

"What did she say?"

Carline shook her head, a slow smile dawning. "Mama asked me why it took me so long to tell her."

Yancey broke into peals of laughter. "I told you. Didn't I tell you?"

"Yes, now let me finish."

Thus chastised, Yancey bit her bottom lip.

Carline shifted on the seat, pulling her hand from Yancey's grip. "Mother said that you and I were opposite sides of the same coin—you too obvious in your romantic infatuation with Hale Adams and me too coy regarding Windsor Buchanan."

Yancey's jaw loosened. "She actually said that?"

Carline nodded. "Mother said no man is brave enough to approach a woman without having received some indication of her interest. To cover my attraction to him, I've always treated Windsor the same way I have Geddes. I've been too coy."

"That's true." Yancey thought back to the play at Ming's Opera House, where, in an effort to get Windsor and Carline to sit together—without Windsor realizing that was the plan—they'd swapped chairs several times until Zoe put a stop to it. "So what are you going to do?"

Another blush pinked Carline's cheeks. "I was hoping to ask you for advice."

"Me?" Yancey pressed her fingertips to her sternum. "I'm the last person you should ask."

Carline shook her head. "I don't think so. We're almost twenty-one now. Between the two of us, we should have enough maturity to figure out the proper way to go about letting a man know we're interested in his attentions."

"And, if not, we probably aren't ready to leave childhood behind and step into the roles of wives and mothers."

"Exactly what I was thinking."

Yancey pulled Carline into a sideways hug. "Oh, how I cherish you. I'm so glad you aren't leaving town."

"I second that." Carline squeezed Yancey's waist. "Let's pray we both find husbands and raise babies here in Helena."

"Oh Lord, hear our prayer," Yancey supplied the rest of the special way she and Carline expressed their hopes and dreams for the future.

As though it had waited for the conversation to end, the telegraph machine began to tap. Yancey jumped up, counting dots and dashes and converting them to letters inside her head as she hurried back behind the counter. She sat down, picked up the pen, and acknowledged Carline's wave goodbye by nodding once as she scratched out the message.

Yancey finished translating and reached out to replace the pen. A paper calendar sat partially hidden under the wooden tray holding the inkpot and pen holder.

I shall have to mark today in the calendar, she'd once heard Isaak say when Jakob did something surprising.

Doing something significant also counted.

Before she changed her mind, Yancey drew a tiny star on June 29, 1888, the day she truly put Hale Adams behind her.

July 4, 1888

Hale licked his lips. The salt from his sweat made his dry mouth long for another glass of lemonade. He'd already drained two and the brunch hadn't even started yet.

Why would God punish him with the hottest day of the year when he needed to appear calm and cool? And where was Yancey Palmer? She had first shift of standing by him as he wandered from group to group. She'd left him on Mrs. Hollenbeck's wide veranda, saying she'd be back in a moment. That was—he pulled out his pocket watch—a full five minutes ago.

He needed no mirror to tell him his face was bright pink and his hair was matted under his black top hat. Mrs. Hollenbeck's lawn was dotted with linen-draped tables, almost in the same configuration as for Luanne and Roy Bennett's wedding fourteen months ago. The tables were set with blue-and-white china plates, crystal glasses, and bowls of red and white flowers. Except that the bridal table had been replaced by a small platform, it looked like a wedding reception.

"You're glaring at that thing like it's a hangman's noose." Mac McCall jutted his chin toward the podium sitting center stage.

Hale turned to his friend. "I've not seen much of you lately. Enjoying married life?"

Mac's grin answered. "If I'd known marriage was going to be this great, I'd have tied the knot the day Emilia arrived in Helena."

Jealousy reared its green head before Hale ruthlessly

chopped it off at the neck. Mac's path to marital bliss had been rocky. No one wanted that kind of courtship.

"Looks like you have a nice turnout for this shindig." Mac turned his head from left to right. "I don't see your uncle."

Hale searched the crowd for Uncle Jonas's gray hair and Aunt Lily's green hat. "Is that why you're here?" Mac, although a good friend, didn't have either the political clout or financial means of the other guests.

"I need him to sign a search warrant." Mac pulled open his brown jacket to reveal a piece of paper sticking out of the inside pocket. "It's important or I wouldn't be barging in."

"I presumed as much. Is it confidential, or may I know what it's for?" Hale searched the crowd.

"Counterfeiting operation down in Bear Gulch."

"Solid evidence?" Hale spotted his aunt and uncle and pointed. "There."

Mac reached out to squeeze Hale's bicep. "Best evidence I've had in months. Thanks, and good luck today." He hurried off, pausing just long enough to whisper something in Isaak Gunderson's ear before moving past, then pulling Uncle Jonas to the edge of the crowd.

Hale was about to make his way over when he spied Yancey. He checked his watch again. Six minutes. "Where have you been?"

She frowned, then looked pointedly at the group a few feet away, as good as shouting, *Be nice. We're on display.* "Thank you for being so patient."

"Is everything all right?" he tried again.

She beamed at him. "Nothing for you to worry about. Now, shall we go chat with Mr. Fisk?"

He snapped closed the silver lid of his watch and tucked it back inside his vest pocket. "Might as well get this over with," he muttered so only she could hear.

She chuckled, the sound rich and soothing. "Don't be such a Scrooge. You might even find you enjoy yourself."

He held out his elbow, and she tucked her hand in the bend. He leaned close to her ear. "I'll have you know, I have nothing against Christmas."

She pulled away slightly to look at him. "Perhaps not, but you are as stingy with your goodwill as he, so I stand by my comparison."

The criticism jarred him. Was his discomfort in social situations stinginess? Before he could think of a retort, they reached Mr. and Mrs. Fisk, who were talking with another couple Hale didn't recognize.

"Mr. and Mrs. Stafford," Yancey identified them as per the plan, "how lovely to see you. How is the construction on your new bank coming?"

Hale waited to insert himself into the conversation until he knew which of his ideas for improving city government would most appeal to the banker. While he chatted with Mr. Stafford and Mr. Fisk, Yancey discussed children and grand-children with the ladies. His ears perked up when one of the ladies asked whether she and Hale were now a couple.

"Goodness no, Mrs. Stafford. We have overcome our past mistakes in order to work together for the common good of Helena."

It was no different than what she'd said at Gibbon's Steak House. But today it was as jarring as when she'd called him a Scrooge.

A touch on his elbow turned his attention. "Uncle Jonas. Is something wrong?"

He shook his head, but his skin was an unnatural shade. "I need to speak with you privately for a moment."

Hale excused himself from the group and followed his uncle to a small clearing at the veranda railing. "What's wrong? You look pale."

"It's nothing. Nothing at all."

Which meant something *was* wrong. Uncle Jonas never repeated himself unless he was trying to cover a lie. It was a nervous tic Hale uncovered on his twenty-third birthday, when Aunt Lily endeavored to throw him a surprise party. She'd enlisted Uncle Jonas's help and, in his attempt to dissuade Hale when he'd guessed the plans, had repeated himself on several occasions.

"I must leave. Sheriff McCall has brought a search warrant and I've forgotten my reading glasses." Uncle Jonas patted his jacket as though to demonstrate the lack of glasses. "I may not make it back here for a significant amount of time. I hate to abandon you."

Hale spied Yancey approaching. "I'll be fine. Go issue your warrant."

"Warrant for what?" Yancey joined the conversation.

Hale extended his elbow toward her. "Counterfeiting."

Yancey's face went white. She gripped Hale's arm as though she needed support to remain upright.

Hale gripped her hand. "What's wrong?"

She shook her head. "You'll say I'm being silly."

He'd said it about her often enough in the past. But it was far from what he was thinking now. "I promise I shall say no such thing."

When she looked up at him, there were tears in her eyes. He'd never noticed how blue they were. Not pale like the sky or cool like ice, but vibrant and warm like a sun-soaked wildflower. The ones that bloomed in spring just after the snow melted. The ones whose proper name he'd never bothered to research.

"Joseph was killed by counterfeiters."

He was so absorbed in her eyes, he almost didn't hear her words. "He was?"

Uncle Jonas cleared his throat, drawing Hale's attention.

"Everyone knows Mr. Hendry was killed by disgruntled brothel owners, but Miss Palmer won't be convinced."

Yancey's fingernails dug into Hale's forearm. He frowned at his uncle. It was the duty of a gentleman to protect a lady from both physical and emotional harm. Why would his uncle be so callous? "If you will excuse us, sir, I believe the lady requires some refreshment and a moment to collect her thoughts." Not caring how his uncle reacted to being dismissed, Hale escorted Yancey toward the house. "What makes you believe Mr. Hendry was killed by counterfeiters?"

Her pace slowed. He matched it and waited for her to speak. "I probably am being foolish."

"We won't know that until we've examined all the facts, now will we?"

She tugged her hand free. "That's just it. I only have one fact. Joseph went to Dawson County to investigate counterfeiting and was killed as soon as he returned to Helena."

"Did he say anything to you about what he found?"

She shook her head. "We only spoke for a moment. He was on his way to his office at the *Daily Independent* to write his story. He seemed excited . . . and sad, which doesn't make any sense."

"It could make perfect sense. A reporter would naturally be excited to uncover a big story and sad if he knew or admired the person he discovered was responsible for the crime." Hale knew all too well how it felt to be disappointed by a father he'd looked up to his entire life.

"You believe me?" Had she said, *I never thought you would take me seriously*, he couldn't have felt more chastised.

He glanced around to be sure they were far enough away from listening ears to have a somewhat overdue conversation. "Miss Palmer, my past behavior toward you has been . . . combative."

She didn't laugh or nod, just stared at him with those deep blue eyes.

"We have apologized to each other for past mistakes and agreed to be on friendly terms. But I would very much like for us to go one step further by becoming friends." He'd been tossing around the idea ever since rereading her letters as Portia. And yet, that he now spoke his feelings aloud surprised him as much as it appeared to surprise her.

Her silence confirmed his suspicion that she didn't know how to respond to an overture of friendship from him. Had his past dismissal of her irreparably damaged their chances of camaraderie going forward?

Maybe it was best to keep the conversation to the facts of Mr. Hendry's case.

"Did Mr. Hendry indicate he had written notes of what he'd found in Dawson County?" Nothing in the reports of his death mentioned as much, but Mac—or more likely Marshal Valentine, as Hendry was killed inside the city's limits—might be keeping certain facts out of the papers while the investigation was still ongoing.

Yancey squinted as though trying to see into the past. "If he made notes, he didn't mention it to me, at least not that I can remember. I confess, I usually got lost in the details because he so often discussed his work when we . . ." *were engaged*, was what he suspected she left unsaid.

Was she embarrassed by their courtship? Or just uncomfortable speaking of another man in front of someone for whom she'd once professed undying love?

Hale checked to make sure they were still too far away from anyone to be overheard. "May I ask you a somewhat personal question?"

"About Joseph?"

"In a manner of speaking." Hale waited for her to give

permission. "Is your . . ." *Insistence* was too strong a word, but *feeling* wasn't strong enough. He started his sentence again. "Is your belief that Mr. Hendry was killed by counterfeiters—rather than by brothel owners, as everyone else insists—some sort of self-inflicted guilt?"

"It was for a few months after he died, but"—Yancey's brow furrowed, and she paused, as though considering what to say next—"not anymore. I can't explain how I know it was counterfeiting, other than a feeling I have. I know it's true. I just do." Her skin flushed. "Please don't misunderstand what I'm about to say next."

Intriguing. "As I am hoping to persuade you to be my friend, I promise to do my best."

A small smile rewarded him. "This feeling I have about Joseph? It's the same one I had about you. That first day we met."

"When I punched that boy?"

She nodded. "And I immediately made an enemy of you."

"Do you know why?" He didn't give her time to respond. "Because I acted the bully, bloodying a child's lip, rather than as a gentleman should."

"But he was bullying me."

"All the more reason I should have shown him a better way. It was disgraceful behavior on my part."

She touched the base of her neck. "And I kept rubbing salt into your shame with my hero-worship."

"You were ten. I should have taken that into account when . . ." He broke off, not sure how to politely say the next half of the sentence. *This* was why he preferred to write out his words ahead of time.

The right side of Yancey's mouth lifted into a lopsided grin. "When I immediately made you my ideal and, consequently, broke up your courtship of my sister?"

He nodded, grateful she was the one to say it.

She sobered and looked down. "May I ask you a somewhat personal question?"

"I believe that's only fair."

She slowly lifted her head. "Did you love Luanne? Truly love her?"

"No. I loved the idea of making a home in Helena with a loving family. Luanne happened to be the first girl who caught my eye when I arrived." The admission was less painful than he expected it to be.

Yancey caught the corner of her bottom lip in her teeth for a moment. "Would you have ended your courtship of her without my interference?"

"I would have."

"I'm not sure if I should say, 'I'm sorry,' or 'I told you so.'" Spoken with such wry humor, Hale couldn't help but chuckle.

He smiled down at her. "How about we agree to put it behind us and celebrate your sister's good fortune in marrying Mr. Bennett?"

She matched his smile. "An excellent suggestion."

"May I make another suggestion—though you'll have to judge its excellence."

"I believe that's only fair." The way Yancey picked up on his banter reminded him of the way his aunt and uncle teased each other.

He liked it. A lot.

Hale coughed into his fist to cover his surprise at the realization. "I . . . uh, I want to return to the subject of Mr. Hendry."

The light went out of her eyes. "Yes. Of course."

"I know the official ruling on his death was murder, but was anyone ever caught?" Hale knew the answer but wanted her to say it aloud.

"No."

"Then there's no basis of fact to back up your feeling that

he was killed over counterfeiting?" He said it as gently as possible, but facts were facts.

Yancey shook her head.

"Then how about we let Marshal Valentine finish his investigation before we jump to counterfeiting as the cause."

"I've tried, believe me I've tried." She ducked her head as though the admission—or the slight whine in her voice—embarrassed her.

Hale took out his pocket watch and wound the stem while he considered a different way to relate the same truth. "When I was in law school, I had a class on the origins of justice. May I pass along some wisdom I believe applies here?"

She peeked up at him. "As long as you limit yourself to no more than three points."

He chuckled at her teasing. "I shall go above and beyond by limiting myself to just one."

Her eyes began to sparkle. "If you adhere to your limit, I shall have to borrow our good friend Mr. Gunderson's response to such a rarity by marking it in a calendar."

He laughed outright. She really was a delightful conversationalist. He sobered and put his free hand on top of hers. "My professor said that every one of us would come up against a case where justice would not be served here on earth. We would then have to decide if we truly believed God was sovereign and not only could but *would* see justice done whether now or in the future."

"Whether I see the proof to validate my feelings or not." After a long silence, she squeezed his arm. "Thank you, Hale. By speaking the truth even when it was a difficult one, you've just acted as a friend. I appreciate it."

Her understanding and gratitude felt like a cool breeze across his skin. "Are you ready to return to the task of mingling with the high and mighty, or do you need a few more minutes?"

She straightened her shoulders. "It's time for me to repay your friendship with my own. By the time we are done here, every one of these people will not only be giving you their vote, they'll be giving you their money as well."

Hale laughed. "I think I'm going to like being your friend, Yancey Palmer."

Chapter Twelve

As soon as Sheriff McCall left Mrs. Hollenbeck's house, Jonas headed straight for the downtown telegraph office to send the prearranged signal to Smith, his man in Bear Gulch. A message with one STOP meant "be careful, law enforcement is suspicious," two STOPs meant "move the press to a new location," and three STOPs meant, "Abandon operations. Save what you can. Burn the rest."

Depending on how hard they pushed their horses, Sheriff McCall and his deputies would reach Bear Gulch in ninety minutes to two hours. Barely enough time to move the press. Jonas mentally composed his two-STOP message as he hurried closer to the telegraph office, cursing under his breath when he saw the CLOSED sign in the window. Stupid mistake on his part. Of course the office would be closed for the holiday.

What reasonable explanation could he give for going all the way down to the train station to send a telegram? He'd stretched credibility already by saying he'd forgotten his reading glasses at his office and couldn't sign a search warrant he hadn't read. Stopping by the telegraph office to send a message—another thing he'd *forgotten*—along the way was believable as long as no one thought too hard about it.

Jonas turned toward City Hall. When he was done there,

he'd have to go to the train depot. He was a man who did what was necessary, from figuring out an excuse for delaying his return to the brunch to sending a three-STOP message. The press would be lost, but hopefully, the men could save the plates and latest run of counterfeit bills.

He passed Wood Street, glancing up the hill at Madame Lestraude's Maison de Joie. He couldn't be certain the madam had informed her son about the counterfeiting operation—Sheriff McCall was an excellent lawman—but Jonas couldn't afford to underestimate the woman. Whether or not this strike was of her hand, he needed to put more pressure on Mr. Green. Who knew a brothel accountant would be so difficult to break?

If only she hadn't thwarted his best move by involving Jakob in her rescuing ring before Jonas even knew they were at war.

Had he erred by telling her he'd orchestrated Hendry's death? Jonas regretted the necessity more than she could know. Unlike most of his peers, Hendry was that rare newspaper man interested in truth rather than sensationalism. It was why people believed him when he wrote that Madame Lestraude and Finn Collins were kidnapping women *into* prostitution. Lestraude had used the reporter's reputation to manipulate the truth in order to save her own skin. Jonas had planned to use it to disqualify Isaak from running for mayor as a last resort to get him out of the campaign and make way for Hale.

Hendry would have believed a carefully worded hint at scandal from a man close enough to the Gunderson twins that they called him Uncle Jonas. And it would have done no harm, not in the long run. Isaak might have suffered some initial embarrassment, as would Hendry when it came out that he'd published a false story, but all would have been well in the end.

But the newspaper correspondent had been too good at his job. He'd uncovered the counterfeiting operation and that the Honorable Jonas Forsythe was behind it. Needing a distraction from the truth, Jonas stirred up hatred against the reporter in the one quarter of town where the residents would do more than silently fume—the red-light district. He'd merely stretched the truth about Hendry's involvement in the rescue of brothel girls, and those already losing money because of the man's articles calling for stricter enforcement of the laws against prostitution were primed for murder.

Jonas mentioned it to Lestraude to scare her into backing away from her declaration of war, but it seemed he'd achieved quite the opposite.

If only he could get Green to cooperate.

And then there was the matter of Yancey Palmer. Last time she'd spouted her suspicions that Joseph Hendry died because he'd uncovered a counterfeiting operation, Jonas silenced her by convincing her parents to send her to Denver for a few months. That option wasn't open to him now. The girl was too valuable to Hale's campaign.

But she needed to hush.

Later that day

Yancey searched the crowd for Isaak Gunderson's blond head. The tall man should be easy to find, but the turnout for Hale's dinner was twice what they'd expected. There were places where people were so thick, it was difficult to see three feet in front of her. She kept moving toward the food, the place they'd designated for changing who was escorting Hale from group to group. Her turn started in two minutes.

She kept her eyes ahead as she excused herself, hoping to see Isaak's black bowler come into view.

There it was. And sure enough, Hale stood beside him checking his pocket watch.

Last year, Yancey would have sighed to think he was anxious for her arrival. But now? It was just Hale through and through. If someone said they'd meet him at eight in the evening, he expected it meant seven fifty-nine.

She smiled, proud of herself for yet another instance where she'd not made too much of his gesture. It was proof she could be his friend, as he'd suggested that morning.

Someone tapped her on the shoulder. She turned around to see Windsor Buchanan. "Windy? How on earth did you sneak up on me when your shadow is big enough to encompass both of us?"

He shrugged. She waited for him to speak, but he stood mute, twisting the bottom edge of his long beard into a roll.

"Did you want to ask me something?" Yancey prompted, hoping it had something to do with Carline Pope now that she'd launched Operation Mrs. Buchanan, which they had come up with four days ago.

"I . . . uh . . ." Windsor kept twisting his beard until it pulled tight against his chin like an upside-down funnel.

Yancey's eyes were drawn to the puckered skin snaking up his neck and disappearing into the beard. Windsor had been *burned*. And his long hair and beard were his way of hiding it.

He let go of his beard, combing it out quickly to cover up the scar.

Yancey rearranged her expression to hide her surprise and met his eyes. "Tell me what I can do to help you."

"I was thinking it might be time for me to . . . but I'm out of practice. You . . . know what I mean?" His hesitancy reminded her of Isaak at the train depot before he ran after Zoe.

Whoever had captured Windsor's heart, he was already in love, whether he knew it or not.

Please let it be Carline, oh please, oh please, oh please.

Yancey took a moment to untangle his words. "If I understand what you're"—*not*—"saying, you want to start courting a woman, but you're out of practice. Is that right?"

He nodded his shaggy head.

"Then I suggest you start small. Ask the girl out for a buggy ride." When what she could see of his face turned ashen, she placed her hand on his forearm as a gesture of reassurance. "Any girl. It doesn't have to be the one who is making you so nervous right now."

Windsor's color returned. "Just for practice, you mean?"

"That's right. Just get the words out so the next time they aren't so difficult."

He grinned, and Yancey wished Carline was around to see it. He really was handsome under all that hair. "Then, Miss Palmer, may I have the pleasure of your company on Sunday after church?"

She gave him her brightest smile. "It would be my very great pleasure to go on a Sunday drive with you, Mr. Buchanan."

A growl from behind her spun her around. Isaak stood there with Hale in tow. The first looked ready to wring her neck, the second . . . ? She'd seen that expression on Hale's face too many times not to recognize it immediately.

Chilly politeness.

Isaak stomped forward and gripped her bicep. "A moment of your time, Miss Palmer." He pulled her aside without waiting for her permission.

"Whatever is the matter with you?" She yanked her arm out of his grasp, rubbing the pain away.

"Me?" Isaak's displeasure was as loud as his voice was soft. "I'm not the one using Windsor to make Hale jealous."

"I did no such thing." Yancey kept her words quiet, her desire to avoid another public scene strong. She hadn't even been *thinking* about Hale while talking to Windsor. Only about helping him so he and—hopefully—Carline could have their own happy ending. "How dare you."

"How dare I? Because you promised me you wouldn't play any of your games."

"I wasn't."

Isaak crossed his arms and stared down his nose at her.

Yancey made a fist, tempted to plow it into his shoulder. "Oh. You are impossible, Isaak David Gunderson." She marched off, not caring that she was neglecting her shift with Hale. Let Isaak do double duty. She wanted nothing to do with Hale.

Because what really hurt was the look on *his* face. This morning he'd asked her to be his friend. They'd talked about Joseph. They'd talked about Luanne. And he'd said they should put the past behind them.

Well, *he* certainly hadn't. And it wasn't just her feelings overruling logic. The look on his face was as readable as a sign. He saw her chatting—not flirting but *chatting*—with a friend and immediately jumped to the conclusion that she was breaking her promise to never be the silly girl who'd chased him in the past.

Isaak had drawn the same conclusion, but as she strode through the crowed, it was Hale's face she pictured as she pounded a fist into her palm.

She searched the faces around her for Carline. Whether she was the object of Windsor's carriage ride invitation or not, she needed to be forewarned. And Yancey needed her best friend beside her if she was going to keep from breaking down in tears or screaming with rage.

Both were viable options at the moment.

Several startled looks were directed at her, so Yancey

fixed a smile on her face lest she—once again—be the subject of gossip.

She passed Royal Easton, who was chatting with Luci Stanek and Melrose Truett. Melrose had longing written all over her face as she stared at Royal, but she seemed incapable of doing anything but fiddling with the navy-blue satin ribbon tied in her red-gold hair. Her navy-and-white-polka-dot dress was accented with a wide red sash, a testament to her parents' wealth and patriotism. Luci's dress, a plain navy, was the poorer version—as was the red cotton ribbon in her dark hair—but she looked just as pretty in it. At least Royal appeared to think so. His gaze never left Luci's face.

Poor Melrose. Yancey knew what it was like to have the man she desired ignore her. Oh, how she knew. At least Melrose wasn't suffering the indignities of having Royal believe she was a lying, manipulative, scheming promise-breaker.

Yancey spied Carline talking with Emilia McCall. Both of them had concerned looks on their faces.

Carline kept turning her head left and right.

Yancey waved to catch her attention.

The instant their eyes met, Carline broke away from Emilia, pushing past the ten or eleven people in her way. "Yancey, thank goodness you're here."

All her frustration disappeared at the frantic look in Carline's eyes. "What's wrong?"

"Check your pockets." Carline reached out and patted Yancey's left side.

"Why?"

"Just check them."

Patting the other side of her skirt, Yancey felt a slight irregularity. She slipped her hand inside and pulled out a slip of paper.

Carline gasped.

Emilia stepped close, both hands over her stomach. Her light brown eyes were filled with anxiety.

Her heart picking up speed, Yancey unfolded the note.

STOP TALKING ABOUT PHONY MONEY OR YOU'LL BE SORRY.

Carline took the paper from Yancey's hand. "Mine's the same."

"Yours?" Yancey snapped her focus to her friend. "You have one, too?"

Carline opened her fist to reveal a crumpled scrap. She peeled it open. The words and handwriting were identical.

Yancey stared at the notes. Over the years, she'd received hundreds, if not thousands, of handwritten messages. Was the penmanship of this one recognizable? And even if it was, would anyone in law enforcement believe her? "We need to show these to Marshal Valentine."

Emilia was pursing her lips. Quinn Valentine wasn't her favorite person. He'd wrongly arrested her and her brother, Roch, for murdering Edgar Dunfree. Yancey never quite understood why, and no one had ever answered her questions about it to her satisfaction.

Carline stretched tall. "How are we ever going to find the marshal in this mob?"

Yancey stood on tiptoe. "If he took off his hat, his red hair should be easy enough to see."

Emilia, who was only five feet and a few inches and wouldn't have been able to see much no matter how tall she stood, was on her toes and looking around anyway.

"There he is." Carline grabbed Yancey by the arm and started pulling her forward.

They soon outdistanced Emilia, but she waved in what Yancey hoped meant, *Keep going. I'll catch up.*

As soon as she and Carline got close to Marshal Valentine, Carline held out the notes. "Look at these."

Quinn Valentine was the rare redhead who didn't have freckles. His eyes, an icy blue at all times, seemed particularly cold now. Although Yancey suspected she mistook the chill in his eyes for the one in her bones and needed a reason other than the note he'd taken from Carline's hand. "Who gave these to you?"

"I don't know," Carline answered first. "I found a penny on the ground and put it in my pocket. That's when I discovered mine."

Quinn pulled a notebook from his inside jacket pocket. A short pencil was tied to the binding with a strip of leather. He opened the notebook, tucked the scrap of paper in the binding, and took up the pencil. "When was this?"

"Five or ten minutes ago." Carline pressed two fingers against her forehead. "I can't quite remember."

Quinn scratched something in his notebook. "What about you, Yancey?"

"A minute ago. Maybe two."

"And neither one of you saw or felt anything?" He looked at Carline first. When she shook her head, he shifted his gaze to Emilia who had just caught up to their group. "Did you get a note, too?"

"No, but I was there when Carline discovered hers."

"How about you, Yancey?" Quinn looked at her expectantly. "Did anyone bump into you or get suspiciously close?"

"I'm not sure how to judge *suspiciously* close in a crowd this size." She swung her hand to encompass the park. How proud she'd been of the huge turnout. Now it seemed threatening.

"Good point." Quinn tapped his pencil point on the open page. "I imagine the reference to 'phony money' is because the two of you have always thought Joseph Hendry's death was tied to counterfeiting."

Emilia crossed her arms over her stomach. "And you should also know that my husband secured a search warrant this morning and left town a few hours ago because he thinks he's found a counterfeiting operation down in Bear Gulch."

Yancey nodded. "He came to the brunch at Mrs. Hollenbeck's house to ask Judge Forsythe to sign it."

"Who else was there?"

Yancey listed off the names of the twenty-five couples while Quinn scribbled in his notebook. She then told him about her conversation with Hale. "No one else could have overheard us."

"Hm." The unhelpful sound made Yancey want to shake the marshal into revealing his thoughts. Quinn finished writing and looked up. "Outside of Hale, have you been talking to lots of people about the search warrant?"

"Goodness, no."

Quinn appeared to weigh her denial. She was about to declare her innocence again—she'd had quite enough of people believing the worst of her—when he swung his gaze to Carline. "What about you?"

She shook her head, and then gasped.

"What?" Yancey and Emilia asked in unison.

Carline scattered looks around the circle. "Mrs. Hess approached me as we were setting up the tables. She asked if I'd heard about the search warrant, and then if I thought it was connected to counterfeiting. I said I hoped it was because if—and I distinctly remember saying *if*—it was connected to Joseph's death, it would prove Yancey and I had been right all along."

Quinn looked at his notes. "Mr. and Mrs. Hess's names aren't on here."

"But she and Mrs. Watson are close friends." Yancey

pictured the two women in the church yard as they whispered about her. "Whatever one knows, the other does as well."

"And whatever Mrs. Watson knows—as well as anything she suspects—she'll tell to anyone who'll listen." Emilia spread her hands. "I'm sorry to say it, but I've seen it over and over again when she shopped at The Resale Company."

"Meaning"—Quinn picked up the note again, squinting at it as though something about it puzzled him—"the list of suspects is everyone who's been here between setup and three minutes ago."

"So what do we do now?" Yancey put her arms around both Carline and Emilia.

"There's not much I *can* do at this point, but I'll tell my men to be on the lookout for any suspicious characters or activity." He was still staring at the note. "It just says to stop talking or you'll be sorry."

Yancey glanced at the other two women to see if either of them understood why that seemed to bother the marshal.

"Doesn't that seem rather vague?" He looked at each of them in turn, as if he expected an answer.

Emilia frowned at him. "I'm not sure we know what you're trying to say, Quinn."

He set the note in the binding of his notebook again. "It sounds like whoever wrote this didn't intend you any *specific* harm."

Yancey tapped her finger against her lip as she considered his assertion. "You mean like when we were in grade school and wanted Billy Sexton to stop picking on us—"

"—but there was really nothing we could do because he was so much bigger than we were—" Carline inserted.

"—so we just told him to stop it or he'd be sorry?" Yancey finished.

"Exactly like that." Quinn snapped his notebook closed.

"Again, I'll tell my men to keep an eye out, but I don't think you're in any real danger."

Maybe he was right, but Yancey didn't want to be at the park any longer. All her joy over the large turnout was gone. She just wanted to go home.

And it had less to do with the notes than the expression on a certain mayoral candidate's face.

Chapter Thirteen

Across the park

Hale stood alone on the edge of the crowd. He checked the time. Eight twelve.

Yancey wasn't back.

He'd started after her as soon as she turned on her heel and stomped away from Isaak, but the gawking stares of the people around them convinced Hale to turn around. Jakob said gossip ate at her. There was already going to be some after the red-faced argument between her and Isaak, so Hale wasn't going to add more by running after her. Instead, he'd smiled, looked over the crowd, and struck up a conversation with the closest person he knew.

Who happened to be Zeb Inger.

The bootmaker had a long list of items to discuss. By the time he was on his twelfth, Hale had stopped listening and was envisioning Yancey—fingers wagging at him—saying, *Three things. Just three.*

He'd suppressed a grin, nodded his head, and said, "Mm-hm. I see. Yes, I understand," until Inger finally ran out of complaints and moved on. Hale had retreated to the edge of the park to await Yancey. Was she coming?

He checked the time again. Eight thirteen.

Windsor Buchanan and Isaak returned from wherever they'd gone. Buchanan was Hale's image of Sampson—lots of muscles and lots of hair with a heart for God. Was Yancey interested in him? It certainly appeared as though she was enraptured with the man

Hale snapped his pocket watch closed and stuffed it in his vest. He'd stopped cold at the sight of her hand on Buchanan's arm. At her obvious delight in accepting his invitation to take a buggy ride with him. Hale had smiled to cover his shock—or had his face just frozen with the smile he'd worn all day?

As they came within earshot, Hale heard Windsor say, ". . . always told you I have your back, but not this time."

Isaak's lips were pressed into a flat line.

Hale waited for the two men to reach him. He turned his attention to Windsor first. "Why don't you have Isaak's back this time?"

"Because he's wrong about Miss Yancey making me think it was all my idea to ask her on a buggy ride."

Isaak inhaled and opened his lips, but Hale put a hand up to stop him. "In a moment." Aware of how overbearing the gesture was, and not caring one whit, he addressed Windsor. "I'm not sure I follow. Please start from the beginning."

Windsor crossed his arms over his chest, lifting his chin until his beard came free. "I aim to start courting Miss Carline Pope—even though Isaak wrongly insists she likes Geddes."

"She's always flirting with him"—Isaak inserted—"and she spit tea all over your shirt when you asked her out the last time."

"That was two years ago. This"—Windsor circled a hand around his hair and beard—"takes some getting used to. And I don't believe Miss Carline has ever flirted with Geddes. She spends half her time at the Palmer house, so of course she's friendlier with Geddes than with most other men."

"So why did you ask Miss *Yancey* on a buggy ride?" Hale brought the subject back to the important point.

Windsor combed his fingers through his beard. "I'm not proud of it, but the idea of asking Miss Carline out makes my knees wobble. I've not asked a woman out for . . . a very long time. Seeing as I'm out of practice, I asked Yancey what I should do about it. She suggested I ask *any* woman out, just to get the words out of my mouth."

"Seems reasonable." And made breathing easier. Hale turned to Isaak. "What's your dispute with Mr. Buchanan's story?"

Isaak tugged at his shirt collar. "I haven't told you the whole truth about what I made Yancey promise before agreeing to help with your campaign."

Hale lowered his chin and raised his eyebrows. "Oh?"

"Before I met Zoe"—Isaak's voice softened when he spoke his wife's name—"I didn't see how Yancey could pursue you with such single-mindedness."

It was because she knew—just *knew*—they belonged together. Which wasn't logical, and yet her reasoning had repeated itself inside Hale's head since she'd said it that morning. "And now?"

Isaak looked to his right before bringing his eyes back to Hale. "When you love someone as much as I love my wife— as much as Yancey claims to love you—you don't just get over it. I asked her to put aside her designs on you until the election was over. Not forever, just until November."

Hale blinked. "You what?"

"You've said yourself that campaigning is difficult for you. I wanted to make sure you didn't have any distractions until it was over." Isaak jutted his chin. "I didn't count on you smiling at her or asking her to be your friend."

"So you think she broke her promise to you because I

encouraged her?" Hale crossed his arms over his chest. "That she's reverted to trying to make me jealous?"

Despite her promise to him to never chase after him or make him the subject of her romantic silliness again?

He rubbed a sudden pain in his sternum. His mind whirled with the various facts and interpretations. *Had* he fallen into a trap? He slowed his thinking. Ran the entire incident through from start to finish. "Windsor said *he* was the one to approach Yancey. Unless he lied about that—"

"Windsor doesn't lie."

"I don't lie."

Hale looked between the two men, his arms falling to his sides. "Then I don't see how Yancey manipulated him into approaching her about a carriage ride."

"Maybe"—Isaak shrugged—"but it still seems rather convenient for the conversation to happen just as we came upon it."

True. "Is that what your discussion was about?" Hale cut a look at the spot where Yancey and Isaak had argued. "And what did she say?"

"That I was impossible . . . and wrong." Isaak's shoulders dropped an inch. "I guess I'm not as over being benevolently arrogant as I thought. I'm sorry, Hale. This is a matter for you to decide, not me."

Hale thought through his options. Yancey had promised to *never* chase him again. Not to *stop* chasing him or *quit* chasing him, or any other word which could be misconstrued for delaying her pursuit. She'd said *never*. Had she lied or told the truth? Was the hurt on her face when she saw his face frozen in shock real or an act? If she'd falsified her reaction, she belonged on the stage. It wasn't beyond the realm of possibility, but . . .

Hale lifted his chin to look Isaak in the eye. "I've jumped to conclusions about Yancey's intentions quite enough over the past two months. I think it's time I gave her the benefit of the doubt."

Isaak stretched his neck from side to side. "Then I will do the same."

Windsor bobbed his head as if to say, *I approve*.

"Now, if you will excuse me, gentlemen, I need to find Yancey." Hale bowed and left. He needed to find her quickly. She might think he'd assumed the worst of her. It was logical on her part—especially when Isaak already had.

Hale headed in the direction he'd last seen her. Too many people wanted to chat, shake his hand, and congratulate him on his speech. He did his best to be polite, but he wanted to make them all disappear with a wave of his hand. He finally caught a glimpse of Yancey through a small break in the crowd ahead. She was looking around as though searching.

Relief wilted his posture. She was trying to find him.

Only the instant their eyes met, her face hardened and she looked away. She was most definitely angry with him.

His chest tightened, but he kept a smile on his face. She wouldn't want him to make a scene. As he moved closer to her, he continued to greet everyone as though they were the most important people in the world at that moment. Just as Yancey had taught him.

The tactic worked. By the time he reached her side, her expression had softened. "You're getting better at this."

"Thank you." He offered her his arm. "I learned from the best."

She shot him a skeptical—or was it perplexed?—glance before putting her hand on his sleeve. "I'm looking for my parents."

I was hoping you were looking for me. Hale's heartbeat picked up speed. What would happen if he said that aloud? He didn't like the tension between them. Not after the way they'd cleared the air that morning. But he didn't know how to start this conversation. Tease her for thinking ill of him?

Ask her what she'd thought he thought when he observed her with Windsor? Hale foresaw multiple ways either could end badly. His fingers itched for a pencil and paper to write out his options before deciding on the best one.

He cleared his throat. "I have something I need to say to you, but I'm finding it difficult to know how to start."

"How about we begin walking so we don't draw attention to ourselves." She was looking away from him, a smile fixed on her face.

"Of course." Hale glanced around the area and started walking in the direction with the least number of people. "I believe you said you were looking for your parents?"

"I am."

He followed her lead, smiling at everyone around them. "Because of what Isaak said to you?"

She flinched.

He drew her to a halt and turned to face her. "I hope you know that—although I was shocked to see you with Windsor—I did not assume nor do I believe . . ." Hale looked left and right to be sure no one was stretching their ears toward them. ". . . what Isaak said."

Yancey didn't smile. Or move. She just stared up at him for the longest time.

Hale held his breath. Her verdict mattered. More than he'd ever imagined it would.

She exhaled and ducked her chin. When she looked back up, there was a sardonic smile lifting the corners of her lips. "I guess you aren't the only one who can jump to a wrong conclusion."

He let out the breath he'd been holding. "We are quite the pair."

She turned and held out her hand, tucking it in the crook of his arm when he offered it to her. "Then I guess we'd better get back to the business of getting you elected."

Dusk was smudging the edges of the landscape, but Hale felt as though the sun had just risen.

Pounding on his front door awakened Hale with a start. He hunted for his glasses on the table beside his bed with his left hand while tossing off the covers with his right.

The pounding continued unabated.

"Coming," he yelled, but doubted he'd been heard over the constant banging. His fingertips touched wire. Not caring that he was smudging the lenses, he grabbed his glasses and put them on.

What time was it?

After quickly dressing, he hurried out of his bedroom, through the living room—where moonlight illuminated the clock on his mantel just enough for him to see that it was twenty minutes past midnight—and down the steps.

"Coming!" he shouted again, the pounding so ruthless, he feared his front door would come loose from the framework.

"Hale? Hale?" He recognized Isaak Gunderson's voice through the wood. "Hale! Open up!"

He turned the doorknob and threw open the door. "What's wrong?"

"It's Mac. He's been shot."

Hale stumbled back. "Where?"

"In Bear Gulch."

"No, I mean in the shoulder? In the arm? Where?" *Don't let it be the heart. Or the stomach. Or the kidneys.*

Hale kept praying over various vital organs until Isaak said, "In the leg. He managed to bind it up and ride back to Helena, but he's lost a lot of blood."

Hale lifted his hat off the stand beside the door and stepped outside. "Where is he now?"

"St. Peter's Hospital."

Hale pulled his door shut. "Let's go."

Isaak ran to the opposite side of his new carriage and hoisted himself into the seat in a smooth, athletic motion.

Hale clambered up, missing his footing and knocking his chin on the floorboard when he fell. The coppery taste of blood filled his mouth. He climbed up more slowly, running his teeth along the inside of his cheek until he felt where he'd bitten it. As soon as he was seated, he pressed the spot between his fingers and tongue to stop the bleeding.

Isaak snapped the reins over the horses and the carriage jolted into motion. "There's more. Deputy Alderson was killed. So was Mac's horse. He had to ride Alderson's horse home."

Hale closed his eyes.

"There's one more thing."

Hale looked over at Isaak and prepared for something worse.

"Emilia is with child. She announced it to her family several days ago, before Mr. Stanek left for Chicago."

To testify against their former landlord. Mr. Stanek had asked Hale for advice about what to say. Even if only half of what the Staneks endured at the hands of that man were true, Hale hoped they sentenced him to living the rest of his days in one of his own tenement buildings.

"She told me because she wanted to give us plenty of time to find a replacement for her at the store."

"When is she due?" Emilia and Mac had only been married four months.

"Late January, early February." Isaak cracked a small smile. "Ever the responsible Emilia."

"How's she taking the news of Mac's injury?"

"I haven't seen her yet. Zoe and I were already at the hospital when she suggested you'd want to be there, too." Isaak slowed to turn right. "I hope you don't mind, but I told Zoe I would wait for Emilia as long as she wants. Zoe is going to get a ride home with someone already at the hospital. Can you find your own way home?"

"If nothing else, I can walk." Hale spent the remainder of the trip praying for Mac, Emilia, the Alderson family, and all the lawmen whose job was to keep civilization and criminal chaos on opposite sides of a squat, flimsy wall.

When they reached the hospital, Hale jumped down from the carriage before it stopped rolling. The three-story brick structure looked more like a home on Millionaire's Hill, with its steep-pitched roof on the right side and rounded turret on the left. By day it welcomed patients, but by moonlight it loomed like the setting of an Edgar Allan Poe story of the macabre.

Hale ran inside but came to a halt when he saw Yancey Palmer, her face wet with tears, holding Carline Pope, who was weeping uncontrollably. Marshal Valentine was standing next to them, his face white.

"Mac?" Hale managed, although his lungs had solidified inside his chest.

Quinn leaned down to say something to Yancey. She scattered glances around the room until she found Hale.

In that moment, an invisible but tangible cord bound him to her in a way that defied description. It wasn't love—it couldn't be—but whatever it was, he found himself walking toward her as though his feet had developed their own will.

"A moment, Hale."

He heard the words, felt the hand on his shoulder, and still couldn't look away from Yancey.

"Mac is still in surgery."

That jerked Hale's attention to Quinn. "What did you say?"

The marshal lifted his chin to acknowledge someone behind Hale.

An instant later, Isaak appeared. "Don't tell me Mac is dead."

"He's not." Quinn didn't sound or look as if he was delivering good news. "I was just telling Hale that Mac is still in surgery."

Isaak spun around so he no longer faced Yancey and Carline. "Then what are they crying about?"

Quinn's gaze dropped to the floor. He took a breath, then squared his shoulders to look Isaak in the eye. "Carline's parents were killed in a carriage accident on the way home tonight."

Hale started for Yancey. His need to comfort her was so fierce, it shocked him.

She kept her left arm around her friend as she reached toward Hale with her right hand.

He took it between both of his. Carline's face was buried in her shoulder, so he addressed Yancey. "I'm so sorry."

Her chin trembled, a tear dripping onto her blouse.

"What happened?" The lawyer in him needed facts. Facts could be understood. Facts could be put in order. He could make sense of facts.

Nothing about the emotions vibrating through his body made sense. He'd never felt them before. He didn't know what they meant. Or what he was supposed to do with them. Or how to put them into words.

But something had just changed inside him.

Hale wanted to press her hand to his heart and let her feel the pounding inside his chest—to let it explain what he couldn't put into words.

"Where's my son?" Madame Lestraude's brash voice assaulted his ears, breaking the spell.

Hale took a step closer to Yancey and Carline, intent on shielding them should the brothel owner turn crass in her distress. When he turned around, he was surprised by the number of people crowded into the foyer. His aunt and uncle stood with Yancey's parents and the Pawlikowskis— the women watching Yancey as if they were waiting for permission to take their turn consoling Carline. Quinn had joined Jakob, Isaak, and Zoe Gunderson. They were facing away from Hale, the twins' broad backs hiding whoever was behind them, although Hale thought he saw Windsor Buchanan's profile. Off to the side, Mac's county deputies and Quinn's city marshals huddled together, their eyes scanning the room. The rest of the foyer was filled with people Hale recognized but couldn't name.

And in the center of them all— but standing alone—was Madame Lestraude, a bejeweled hand at her neck. Nico squeezed between Isaak and Zoe. He walked straight to the madam, wrapped his arm around her shoulders, and leaned close to say something. The madam nodded, and the two of them walked closer to the window overlooking the front lawn, the people in their way shifting like an invisible force pushed them aside.

"Mrs. McCall?" Hale snapped his attention toward the voice. Miss Young, the superintendent of the hospital, was making her way across the crowded foyer.

Emilia pushed between Isaak and Jakob. "I'm here. How is he?"

"He's going to be fine."

A cheer went up, prompting Miss Young's immediate, "Please. We have other patients who are trying to rest."

"When can I see him?" Emilia wrapped both hands around her waist.

Hale's eye caught on Madame Lestraude. She was glaring at Uncle Jonas.

What was between the two of them?

Sure, the woman had shown up at the picnic today—was it still today?—wearing a "Vote for Hale" ribbon, but that didn't explain the antagonism sparking between her and his uncle. It was too . . . personal? Or maybe *vitriolic* was a better word.

"Madame?" Emilia drew Hale's attention. She held out her hand, palm up, toward her mother-in-law "Would you please join me? I'm sure Mac will want to see you."

Madame licked her lips, raised her chin, and walked straight to Emilia. The crowd between them parted, as if the madam was the one who was sick instead of her son. The two women held hands as Miss Young led them away.

As soon as they disappeared from view, everyone started talking at once. The only one Hale paid attention to was Mrs. Palmer, who hurried to her daughter. "Come, Yancey. Let's take Carline home. There's nothing more for us to do here."

Yancey pulled a few inches away from Carline. "Now that you know Mac is going to be all right, are you ready to go?" Carline must have whispered she was, or else the two friends spoke without words. Yancey shifted her embrace to wrap one arm around Carline's shoulders, leaving room for Mrs. Palmer to wrap her arm around Carline's waist. As the trio shuffled past, Yancey gave Hale a sad smile that pierced him to the heart.

Everyone who'd been talking a moment ago ceased to do so as Yancey, Carline, and Mrs. Palmer crossed the foyer. Mr. Palmer, the Pawlikowskis, and Aunt Lily trailed behind them like a funeral procession. The crowd parted to let them pass.

Isaak bent close to his wife's ear. She nodded, then joined Aunt Lily.

Uncle Jonas stepped into the center of the wake. "Go home, everyone. There's nothing more to be done here tonight. You"—he pointed his finger at the lawmen, who weren't moving—"go on. You're going to have a busy day tomorrow. Marshal Valentine and I will stay behind and keep you informed if anything changes."

They grumbled their insistence on staying with their fellow officer until Quinn added, "Judge Forsythe is right. I'm going to need you sharp tomorrow, so get some sleep and we'll talk in the morning."

Soon the foyer was empty save for Hale, Isaak, Jakob, Uncle Jonas, and Quinn.

Hale went directly to the city marshal. "What happened?"

Quinn reached inside his vest pocket and withdrew a notebook. "I'm fairly sure the accident has nothing to do with the notes Carline and Yancey—"

"What notes?" Hale's question was repeated by the rest of the men almost simultaneously.

Quinn opened his notebook and took out a scrap of paper. He handed it to Uncle Jonas first.

"I never authorized—" His skin turned red.

Hale snatched the note from his uncle's hand. **STOP TALKING ABOUT PHONY MONEY OR YOU'LL BE SORRY.** "What didn't you authorize?" He barely felt the paper being tugged away.

Uncle Jonas coughed into his fist. "I'm sorry, Marshal Valentine. I forgot myself for a moment. This is city business. It's not within my jurisdiction to deny the release of evidence in an ongoing investigation."

The words rang false in Hale's ears, but a logical reason why escaped him.

"Do you think Mac's search and this"—Hale looked at his uncle while pointing at the note now in Isaak's hand— "are connected?"

"Hard to know." Quinn glanced to where Emilia and Madame Lestraude had last stood. "I only spoke with Mac for a minute before he passed out. He and Alderson found the place easily because it was on fire. Mac figures someone must have warned the counterfeiters."

And to shoot the men who'd come to arrest them, all of which had happened while someone was warning Carline and Yancey to keep quiet about the same thing or they'd be sorry.

Hale's stomach squeezed into a hard lump. "Mac came to the brunch this morning so Uncle Jonas could sign the search warrant. There were approximately fifty people in attendance. Do you think one of them could be involved?"

Quinn stared down at his notebook. "Were it not for the notes the girls received, I would have said no. Illegal operations usually have their own lookouts posted."

"You said both Carline and Yancey received one of these." Jakob took the note from Isaak's hand.

Quinn nodded. "They brought them to me at the picnic, but there wasn't much more they could tell me. They didn't remember seeing anything or anyone unusual, but that doesn't surprise me. So many people were there, it would be as easy for a skilled pickpocket to put something in a pocket as it would be to take something out." He lifted the pencil dangling from the end of his notebook by a leather strip and began tapping it against the open page. "Nothing about the Popes' deaths suggests foul play. It just appears to be a tragic accident, but I wish I'd taken this threat more seriously. I even told Yancey and Carline not to worry too much because 'or you'll be sorry' was such a vague and almost juvenile warning."

Isaak frowned. "I've given Carline and Yancey a hard time about their irrational adherence to the belief that Joseph Hendry was killed because of counterfeiting. That"—he pointed to the note still in his brother's hand— "makes me think they've been right all along."

I can't explain it other than a feeling I have. I know it's true. I just do. Yancey's declaration—the one Hale dismissed because it wasn't logical—rang in his ears. What else might he be wrong about?

Isaak rubbed the corners of his lips between his thumb and index finger. "A few months ago, Mac came to The Resale Company asking whether we ever sold a leveling foot to someone in town. He found one in Finn's barn after he was killed. I was supposed to check our ledgers, but I put him off until Ma and Pa came home from their trip."

Jakob jerked his attention to his brother. "You never told me that."

"I didn't?" Isaak frowned and glanced at the floor. He shook his head. "Sorry about that. Anyway, I'm starting to think that Mac asking for our ledgers, the store burning right before I was going to check them, and the fire marshal's ruling of probable arson are all connected."

"I"—Jakob raised his hand as if he were a schoolboy needing the teacher's attention—"also find it suspicious that the fire started in the office instead of the storage area, where we kept varnish and other flammable chemicals."

Hale shifted his focus between the twins. "Are you saying you think The Resale Company was deliberately burned to keep you from going through your ledgers?"

Isaak raised both shoulders. "Maybe I'm stretching things here, but I remember we briefly had a printing press in stock. Between Pa and me, we can usually fix just about anything, but that press was beyond us. Pa set the price at a tenth of what he thought a functional one would sell for, and we were thrilled that it was gone by the next week."

"Who bought it?" Quinn gripped his pencil and held it over the open page of his notebook.

"I don't remember selling it myself. Do you?" Isaak looked at Jakob, who shook his head. "We can ask Pa, but the reason he was so methodical with his records in the first place was because he couldn't remember which whos bought which whats."

"Or which whos sold him which whats," Jakob added.

"Here's the thing"—Isaak tapped the fingers of his right hand into his left palm—"printing presses use leveling feet, and sometimes when we couldn't fix things, we'd send them to Finn Collins. I'm wondering if whoever bought that press paid Finn to fix it, then killed him before he figured out they were using it to make counterfeit money."

"That's rather far-fetched." Uncle Jonas scowled with—what? Anger seemed too strong an emotion, yet his glare was identical to the one he'd given Madame Lestraude earlier.

Quinn scribbled notes in his book. "Maybe, but it's at least worth pursuing."

"You're chasing a rabbit down a hole." Uncle Jonas shifted his glare to Quinn. "There's no reason for you to waste valuable time and money. No reason at all."

His repetition caught Hale in the stomach. His uncle was lying. But why? And about what?

Quinn returned the notebook to his inside pocket and then tugged the lapels of his jacket together. "You've made yourself quite clear, sir, but as you stated earlier, your jurisdiction doesn't include mine." He bowed. "Now, gentlemen, if you'll excuse me, it's been a long day and it's going to be an even longer night."

"I'll go with you." Jakob clamped a hand on Quinn's shoulder as they left, their footsteps thudding across the floor.

Uncle Jonas waited until they were gone before turning his attention to Isaak. "I hope that, in the future, you will think through your presumptions before spouting them." He patted his arm. "Where's my cane? Never mind"—he stomped away—"I have more important things to do than stand around listening to puppies yap about . . ."

Whatever else he said was lost when he lowered his voice and turned the corner to leave.

Isaak turned wide eyes on Hale. "Do you know what that was about?"

Hale shook his head. "No, but I intend to find out."

July 5, 1888
City Hall

"You did what?" Jonas marched to the door and flipped the lock. His only appointment for the day was this one, but it wouldn't do to have an unexpected interruption. He turned and walked back to his desk. His hands curled as he walked past Lombard. How hard would it be to wrap his fingers around the dolt's dirt-creased neck and squeeze? Jonas stood behind his chair gripping the top of the leather. "I never told you to do anything beyond listening and reporting back to me. And I certainly didn't authorize writing notes to those girls. Of all the stupid, idiotic, asinine things to do."

Lombard didn't bother to take the toothpick from his mouth. "I don't hold with killin' women."

Jonas balled his fingers into fists. "I would never kill Yancey Palmer or her parrot of a friend."

Lombard shifted the toothpick from the left side of his mouth to the right with his lips and tongue. "How was I supposed to know that? All I know is that you had that reporter killed to hush him up about the counterfeiting, and like I said, I don't hold with killin' women."

Jonas had killed for incompetence, too, and he still had the hemlock he'd used on Dunfree. It would be easy—so easy—to invite Lombard over to the house, pour him a glass of wine, and watch him choke on his stupidity.

But he wouldn't defile his wife's home, and getting rid of two men in the same manner might raise suspicions.

He could pay Smith to do it. The man would ask no questions. Jonas could even specify that he didn't want to know how the deed was accomplished, just that it was done.

If only Lombard weren't so valuable in his own slothful way. Yesterday's picnic was the first of many events leading up to the election. Jonas needed the names of men whose votes could be bought for five dollars of counterfeit money. Lombard was a fixture in Helena. He sat on the front porch of Babcock's Hardware Store like it was his job. He knew names, could blend into a crowd, and would be dismissed by law enforcement as incapable of criminal activity because he was too lazy and stupid.

A fact he'd just demonstrated to perfection.

Jonas forced his hands to his sides. "I will forgive this lapse in judgment on your part. But I'm warning you, Lombard, from now on, you do precisely what you're told. Nothing more, nothing less. Do you understand me?"

The man was impressed enough to take the toothpick from his wet lips. "You got it, boss."

Jonas walked him to the door and watched him go, tempted to call him back and pour him a hemlock-laced drink after all. Stupid men were a liability. So were intelligent ones. The first didn't ask questions but the second asked too many. If only he could be multiple places at once and not have to rely on anyone but himself.

Chapter Fourteen

July 24, 1888

Hale stared at his calendar. *Debates* was written in pencil on today's date. In light of the dual tragedy on the Fourth of July, he and Kendrick agreed to put the campaign on hold for a month while the city mourned. Hale withdrew an eraser from the top drawer of his desk and rubbed out the gray letters.

If only the last three weeks could be erased as easily. Better yet, if they could go back in time and relive the day so Uncle Jonas refused to sign the search warrant, Mac and Nick Alderson never went to Bear Gulch, they could see who put those threatening notes in Yancey and Carline's pockets, and the Popes stayed longer—or shorter—at the park so they weren't at the intersection at the same moment as a runaway horse.

Their deaths were officially ruled an accident. Yancey and Carline had received no more threats. And Mac was recovering well.

But three people were dead.

Deputy Nick Alderson's funeral was held at the largest church in Helena, every seat taken by residents. Law enforcement officers dressed in uniforms representing the cities and counties from all around the territory stood at attention along both side walls. Mac—against doctor's advice—came in a wheelchair, his right leg in a long cast. Emilia stood beside him until halfway through the service, when she sat beside Madame Lestraude, who'd saved a seat for her. The entire Palmer family was there surrounding Carline. They left as soon as the ceremony was over.

The Popes' funeral was held at Hale's church. Carline and her uncle sat in the front row alone, but halfway through the service, she was weeping so uncontrollably that Yancey and her mother left their pew to sit on either side of her. When the service was over, the Palmers hosted a reception at the grange hall.

Hale was able to express his condolences but moved along quickly, as was proper.

A few days later, Carline's uncle abruptly announced that—as her legal guardian—he was taking her back to Butte with him to recover. Yancey had burst into Hale's office, begging him to break the guardianship, but the terms were clear. Carline would remain the legal ward of Eugene Nordstrom until she turned thirty or married, whichever came first.

Poor Yancey.

Hale consoled her as best he could, but there was nothing he could do to stop it.

He went to the train station the day Carline departed and stood behind the Palmer family as they waved her goodbye. He would have offered to add another event to the calendar to give Yancey something to plan, but the campaign was on hold.

She needed a friend. Hale was doing his best to step into that role, but Yancey had little time for him.

As though his longing for her had conjured up a response, Mrs. Palmer entered the office. "I've come to ask you for your help."

Hale stood to honor her presence. "Of course."

"It's about Yancey." Mrs. Palmer walked deeper into the office. "Her birthday is two weeks from tomorrow. For years, she's planned a huge party. I don't know how many times I've heard her say, 'August 8 of '88 only comes around once every hundred years. I plan to invite a hundred people.'"

"Sounds like her." Hale flipped over the final adoption papers turning just plain Nico into Nico Lester.

Mrs. Palmer's lips quirked into a sad substitute for a smile. "Now Yancey wants to do nothing but have a quiet celebration with just our family."

Hale frowned. The words *quiet celebration* and *Yancey* didn't belong together in the same sentence. "Is there something I can do to help?"

"I was hoping I could interest you in a small subterfuge. I'd like to plan a surprise party, but since Carline left, Yancey's done nothing but work and go to church. And as much as I appreciate her revived interest in cooking, I need her out of the kitchen." The last was said with a bit of heat. Mrs. Palmer was one of the most compassionate women he'd ever met, but even she must have limits.

"What did you have in mind?"

"I was hoping you'd plan another event, now that there's been a sudden cancellation in a reservation at the grange hall." Mrs. Palmer waved her hands in small circles. "You can put Yancey in charge of decorations and the like."

Hale couldn't help but grin. "Am I to understand that you want Yancey to plan her own surprise party?"

She tilted her head to the left. "Can you think of a better way to keep her from suspecting anything?"

He thought about it for a moment. "Indeed, I cannot."

"But it won't fool her for long if she's not busy with other things for the next two weeks." Mrs. Palmer sat down. Was she planning to stay until they'd worked out a schedule?

Hale glanced at his appointment calendar. Nothing for another hour. He returned his full attention to the lady. "Such as?"

"Send her door-to-door to spread the word about your plans once you're elected, or have her deliver messages around town. I don't care. Just give her a reason to get out of the house." Mrs. Palmer pressed gloved fingers against the corner of her eye. "I'm sorry, Mr. Adams. I don't wish to be rude. I'm just worried about my girl."

Hale walked around the side of the desk. "No need to apologize, ma'am."

She gave him a tremulous smile. "I need to get my daughter back, Mr. Adams. She needs people. She's withering like a late summer rose without them."

"Would you like me to go speak to her now?" He perched on the edge of the desk so he didn't look too eager.

"If it's not too much trouble, that would be lovely."

"No trouble at all." He held out his hand.

"Thank you." She put her hand in his and rose. "She's at the telegraph office."

"Downtown?" he asked, although he already knew the answer. In light of the note his daughter received, Mr. Palmer had rearranged his staff. His son now worked primarily at the train depot alone, while Yancey worked at the downtown office with her father. As the office was only a few blocks away, Hale had found several reasons to send telegrams when a letter would have done.

Just to check in on her, because that was what friends did.

"I think it might be better"—Mrs. Palmer shifted her hand to the crook of his arm as they walked out of the office and into the waiting area—"if you joined us for dinner tonight. You can talk about the assistance you need, and Mr. Palmer, Geddes, and I can work to convince Yancey to help."

"Are you making another cherry pie, ma'am?" Hale

placed a hand on his stomach. "I've not been able to get the delicious smell of the one you were baking back in May out of my memory."

Her smile wobbled into and out of existence. "If it will get you around my table so we can bring our Yancey back, I'll make one for tonight and one for you to take home with you."

He chuckled. "I think that might be the best deal I've ever negotiated in this office."

They reached the small foyer beyond the waiting area. Mrs. Palmer withdrew her hand. "Dinner will be at six, unless you need us to push it back by half an hour."

"Six will be fine, ma'am. I'll see you then." He opened the door, startled when—instead of leaving—she put a hand on his cheek.

"Thank you, Hale. Thank you very much."

"No, ma'am, it is I who must thank you. I've been looking for a way to regain your daughter's"—*trust? something more?*—"assistance. With the campaign." Because they were friends. And because the four-week hold on the campaign was ending soon. Those were legitimate reasons, so why was heat creeping up his neck?

Mrs. Palmer patted his cheek. "If this works, we shall agree to be equally grateful. Until this evening."

"Until then." Hale watched her go, closing the door only after she turned the corner of Jackson and Sixth.

The rest of the day passed at a snail's pace. Hale opened up his watch six times an hour, frustrated every time that only ten minutes had passed since the last check. Work was impossible, so he decided to reorganize his piles. By five to five, he was sweaty and coated with dust, but his office had more floor space and both chairs were free for clients.

He took the stairs two at a time, gathered together clean clothes, ran back downstairs, and then stood by the door,

pocket watch open, waiting for the instant the second hand
ticked onto the twelve, indicating precisely five o'clock.

Five, four, three, two, *one*.

He stepped outside, locked his door, and hurried toward
Chen's Bath House and Laundry. He paid extra for hot
water that hadn't been used by any previous customers,
scrubbed himself clean from head to toe, and then dressed
in the clothes he'd brought with him, leaving the dirty ones
with Mr. Ling to be laundered. It was five thirty by then,
which was just enough time to get to the florist and pick up
a bouquet for his hostess before heading to the Palmers'
house.

Only . . . maybe he ought to bring a present to Yancey
as well.

A picture of the letters bundled together in his safe
flashed into his mind. He wouldn't have time to get them
and the flowers, but he suspected Mrs. Palmer wouldn't
mind the lapse in bringing her a hostess gift if bringing the
letters instead made her daughter smile.

He hurried home, gathered up the letters, and rushed
back outside. A flower seller was rolling her cart along
Sixth Street just as he turned the corner, so he purchased a
bouquet of mixed blooms in yellows, blues, and deep reds.
He arrived at the Palmers' house a little out of breath with
the flowers in one hand, the letters in the other, and a dribble
of sweat trickling its way down his neck.

Mr. Palmer opened the door. "Good evening, Hale. It's
been too long since we've had the pleasure of hosting you
in our home."

Over four years, to be precise.

He stepped across the threshold, the scents of roasting
meat, baked bread, and sweet cherries in a competition to
see which one could make his mouth water the most.

"Are those for my wife?" Mr. Palmer dropped his gaze to the flowers.

Hale handed them over. "A small token of my appreciation for her kind invitation."

Mrs. Palmer appeared. "Hale. We're so happy to see you."

She might be, but behind her, Yancey had a confused frown on her face. "Hale? I didn't realize you were joining us tonight." The last was said with a sidelong glance at her mother.

"Miss Yancey." He bowed and then held out the letters. "I thought you might wish to have these back."

She stared at them, the expression on her face difficult to read. "Are those . . . ?"

"Both yours and mine," he answered her unfinished question.

She scratched her eyebrow. "I thought you would have burned them by now."

He extended his hand a bit farther. "You are welcome to do so. I've read them and am satisfied that Miss Archer told the truth. I don't remember precisely what I said, of course, but these match my memory well enough. She told no lies other than about living in Denver and using a typewriter because my handwriting was illegible."

Yancey nodded. "I asked why they were typed."

"I know." That jolted her attention to him. "As I said, I read them all."

After another nod, she took the packet. "I'll just take these back to my room."

"Don't be too long, dear," Mrs. Palmer called after her. "Dinner is ready."

Geddes passed his sister on his way into the living room. "Hale. Good to see you." He stuck out his hand in greeting.

Hale shook it. "Good to see you too, Geddes."

They wandered through the living room and into the

dining room, where the table was set with plain white china and a floral tablecloth in pale pinks and greens. Mrs. Palmer took a vase from her corner cabinet and disappeared with it and the bouquet. A few minutes later, during which Hale and the Palmer men talked politics, she reappeared with the vase and bright flowers, placing it in the center of the table.

Yancey entered the room, then followed her mother into the kitchen. They brought out bowls of mashed potatoes, gravy, green beans, pickled beets, a basket of golden brown rolls, and a platter with a whole roasted chicken.

Hale stood behind the chair appointed to him until the ladies both sat, Yancey choosing the chair directly opposite him.

"Everything looks delicious, darling." Mr. Palmer smiled at his wife. "Let's give thanks, shall we?"

All through the prayer, Hale battled to focus on Mr. Palmer's words because the phrase that kept getting in his way was, *I come from a happy family*. And suddenly he realized why he'd declined every invitation to sit at this table after his courtship of Luanne ended. It wasn't because Yancey had come between him and her sister but because this family was everything he'd ever wanted. It hurt to watch.

"Amen."

Hale failed to add his amen to the rest of the family's but had kept his head bowed, so it was unlikely any of them noticed.

Mrs. Palmer picked up the bowl of potatoes and handed it to Hale. "There's plenty more in the kitchen, so take as much as you like."

Conversation was plentiful, and the food was delicious. Geddes and Mr. Palmer drew Hale into their concerns that Helena would fade into a "once was" city if it didn't retain the title of capitol once Montana became a state. The topic moved to the impact the telephone would have on the telegraph business Mr. Palmer had spent twenty-three years building. By the time the cherry pie was served, they all were laughing and poking fun at one another like old friends.

No, like family.

Hale stared at Yancey Palmer across the table from him and realized this was what he wanted. Her. On the opposite side of the dinner table from him. Friends and family filling in the chairs to their left and right. Him at the head like Mr. Palmer. Her at the foot, like his wife. He should be startled, but instead he was delighting in the irony of his stubborn refusal to yield to what he now recognized as both inevitable and extraordinary.

He loved Yancey Palmer.

She looked up at him. Her eyes went wide an instant before she tossed her napkin to the side of her dessert plate. "I'll clear the dishes."

"Nonsense," Mr. Palmer responded. He turned to Hale. "In our house, the men do the dishes. As you are our guest, you are free to either join Geddes and me in the kitchen or join my wife and daughter in the living room."

Knowing he should use the time to request Yancey's assistance with the campaign, Hale nonetheless chose to join the men. He needed time to think. It was absurd—wasn't it?—that he wanted to spend every minute of the rest of his life with Yancey.

As soon as Hale left, Yancey sprinted to her bedroom, locked the door, and sat on her bed, panting as though she'd run a mile. The look he'd given her across the table . . .

She pressed the heel of her hand against her racing heart.

How many times had she longed to see that exact expression on his face? A thousand? Ten thousand?

She closed her eyes.

Lord, You know my heart better than I do, and You know

I haven't always been wise with it. Help me now, I beg You.
She reached for the letters, feeling her way across the
quilted bedspread until her fingers touched the tightly
wrapped bundle. She lifted it into her lap. *What should I do
with these, Lord? If I read them, I'll fall in love with Hale
again. I know I will. And I don't want to. I don't.* Tears
squeezed between her eyelids. She let them fall, unwilling
to let go of the letters until she heard God tell her what to
do with them. *Please, Lord. Please tell me what to do.*

She waited, listened, and prayed some more, but she
couldn't hear past the desires of her heart. To make matters
more difficult, she kept picturing Hale sitting across the table
from her tonight with love shining from his brown eyes.

After what seemed an hour—but was probably no more
than a minute or two—Yancey whispered, "Amen." She
wiped her cheeks with one hand as she stood. The wooden
box she'd used for her Hale treasures was still under her bed.
She pulled it out, put the letters inside, and shoved it back
into place. Until she heard clear direction from God, that's
where they'd stay.

Oh, how she wanted Carline. If only telephone lines
stretched between Helena and Butte.

Yancey sat down at her desk. It was topped with stationery she'd failed to put away after her last letter. She
reached for the pen and dipped it in ink.

My dearest friend,

    *Please come home. I need you more than
words can convey. Hale came to dinner tonight
and, unless I'm blinded by longings I thought
I'd put behind me, I think he might . . . I don't
even wish to write the words for fear I'll sound
foolish. I need your eyes to help me see clearly.*

Should she mention that Windsor Buchanan had asked after Carline for the past three Sundays? He'd even admitted she was the girl he'd wanted to ask on the buggy ride.

Yancey held the pen over the inkpot. She'd not mentioned it in her prior letters to keep from manipulating her friend into crying, begging, or otherwise making her Uncle Eugene's life miserable until he agreed to bring her back to Helena. But was withholding information an even greater transgression?

Perhaps it was time for a little truth.

Yancey dipped her pen and wrote everything Windsor had said and how miserable he'd appeared since Carline left town.

I tell you these things with fear and trembling lest I live up to the accusation of being manipulative and scheming. You must make up your own mind if you are better off in Butte with your uncle or here with me.

Your dearest friend who misses you terribly,

Yancey

P.S. I've received no more threatening notes.

Satisfied she'd been as honest as possible, Yancey blew on the ink. After testing it with a tentative finger to assure it was dry, she folded the letter and stuffed it inside an envelope. She knew the address by heart. When she'd finished writing it on the front, she turned the envelope over and sealed it with wax.

There.

She felt better.

For now.

But as she suspected, the moment she entered Hale's office the following day, the tightness in her chest made breathing difficult. "Reporting for duty as ordered, sir." Her attempt at teasing fell flat to her own ears.

If Hale was offended, he kept it from showing. He stood to greet her, a smile on his face. "I'm glad you're here. Please have a seat." He pointed to the chairs across from his desk.

Wonder of wonders, *both* were clear of files and books.

Rather than risk another teasing comment coming out wrong, she remained silent as she settled into the chair.

Hale waited for her to sit before coming around the desk and perching on the edge. "I'm glad you're here." He'd said that already, and both times it had made swallowing difficult.

Yancey squeezed her gloved fingers together. "How can I help?"

He put one hand on the desk and leaned on it. "I think another major event is in order. I checked at the grange hall to see if I could book a date and they only had a few. I booked the nearest one, but I need someone with your talents and abilities to make it less boring. Otherwise it will be up to me, Uncle Jonas, and Isaak."

Yancey laughed despite her resolve to keep herself from responding to him. "I can only imagine what the three of you would plan." She shuddered for effect.

"Whatever you're imagining, I can almost guarantee the reality would be worse." Hale took a piece of paper from the top of his desk and handed it to her. "I drew this up and showed it to Mr. Wiggans. He's printing flyers as soon as he can."

She glanced at the date. "But this is in two weeks."

"The grange hall opened up unexpectedly and we thought it was too good an opportunity to pass up. I know it's a short amount of time, but if anyone can do it, you can."

She stared at the date. Her birthday. The one she'd planned as the celebration of the century. In light of the tragedies and with Carline gone, Yancey hadn't wanted to celebrate much of anything. But Mother kept saying life had to go on. She was right, but it hurt to think how different the night would be compared to the way she'd originally planned it. But that was another one of life's little lessons.

Yancey took a deep breath. "All right. I'll do it."

The smile on Hale's face almost made up for the pang of losing her birthday celebration.

She spent the week in a flurry of activity, enlisting help from everyone she knew in order to make Hale's event memorable. She met with him daily to be sure her plans were in keeping with his wants.

And her mother was right. Getting out of the house and moving forward with life was good for her. She took on some extra campaign work, going door-to-door to distribute flyers and talk about why Hale was the best man for the job of mayor.

On Monday, before the big event, she was in the downtown office when a telegram came through that made her whoop with joy. "It's a *girl*."

Her father dropped the papers on his desk and came close to the telegraph machine as it tapped out specifics on the birth of his first grandchild. Luanne had jokingly promised Yancey to deliver on her birthday, but two days ahead of time was close enough.

GRACE HARLOWE. STOP
11:28 AM. STOP
MOTHER AND BABY FINE. STOP

Papa beamed. "Can you handle things here while I go tell your mother?"

"Of course."

He rushed out the door. "It's a girl!"

She laughed at his enthusiasm, then tapped out the news to Carline, marking it urgent and including an address for delivery. Yancey withdrew some coins from her purse and put them in the till to pay for the message, then sat in the silent office wishing she could also tell Hale.

Her jaw dropped when the next instant he walked through the door. "I was just thinking about you." Oh, goodness. That came out too enthusiastically.

But Hale didn't seem to mind. His face brightened. "May I ask why?"

"Luanne and Roy had their baby. It's a girl." Yancey's cheeks hurt she was smiling so big. "I just wanted to share the good news. I already sent a message to Carline."

He smiled. "And I was next on your list. I'm flattered."

Yancey's breath hitched. Oh dear. That look was in his eyes again.

His expression grew more serious. "Yancey, may I ask you for a favor? A personal one?"

She gripped the armrests of her wooden chair before responding. "What is it?"

He took out his pocket watch and began winding the stem. Which meant he was nervous. Was he going to ask her out to dinner? Or on a buggy ride? "Do you still have our letters, or have you burned them already?"

"I have them." Locked inside a box and shoved to the wall under her bed.

He popped the cover of his pocket watch open, clicked it shut, repeating the action as he spoke. "I was wondering if we could get rid of them. Together. A symbol of putting the past behind us so we can move forward as friends."

Was it her imagination, or had he paused for a fraction before saying *friends*? Like he wanted to say something different or wanted more than that.

No. She wasn't going to read anything into his request.

Hale liked to craft words instead of speaking extemporaneously, a preference he'd shared—like she didn't already know—when they were discussing how to best thank the many volunteers helping with his campaign. Yancey said he needed to express his appreciation aloud, and he'd countered with the idea of writing thank-you notes. Because words mattered. He wanted to be clear. Just as he'd done now.

He'd chosen the word *friend*, so that's what he meant.

"I would like to be friends . . . again. Because we already agreed to that . . . at the brunch." Could she sound any *more* flustered? "But perhaps we should hold off burning our correspondence until next week when all this craziness is over. With the rally in a couple of days, I mean."

"Agreed, although"—he shook his head—"somehow I think we will find even more craziness awaits us on the other side."

No, Lord. Please, no. Oh please, oh, please, oh please.

Yancey repeated the prayer, this time with a different connotation, when she pulled out the letters to reread them later that night. The Lord knew how much she feared turning back into a mushy-headed girl over Hale Adams. She needed miraculous strength because the feelings inside her chest were threatening to boil over like soup left too long on the stovetop.

And praise be, once she got over the initial disquiet of seeing her words written in someone else's handwriting, the answer to her prayer was peace within her soul. As she'd said, Antonia had changed Yancey's name to Portia, her hometown to Denver, Colorado, and deleted specifics like the names of her family members and best friend.

Which meant Hale had fallen in love with *her*, just as she had with him. So why did he only want to be friends now?

She must have misinterpreted the look in his eyes when he came to dinner.

Something Carline said when they'd planned Operation Mrs. Buchanan replayed inside Yancey's mind. *I will be a wonderful wife and—should God bless me with children— mother. If some man doesn't recognize as much, that's his loss, not mine.*

Yancey straightened the stack of letters and retied the string around them.

She refused to fall back into the trap of thinking Hale Adams determined her value as a woman. Tomorrow was a new beginning. She'd show everyone—including herself— that her days and worth were determined by God. No one else.

The Lord is my light and my salvation; whom shall I fear? The Lord is the strength of my life; of whom shall I be afraid?

She had memorized the Bible verse in Sunday school years ago, although she couldn't remember the reference. Somewhere in Psalms? She'd look it up later. For now, she returned the letters to the former treasure box, but instead of shoving it back under the bed, she placed it on her desk as a reminder of her resolve.

But no matter how many times she repeated the verse the following afternoon, her hands were shaking when she knocked on Hale's door at five ten the following afternoon for her final report before the rally tomorrow.

He opened the door, pocket watch open. "You're here."

"You sound surprised."

He glanced at his watch. "It's five ten. On the dot."

She shook her finger at him, smiling over his teasing at her surprising promptness. "None of your cheek, Mr. Adams, or I'll deliberately keep you waiting a full fifteen minutes next time."

His grin set her heart to fluttering.

The Lord is my light. The Lord is the strength.

"Come in." He stepped back to allow her to enter.

As soon as she turned to walk through the double doors open between his foyer and office, she gasped. "Mac. It's so good to see you." She hurried to his chair, laying her hand on his arm. "Don't get up. Hale can be gentleman enough for both of you."

Mac smiled, but pain pinched the edges of his lips. "Yancey. Good to see you, too."

Hale walked over to pull out the second chair. It was still free of piles. Even more surprising was the neatness of his desk.

Yancey sat down beside Mac, grateful for his presence as it had quieted her nervousness. Except . . . he and Hale shared a look that kicked her heart back into double speed. "What's wrong?"

Hale sat on the edge of his desk and picked up an envelope. "Charles Cannon found some counterfeit bills in the money you gave him to pay for the fabric you bought last week."

She'd used it for banners to decorate the grange hall. "I can't return it now that it's been cut, but I could repay him."

"That's not necessary." Hale set down the envelope. "I'll reimburse him."

Then why was he asking her about it? She looked between him and Mac, trying to decide why they looked so upset. She gasped. "Is Mr. Cannon accusing me of deliberately passing on counterfeit money?"

"Of course not." Mac sliced his hand through the air. He winced and then rubbed his thigh. "Amazing how many muscles are connected to the one that's been shot."

"Next time be more careful." Hale's admonishment was spoken with the kind of teasing only good friends could share.

Mac acknowledged it with a mocking, "Ha, ha."

Yancey turned her chair to better see the sheriff. "How are the Aldersons?"

"As well as can be expected, considering they lost a son and brother."

"I heard Eli has joined your deputies." Hale gripped the edges of his desk with both hands. "How is he doing?"

"He's green—like we all were when we first started. I'm keeping him close." Mac rubbed his thigh again. "But back to that money. I need to see the record of your contributors."

Hale stood, walked around his desk, leaned over to open a desk drawer, and pulled out the top file. "Here, but I'm not sure how helpful it will be. Yancey has elicited contributions from half of Helena." The last was said with admiration.

The real kind. Not what in years past she would read into his voice afterward, using her imagination.

The Lord is my light. The Lord is the strength.

Mac ran his finger down the list. "Is this everyone?"

Yancey sat taller, trying to see over the file edge. "I've written down everyone I've received money from, but I'm not the only person who's solicited contributions."

Mac looked at Hale. "Who else?"

Hale recited several names, his fingers ticking them off as he went. He looked to Yancey. "Am I missing anyone?"

"Did you mention your aunt and uncle?"

"Right. Sorry"—Hale shifted his gaze to Mac—"that goes without saying."

"No, it doesn't," she countered in the same mocking tone Mac had used earlier.

Her teasing had very different responses. Mac jerked his attention to her, the surprise on his face quickly replaced by a wince. Hale, on the opposite spectrum, laughed outright. "Yancey tells me I think too much and don't speak enough."

She communicated her justification by raising her brows.

"Like the other day, when you neglected to tell me that Mollie Fisk and Jefferson Brady reconciled—again—so the wedding is back on—again—because you thought I would already know."

Hale inclined his head toward her. "A hit, madam. I acknowledge it."

Mac's gaze alternated between her and Hale, but he said nothing.

Men. Why were they so uncommunicative? What she wouldn't give to know what both he and Hale were thinking.

She turned the topic of conversation to business before she let her imagination run amok. "Everything is set for tomorrow night, so we need to talk about what's next on your agenda."

Hale pushed his glasses back into place. "I was hoping you'd tell me."

Of all his little mannerisms, his constant readjustment of his glasses was the one she found most endearing. Yancey lowered her gaze to her lap until she was certain that particular truth wasn't written on her face. "Are you up for another speaking event? People like hearing your ideas."

"Or like attending your"—Mac cut a glance at Yancey—"parties."

She didn't hear any mocking in his voice, nor did she see any humor in Hale's expression. "Does that bother you?"

"Not at all." Hale perched on the edge of his desk. "You're great at making people feel welcome. I'd be a fool not to recognize that as a gift and appreciate how you're using it on my behalf."

The praise warmed her heart. Should she compliment him in return? Or would that be too brazen when they were just friends? If he was anyone but Hale, she wouldn't hesitate, so she needed to treat him the same way. "In return, let me say you're now much better at handling crowds. A number of people have remarked that you aren't as"—*rigid* seemed too mean, but she couldn't think of another word.

"Stodgy?" Hale supplied.

"I was trying to think of something nicer, but yes." She opened the drawstrings of her reticule and pulled out the small calendar she'd made for herself. "When would you like to have this event, and don't say next week."

He chuckled. "How about a month from now, and then another a month after that?"

"That will be around the time of the Harvest Festival." She turned to Mac. "Do you remember the dates?"

"Why are you asking me?"

She huffed. "Because it takes place outside the city limits and you *are* the county sheriff."

Mac crossed his arms over his chest. "Doesn't mean I know the dates."

"Fine. I'll talk to Carline . . . no." Yancey swallowed down the pain of missing her best friend. "I'll talk to Geddes about the dates. He's planning on entering the hot-air balloon race again, and I'm sure he'll let us paint 'Hale for Helena' on his balloon." Too bad their brother-in-law, Roy, wasn't planning to come. He'd be too busy with his new daughter.

"I take it by the crease between your eyebrows"—Hale drew her attention—"that you're thinking about scheduling a campaign event at the same time."

"Maybe even having a booth at the festival, if Superintendent Watson will allow it." The man wasn't her favorite person after the way he'd fired her sister almost two years ago. "I'll have to be charming."

Hale's smile warmed her to her toes. "I believe in your charm."

If she didn't know better, she'd think Hale was flirting with her. Yancey stood. "Don't get up, Mac. I just remembered I need to be somewhere." It wasn't a complete lie. She had nowhere specific to go, but she needed to be somewhere other than Hale's office.

Because being friends with Hale Adams was becoming a problem.

Chapter Fifteen

Hale walked Yancey to the door where, like her mother, she stopped. Unlike her mother, she didn't pat his cheek.

Which was disappointing. He wanted to know what her hand would feel like against his skin. How he would react. He needed to know if the strange emotions in the hospital foyer and the longing to make a home with her were real or illusions. If her touch would ignite his soul.

He wasn't a cold man, though some had accused him of such. He had a deep reserve of love and passion. Standing near her, he felt it bubbling up in anticipation of the moment a woman's caress set it free.

She was tying the strings of her straw hat under her chin. He started to do it for her—a small way to make contact— but she jerked away, the shock on her face clear. "I, uh, I'm happy to reimburse Mr. Cannon. That's what friends do, you know."

Was he imagining it, or did she put greater emphasis on the word *friends* than the rest of her sentence?

"Because that's what we are," she continued. "Friends." This time the emphasis was unmistakable.

What was he supposed to do now? Say now? He'd flirted

with her a little bit. No, that wasn't right. He'd *tried* to flirt and failed. Even that didn't seem like the right word.

Was there a verb stronger than *failed*? Maybe *crashed*. Or *flunked*.

He'd assumed that, once he made his feelings known, she'd be delighted. Instead, she'd recoiled from him.

Now that was the perfect word. *Recoiled.*

"Don't worry about Mr. Cannon," he managed through his dejection. "I'll take care of it."

Yancey dipped her chin, then scurried out the door, tying the knot as she went, clearly eager to be away from him.

Even though they were *friends*.

The moment he returned to the office after escorting her to the door, Mac pierced him with a frown. "What's going on between you and Yancey?"

Hale strolled to the window, watching her until she turned right onto Sixth Street. He shifted his focus to Mac. "That's a good question."

"To which I assume there's a good answer." Mac gripped the lapels of his brown jacket, the badge on his chest gleaming where it caught the late-afternoon sunlight.

Hale walked to his desk and sat down. "I've had a slight change of heart."

Mac's face broke into a grin. "Don't tell me Yancey finally caught you."

"She has, but now it seems her interest in me doesn't extend beyond friendship." Hale pushed his glasses back in place while Mac hooted with laughter between grunts of pain. "You're going to reopen your wound."

Mac nodded as he gripped his thigh, his mirth unabated.

"Were you anyone other than an injured sheriff, I would throw you out of my office." Hale pointed toward the foyer attached to his waiting area.

Mac brought his laughter under control. "Injured or not,

I'd like to see you try." He took several deep breaths. "Sorry, but you have to admit, after five years of avoiding Yancey Palmer like an infectious disease, this turnaround is funny."

Hale rubbed his forehead. "I'm well aware of the irony of my situation, but I find myself ill-prepared to handle it. I thought it would be a simple matter of telling Yancey about my change of heart, but she only wishes to be *friends*. I'm beginning to hate the word."

"I wonder if all men find themselves at a complete loss when it comes to loving a woman."

"God's way of keeping us humble, you think?" Hale shifted the clay mug sitting between his cast-iron telephone and typewriter a fraction to the left, well aware that it was a new nervous habit now that he was determined to keep his desk clean. "If you've any advice for me, I'm listening."

Mac's eyes went wide. "From me?"

Hale's lips twitched despite the misery in his stomach. "I don't see anyone else here. What do you think? Can I overcome Yancey's determination to be nothing more than friends, or did I miss my chance with her?"

"Talk to your aunt or Emilia." Mac twisted to grab his cane from where it hung on the chair back. "Speaking of my wife, I told her I'd be gone no longer than an hour. Before I go, if more counterfeit money shows up around town, I can't guarantee others will be as fair-minded as Cannon."

"Understandable. I'll reimburse him." Hale picked up the envelope with the fake five-dollar bills. "You think this came from Bear Gulch?"

Mac picked his hat off the floor and put it on. "I can't say for sure, but it seems a bit too coincidental that, almost as soon as we raided it, fake bills started showing up in Helena."

"We've been luckier here than other places around Montana." Hale subscribed to all the major territorial newspapers. They'd been full of stories about counterfeiting for several years.

"Too lucky." Mac pressed his hat lower on his head.

"You think whoever heads up this operation"—Hale waved the envelope—"has intentionally kept it out of Helena?"

Mac nodded. "Leads me to believe this is home."

"Kendrick?"

"Quinn and I wondered the same thing." Mac poked the brim of his Stetson higher with a finger. "Last election cycle, your uncle was sure Kendrick was passing out counterfeits. Quinn looked into it but could never prove anything."

"So either Kendrick was using real money or his fakes were impossible to detect." Hale pulled the paper dollars from the envelope. "How did Cannon know these were counterfeit?"

"Do you have a five-dollar bill handy?"

"No. That much money goes to the bank immediately."

"Good point." Mac leaned forward, pointing to the picture of James Garfield. "See his hair? On real bills, the fine hairs on the top of his head are less defined."

Hale brought the bill closer to his glasses. "I guess I'd have to compare it to the real thing in order to see the difference."

Mac's grunt said, *Which is why I asked if you had one.* "Makes me think that either Kendrick never used counterfeits last campaign but is this time, or whoever printed those"—he directed a look at the bills—"is a new player."

Hale replaced the dollars inside the envelope. "Any guesses as to who?"

"A few, but no proof." Mac struggled to his feet. "I need to go."

Hale stood up and walked around the desk. "Before you do, may I ask you for a favor?"

"You can ask." Mac pushed his cane into the floor.

"I need to court Yancey without letting her know I'm courting her."

Mac squeezed one eyelid shut. "Seems to me a girl that's been in love once would be easy to convince to fall in love again."

Or harder.

Hale rubbed his left bicep with his right hand. "I was hoping you and Emilia would agree to attend a play or go to dinner or . . . I don't know. Something Yancey would enjoy."

"So ask her. Why involve Em and me?"

"Because last time I asked her to dinner, she insisted that others accompany us." Hale stopped rubbing his arm. It wasn't making him any warmer. "I need to show her that I'm not just a stodgy lawyer who stays inside his office all day. At least I'm not anymore," he added when Mac lowered his chin.

He tapped his cane as he walked toward the door. "I'll ask Em, but you might want to enlist Isaak and Zoe, too."

Yancey often said, *The more, the merrier*, but Hale didn't want to expand the circle of those knowing about his change of heart too far. However, if any men knew how rocky the path to love could be, they were Mac and Isaak.

Hale opened the front door. "I'll do that. And Mac?"

He turned on the front step.

Gratitude swelled Hale's throat. "I'm glad you are well."

His friend nodded and stepped into the street.

As Hale watched him go, he wondered what it would be like to go home to a wife. Someone who cared about him more than anything else. Yancey's face came to mind, and his heart picked up its rhythm while warmth crept up his neck.

But what if he told her of his change of heart and she laughed? His heart wouldn't be able to take it.

Wednesday, August 8, 1888

"Carline!" Yancey threw her arms around her friend and pulled her into the living room. "Oh, this is just the best birthday present ever. Why didn't you tell me you were coming? When did you get in? Did your uncle come with you? Are you all right?"

Mother came out from the kitchen. "Yancey dear. Give Carline a moment to breathe."

Carline's sad eyes brightened for an instant. "Good morning, Mrs. Palmer." Mother held out her arms. Carline pulled away from Yancey to seek shelter in matronly arms.

"We're glad you're home, dearest." Mother rubbed Carline's back, the black bombazine fabric making a soft, shushing sound. "Whatever you need, you've only to ask."

Yancey wiped the corners of her eyes. "How did you get your uncle to agree to let you come home?"

Carline stepped out of Mother's embrace. "I stopped crying, packed my bags, and was halfway to the train station before he caught up with me. I told him that either he took me home, or he'd have to lock me in my room. I wasn't missing my best friend's birthday for anything."

Impressed, Yancey clapped her hands, then gripped them together. "Are you home for good? Please say you are. I've missed you so much."

Carline's cheeks pinked in the most becoming way. "I'm hoping it's for good."

Yancey gasped. "Carline Elizabeth Pope, you tell me everything right this instant."

Instead of replying, she pulled a letter from her skirt pocket. The folds were frayed, as though they had been opened and closed a hundred times. She handed it to Yancey. "It's from Windsor."

Mother cut a startled glance at Carline. "Windsor Buchanan?"

Yancey kept her eye on her friend as she peeled back the edges.

Carline's smile was tinged with grief. "Go ahead and read it aloud."

Yancey cleared her throat and read.

> Miss Pope,
>
> I am sorrier than I can say about your parents. I hope you are planning to return to Helena soon. All your friends miss you. You probably heard that I was hoping to ask you out on a buggy ride. I still would, if you come home that is. Sorry for the poor penmanship. I'm a little out of practice.
>
> Your friend,
> Windsor Buchanan

Carline held out her hand to take back the letter, her fingers trembling. "What do you suppose he meant by being out of practice? Writing letters?"

Yancey shook her head. "I didn't tell you everything about my conversation with him at the Independence . . ." She trailed off, not wishing to bring back the horrible memory attached to the end of that day.

"It's all right." Carline placed a hand on Yancey's wrist. "We have to take the good with the bad. Uncle Eugene keeps telling me that."

"He's right." Mother patted Carline's shoulder. "I'll leave you two to chat while I finish washing dishes."

"So let's talk about the good." Yancey tugged Carline down the hall. When they were in Yancey's bedroom, she relayed the entire conversation she'd had with Windsor, including his nervousness, how he said he was out of practice asking a woman on a buggy ride, and—most interestingly of all—that his shaggy beard hid a burn scar along the left side of his neck. "I'm not sure how far up it goes, and I didn't dare ask him about it because he went stiff as soon as he noticed that I noticed and . . . oh. Listen to me ramble. I'm just so happy to have you here."

Carline refolded her letter and tucked it inside her bodice. "Good, because I have an enormous favor to ask of you."

"Anything."

"Would you ask your parents if I could stay here instead of going back . . . home?" She choked on the last word. "Uncle Eugene made me promise that, if he brought me back to Helena, we would find a new house to live in. I told him we would, but before we can sell the house, I need to decide what can be donated to charity and what I want to keep for sentimental reasons."

"I'm certain Mother will say yes, but let me run and ask." Yancey hurried out the door and down the hall to the kitchen. As expected, Mother was thrilled to have a houseguest. Yancey returned to her bedroom. "Mother wants to know if you'd like to have Luanne's bedroom or if you want to stay with me in my room."

Carline rubbed the back of her left hand. "With you, if that's all right."

"I was going to beg you to stay here had you chosen Luanne's room. Now"—Yancey held out her hand to help Carline stand—"what do you wish to do? We can help Mother bake, go to your house and begin sorting together, or take a walk to town and pass by a certain bladesmith's shop. Your choice."

"Then let's go over to my house. Uncle Eugene is waiting to hear from me before booking a room at the Grand Hotel. He said he'd book one for me, too, if I couldn't stay here."

"And then we'll walk by a certain bladesmith's shop?"

Carline blushed and nodded.

Half an hour later, they walked to Windsor Buchanan's shop. When he glanced up and saw them, he dropped the ax he was holding against the revolving sharpening rock. The ax bounced twice, then flew into the air. Windsor jumped up, reaching for it with flailing hands as though he couldn't decide which was less dangerous—catching a sharp blade with his bare hands or letting it decapitate whatever it landed on.

Once the ax was safely back in hand, even his beard couldn't hide the smile that lit up his whole face. Yancey looked at her dearest friend and her heart swelled. The man's reaction was everything Carline could want.

But a few hours later, when Yancey walked in on her own surprise party, the smile on Hale's face was everything she had ever wanted.

And more.

Chapter Sixteen

Monday, August 13, 1888

"Adams? You in here?"

The sound of Windsor Buchanan's voice made Hale check his appointment book. He didn't remember scheduling anything with the bladesmith, but his mind was scattered of late.

The birthday party had been a huge success. Every time Hale settled in to work, he saw the delight on Yancey's face. And he'd helped to put it there. Amazing.

Hale stood and walked to the waiting area, where Windsor was staring at the cushioned love seat like he wasn't sure if its legs were sturdy enough to hold him.

"Windsor." Hale stepped forward and held out his hand in greeting, bracing for it to be crushed. "What brings you to my office today?"

Windsor's handshake was short and blessedly gentle. "I need to ask you a favor."

"Of course."

"Now that Miss Carline Pope is back in Helena, I aim to court her but . . ." He shrugged his wide shoulders.

"It's not proper etiquette," Hale finished the sentence. The proper mourning period was a full year.

Windsor's cheeks filled with red. "I'll be as respectful of her grief as a man can be, but I'll not have her dragged out of Helena against her wishes by that no-account uncle of hers. Not again."

"I see." Hale was taken aback by the dismissal of the mourning etiquette. And a little impressed.

"I asked Isaak if he and Zoe would mind going to Ming's Opera House again. He said he'd have to think about it and to ask Mac. But when I asked Mac and his wife to join us, he said I should ask you and Yancey." Windsor ended the sentence with a slight elevation in pitch, as though not sure if he was making a statement or asking a question.

While he wasn't a good friend, Isaak trusted him, and apparently Mac did as well. Hale took a deep breath, preparing for more laughter. "I'm looking to court Miss Yancey Palmer, but I need to ease into it because she only wishes to be friends."

Windsor squinted one eye. "Seems like a pretty big change of heart on her part. Yours too, if you don't mind my saying so."

"I don't mind. Truth is truth, after all."

Windsor's expression cleared. "I agree. Mozart's *Magic Flute* is on the program at the opera house for the next two weeks. It has a happy ending, which is more than can be said for most operas."

Hale regarded Windsor. The man was as shaggy as they came but spoke like an educated man. "Where did you go to school, Mr. Buchanan?"

"Dickinson."

Hale knew it well, having gone to Harvard, its rival. "President James Buchanan graduated from there. Are you related?"

Buchanan shook his head, his mane of brown hair

swaying back and forth. "No, but I sure liked to pretend I was during college. For a time, at any rate. It didn't end well."

Several questions begged to be asked, but Hale decided on only one. "What brought you to Montana?"

"I got tired of playing the East Coast games and came West to be my own man." And now he wanted to be Carline Pope's man. Given that the woman was set to inherit ten million dollars—unless her uncle lost his fortune, as others had before him—someone with education and a strong streak of independence was probably a fine choice. Buchanan reached under his beard to scratch his neck. "I think we'd best tell Isaak you're sweet on Miss Yancey."

"You're right"—much as Hale hated to admit it—"I'll tell him this afternoon." They were meeting to discuss the insurance money from The Resale Co. fire, which still hadn't been paid out.

"I'd best be going." Windsor headed for the door. "Let me know what Isaak says."

Three hours later, Isaak's jaw dropped. "You're what?"

Hale repeated that he was going to the play at Ming's Opera House with Yancey, Windsor, Carline—if she agreed—and whoever else was joining the party.

Isaak looked out the window, presumably to check if his stepfather was about to arrive, as the meeting was supposed to be with both of them. "Are you telling me"—he swung his gaze back to Hale—"that you're pursuing a romantic relationship with Yancey Palmer?"

Hale nodded. "But I have to be careful about how I go about it because I've no wish to jeopardize our friendship."

Isaak scratched his left eyebrow. "Let me see if I have this right. After all my warnings to her about not entrapping you, now *you're* the one who wants to trap *her*?"

"A fairly accurate summation."

Isaak covered his mouth with a fist. His shoulders began

to bounce. And then he let loose with the loudest laugh ever to shake the walls of Hale's office.

Hale snapped the pencil in two. Both Mac's and Isaak's reactions were normal. Expected even. But still annoying.

Mr. Pawlikowski hurried past the window, waving an apology for his lateness.

Isaak waved back and brought his laughter under control. "I'll ask Zoe. Our last outing to Ming's was something of a mixed blessing, so I can't promise she'll want to attend."

"I understand. Please let me know as soon as possible." Hale opened the top right drawer of his desk and dropped the broken pencil inside. "Do you think you can have an answer for me in the next few days?"

Isaak nodded, and then his stepfather entered the office. The rest of the hour was taken up in discussing how to address the insurance company's failure to pay the fire claim even after Mr. Booker, the fire chief, and Quinn Valentine wrote letters stating they'd cleared the family of any suspicion regarding the arson.

As Isaak was leaving, he gripped Hale's hand with extra force. "Be careful with Yancey's heart."

"I will."

But would Yancey be careful with his?

Tuesday, August 28, 1888

The moment Hale showed up unannounced at Ming's Opera House, Yancey knew she was in trouble. But when Isaak Gunderson gave up his seat so Hale could sit next to her, she knew she was in *real* trouble.

And the smirk on Zoe's face said no help would be coming from her friend.

Was she in on this little surprise? Certainly Carline was. She'd dismissed every one of the concerns about going to an opera only six weeks after her parents' passing until

Yancey was already in the carriage with Isaak and Zoe. Carline was then suddenly unable to bring herself to attend. She and Windsor were going to spend a quiet evening on the front porch, talking.

Mourning or no mourning, Yancey was going to give her *dear* friend a piece of her mind when she returned home.

The first half of the opera passed in a blur. The singers and orchestra could have played two pieces of music in four different keys and Yancey wouldn't have noticed. Her entire attention was on Hale's leg next to hers, his arm next to hers, his entire being next to hers. There were a thousand people in the red leather seats, and her attention was focused solely on the one.

Hale Adams.

The man she'd loved, then given up, then hated, then made peace with, then became her friend, and was now . . . what?

She leaned as far back in her seat as possible, sliding her gaze left to observe him. He turned his head and their eyes met.

She yanked her gaze back to the stage. She felt rather than heard Hale chuckle. Or was she imagining it? Hale wasn't a chuckling kind of man. Then again, he wasn't an opera kind of man either. He attended the symphony, lectures, and the occasional benefit concert, but never the opera. Yet here he was. Sitting next to her.

She smoothed the skirt of the green gown Carline had loaned her—the one Mother had altered by removing the extraneous frills. As soon as the curtain fell for intermission, Yancey rose to her feet, took Zoe by the arm, and practically dragged her out of the auditorium.

The moment they were far enough away from Isaak and—more importantly—Hale, Yancey leaned close to Zoe's ear. "Did you know about this?"

"Know about what?" Zoe's expression was without guile.

Yet Yancey repeated her question.

Zoe frowned. "Are you unhappy zat Hale wanted to sit beside you?"

She wouldn't be had he not declared three weeks ago that he wanted to be *friends*. Yancey narrowed her gaze. "If you weren't in on this surprise, why were you smirking at me?"

"I was not smirking."

"You most certainly were."

Zoe shook her head, her dark curls shimmering under the lights. "I might have been smiling with a little bit of appreciation for ze irony of us once again at ze opera house and changing chairs, but I did not smirk."

Yancey inhaled and blew out with a *whoosh*. "What am I going to do?"

"*Carpe diem*." And with that, Zoe turned and returned to Isaak's side.

Yancey continued toward the ladies' room until the smirks—and these were *definitely* smirks—of a hundred women drove her back to her party.

The rest of the evening dragged while she did her best to ignore Hale without anyone noticing that she was ignoring him. She followed this same plan the next night when he arrived for dinner—a guest of her parents'.

"Did we forget to tell you, Yancey dear?" Mother's question was a shade too innocent.

The next night, Hale just happened to be coming past the church at the exact time the Ladies' Aid Society meeting ended and he offered to walk her home. And Mrs. Hollenbeck chose that precise moment to announce she needed to speak with Mrs. Pawlikowski, so Yancey should "take Mr. Adams up on his generous offer."

There were no smirks, but there might as well have been.

Three nights in a row. It was time to deal with this in an adult and *friend*-like manner. "What are you doing?" Yancey demanded as soon as they were outside.

"Walking you home." Hale offered his right arm.

Courtesy demanded that she take it. But in her haste to leave, she'd forgotten to put on her gloves. Which was worse, being discourteous or improper? The last of the sun's light was fading. Unless someone walked directly past them, they wouldn't be able to tell that her hand was bare.

She drew in a steadying breath and took his arm.

He kept an easy flow of conversation between them as he told her about his interactions with various townsfolk he'd spoken to that day. It included a rather humorous one involving Mrs. Nanawitty, the woman who carted blocks of ice around town in a wheelbarrow pulled by a buffalo. She wanted Hale's promise that—if he was elected—he'd get horses banned from Main Street because of the plethora of manure piles they left. But the funny part was that her entire diatribe took place while her buffalo added his large and odorous deposit to the sum total in the street.

Yancey laughed so hard, she stopped walking, pulling her hand from his arm to cover her mouth.

When she took his arm again, he placed his left hand over hers. His skin was warm, yet she shivered. She looked up to see his reaction. He was staring at their joined hands as if he'd just received the best gift ever.

Propriety said she should withdraw her hand, not allow a man who wasn't in her family to touch her skin, but this was Hale. The man she loved. There was no point in denying it. She had fooled herself into thinking they could be friends when—in her heart of hearts—she'd always wanted more. Always wanted this. To be alone with him, their hands joined and her heart pounding.

He lifted his eyes to hers. Was that love in his, or was she fooling herself again? Hale had the power to confuse her more than any person she'd ever known.

Please, God.

But as she repeated the prayer in her head, she couldn't complete it. Did she want permission to move forward or strength to pull away?

Hale's gaze lowered to her mouth. Was he about to kiss her? In public? Hale Adams was the most upright, moral man in Helena. If anyone observed the way they were standing gazing at each other, it was as good as a declaration of intent to marry. Did she have the power to move him as much as he moved her?

Yancey's heart hammered against her rib cage. Her whole life—the part that counted anyway—she'd waited for this. To feel Hale's lips on hers, to know the power of his kiss, to *be his*. She wetted her lips, dropping her gaze to his mouth.

Waiting.

Lifting her face a fraction closer.

Holding her breath.

Had he ever pressed his fingers to his mouth and imagined they were her lips against his? She had. Hundreds of times.

Her lungs burned. She inhaled a shaky breath.

He shuddered and took a step back, dropping her hand as though it was a hot coal.

She leaned forward to follow him, catching herself at the last moment before she stumbled.

"We need to go." He adjusted his glasses with two fingers, poked them higher on his nose with his index finger, blinked and readjusted them a fraction lower.

She nodded, not trusting herself to speak.

He turned so they were side by side and offered his arm again, as any gentleman would.

Yancey laid her hand on his black sleeve, her skin almost as white as her absent gloves.

* * *

After dropping Yancey off at her doorstep, Hale walked home in a daze. He'd not expected his feelings to overpower him in the middle of the street. But then again, why not? He'd loved Yancey Palmer since April—only he'd known her as Portia York back then.

And she returned his affection. She'd wanted his kiss—Hale knew it the way Yancey knew he was hers from the time she was ten—and he'd wanted to kiss her more than he'd ever wanted anything in his twenty-eight years. What a *fool* he'd been. Had he not dismissed her infatuation as beneath him, he could have started his life with her two or three years ago. He could have lowered his mouth and claimed hers rather than pulling away because propriety demanded that no man kissed a woman who wasn't his betrothed.

Sweat broke out on the back of his neck.

There was an order to follow. Hale needed to speak of his affection rather than—as she'd teased—assume she knew. Then he could speak to her father to gain permission to officially pursue a courtship leading to marriage. But before he spoke to her father, he needed to share the secret he'd kept from her and all of Helena, save his aunt and uncle.

Only then could Yancey decide if she wished to marry into his tarnished family.

Chapter Seventeen

Saturday, September 8, 1888

Yancey lifted the letters between Portia York and Nathan St. John from the box sitting atop her desk. After multiple social outings with friends, today Hale was taking her on a picnic. Just the two of them.

He wanted to burn the letters. And he had something *important* to tell her.

She pressed one hand against her jittering stomach, checking the mirror to make sure she looked her absolute best. The dress was a lovely concoction of white cotton with printed pink roses and mint leaves, a matching pink satin sash, and stylish ruffles along the hemline and down the bustled back. It had been purchased by the Fisks back in March for Mollie's bridesmaids. But then Mollie and Jefferson had an enormous fight and the wedding was canceled. They'd reconciled, but not in time for their June wedding. The ceremony was rescheduled for the fall, which—for people as wealthy as the Fisks—meant an entirely new color scheme. New dresses were being made, so all eight of the bridesmaids got to keep their original dresses.

Yancey was half-sure the entire fight had been staged because Mollie saw a new design she liked better.

The only problem was that either the dressmaker took wrong measurements or Yancey had put on weight since her fitting in March. She had to pull the strings of her corset so hard, she almost gave up wearing the dress. But it was the very height of fashion. The straw hat with matching pink ribbon was secured to her bun with a long, pearl-tipped hatpin. She turned her head left and right, making sure the curls along her neck and beside her ears weren't encumbered in the hat.

She took a breath as deep as the corset would allow and blew it out. She was as ready as she'd ever be.

The distant sound of a knock and her father's, "Good morning, Hale," spurred her into action. She snatched up the pink satin reticule on her bed and the box stuffed with their letters as she hurried out her bedroom door and down the hall.

"Good morning, sir." Hale sounded nervous.

"Yancey is almost ready." Papa sounded like he was holding back a chuckle. "Would you like to come in?"

Yancey stopped at the edge of the hallway to catch her breath before turning the corner into the parlor. "I'm here, Papa. I know better than to keep Hale waiting."

The stunned look on Hale's face was worth every bit of her considerable effort and constricting corset. "I'll, uh, I'll have her home before one this afternoon, sir."

Papa nodded at Hale, kissed Yancey's cheek as she passed, and shut the door. His rich chuckle penetrated the wood.

To cover her father's laughter, Yancey said the first thing that came into her head. "I see Windsor loaned you his carriage again."

"He needs it back by one. I hope you don't mind." Hale turned so they were side by side and extended his elbow.

Yancey laid her hand on his arm, noting the stark contrast

between her white glove and his black jacket. "I don't mind at all."

They descended the steps and, after tucking the box under the seat, he assisted her into the carriage. Once he was settled in the driver's seat, he said, "I thought we could picnic on the field next to your church. In addition to having a firepit, it's public, but large enough that our conversation won't be overheard."

Yancey's stomach somersaulted inside her torso. He wanted to be private, to speak to her and her alone. "That sounds lovely."

Oh, so lovely.

The ride to church never lasted so long or went so fast. Hale pointed out landmarks as though she was new in town. Yancey remarked on the beautiful sunshine and cool autumn breeze. It was an inane conversation—he must be as nervous as she—but between his tour and her weather commentary, they made it to the other side of town and parked the carriage in the dirt lot next to her church.

The green field was dotted with Aspen leaves and pinecones that had fallen from the bordering trees. An occasional gust of wind sent the leaves dancing in the air before they settled again.

Hale helped her down from the carriage, took a large wicker basket from under the back bench, then offered her his arm again. How delightful to walk with this man who owned her heart. They reached the center of the clearing, where stones circled the charred remains of last month's bonfire.

He stopped, and she reluctantly let go of his arm. He set the wicker basket on the ground and withdrew a blue-and-green-plaid blanket. After flapping it open, he let it float down to cover the grass. "I hope this will protect your lovely dress."

His compliment made her giddy with delight.

Yancey bent her knees, inching closer to the wool blanket

while her tightly laced corset kept her from bending sideways. Which, as it turned out, made it quite impossible to gracefully sink to the ground and lean on one arm like the women in paintings. Stuck halfway between sitting and standing, Yancey started to giggle.

Hale frowned at her. "Is something funny?"

"I . . . I . . ." Her inability to speak over the giggling made her laugh until she snorted.

"Do you need some assistance, madam?" Amusement sparkled in Hale's voice.

"Hand," she managed. One appeared. She gripped it, then didn't know if she wanted it to help her rise or sit, which increased her hilarity until she started to hiccup.

Oh, what a disaster, but as there wasn't a thing she could do about it, she might as well make the best of it.

She balanced herself against Hale's hand, but it didn't work for long. She started leaning sideways and—before she could recover—toppled to the ground. It knocked out the small amount of air she'd managed to get into her lungs, but at least her hiccups were gone.

"Are you all right?"

Yancey craned her neck to look up at Hale.

His shoulders were shaking and his face was pinched as though in pain.

"Go ahead and laugh before you hurt yourself."

He obeyed with staccato bursts of mirth, dropping to his knees and flopping sideways in a perfect imitation of her descent.

Seeing proper, stodgy Hale Adams lying on his back with both hands pressed against his bouncing stomach was worth every bit of embarrassment and her current inability to take a full breath.

"I . . . I don't think . . . I've ever . . . laughed this . . . hard."

He hadn't. At least not that she'd ever seen. And she'd

make a fool of herself every day if it would keep that smile on his face.

"I'm sorry." He wiped tears from under his glasses. "I shouldn't laugh at you."

"You most certainly should." Yancey pushed herself into a respectable lean, the corset digging into her hip. "But I'm warning you now. If you thought getting down was bad, getting up is going to be much worse."

That sent him into a fresh round of hilarity.

She gloried in the sound of it, knowing she had given him the gift of joy.

Hale slowed his laughter with longer and longer breaths until he drew in a deep one, held it, and let it out in a long exhale. "Tell me honestly, which is going to be more comfortable for you, picnicking here or going to a restaurant?"

"I'd rather we stay here"—because she wasn't giving up her private time with him for anything—"but could we move up the hill so I can sit on that tree root?" She pointed with her head because both hands were needed to keep her propped in her current position.

"Of course." Hale eyed her. "How do you propose we get you to your feet?"

"I think you're going to have to grab me under the arms and hoist." Not a sentence she'd ever expected to say, but there it was.

Hale grinned as though he'd read her mind. He stood and came around behind her, fitting his hands under her arms. "Ready?"

"As I'll ever be."

"One, two, three-ee." He lifted with such strength, her feet left the ground for an instant. As soon as she landed, he let go.

Unfortunately.

"Are you all right?" He came alongside her, the amusement

in his eyes replaced by genuine concern. "I didn't hurt you, did I?"

"No. I'm fine." She stepped off the blanket so he could gather it up again.

They set off for the small rise where a large tree stood, its roots visible. When they got there, Hale folded the blanket into a square and set it on the largest root. "Allow me to help you down."

Yancey took his proffered hand and, with great effort, managed to sit with respectable grace.

By the time he'd unpacked pork pies, pickled asparagus, golden brown rolls, slices of three different cheeses, potato salad, lemonade, meringues filled with sugared berries, and custard tarts, Yancey suspected he'd enlisted Zoe Gunderson's help.

There was a time to enjoy the company of the person you loved and there was a time to eat. If the book of Ecclesiastes didn't include that bit of wisdom, it should.

Hale seemed to agree. They enjoyed the wonderful food while conversing about a variety of topics—how he was beginning to fear approaching strangers less, her decreasing fear over the anonymous notes now that Marshal Valentine had ruled out any foul play in the Popes' carriage accident, Luanne safely delivering a baby girl, Emilia's pregnancy, and Carline and Windsor's progressing romance. They were two people in love talking about the people they loved. It was more delicious than the custard tarts.

"Yancey . . ." Hale brushed a crumb from his trousers. "I believe the time has come for me to . . ."

Her heart sped up. Was this the moment? Was he about to ask if she'd consent to be his wife? "Yes?"

"What I'm trying to say is, I think it's important that I share a bit more about my family with you."

She ducked her head to hide her disappointment. "Please do." She'd always been curious, because the only thing she'd heard—when she was ten years old—was that there was some *unpleasant business* between his father and mother.

Hale continued brushing at his pant leg, his eyes not meeting hers. "On my eighteenth birthday, my father announced that he could no longer live a lie. He had a second family, and now that I was grown and off to college, he needed to spend more time with his sons who were five and three."

Yancey covered her mouth with her hand. What could she possibly say to counter the hurt of something so terrible? Nothing. There were no words to make it better. And while she ached for him, she also realized that by sharing this incredibly intimate secret with her he'd given her a gift as rare as his earlier laughter.

If only a box could contain such a treasure.

He peeked up at her for an instant before dropping his gaze again. "It wasn't until several weeks later, when Uncle Jonas came to support my mother, that we found out my father had, in point of fact, illegally married this other woman."

"He was a bigamist?" She barely got the words out of her covered mouth.

But he heard and nodded.

She lowered her arm. "You must have been livid."

"I was, but mostly because my mother refused to let me stay and help her. She and my uncle—"

"—sent you to Helena," Yancey finished, then gasped at her interruption of his story. "I'm sorry. I didn't mean to be rude. I was just fitting the pieces together."

He smiled at her, but his eyes remained serious.

"So when you punched Bruno Carson in the nose, you weren't defending me as much as you were taking out your anger on the nearest target."

He nodded and looked down again. "It was unforgivable of me."

And she'd praised him from one end of Helena to the other, spreading the tale of an incident he regretted. More than that, was mortified by. She wished she could lean forward and place a hand on his arm in a gesture of support, but her corset wouldn't allow it. "I'm so sorry, Hale. I had no idea."

"No one did, which was what I wanted. I still want it, but I thought it only fair that you know the truth." He took out his pocket watch and clicked open the lid.

"What happened next?"

Hale frowned. Did he not expect her to ask questions? "With my mother?"

"Well . . . yes. I'd like to hear about her, too, but I was asking about your father."

"He and my mother divorced, and he legally married his other woman." He snapped his watch closed and stuffed it into his vest pocket.

"What's she like?"

Hale tipped his head to the left, his eyes narrow. "Who?"

"Your stepmother."

"Don't call her that."

Yancey blinked, shocked at the harsh tone of his voice. "What else should I call her?"

Hale looked away. After a long moment, he said, "Her name is Jeanette. I've never met her."

Yancey's mouth fell open. "Never?"

Hale shot her a perturbed glance. "That's what I said."

"What about your . . . ?" Should she call them stepbrothers? Hale would hate it, but was there anything else to call them? "Your stepbrothers? Have you met them?"

"I don't understand why you want to know about them."

"Because they are your—"

"What? My family?" Resentment filled each syllable. "They most certainly are not. At best, they are my father's wife and sons. I want no part of them."

Yancey snapped her teeth together with a clink. "Do they want a part of you?"

"I think it's time we burn those letters." He pointed his chin toward the carriage where they had agreed to leave the letters until after their picnic.

But Yancey wasn't ready to give up on the conversation just yet. "After you tell me how your mother died."

Hale jerked back. "What makes you think she's dead?"

"You mean she isn't?"

"Of course not."

"But you never talk about her."

His squint said, *Why does that matter?*

"When's the last time you visited her? Because in the five years you've lived in Helena, the only time you left town was for that conference in Denver almost a year ago." Yancey brightened. "Wait. Does she live in Denver now?"

"She lives in England. It's not an easy journey."

Yancey stared at Hale, trying to mold the resentful man before her into the model of perfection she'd made him out to be.

He didn't fit.

She tried one more time, hoping to squeeze him back into the Hale Adams of her dreams. "Then I presume you write to her often."

"Not since she remarried and started her own second family." The vein at his temple pulsed. "I'm an orphan, you see, left behind by both my father and my mother."

Wanting to pull him into a hug and also punch him, Yancey crossed her arms to keep from doing either. "I can understand why you're upset with your father but not your mother."

"Then it's a good thing I didn't ask for your opinion." He stood and held out his hand. "It's time for us to go."

Yancey remained seated. "I'm not going anywhere until you and I finish this discussion."

"I've no wish to continue."

"Too bad, because I do."

Hale blinked, as if he didn't recognize her.

Yes, well, she didn't recognize him either. And his harsh description of his family didn't sound the same as the one he'd described in his letters. He'd written about trips to New York City, Niagara Falls, and Toronto. He hadn't sounded bitter about them, so either he'd lied —which wasn't like him—or he was blinded by his hurt. "When you were seventeen, how would you have described your family?"

"Ideal." Spoken with a resentment at odds with his declaration.

"And now?"

He withdrew his hand and raked it through his hair. "It was all a sham. None of it was real."

"Wrong."

He blinked and stared at her again. "My father ruined everything."

"No." She gripped her hands in her lap. "He ruined the ideal picture you had of your life. That isn't the same thing."

"Close enough."

"Wrong," she repeated, infusing it with as much gentleness as her mounting frustration at his thick-headedness allowed. "Do you know what Carline's uncle keeps telling her about the death of her parents? That she must take the good with the bad. Now, it's no secret that Mr. Eugene Nordstrom and I have some serious disagreements, but he's absolutely right in this instance. If Carline sees her life before July of this year only through the glasses of grief, she will lose twenty years of happy memories with wonderful parents who loved her."

"My father never loved me. Or my mother."

She shook her head. "Are you so committed to seeing only the bad that you cannot—you will not—see the good?"

He looked away.

"I'm not blind to what is happening between us, Hale. I know you wanted to kiss me last week, and you certainly know I wanted you to."

He crossed his right arm over his chest to rub his left bicep. "I concede your point."

He'd reverted to being a lawyer, so she matched his logical word choice. "You must also concede that I've made no secret of my desire to be your wife since I was ten years old."

He nodded.

"Then I hope you understand how difficult it is for me to say these next words." She took several shaky breaths while gathering her courage. "I cannot bind my future to a man who may at some point decide that I or our children have disappointed him so deeply that he sees us as lost causes."

He jerked his attention to her. "I would never—"

"You've already done it to me once. When I was fifteen and came between you and the happy future you wanted. I will not be the nearest woman at hand to help write over the first eighteen years of your life with your new, ideal family. No family will ever be ideal, Hale. You must find a way to forgive yours if you ever want to forge a happy—not ideal, but happy—one in the future."

"What should I do?" He stared at some point over her left shoulder. "Pat my father on the back and congratulate him on his lovely wife and delightful children? Thank my mother for moving to an entirely different continent to start a new life without me?"

"I don't know. But I *do* know you need to figure out what forgiveness looks like, regardless of what happens between the two of us." Yancey held out her hand so he could assist her to stand. When they were eye to eye, she added, "Please learn how to take the good with the bad, Hale. More than just your future is dependent upon it."

* * *

Jonas shifted in the saddle. He was getting too old to ride for weeks on end covering his quarter of the Montana Territory. If only the train lines ran where he needed to go and the government reimbursed him for travel. When he became senator, the first bill he'd sponsor would allot funds to cover the necessary expenses required for his job.

At least the weather was cool and his saddlebags were full of the last counterfeits printed before Smith destroyed the press. They'd met up in Deer Lodge at Jonas's mine. It was a shame to let a good employee like Smith go, but he'd served his purpose and was off to another job somewhere in Wyoming. With the printing press gone, Jonas needed to conserve every penny anyway.

He plodded through the valley east of Helena, his eye catching on the cabin where Marilyn Svenson Pawlikowski once lived. After she and David married, they'd used the place to shelter less fortunate souls. Currently, it was inhabited by Mrs. Mitzi Oren, a middle-aged widow with four children, who did housekeeping duties for various families around town. As he hoped, she was home working in her yard. He lifted a hand in greeting. She pushed her shovel into the dirt and waved back, calling, "Welcome home, Judge Forsythe."

He laid the reins on his black stallion's neck. As much as Jonas wanted to hurry home and kiss his wife, the reason for detouring so many miles out of the direct route between Deer Lodge and here was so Mrs. Oren or someone else would see him. The horse picked up his sedate pace, perhaps because the tall, scrawny widow had fed him a carrot the last time Jonas stopped to chat. "Good afternoon, Mrs. Oren. I see your pumpkins are coming in nicely."

She beamed. "That they are. Mrs. Zoe Gunderson is

going to teach me how to make pie crust in exchange for a couple of them."

Jonas pulled up next to the split-rail fence bordering her property. "What have I missed in the last month since I've been gone?"

"You heard about the Popes?"

"I did. Was it ruled an accident?"

Mrs. Oren frowned, the expression unflattering on a woman with her angular features. "Why wouldn't it be an accident? You know something I don't, Judge?"

He smiled down at her, cursing himself for the slip. "I'm sorry. I was confusing them with a case I heard up in Lincoln. When I'm tired, the things I hear at work and what I've left behind at home tend to blend together."

"Like eggs and cream in custard." Clearly the woman had cooking on her mind. "I guess the only other real big news is that Sheriff McCall's mother is buying him a new horse to replace the one that was killed."

"A terrible business," Jonas replied, meaning every word of it. The counterfeiting operation was already aflame when the sheriff and his deputy arrived in Bear Gulch. There was no reason for his men to exchange gunfire. Worse than unnecessary, it combined with Lombard's stupidity to make Marshal Valentine suspicious. What had he discovered during the past three weeks while Jonas was out of town? Perhaps the widow knew. "Is there any news about who killed Deputy Alderson and injured Sheriff McCall?"

"Not yet, but whoever he is best not come near me or I'll"—she stabbed the dirt—"his miserable neck."

Jonas felt the jab in his throat.

Mrs. Oren leaned on the shovel, pressing it deeper into the earth. "I understand a mother wanting to help her son recover after losing his horse—although I think it's more about buying her way back into Sheriff McCall's favor after she went and replaced him by adopting that Nico—"

She had? How very interesting.

"—but why didn't she go to Wichita herself? Why send Jakob Gunderson?"

Jonas barely managed to keep hold of his horse. Madame Lestraude had sent *Jakob* on an errand for her? Why? As revenge for what had happened to Mac?

"I won't keep you any longer, Judge. I know you want to get home now."

"Yes," he managed. "It was . . . nice talking with you."

If she noticed his hesitation, she didn't let on. "Give my best to your missus."

He reined his horse to the left and kicked him into a gallop. As he raced toward town, Jonas pictured charging straight to Madame Lestraude's brothel and letting his horse's powerful hooves trample through her doors, across her furniture, and over her wretched, miserable body until everything lay shattered.

He'd miscalculated. Badly. Green wasn't her weakness, that street urchin was. And she'd revealed it the day she declared war between them. Jonas had failed to notice because he was so taken aback that she'd figured out his part in Finn's death.

Stupid, *stupid* mistake.

But now that he knew, he would make her pay. Jakob was more a son to him than that insignificant brat she'd adopted would ever be to her. What had she said? Their deal was not that no harm would come to their family but they were not to even be *threatened*.

Involving Jakob in the periphery of her little rescuing ring was one thing. Sending him out of town under a pretense so flimsy it would disappear with a huff of breath was quite another.

Zuzim's powerful stride ate up the miles. Named for a race of giants, he inspired envy wherever Jonas rode him. On the edge of town, he drew the horse into a sedate walk and ran a hand over the sides of his hair to smooth down the tufts of gray.

He stopped to chat with several people—casually mentioning that he was headed to Maison de Joie to inform the madam of a new business opportunity in Butte per her request. He'd used the same excuse to good effect with Hale after Sheriff McCall was shot. Jonas hated using it again, but it couldn't be helped.

Mrs. Nanawitty asked why he was going to the brothel instead of home. "The opportunity requires immediate action," he replied, but the truth was, he'd not sully his wife's home. His current clothing needed to be burned. He'd not wear the filth of the road—or of a brothel—in front of Lily for longer than it took to change into a gentleman's attire.

He dismounted Zuzim and tied him to the hitching rail outside Maison de Joie. The three-story brick building looked exactly like what it was—a combination of store and hotel. Jonas made a show of removing a notebook from his saddlebags so everyone in the street could see he was there on business.

Mr. Lui answered Jonas's knock. The giant Chinese man stared down from his superior height, not a muscle in his face moving or offering any hint of his thoughts.

Just as Jonas was about to demand the madam's presence, the wall of flesh stepped aside, allowing him entrance.

Madame Lestraude was standing at the head of a long table, the wooden stick in her hand pointing at a movable chalkboard. The black surface was filled with basic addition and subtraction equations. "Judge Forsythe. What a pleasure to see you this afternoon."

He bowed to acknowledge her greeting. "A moment of your time, madam. We have some business to discuss."

Lestraude quirked one eyebrow higher than the other. "If you mean about the 'Vote for Hale' ribbons my girls and I have been wearing, Mr. Adams realizes they have done him no harm." Was that a sly way to say Jakob was in no danger?

"While that's most gratifying to hear, I'm here about that business in Butte you asked me to look into while I was away." Jonas repeated his story in case any of her girls gossiped with their clients tonight. "By the way, I offer you my congratulations."

Her eyebrow lowered.

Good. He had her wondering what he meant. "I hear you are a proud mother. Again."

Her expression froze for an instant. She recovered quickly, but it was enough to let Jonas know his arrow had struck true. "I'm soon to be a grandmother too."

"My goodness. I have missed a great deal while I've been out of town." His patience with their banter was growing thin. "I suggest we withdraw to your office where we can discuss specifics in private."

"Susan"—Lestraude turned to a striking redhead seated close to the chalkboard—"please continue our arithmetic lesson until I return."

"Yes, ma'am." The girl rose and took the wooden pointer from Lestraude's hand.

"This way, your honor."

Did she think he missed the mockery in her tone? Or that she was safe to taunt him because Jakob was away doing her dangerous business? He would teach her to respect him. To fear him now that he knew which piece to play in this game of theirs.

He followed her to her office, brushing dust from his jacket as they walked.

"Might I offer you something to drink? You look quite parched." She closed the door and all pretenses dissolved. "How dare you come here with your threats? My son—my oldest son—is still recovering from the wound that nearly killed him seven weeks ago."

He stretched to his full height and leaned marginally closer. "So you retaliated by sending Jakob into harm's way?"

She took a step back, the fear that flashed in her eyes a small reward. "He's in no danger, I assure you."

"As though your assurances mean anything."

She spun away, the stiff tatteta of her skirt swishing as she hurried to put distance between them. When she was behind her desk, she pulled back her heavy chair and sat. "I am not the one who broke our agreement. You are."

"In so convoluted a way, only a disordered mind could follow it." Jonas held back a smile. Not so long ago, he'd been the one sitting while she towered over him. The tables were reversed, and he intended to make full use of his advantage. He walked to the opposite side of her desk, placed both hands on the smooth surface, and leaned over her. "I have you now. You will abandon this little war of yours or I will find a way to implicate Nico in a crime. It shouldn't be too difficult, given his confession to vandalism."

She eyed him, measuring his sincerity. "Then you leave me no choice."

He straightened, satisfaction filling his frame. He'd finally bested her.

Only . . . she didn't look bested. That smug superiority he despised so much was back. She removed a gold necklace from around her neck, a small key the only pendant. After unlocking the top drawer, she withdrew a page torn from a ledger. "Before you burn buildings, my dear Jonas, you might want to be sure the evidence you wished to destroy wasn't already removed."

He stumbled back, catching himself against the chair behind him before he fell into it.

"This"—she waved the paper—"will find its way to Marshal Valentine if you so much as breathe another threat against my Nico."

Jonas wasn't taking her word that she'd torn the page proving his former associate, Edgar Dunfree, had purchased the printing press from The Resale Co. Before it became necessary to eliminate him, Dunfree used to brag about his close relationship with the Honorable Jonas Forsythe. With Marshal Valentine already suspicious because of Isaak's too accurate description of why the printing press was purchased—and that Finn Collins was killed for repairing it—Jonas couldn't take any chances that Madame Lestraude held evidence in her hands which could be traced back to him. He reached across the desk. "Let me see that."

She snatched it back. "Oh no. You are too close to the door. I'll not have you run away." *Like a coward* was insinuated in her tone of voice.

"And I'll not trust the word of a woman such as *you*."

Her face suffused with red at the insult. "Of the two of us, I am the one with the greater honor, your *honor*." She returned the page to the drawer and locked it. "Believe me when I say my threat is not idle. You will leave Nico alone or I shall ruin all you hold dear."

Jonas slapped his hands on her desk and leaned as far as his six-foot frame allowed. "I swear to you on all I hold dear, if any harm comes to Jakob Gunderson or anyone else I love, I won't even bother accusing your precious Nico. I will string him up from the nearest tree and watch him swing."

"You wouldn't." But she was shaking. "I will expose you as the base, vile criminal you are."

"And who's going to believe you? Hm? I am a sitting judge. A personal friend of the President of the United States of America. You"—he summoned every ounce of his considerable disdain—"are nothing but a *prostitute*."

Chapter Eighteen

Hale left the Palmers' porch, his mind racing.

    The day had not gone as planned. He'd intended to enjoy a special meal prepared by a trained French chef—also known as Zoe Gunderson—burn the letters with Yancey as a symbol of leaving the past behind, and then declare his affection.

The logical part of him knew she was right to say he needed to forgive his mother. In truth, he'd been thinking about doing that for some time. But his father?

No and never.

And yet Yancey made it abundantly clear that her terms were nonnegotiable.

What should he do?

Going back to his office was out of the question. He would go crazy replaying what he said, how she responded, what he *should* have said, and how the better choice of words would have resulted in a better outcome.

After returning Windsor's carriage, Hale set out toward City Hall. Perhaps Mac would have some sage advice.

He continued walking and thinking until he stopped cold at the sight of Uncle Jonas stomping out of Madame Lestraude's Maison de Joie, his face shiny red and his neck veins visible from a block away. His suit was covered with dust, a sure sign he'd just returned from his three-week trip.

Hale ducked into an obliging alley between two buildings he didn't recognize. He'd never been through the red-light district, and only came today because he'd been so lost in thought over Yancey, he wasn't paying attention.

What was going on between his uncle and the brothel owner? No business transaction would make his uncle go directly to Madame Lestraude rather than his wife after weeks of travel.

Hale peeked around the corner of the brick building. Uncle Jonas mounted his big black stallion, reining him in the direction of home rather than City Hall. As soon as he was out of sight, Hale jogged to the end of the block, watching until he was sure his uncle was gone. He looked over his shoulder at Maison de Joie. His inclination was to confront the madam on his own, but although he'd never been inside her establishment, he knew well that she employed a Chinese man so large, he'd intimidated Isaak Gunderson and, last year, had picked up and tossed both Mac and Quinn Valentine into the street.

Hale needed reinforcements if he was going to confront Madame Lestraude to find out what scandal she was threatening to expose. Or—more likely, because it involved Uncle Jonas, who was as upright as any man who walked the earth—the lie she was planning to tell.

Not caring if he drew attention to himself, Hale raced down Wood Street and turned left on West Main. Once inside City Hall, he headed straight for Mac's office. Eli Alderson and Undersheriff Keenan looked up from whatever they were studying on the latter's desk.

Alderson broke away and approached Hale. "What can I do for you, Mr. Adams?"

"Is Sheriff McCall here?"

Mac poked his head out of his side office. "I'm here. Come on in."

Hale pushed through the small gate on the side of the wood counter between him and the deputies. He weaved through their desks, noting the WANTED posters and delinquent tax notices as he passed.

Mac stood in the doorframe between the open space and his private office, waiting until Hale came inside to close the door behind him. "Have a seat."

Hale gripped the back of the chair instead of sitting in it. "I need to speak to your mother, and I'd like you to go with me as a witness. And so her man doesn't toss me out on my rear before I can get to her."

"I see. What's this about?" Mac walked to his side of the desk.

"I wish I knew." Hale scratched the back of his head. "For the past few months, I've noticed tension between my uncle and your mother. You should have seen them when we were waiting to hear how your surgery had gone. You could have roasted a chicken with the fiery looks passing between them."

"Did you ask him about it?" Mac sat down, his expression calm.

"I did. He gave me a story about how he'd advised her to invest in a somewhat risky venture that went bankrupt, and she was angry with him."

"Sounds reasonable."

"For her to glare at him, maybe, but not for him to return it." Hale yanked back the chair and sat so he was eye to eye with Mac. "I saw my uncle coming out of your mother's brothel less than five minutes ago. Based on the amount of dust on his clothing, he'd just arrived back in town. Why go there instead of home? You know as well as I do that your mother loves to stir up scandal. That business about Finn last year is a prime example."

Mac cocked his head to the side. "What do you mean by that?"

"I never believed a word of that hogwash about Finn selling Emilia and her sister into prostitution. Emilia inviting your mother to your wedding and then your bedside after the surgery confirms it. No one is that forgiving."

"My Em is." Mac sat back in his chair and crossed his arms over his chest.

Hale studied his friend. "Maybe she is, but I find it hard to believe that you are. I don't say that to offend you, but we've been friends a long time. You need truth and justice. It's why you became a lawman."

"Men can change."

Hale narrowed his eyes. "What aren't you saying?"

"My mother has secrets which are best kept."

The phrase was word for word what Isaak had said. Hale respected it then. He couldn't afford to now. "I'm going to confront your mother. Would you like me to do that with or without you?"

Ten minutes later, when they reached Maison de Joie, Mac went in first. Hale waited outside, pacing back and forth for eight minutes and twenty-four seconds until the door opened a second time. Nico escorted Hale to the madam's office, the look on his young face a combination of interest and apathy, as only a fifteen-year-old could manage.

Hale vaguely noted that the brothel was laid out like a regular house, with an entry, parlor, and stairs leading to a second floor. The walls were papered in burgundy, a color the madam favored in her dress and used for the "Vote for Hale" ribbons her girls wore around town.

Hale stepped inside the madam's office. The mahogany desk she sat behind was so like his, he gawked. Same rich wood, same size, same depth. The differences were in the carvings—his were geometric, where hers were flowers and vines—and her vase of pink hothouse roses as opposed to his phone and typewriter. A picture behind her desk mimicked the flowers on her desk, pink buds in a blue vase.

Another surprise was Mac standing behind his mother's chair, one hand on her shoulder. But the biggest surprise was the madam herself. Whenever Hale had seen her around town, her entire demeanor was one of haughty disdain.

This woman was pale and shaking, the paint on her face smeared from where she'd wiped tears off her cheeks. "Please have a seat, Mr. Adams. It seems the time has come for you and me to chat."

Hale sank into the padded wing-back chair, his worked-up bravado gone. "I need some answers, ma'am."

She lifted a hand to grip Mac's. "My son told me what you observed earlier today. Allow me to set your mind at rest on one point. Your uncle has, to my knowledge, always been faithful to your aunt."

The reassurance loosed the knot of uncertainty in Hale's gut. "Thank you for that."

Madame Lestraude smiled, but it wasn't reassuring. "It would be better if that *were* his sin, Mr. Adams."

Hale gripped the armrests and scooted back in the chair.

She patted Mac's hand. "Son, you need to sit next to your friend. I have much to tell you."

By the time she finished, she'd regained her composure, but Hale was drained of every bit of his. Simply put, he was a wreck. His uncle was the counterfeiter at Bear Gulch.

Hale took off his glasses. Polished them with his vest. Replaced them, but his vision was still blurry. "Do you have any proof?"

She shook her head. "None that's usable."

"Meaning what?" Mac leaned forward in his chair.

Madame Lestraude pulled a necklace from around her neck. The pendant was a key. She unlocked the top right drawer of her desk and pulled out a single piece of ledger paper. Every line was filled, but the handwriting varied. One edge was torn. "I ripped this from one of the ledgers at The Resale Company before it burned. I was looking for proof that Jonas purchased the printing press but couldn't find any because I had no idea when the press was purchased, and David Pawlikowski has recorded every transaction since the beginning of time. Nevertheless, I thought it prudent to pretend I did. I showed this"—she waved the paper—"to Jonas today. I don't think he believed me, but it will keep him from doing anything rash until Jakob gets back to town, which should be in a couple of weeks at the most."

"What does Jakob have to do with any of this?" Mac put his hands on his knees, elbows out.

Madame Lestraude returned the ledger sheet to her desk drawer, locked it, and replaced the chain around her neck. "He's escorting some of the girls I and my little ring of rescuers have liberated from prostitution to a private school in Kansas."

"Including Finn," Mac added with a sidelong glance at Hale.

"Wait." Hale put up a hand, palm facing the madam. He looked at Mac. "How long have you known that Finn was killed because he was helping rescue girls?"

Mac pushed his arms straight and sat back in his chair. "Since the week before my wedding."

Madame Lestraude cleared her throat, drawing the eyes of both men. "He wasn't killed for that."

"He wasn't?" Mac and Hale spoke in unison.

Mac recovered first. "Why didn't you tell me?"

"Because I didn't have proof." She looked to the side. "I still don't, and accusing a territorial judge who is friends with the President of the United States without irrefutable proof is not good for one's health."

Hale's head filled with bits and pieces of the conversation at the hospital. "Are you telling me that Isaak was right?"

"About what?" Madame Lestraude snapped her attention to Hale.

He closed his eyes to keep his focus on the memory. "We were discussing the notes Yancey and Carline received warning them to stop talking about phony money. It made us think that perhaps they were right to think Joseph Hendry's death was tied to counterfeiting after all. Isaak remembered having a printing press he and his father couldn't fix, that they sometimes sent work to Finn, and that if the press was being used for counterfeiting, perhaps Finn was killed before he could make the connection." Hale opened his eyes to gauge the madam's reaction. "He was right, wasn't he?"

"And you didn't think you could trust me with that?" Mac asked.

Hale was about to answer that he assumed Quinn had passed along the information, but the question was directed at Madame Lestraude.

She bowed her head. When she looked up, the regret on her face made her appear ten years older. "This relationship we have forged"—she waved her hand between herself and her son—"has been tenuous at best. We're just learning to trust each other. I wasn't about to endanger it when I was accusing a sitting judge, a man you admired, and an uncle or pseudouncle to some of your best friends without proof."

Mac hung his head. "I need you to trust me now, Mother. With the whole truth. All of it."

By the time she was finished with the second round of revelations, Hale was covering his mouth and swallowing down bile.

Not only was his uncle involved in the counterfeiting, he had admitted to orchestrating Joseph Hendry's murder. And though she had no proof, she firmly believed he'd killed or hired someone to kill Sheriff Simpson—maybe more people—and to set fire to The Resale Co.

"What are you going to do?" Madame Lestraude directed the question to her son.

"Find proof."

"How?" Her tone was sharp with either scorn or concern. Maybe both. "You can't let him know you suspect him." She slid her gaze to Hale. "How are you at acting?"

"Terrible." It was why he hated arguing in front of a jury. They were usually more interested in the theater of a case than the truth.

Madame Lestraude turned to her son. "What about you?"

"Worse than terrible."

"Then I suggest you learn." She looked between Mac and Hale. "Quickly."

Chapter Nineteen

Saturday, September 22, 1888
Mrs. Hollenbeck's house

Yancey wandered to the gazebo on the far edge of Mrs. Hollenbeck's lawn. As it had been at Roy and Luanne's wedding, the enormous back patio held two dozen round tables set with china and crystal. The only difference between now and then was the color and size of the floral arrangements. Luanne had chosen small bouquets of white carnations. Mollie Fisk—now Mrs. Jefferson Brady—had chosen pink and brown bouquets so large, guests had to duck or lean to see the people across the table from them.

For the last hour, Yancey had fulfilled her bridesmaid duties with a smile on her face. But she was ten minutes away from taking her turn accompanying Hale from group to group, and she didn't know how to behave around him.

She stepped into the gazebo and sat on the bench. Usually, she loved weddings. Not this one. It had been a trial from the moment she walked down the aisle—the last of eight bridesmaids.

Hale had said and done nothing in the past week to indicate he was planning to forgive his family so they could have a future. He was polite—if somewhat chilly—when they were together. Which wasn't often. The next event on the campaign schedule wasn't until next month at the Harvest Festival, and he was busy preparing for his debates with Mayor Kendrick.

But the worst had been a few minutes ago, when Hale asked what she was doing on Tuesday. Thrilled that he was finally going to resume their as-yet-undeclared courtship, she was crushed when he said he needed her to ask his aunt to tea.

She looked down at her pink-and-brown-plaid skirt. This was so much worse than the first bridesmaid's dress. It was almost as though Mollie had deliberately chosen something unflattering. Had she always wanted a fall wedding and was trying to make up for these awful dresses with the first ones, which were so different—and so lovely?

"Are you over here pouting?" Jakob put one foot on the floor of the gazebo. "Because if you are, I'd like to join you."

Yancey quirked a smile at the repeat of her exact words to him a little over a year ago. They'd been at the Independence Day picnic. Jakob was moping because he'd been trying to impress Emilia, but she only had eyes for Mac. Yancey was moping because Hale was ignoring her, and a good number of people were still looking at her with skepticism after the scandal linking her to Finn Collins and his scheme to lure unsuspecting women to Helena on the ruse of a mail-order marriage in order to sell them into prostitution.

So much had happened since then. She picked up a brown leaf from the bench beside her and crushed it between her fingers. "I haven't had a chance to talk with you since you came home. How was your trip?"

"Good."

She slanted a look at him. Leading up to the trip, he'd talked about taking some extra days to visit a few places along the route. His curt answer didn't match his excitement before he left. She ought to ask him what was wrong, but then he'd ask her what was wrong with her, and she couldn't tell him. Hale's family background was his secret to tell, not hers.

She chose another topic that would account for her melancholy. "Have you been by to see Carline?"

Jakob blinked and stared at her for a long moment. "I took Carline to dinner a couple of nights ago. She shared that Windsor is courting her. Isn't that a little soon, considering her parents died less than three months ago?"

Yancey brushed bits of leaf from her skirt. "Better that she is here with friends and a man who loves her than for her to be in Butte with an uncle who wants to control her life."

Jakob nodded and stepped into the gazebo to sit beside her. With him no longer blocking her view, she caught a glimpse of Hale standing next to his uncle as they chatted with the groom's parents. He looked like he'd eaten something sour but was doing his best to hide it. Was that because he knew her turn was coming and he didn't know how to act around her either?

"What is going on between you and Hale?"

Yancey dropped her gaze to her lap. Between her staring at Hale and how everything up to this point in her life had always been about him, Jakob's question was natural. But the thoughts plaguing her on this beautiful fall day weren't about Hale per se. They were about *her*.

Hale was neither the knight nor the villain in her fairy-tale future. He was just a man with a flaw. She believed he'd one day fix it—or most of it. But how long would it take? Should she wait for him or let him go? She believed God was sovereign. That He would pursue Hale with a love more relentless than anything he'd ever experienced. That God would teach Hale to take the good with the bad. To forgive.

Only . . . what if it took another fifteen years? Or fifty? Or days instead of years?

God knew but He wasn't telling, so where did that leave her? In a jumbled sort of way, she needed to forgive Hale for not fitting into the mold she'd made for him. What did that look like? She didn't know. And she was running out of time.

Jakob was staring at her.

She gave him the best smile she could muster. "I gave a friend some excellent advice a couple of weeks ago, and now I have about five minutes to decide how to follow it myself."

He opened his mouth but didn't say anything. The silence stretched between them. She was just about to excuse herself when he said, "Hey. Did you ever find out who wrote those notes to you and Carline? If not, I have time. I can look into it."

She shook her head. "I've decided to leave that entire situation in God's sovereign hands." At least in this one case, she could take the good advice Hale gave her and put it into practice.

"It's never going to go back to the way it was between us, is it?"

She jerked her attention to Jakob. Why would he ask such an odd question? They were friends. Almost siblings. Nothing could change that.

And yet . . .

Before now, they'd always shared the ups and downs of their separate romances. Yancey had known Jakob signed up for the Archer Matrimonial Company when no one else did. He was the only person outside her parents and Carline who knew she'd done the same. But if Hale didn't overcome his unforgiving spirit—or even if he did, but never wanted Yancey to speak of it to anyone—she couldn't reveal the reason she'd let him go. She always prided herself on her ability to keep a secret. Now it was a wedge between her and dear Jakob.

Tears pricked her eyes. She blinked to keep them at bay. "Maybe not."

"No one's been the same since I returned." He looked up, as though the ceiling of the gazebo held answers. "You're all the same. It's me who's changed. I thought Helena needed me, but life continued on."

"Of course it did." Mrs. Hollenbeck's voice startled Yancey.

Jakob jumped to his feet.

Mrs. Hollenbeck eyed him narrowly. "I'll deal with you in a moment." She turned her gaze to Yancey. "It's time."

Her five minutes were up and she still hadn't figured out what to do. She glanced to where Hale was conversing easily with the Cannons. "Hale no longer needs me to help with his campaign."

"He needs you now more than ever."

She returned her attention to Mrs. Hollenbeck. She wasn't talking about the campaign, but she didn't know what had transpired at the picnic. Or did she? The lady had a way of inviting confidences. Had Hale told her about Yancey's condition that he learn to forgive before they could be together? "I don't know how to act around him."

"I suggest you start by being the same Yancey Palmer who thought he was the best candidate for mayor and agreed to help get him elected." Mrs. Hollenbeck's expression softened. "Don't try to figure out everything, just the right thing to do at this moment. God will light your path— although maybe no more than two or three steps, so you must trust Him as you walk."

Now that was some good advice—which Yancey didn't want to follow. She suddenly understood why Hale needed some time before getting back to her. Two weeks was a bit much in her opinion. But his lack of action would not excuse hers.

Yancey rose from the seat. "You're absolutely right."

Mrs. Hollenbeck smiled. "Dear girl, of course I am. Now go. And smile."

Tuesday, September 25, 1888

The sound of footsteps coming up the stairs drew Jonas's attention. "Lily?" She was supposed to be having tea with Emilia McCall and Yancey Palmer.

"No, sir. It's me." Hale appeared in the doorway to the library. "We need to talk." He stepped into the room, followed by Sheriff McCall and Nick Alderson's younger brother, Eli.

The serious expressions on their faces were worrisome. Could they know about the counterfeiting? Had Madame Lestraude delivered her latest blow in their ongoing war? No. He'd put the fear of God in her the last time they met.

Jonas removed his reading glasses and stood. He wasn't going to sit while the three of them towered over him.

He came around the desk to greet them. "What can I do for you gentle—whoa." Jonas jerked to a stop when the Alderson boy pulled out his gun.

Fear and retribution filled the young man's eyes. He was short, and his light brown skin announced his mixed heritage. His parents had come to Montana to escape the stigma of being the children of slave mothers and white masters. Jonas had performed their wedding ceremony when no one else would. Did young Alderson know that? If so, the hatred in his dark brown eyes said he didn't care.

Mac slowly raised his open hand, palm facing Alderson. "Put the gun down, Deputy."

Alderson didn't move. "He killed my brother, Sheriff. I'm not letting him get away with it."

"We aren't, but you promised you'd follow my instructions

to the letter when I agreed to let you come. Now, put the gun down." Mac demonstrated the action. "Judge Forsythe is under my protection."

Alderson flicked a look at his boss before letting out a huff. He lowered his arm to his side but didn't return the gun to its holster.

Jonas released the breath he'd not realized he was holding.

Mac pulled a folded piece of paper from inside his jacket. Jonas knew what it was even before Mac unfolded it and laid it on the desk. "This search warrant is for both your home and downtown office. It allows us to look for counterfeit money and any records connecting you to the operations of such."

Jonas glared at the warrant. The records they sought—and the ones for the mine—weren't here. This was Lily's home. He'd never tarnish it with his necessary evils. And now they wanted to make a mess by rummaging through their private belongings? *No.* Lily kept a neat house.

But he needed to hear exactly what they suspected.

"What proof do you have?"

Hale brought his hands in front of his body, several sheets of paper in varying sizes and shades of cream in his left hand. "These are sworn statements from six men testifying that you hired them to print and distribute counterfeit bills, further testimony from a Mr. Smith that you hired him to set fire to The Resale Company and the printing press, and that he—under your orders—attacked Sheriff McCall and Deputy Alderson."

Jonas picked up the search warrant, needing to focus on something other than the disappointment on his nephew's face.

"We also have a written statement"—Sheriff McCall picked up the narrative—"from Miss Mary Lester that you admitted to inciting violence against Mr. Joseph Hendry, resulting in his death. Furthermore, she stated that you once employed Edgar Dunfree, that in his capacity as your employee he killed Phineas Collins, and that you murdered Dunfree to keep him quiet."

Jonas read the warrant. Each of the charges was listed, along with the proof garnered so far. He should have ripped the ledger paper out of Lestraude's hand when she waved it at him as proof Edgar bought a printing press from The Resale Co. Because she wouldn't let him see it, Jonas dismissed her threat as empty.

It *was* empty, and yet it led to the full truth. At least about the counterfeiting. As he suspected, the woman knew nothing of his mining operation. Was there a way to save that? To make sure Lily had some income if he was convicted of his crimes? He needed to protect her as best he could. Admitting guilt often swayed judges to more lenient sentencing. And if he confessed to the crimes they knew about, perhaps he could keep them from searching his office and discovering the mine.

Mindful of the gun young Alderson hadn't returned to its holster, Jonas kept his voice calm. "I never told Dunfree to kill Finn Collins. I was as upset about that as you are, Sheriff."

"Doubtful."

"Nevertheless, I didn't know about it until after the fact. As for the rest . . ." He wet his lips and took a breath. "The rest is true."

"No!" The shocked cry of his wife jolted Jonas's attention to the door. He started for her.

Young Alderson spun around, his right hand swinging high.

Mac shouted, Hale pushed against him, and Jonas tried to get to her before—

Bang!

Time froze for an instant as he and Lily stared across the space between them.

Her eyes went wide, red blooming from her chest. She wobbled, her hands reaching for Jonas.

He ran to her, caught her before she fell to the ground. "I'm sorry, my darling. I never meant any of this to happen."

"How . . . how could . . . you?"

Jonas stroked her hair, a sob in his throat. "I did it for you—for us. To give you the home you deserved in Washington, as a senator's wife. I promised I would, remember?" He did. He'd promised. It was all for her. For them. Because they deserved that life.

She sagged, her weight dragging them both to the floor. "No, Jonas. Not for me. I . . . never . . . All I ever . . . wanted . . . was you." Her breath brushed over his face as the light went out of her eyes, her body draining of tension.

Jonas bent over her, hugging her close to his chest. "No, Lily. Don't go. Don't leave me. I did it for you. For us. Come back. Come back!"

This wasn't real. It couldn't be. This was Lily's home. Nothing bad happened here. He'd made sure of it. What had these men done? Why were they even here? Jonas blinked several times. It was against the law for them to trespass on his property. Lily would be furious when she saw the mess they'd made. He lifted his chin and rose to his feet, straightening his vest. There were things he needed to attend to. He couldn't remember what they were at the moment, but they were important. *He* was important. There were piles of papers that needed his attention before Lily had dinner ready. And he never kept Lily waiting.

Hale stood over his aunt's motionless body, his own limbs as incapable of movement as hers. She was dead. He knew it intellectually but couldn't make himself believe it. It was like seeing things before putting on his glasses or hearing them from a distance.

Mac took the gun from Eli Alderson's hand.

Eli kept repeating, "I didn't mean to shoot her."

Uncle Jonas stood and straightened his vest. "I have appointments. Yes. I must have appointments. I'm an important man, and important men have appointments." He looked around the room. "Why are you here? You're trespassing. My wife keeps a neat home. She'll be furious with this mess."

What appointments? What mess? Hale snapped his attention to Mac. The looks of confusion on his and Eli Alderson's faces echoed Hale's. Had his uncle gone mad?

"Come, boys"—Uncle Jonas stepped over Aunt Lily's body on his way toward the door—"we need a broom and a mop."

Mac blocked his path. "I'm sorry, Judge Forsythe. But we need to take you down to City Hall."

"Whatever for?" Uncle Jonas frowned, three wrinkles appearing between his brows. "Do you need me to sign another search warrant? Yes. A search warrant. I can do that here." He turned back around and tripped over Aunt Lily as if he'd forgotten she was between him and his desk. "What is . . . Lily? Oh no. What happened here? Lily? *Lily?*" He dropped to his knees and lifted his wife back into his arms. "I did it for her." Uncle Jonas's eyes were wild. "She knows that, doesn't she? She knows I was just trying to give her the life she deserved."

Mac kneeled beside Uncle Jonas. "It was an accident, sir. A horrible accident. Come away, now. I'll take you downstairs while your nephew and my deputy attend to matters here."

"What happened?" Uncle Jonas wouldn't let go. "Who shot my Lily?"

"It was an accident," Mac repeated.

An accident? Hale couldn't believe what he was hearing. It was a deliberate disobedience of orders on Eli Alderson's part, and a fatal mistake on Mac's. But the greater sin was Uncle Jonas's for bringing them all here to arrest him.

Hale spun around to face the bookcases. No. The greater sin was his for asking to keep the arrest a private matter. He'd wanted to spare his aunt—his *innocent* aunt—the humiliation of having her husband arrested like a common criminal in front of the entire town.

"Someone made a mess." Uncle Jonas sounded like a child.

Hale pulled off his glasses so he could cover his face with his hand. Tears burned his eyes while shock, horror, and anguish wrestled with one another inside his chest.

"Jonas Forsythe"—Mac's voice wobbled—"you are under arrest for—"

"Lily!" The scream turned Hale around. Uncle Jonas's face was white and twisted with grief, but the light of reason shone from his gray eyes. "I killed my Lily! Oh, God. What have I done? What have I done?"

Mac flicked a glance at Hale, who still couldn't move, before beckoning Alderson closer. "Let us help you with this"—Mac swallowed hard—"mess."

"Yes. This is a mess." Uncle Jonas let go of his wife again, stood again, stepped over her body again, only this time Mac stayed out of his way and Alderson followed behind.

When they were out of view, Hale stumbled closer to his aunt and fell to his knees beside her.

Dear Lord, why? How could You have let this happen? She was innocent. You should have protected her. You could have. With a wave of Your hand, You could have altered the trajectory of that bullet. Why didn't You? Why?

Now that his brain had started working again, it wouldn't stop. The questions—the tirade against God—wouldn't cease. He wasn't sure how long he knelt beside her until a touch on his shoulder made him look up.

Mac leaned down, the weight of his hand increasing.

"Do you want me to take your uncle to City Hall or stay here with you?"

"What went wrong? Why did Aunt Lily come home?"

"As best I can tell, she forgot her grocery list and came back to get it. I found it sitting on top of a bowl of chicken salad. Emilia said she was craving the salad and asked your aunt to make some for the tea. I put it in the icebox. The salad, not the list." Mac squeezed Hale's shoulder. "I'm so sorry."

The apology felt like a slap across the face. "You shouldn't have brought Alderson."

Mac took a step back. "Are you blaming me for this?"

"Bringing Alderson was a mistake. You shouldn't have done it." Hale turned his head away. He couldn't bring himself to look at his friend, even as a part of him recognized his faulty logic in laying blame on anyone.

It *was* an accident, but someone needed to pay for the anguish burning its way through every muscle and stinging his skin.

Uncle Jonas's voice drifted up the stairs. "On her way home from tea with Mrs. McCall and Miss Palmer, my wife is stopping at Cannon's Grocery Store. She's planning to make croissants again. Have you ever had those, Deputy Alderson?"

"No, sir, but I'm sure they are delicious."

"Zoe taught her how to make them. Did you know that?"

"No, sir."

"My Lily is a wonderful cook. She'll be home soon. She went to tea, and then she's going to the market. She'll be home soon."

The strange conversation broke Hale. He put his hands over his face and sobbed. He'd lost his parents and now he'd lost the people who'd replaced them. Uncle Jonas was as gone as Aunt Lily. Hale reached out a shaky hand to brush his aunt's cheek. Her skin was still warm.

She'd heard her husband's crimes. She'd cried out. Uncle Jonas jerked. Eli Alderson raised his gun toward the threat, but also swung around to investigate what was behind him. The gun went off. Aunt Lily died. And Uncle Jonas lost his sanity.

All because of a forgotten grocery list.

"My Lily loves me. She calls me a good man." Uncle Jonas continued, his voice softer but still carrying. "Do you know how we met?"

"No, sir. Tell me." Eli Alderson was doing Hale's job. Regardless of his feelings, he needed to take charge of his uncle. The responsibility rested with him.

Hale stood, wiped the tears from his face, and—without looking at Mac—staggered down the stairs. For the next half hour, Hale kept his uncle talking. Through the slow footsteps and grunts of men carrying a heavy burden down the stairs. Through a conversation too hushed to distinguish words before it disappeared altogether with the thump of a door closing. Through the emptiness of a house now absent its lady.

Hale kept asking questions—pretending he couldn't remember how his aunt and uncle met, fell in love, and got married—until he thought he'd go as mad as his uncle.

A faint knock was followed by an immediate, "Mrs. Forsythe?"

Yancey's voice. The sound of it acted like ointment on a burn. Hale jumped up from the table before his uncle could. "I'll get it."

"Tell whoever it is that Lily is out for a few minutes." Uncle Jonas sounded almost normal. "She's at the market and will be home soon."

"I will." Hale hurried out of the kitchen, through the dining room, and into the front hall. He pulled open the front door. "Yancey." Her name was like a prayer on his lips.

"Is Mrs. Forsythe here? She didn't show up for our tea,

so Emilia and I started to worry." Her eyes flitted over his shoulder. "What's wrong?"

Hale closed the door to give them a moment of privacy. "There's been a terrible accident." He was determined to keep using the word until it felt like the truth. "Aunt Lily was killed."

Yancey gasped and covered her lips with gloved fingers.

"And Uncle Jonas has lost his reason. One minute he knows she's dead, the next he thinks she's at the market and will be home soon."

As though intent on proving the unbelievable statement, Uncle Jonas started screaming. "Lily! Oh, my Lily! What have I done?"

Hale pivoted, jerked the door open, and, without waiting to see if Yancey followed him, raced up the stairs to where his uncle stood staring at the bloodstained floorboards of his office.

Hale felt Yancey's presence behind him an instant before she touched his shoulder. He moved aside to allow her into the room, regretting the instinctive gesture when she gasped again, her eyes on the stain. "Judge Forsythe, how lovely to see you." Whatever her feelings, Yancey managed to sound as though she was greeting a friend at church or on the street. "I hear your wife is at the market."

Uncle Jonas turned his attention from the floor to Yancey. "What? What's that you say?"

She held out her hand. "I wonder if I might trouble you to escort me downstairs. I hear your wife is at the market. Would you honor me with the pleasure of your company while I wait for her?"

Uncle Jonas took Yancey's hand, allowing her to lead him out of the room, as though he were a child and she his mother. Halfway down the stairs, he said, "Miss Palmer, I thought you were having tea with Mrs. McCall and my wife."

"We were . . . are. She sent me to fetch you because . . . because . . ." Yancey cast a help-me glance over her shoulder.

Hale had none to offer. The events of the past hour were catching up with him, draining his ability to think.

"She made chicken salad," Uncle Jonas announced as though it made sense. Had he figured out that Mac and Hale planned the tea to get Aunt Lily out of the house so they could arrest him?

"Yes." Yancey patted his arm. "Because she made chicken salad and forgot to bring it to our tea."

"She shouldn't have forgotten. It's very bad to forget things." Were fragments of his former brilliance somewhere inside Uncle Jonas's disordered mind? It sounded like he was putting pieces together—figuring out how the forgotten grocery list brought her home too early, led her to hear things Hale wanted to shield her from for as long as possible.

He stopped at the foot of the stairs. His uncle needed to pay for his crime, but what if he never recovered his intellect? Either he would spend the rest of his life in prison or in an asylum for the criminally insane. Both were no less than he deserved.

And yet, Hale shuddered.

Chapter Twenty

Yancey stayed with Hale and his uncle until Mac returned to the house. He brought two deputies—neither of whom was Eli Alderson—to escort Judge Forsythe to City Hall. As the judge was currently in his imaginary world where his wife would be home any minute, Hale asked Mac to forgo the handcuffs. He agreed as long as Hale came along to keep his uncle in check.

Before Mac left, Yancey asked him what had happened. He explained the plan, how it went wrong, and that Hale was blaming him for bringing Eli along. "Maybe he's right." Mac scratched his jaw.

Yancey placed a hand on his arm. "No, he's not, and he'll soon come to recognize it."

When the house was quiet, Yancey allowed her grief to spill down her cheeks. Usually, she would run to her mother or Carline when the emotions were this powerful, but Yancey wouldn't put them through what needed to be done next.

She walked into the kitchen and rummaged through drawers and closets until she found an apron, a mop, and a bucket. Before Hale came back, she wanted the upstairs office floorboards clean.

But they refused to let go of the stain.

Yancey went back downstairs and found a scouring

brush. Back in the library, she pressed so hard that bits of varnish came away, and still the pinewood held on as though determined to never let anyone forget the tragedy soaked into them.

Stupid floor. Why wouldn't it cooperate? She scrubbed and scrubbed, her arms and back aching from the effort. The stain remained. She threw the wet brush at the wall and burst into tears.

She heard the door open, heard Hale call her name, heard his footsteps running up the stairs, but no matter how much she wanted to calm herself, to be strong for him, she couldn't stop blubbering.

Hale knelt beside her and drew her into his arms. She pressed her face against his shirt, obeying his gentle command to go ahead and cry. A moment later, his chest shook and she heard him sob.

Several minutes passed. "I'm so sorry, Hale," she managed to whisper when she'd brought her weeping under control. "What can I do? Tell me what to do."

He pulled away, wiping his face with his forearm. "You've already done enough. Thank you for this." He glanced at the floor.

"It won't come clean. I tried."

"Maybe it shouldn't. Maybe we should always see it and remember where unchecked ambition leads."

Yancey shifted to sit sideways on the floor. "What do you mean?"

"My uncle is the one responsible for the counterfeit money. I think he was planning to use it to buy votes either for my election or for his eventual campaign for senator. Maybe both."

Yancey sucked in a breath. "He's the one Joseph was going to expose as the high-ranking government official involved in counterfeiting, wasn't he?"

Hale nodded.

"Is he the one who killed Joseph?"

"Not directly, but he's responsible for it." Hale pulled away. He took her left hand and rubbed it with his right. "He's also responsible for Finn Collins's death. Finn repaired the printing press my uncle was using. Mac and I have known it for weeks, but we needed to gather proof."

Yancey stared at their joined hands. Unlike the last time they'd touched, this was comfortable and comforting—two friends consoling each other with human contact. "What's going to happen to your uncle now?"

Hale looked away, his hand pulling out of hers. "I don't know. He's guilty, but he won't be able to stand trial." His voice was harsh.

Yancey winced. Should she warn Hale that he needed to add his uncle to the list of people needing forgiveness?

No. Hale needed to become the right person on his own, not because Yancey asked or manipulated him into it. Hale loved her. The way he'd rushed to hold her, crushed her to his chest, and pressed kisses into her hair while she wept told her as much.

And he was looking at her as though she was his salvation.

If he proposed now, she wouldn't be able to say no, even knowing she should. The strength she was developing to detach herself from him was too fragile. It was her turn to push him away without explanation. Hale needed to decide whether he would forgive his uncle, Mac, and everyone else connected to today's tragedy.

Yancey took a shaky breath. "I need to go."

He nodded and stood, extending his hand to help her rise, pulling her close so they stood heart to heart. "Yancey, I—"

"Shh." She put her fingers on his lips. "Please don't say anything, Hale."

He took her hand, pressed a kiss into her palm. "I understand. Now is the time for grieving."

He didn't understand at all. Now was the time for forgiving.

Yancey withdrew her hand and stepped back. "I'm sorry, Hale." For his aunt, for his bitterness, but mostly because she loved him too much to marry him as he was. "I'll stop by The Import Company and let Isaak know what happened. I'm sure he'll come right away."

Hale narrowed his eyes. "What's wrong, Yancey? Why are you leaving me?"

"I'm sorry." It was the only thing she could think to say. "I'm so sorry."

She hurried out the door, down the stairs, and out of the house before she threw herself into his arms and held on, to the detriment of them both.

It was time to get out of Helena.

Mary Lester closed her business ledger and pushed it to the side of her desk. The gleaming wood was a symbol of everything she'd achieved since arriving—at fourteen years old—in her first brothel. She'd fallen in love with an older man, believed his lies when he painted a rosy future where she could wear dresses of the finest silks and satins, eat delicacies every day—every meal, if she wanted—and lounge in her luxuriously decorated boudoir all day.

She snorted. Oh, she'd gotten all those things, but only after spending twenty years on her back. She'd hidden everything from paper dollars to gold nuggets anywhere her various madams wouldn't find, biding her time until the day she broke free and could take charge of her life once more.

She'd spent the next twenty years making more money than she'd ever imagined, and she'd been a *fair* madam. Her girls were treated with respect, received an education while in her employ, and were encouraged to put away part of their earnings for when they were too old or diseased to ply their trade.

That was why her brothel was known far and wide as the best place to work in the entire western territories.

People outside the business might not understand, but Mary was proud of what she'd accomplished, and giving it up wasn't a decision she took lightly.

But Lily Forsythe's death changed everything.

Mary reached inside the top left drawer of her desk and took out her personalized stationery. A few minutes later, she called Nico into her office and gave him strict instructions to deliver the sealed letter into Mrs. Pauline Hollenbeck's hand.

He returned an hour later, during which Mary had written five more letters to her bankers, notifying them of her intention to withdraw her entire balance the day after tomorrow.

Nico handed over a letter, saying Mrs. Hollenbeck insisted that he wait until she'd written it and that she needed an answer to her inquiry as soon as possible.

Intrigued, Mary broke the wax seal and unfolded the paper.

My dear Miss Lester,

Please do me the favor of joining me for tea tomorrow at two o'clock in the afternoon. I guarantee you will be glad you came. Please send your reply by the delightful young man who delivered your missive.

Warmly,

Pauline Hollenbeck

Mary hardly knew what to think. The bond between them was mere business, a brothel madam who happened to rescue young girls from prostitution and a Christian woman who provided those girls with an education at a school in Kansas. But Mrs. Hollenbeck's letter made it sound as if she was inviting her dearest friend over for tea and a leisurely chat.

"I think you should go, Miss Lester."

Mary tilted her head to gauge Nico's sincerity. "Why?"

"Because she treated me like I was something other than a dirty street urchin messing up her carpets by walking inside her house. Same as you did when I first met you."

The comparison formed into a lump that settled in her throat. Afraid she'd turn into a watering pot if she tried to speak, she set Mrs. Hollenbeck's letter on her desk, reached for another sheet of stationery, and wrote out a reply accepting the invitation.

The lump had moved to her stomach by two the next afternoon.

Why had she agreed to this?

The answer eluded her, but she lifted the brass knocker and rapped it three times. She stepped back, waiting for the door to open. Her palms itched inside her black lace gloves. She'd chosen a dark blue dress, was wearing a stylish brunette wig topped with a hat with a netted veil covering the top half of her face, and kept her decorative parasol open to hide what the hat and wig couldn't.

And every moment she stood on the front step of the gingerbread mansion, she was afraid she'd be unmasked. Perhaps she should have come in her hag costume.

Just as her nerves were about to get the better of her, the door swung open. A tall man with round cheeks and a meager amount of silver hair combed over his bald head appeared. "Welcome, Miss Lester. Mrs. Hollenbeck is expecting you."

But why?

The mystery would remain unsolved by staying outside, so Mary stepped across the threshold like she visited great ladies every day of the week. The butler took her parasol, then escorted her across a black-and-white-checkered marble floor and into a cozy breakfast room flooded with light.

Mrs. Hollenbeck rose from the table set for eight. The yellow tablecloth matched the silk-papered walls, the white china a match for the wainscoting encircling the room, and the gold candlesticks gleaming in the sunlight.

The lump in Mary's stomach doubled in size. "Are you expecting more guests, Mrs. Hollenbeck?"

"None more important than you." She crossed the room and took Mary's elbow. "Please be seated. I'd like to introduce you to my friends."

Hardly knowing where to look, Mary allowed herself to be led deeper into the cheerful room.

As soon as she was seated—at the foot of the table, as the guest of honor—Mrs. Hollenbeck called, "Ladies. Please join us."

A steady stream of church-going types filed into the room. Mrs. Ellen Palmer, Mrs. Marilyn Pawlikowski, Emilia, Mrs. Abigail Snowe, and Mrs. Joan Babcock. Each of them paused to greet Mary with a smile and a word of welcome. She stammered through her responses, waiting for the moment their smiles turned to frowns and their fingers pointed to accuse her of harlotry.

But they all sat down, picked up their white silky napkins, and draped them over their laps. One chair remained empty. Was another lady coming late?

Mrs. Hollenbeck waited for her guests to be seated before settling into the chair at the head of the table. "Thank you all for coming, particularly on such short notice." She turned her smile on Mary. "Miss Lester, I'd like to introduce you to your benefactors."

"Excuse me?" The question was harsh, more suited to a brothel madam than the honored guest at a lady's afternoon tea.

"I understand your surprise." Mrs. Hollenbeck looked to her left and lifted her finger. "We're ready to be served now, Katherine."

"Yes, ma'am."

Mary jerked her attention to her right. A young brunette dressed in black with a white apron and a matching cap stepped to the side of the door the church ladies had entered. Five more similarly dressed girls paraded into the room. The first carried two pots of tea, which she set at the ends of the table. The second and third carried triple-tiered serving stands holding scones, crustless sandwiches, small cakes, and miniature china bowls topped with whipped cream. The fourth placed a large platter of fruit arranged in concentric circles near the center of the table. The final girl carried in a single layer cake on a crystal stand and set it next to the fruit platter.

As soon as the young ladies left the room, Mrs. Hollenbeck said, "Shall we pray?"

Every head bowed.

Mary followed suit, but only to be polite. God had abandoned her long ago, so she'd returned the favor.

The prayer consisted of thanking God for a whole passel of things He'd done nothing to earn. Friendship, blessings untold, and the sweet assurance of heaven.

"Amen."

Mary snapped up her head, prepared for them to pass around their condemnation. But the only things that came her way were tea and delicious treats.

Once the china plates were full, Mrs. Hollenbeck stood. "Ladies, I gathered you today because Miss Lester wanted to thank us for supporting her cause and because"—she looked directly at Mary—"if I interpreted your letter correctly, you think we need to be warned." Mrs. Hollenbeck gazed over the food-laden table as though she'd said nothing more sinister than, *Please tell us about your shopping trip to Billings*.

Mary swallowed the bite of chicken salad sandwich stuck halfway between her vocal chords and her stomach. "Am I to understand that the six of you know what I've been doing these past twelve years?"

Mrs. Hollenbeck smiled. "Some of us"—she glanced at Emilia—"have known about it for less time than others, but most of us have known from the beginning. You have assumed I alone was your benefactor. I wanted you to know the truth."

"How is it possible—?" Mary bit back the rest of her surprise. It wasn't polite to ask how a gaggle of women had kept such a delicious secret for years. One woman was somewhat believable, but six? Seven, if whoever was supposed to be filling the empty chair was included.

Mrs. Pawlikowski turned to look at Mary. "You likely aren't aware that I came to Helena before it was even a named city. In those days, we had an area of town we called Prostitute Alley. For a time, I feared I might become a resident there myself."

She would have made a fortune.

Marilyn Pawlikowski was in her late forties to early fifties and was by far the loveliest woman in the room. Like her sons, she had blond hair and those distinctive two-toned eyes. Men would have paid triple what any other girl could expect.

She raised her brows, the look in her blue-brown eyes making Mary feel that her private thoughts were as readable to Mrs. Pawlikowski as a written note. "I vowed that, were

I ever fortunate enough to be in a position to do so, I would help those women."

One by one, the rest of the ladies gave their reasons. It was all Mary could do to hold up her head when Emilia talked about joining the group after the misunderstanding about Finn Collins bringing her to Helena to sell into prostitution.

It wasn't a misunderstanding. It was a rumor Mary had started to protect her own skin.

Shame burned under her breastbone, radiating down her arms and up the back of her neck.

"Miss Lester, there are still good people in this world. We"—Mrs. Hollenbeck swung her hand in a wide arc to include all the ladies seated around the table—"also wanted you to know that, for the past twelve years, we have prayed weekly for you and for each of the girls we've sponsored."

The Bible talked about heaping coals on a person's head. Mary remembered it because she'd never figured out how being nice to someone made their head burn. She understood it now.

"In light of your decision to leave Helena," Mrs. Hollenbeck continued, "we wanted you to know that we intend to continue sponsoring girls at the academy in Kansas. We are creating the Lily Forsythe Scholarship Fund." Her voice splintered. She dropped her gaze to her plate.

Several of the other ladies did, too. Only Emilia and Mrs. Pawlikowski kept their heads up, but both looked at the empty chair.

Mary now understood its significance. It was where Lily Forsythe was supposed to be sitting. Her friends were honoring her memory by including her at the tea in the only way they could. Did they blame her for Mrs. Forsythe's death? Had Jonas said something in his wild ramblings— or his sane ones?

Mary never meant for anyone to die. Her aim had been to prevent bloodshed by keeping Jonas's quest for power in check. Poor man. Death would be better than to live half the time in a fantasy world where his beloved wife was in the next room fixing dinner or on her way home from the market, only to be stabbed with guilt and grief again and again and again when he came to his senses.

Mrs. Hollenbeck pressed a fist against her lips and cleared her throat. "We have heard about your commitment to educating the young women who pass through your house."

Mary shot a look at Emilia, who shook her head to say, *They didn't hear it from me.*

"In light of that," Mrs. Hollenbeck continued, "and knowing this day would eventually come, I took it upon myself several years ago to contact the headmistress of the academy. Should you desire to join the staff there as a teacher, a position is open to you. May I telegraph Mrs. Stillwell tomorrow letting her know to expect you?"

"What about my son, Nico?" Mary cringed at how ungrateful she sounded, but it was only because she was too shocked to keep her voice under control.

But Mrs. Hollenbeck didn't look offended. In fact, her smile was so warm, Mary's scalp began to burn afresh. "I purchased a home near the school in February of last year. It has been used as a guesthouse, but it's ready for you and Nico to occupy immediately should you decide to accept. It has three bedrooms and comes fully furnished."

February of last year was when Sheriff Simpson died getting a girl to the train line. They didn't know if he'd succeeded or failed before he was killed, and Mary had sent a letter like the one she had Nico deliver yesterday. The only difference being that she wasn't *sure* she was leaving town then.

And Mrs. Hollenbeck, God bless her, had made sure Mary had a safe place to hide. What was she supposed to do in light of that kind of generosity?

"Why?" Mary was glaring at the widow when she should be grateful—humble even—but no one had looked out for her interests since she was fourteen. "Why would you do all this for me?"

"Because someone once did the same for me."

Mary shot a look at Emilia, who shook her head again, another denial that she'd shared a part of Mary's life with the circle of ladies.

Eighteen months ago, when they'd first met so she could enlist Emilia's help in keeping the rescuing operation a secret, she'd asked Mary why she—a brothel owner—smuggled young girls out of prostitution. Her answer was, *Because it's what I wish someone had done for me.*

But she'd deserved her fate. Girls who disobeyed their parents and met men in alleys could hardly expect different. Even so, she preferred for people to think she'd chosen her life rather than fallen into it.

Mary narrowed her eyes, trying to bring into focus everything she knew about Mrs. Pauline Hollenbeck. "You were never a prostitute."

"You're right, I wasn't. But I was mired in a mess I couldn't get out of on my own, and a man rescued me."

"Are you getting religious on me, Mrs. Hollenbeck?"

"Would that be so bad, Miss Lester?"

Would it? Forty years of struggle and she was in as much need of rescue as she had been at fourteen. At fifty-four, she didn't have forty more years in her. Mary took in the faces of each of the women seated around the table. They had accepted her into their midst like a friend rather than turning up their noses like she wore the stench of her life into the breakfast room. They had prayed for her—and she believed it was *for* her rather than *about* her—for twelve years. They had paid for her girls to have a home and an education while they unlearned their fear.

She glanced at the empty chair. If nothing else, she owed it to Lily Forsythe to listen. So Mary shoved her antagonism toward God an inch to the left. "I suppose a little religion wouldn't be all bad."

Chapter Twenty-One

For the next five weeks, Hale buried himself in business. There were funeral arrangements, depositions, debates, the funeral itself, settling his uncle's debts, the Cannon v. Fisk land dispute, and the Harvest Festival, where he made the briefest appearance possible because he couldn't stand being surrounded by happy people whose lives weren't shattered by loss and betrayal.

He'd lost Yancey, too.

She came to the funeral, asked how he was doing, but didn't stand near him or offer any comfort beyond laying her hand on his forearm for an instant. The moment he tried to cover her hand with his, she drew back. She came to the office to collect flyers for distribution but always came with her mother or Carline, and they stayed mere minutes. She took his messages across the counter at the telegraph office—ones he didn't need to send and certainly not from the train depot—with the same professional courtesy she showed every customer.

He was at a loss to explain the change. It wasn't retaliation for the way he'd ignored her while gathering proof of his uncle's guilt.

His uncle. Hm. What to do about him?

Hale pushed away the thought. Uncle Jonas was in jail,

where he belonged. Only . . . at the funeral, Mrs. Hollenbeck had pulled Hale into a brief hug and whispered, "Be careful how you respond to this tragedy. People are watching."

He'd taken it as a warning about his candidacy, but was that the only reason?

The sound of the outer door opening made him check his appointment calendar. No one. There hadn't been any new clients since his uncle's treachery was revealed. Maybe it was time to leave Helena and start over somewhere else.

Mac walked through the double doors, his limp gone. "It's time we had a talk." He took off his hat. "What I've come to say won't take long, so please don't kick me out of your office before I've had a chance to say it."

Hale had never heard that particular tone of voice from his friend. It made him feel small. Petty. Guilty.

Mac tapped his hat against his thigh. "How often have you and I sat in this office and talked about people being free to make their own mistakes? Not the least of which was a year and a half ago when Emilia sat here"—he pointed at the wooden chair with his free hand—"determined to pay off Finn's debts when both of us knew she was better off going back to Chicago." Hale opened his mouth to answer, but Mac cut him off. "Don't answer, because that's not my point."

"Then what is?"

Mac tossed his hat on the chair next to him. Picked it back up. Stared at it for a long time before speaking. "I never realized that when you said people were free to make mistakes that the rest of the sentence was, 'And I'm free to cut them out of my life for making them.'"

"That's not—"

"Please don't interrupt me." Mac looked up, pain and pleading in his eyes. "Do you think you're the only one hurting over your Aunt Lily's death? We all are. Zoe Gunderson can't get through a single day without tears. Emilia, whom *I* think should be resting at this point in her pregnancy, is over at The Import Company every day so Isaak can care for his wife. Eli Alderson quit."

"Good."

Mac sighed and shook his head. "No. It's not good. He's a fine, intelligent young man who will make an excellent deputy given half the chance."

Hale dropped his gaze to his lap, the blood in his veins hot and throbbing.

But Mac wasn't done. "I'm speaking to you as a friend now, not as the sheriff. You need to decide what to do about your uncle, and then what to do about the rest of us who have let you down. We'd prefer not to be cut out of your life, but that choice is up to you."

Silence.

Hale raised his chin. "Are you quite finished?"

Mac picked up his hat. "I am."

As Hale opened his lips to declare his innocence, the memory of Yancey's face after their picnic stopped the words in his throat.

She'd asked him to find a way to take the good with the bad—to figure out what forgiveness looked like. Hale had shoved her request aside because there were more important matters needing his attention.

Which made him sound like his babbling uncle. *I'm an important man. I have important appointments. I must have important appointments. Where's my calendar?*

Hale sat back. Was he so sure of his own importance—of his own rightness—that he was becoming his uncle? A man who acted without counsel from friends. Who did what was right in his own eyes.

Something he'd blamed others for in the past.

His mother's choice to move to England, where she could start over as Countess of Devon, leaving behind her name and the shame of being cast aside for a younger woman, wasn't bad from her perspective. But after what his father had done, her decision had felt like a second abandonment to Hale. She'd reached out to him over the years with letters and Christmas cards. But he'd ignored them all.

Because he'd judged her unworthy.

Hale squeezed the bridge of his nose, his glasses lifting out of place. Not too long ago, Isaak Gunderson sat across the desk and admitted he had a problem with pride. Hale had agreed, all the while feeling superior because he'd never had a problem with that particular sin.

What a lie.

He was filled with it, judging himself a better person than those who failed to live up to his standards. In his fierce need for loyalty, he had cut off anyone whose betrayal ran too deep. His father for having feet of clay, his mother for putting her needs ahead of his, his uncle for falling into the trap of pursuing power, and Mac for bringing Eli Alderson along for the arrest.

Mac stood on the opposite side of the desk, waiting.

Yancey once said that speaking the truth was a sign of friendship. She was right. So was Mac.

Hale looked across his desk at his friend. "How did you do it? Reconcile with your mother?"

Mac sat and dropped his hat into his lap. "We're still working through that."

"How did you start?" Because Hale had no idea how to even begin. He'd not spoken with his mother in seven years.

"I had to accept her for who she is rather than who I wanted her to be." Mac rubbed the side of his neck. "Looking at it from her perspective, it makes sense. Who wants to be loved only if they live up to someone else's standards?"

"But shouldn't we want to be our best selves out of love?"

Mac chewed his bottom lip and stared absently out of the window for a long moment. "I think the difference"— he transferred his gaze to Hale—"is between *wanting* to be our best selves and being *required* to be. My mother wanted to be loved by a son. The way she's taken to Nico proves it. That boy waltzed into her life thinking she was the finest example of motherhood he'd ever seen."

It was probably true for him.

"Whereas I waltzed into her life intent on turning her into my ideal mother." Mac shook his head. "My standard was impossible, so she scorned it. Same thing happened with you and Yancey."

Hale sucked in a breath, preparing his heart to hear her name again. "What about us?"

"When Yancey first fell in love with you, it was the knight in shining armor you knew you weren't, so you pushed her away."

True.

Hale stared at his desk, the memory of Yancey's face reflecting in the polished mahogany. Since issuing her condition that he learn to forgive, she'd not brought it up again. She wasn't requiring him to change to earn her love—she'd proved that by staying behind to clean the bloodstain because she knew how hard it would be for him. By remaining faithful to her word to help with the campaign. By being his friend over the past two months, when he withdrew into himself to manage his hurt apart from her. But she wasn't giving him her heart until he fulfilled one of the requirements listed on her application to the Archer Matrimonial Company.

A Christian man.

She didn't want a knight in shining armor, she wanted a man who lived what he claimed to believe. Christ demanded forgiveness. Yancey was asking for no more—and no less.

Hale looked across the desk at Mac. "How do I get her back?"

"Yancey or your mother?"

"Both." And his father, too.

Mac picked up his hat and stood. "You already know the answer to that. Now you just need to put it into practice."

After Mac left, Hale took several blank pieces of paper from his top drawer and laid them on his desk. He dragged the mug of sharpened pencils closer because—for this—he was going to need all of them.

Eight pages later, he recopied his messy draft letter in ink onto six pages, sealed them in an envelope, and addressed it to his mother. He then withdrew several more sheets and started a second letter to his father. The final version was shorter—only two pages—and didn't include any information about Portia York or Yancey Palmer.

By the time he'd spilled his heart on the pages, he was exhausted and more lighthearted than he'd felt in years, just as his Aunt Lily had told him he would be ten years ago when he'd first met her.

Oh, how it hurt to remember her as she was while the picture of her death was still fresh. Would he ever be able to rid it from his mind or recall her wisdom without feeling its loss in the future?

We must take the good with the bad.

Yancey had said that, a repetition of wisdom from Carline's Uncle Eugene about the loss of her parents, but it applied to every situation.

With people.

With past, present, and future.

With himself, for how could a man work for the good of his family or community unless he first recognized his capacity for evil?

People were not perfect. They would make mistakes. They would make terrible choices, often knowing full well that their choices were wrong. Sometimes people would pay for their sins. Sometimes others would—as Aunt Lily had. God hadn't created the world to work this way. He'd created it perfect. Sinless. And beautiful.

But when Adam and Eve decided they could determine what was good vs. evil apart from God's standard, it broke that perfection. Ever since then, mankind had been making their own standards, doing what was right in their own eyes, and the pattern would repeat until God put an end to it.

Hale had grown up hearing the story of Creation, but until now, he'd never understood what was so wrong about humankind knowing the difference between good and evil. It wasn't the knowing, it was making the determination of which was which apart from God.

Including determining which people deserved forgiveness and which didn't.

What kind of husband and father would he truly be if either his wife or children could commit unpardonable sins, if he cut them out of his life because their betrayal ran too deep?

A miserable one, and one Yancey Palmer didn't deserve. Now he just needed to figure out how to convince her he'd changed, so he could start spending the rest of his life creating the happy home he'd always wanted. Not ideal. A happy one.

With her.

His first stop was to the post office, where he mailed his letters. He greeted people along the way, accepting their condolences on losing his aunt and their veiled questions to determine if he'd been aware of his uncle's illegal activities, as Harold Kendrick was suggesting to anyone who would listen—including a reporter who was more interested in headlines than truth. Hale forced himself to express gratitude for the condolences and repeated his innocence, including that he had helped gather evidence against his own uncle.

But as much as his blood pounded at their accusations, his next stop made sweat pool under his hat brim. He stepped into the downtown telegraph office. It was empty save for Yancey's father and brother. "Mr. Palmer. Might I have a word with you?"

Four weeks later

Had every soul in town decided they needed telegraph messages sent from the train depot at this exact moment? The line was out the door and the next train wasn't due for another half hour.

Yancey took a message and money from a stranger, and after she tapped out a notice of departure from Helena and imminent arrival in Billings to his business associate in Missoula, she delayed waiting on the next customer until she sent a request for help to the downtown office.

Less than a minute later, she was stunned when her father showed up. "How did you get here so quickly?"

Papa cut through the line in order to get behind the counter. "Did you send a request for help? Sure looks like half the town is here." There was a distinct twinkle in his eye. "Let me take over the machine while you wait on people."

Sure she was missing something but too busy to ask what, Yancey turned her attention to the next customer. "Mrs. Abbott, how can I help you today?"

Rather than handing over a message, the older woman looked around the room as though searching for someone.

"Mrs. Abbott?" When repeating her name didn't have any effect, Yancey stood on her tiptoes to lean over the counter and touch the woman's arm. "Mrs. Abbott? Did you have a message?"

A commotion at the doors leading to the train depot drew Yancey's attention. She could just see the top of a black hat—either Hale's or one just like it—as it bobbed and weaved through the crowd parting ahead of it, then reforming behind it. Yancey picked out specific people:

Carline and Windsor, Isaak and Zoe, Mac and Emilia, Mrs. Hollenbeck, and strangely, Yancey's mother and brother.

What were they all doing here?

Hale cleared the bulk of the crowd. He carried a large bouquet of red roses. Mrs. Abbott stepped away from the counter to give him her place. All conversations ceased, as though an invisible conductor cut them off with the wave of his baton.

Yancey's heart pounded, the beats filling her ears and rattling her vision. "What . . . what's going on?" She twisted around to look at her father. "What's happening?"

Papa just smiled. Four weeks ago, he'd announced that Hale had asked for permission to show he was learning how to forgive. Since then, he'd made dozens of small steps toward that goal, including meeting with Eli Alderson and encouraging him to rejoin the county sheriff's office.

But nothing had proved it more dramatically than when he'd arranged for his uncle to live under house arrest. Jail was a death sentence, and an asylum for the criminally insane was an even worse fate. Between paid nurses, a bevy of volunteers, and a telephone installed inside the house allowing instant connection to the sheriff's office if needed, the former judge would live out his days trapped between waiting for his beloved wife to come home from the market and the searing guilt of causing her death. Kendrick seized on Hale's decision to work for a more lenient sentence as proof he'd been complicit in the judge's crimes. Knowing it would cost him the election—which it had, as of a few nights ago—Hale stuck to the harder path.

"I don't care what anyone else thinks," he'd told Yancey, "as long as you believe me."

The temptation to pull him into her arms and kiss him would have proved overpowering were they not standing at the front of a huge crowd gathered outside City Hall as the election results were read.

Hale had also told her of the letters he'd mailed to both his parents in an effort to reconcile with them. There'd been no answer from his father, and it was too soon to expect one from his mother.

And with each evidence of change, Yancey fell more in love with Hale Adams in all his wonderful, flawed, glorious Hale-ness.

"Yancey Marilyn Palmer?" His voice sounded as wobbly as her legs felt.

She swallowed hard and turned to face him. "Y-yes."

"Would you come around to this side of the counter, please?" He inhaled and exhaled in shaky spurts. "I have something I need to ask you."

Had the roses not announced his intention, the dramatic sighs and fluttering hankies of the women, along with the wide grins of the men, would have.

Hale was going to *propose*.

She looked to her father again.

You have my blessing, he mouthed.

She gripped the edge of the counter, the gate, and the counter again as she worked her way closer to Hale. Should she clear the room, ask for the privacy she knew he'd prefer, or let him declare himself in front of so many people? She was still figuring out the answer when he knelt in front of her. "Oh, Hale. You don't need to do this."

His face fell.

"No. I mean, do this"—she waved her hands around, trying to encompass his posture and what it meant—"but not like this."

"Excuse me?"

Yancey sighed. Here she was, getting the proposal of her dreams, and she couldn't enjoy it because she knew how much it was costing Hale. He hated crowds. Or at least he once had.

From the opposite side of the counter, she heard her father whisper, "This was his idea, child. Let him carry it out."

This was Hale's idea? To propose in front of a hundred people? Which it wasn't, because only fifteen or twenty could cram into the space, but it sure felt like that many. Tears of gratitude, joy, unworthiness, and a whole host of other emotions Yancey couldn't identify at present stung her eyes. "I'm sorry, Hale. You were saying . . . ?"

He licked his lips and tried to open a folded piece of paper with only his left hand. He lifted the flowers. "Could you take these?" he whispered, a blush creeping into his cheeks.

The dear man. He'd planned out his speech but forgot to take into account his props.

Yancey took the flowers, raising them to her nose to inhale the sweet fragrance. While Hale fiddled with opening his speech, Yancey glanced over her shoulder at Carline, who nodded her understanding. A few months ago, the two of them had crushed the dry, brittle petals of the bouquet Yancey had saved because Hale had brought it as a hostess gift for her mother. This bouquet would be saved for as long as Yancey lived. She smiled at her friend, then returned her attention to the man kneeling before her.

He pushed his glasses into place with a finger. "Ten years ago, you knew we belonged together. I'm sorry it took so long for me to catch up. I'm also sorry for how I've ignored you and worse in the intervening years. I set myself up as judge and jury, interpreting your actions in light of how they affected me. I was wrong."

The tears spilled onto her cheeks. Yancey let them fall, afraid any movement on her part would wake her from what was beginning to feel like a dream.

"As my dismissal of you played out in front of the town, I thought it only right that I beg your forgiveness and ask you to allow me to make it up to you for the rest of our lives in front of them, too."

A sob broke from Yancey's throat. Was she supposed to say yes now? Or was there more?

When he reached into his pocket and withdrew a glittering ring, she sucked in a breath and held it. Hale stared up at her with humility and adoration pouring from his brown eyes. "Yanccy Marilyn Palmer, would you do me the very great honor of consenting to be my wife?"

Epilogue

Four months later

Yancey smoothed the white satin skirt of her dress. Designed by Charles Frederick Worth, it featured a deep ruffle along the hem, a modest bustle trailing into a three-foot train, and a fitted bodice decorated with seed pearls, lace, and fabric roses in pinks, reds, and purples with green leaves. When they were younger, Yancey and Carline had sat on the floor, magazines laid on the floor between them, and dog-eared the pages of elegant dresses never once thinking they would actually get to wear one of them.

Mama had conspired with Hale's mother—a bona fide countess from England—to surprise Yancey with the custom-made dress two weeks ago when the Countess of Devon, her husband, and their six-year-old son arrived in Montana for the wedding. Mama had sent the countess lace taken from the dress she'd worn when she married Papa to be worked into the design.

Something old and something new.

Mama lifted the veil trimmed with seed pearls—the

same one her sister, Luanne, had worn—from the trunk. "Are you ready, my dear?"

Yancey smiled. "I've been ready for years."

As her mother pinned the veil over her hair, Luanne and Carline reentered the bridal room—a converted Sunday school room in the basement of the church. Wearing a dark pink dress and a smile that hadn't left her face since Windsor had declared his love for her, Carline pressed both hands against her cheeks. "Oh, Yancey. You look like a fairy princess."

"I feel a bit like one, if you want to know the truth. I've pinched my wrist so many times today, I think I'm going to have a permanent bruise."

Luanne, wearing a deep purple dress, came close and touched the veil, a nostalgic smile on her face. The veil was the same one she'd worn when she wed Roy.

Something borrowed.

Luanne sighed. "Pastor Neven has given the signal to begin."

Mama stepped aside. "Turn around now, dear, and take a look at yourself."

Yancey obeyed, inhaling sharply when she caught her reflection in the full-length mirror her brother had hauled down the stairs with much grumbling. "I doubt Hale will recognize me."

Mama appeared in the background. "He will think you're beautiful."

Luanne appeared on the other side. "Even if you were wearing a burlap bag."

Carline poked her head in the space between Luanne and Yancey's shoulders. "But he won't be happy if you're late."

Yancey laughed, the nervous fluttering in her stomach easing. She turned around, careful of the dress's ruffled train. "Thank you—all of you—for everything you've done to prepare me for this day."

Mama shook a finger under Yancey's nose. "Don't you dare make me weep. I'm holding on by a thread as it is."

"Weep all you want." Yancey pulled her mother into a light hug.

Knock, knock, knock. "You about ready in there?" Papa's voice came from the hallway outside the room.

Luanne and Carline headed for the door. Luanne reached it first, opening it to allow Papa entrance.

Mama took a step back. She tugged the veil back in place. "There. You look perfect." It was time for her to join the processional party, but she remained.

"Was there something else?" Yancey prompted.

Mama took Yancey's hands. "We know Hale as well as any parent could hope upon the marriage of their daughter, but I'm going to ask once more on principle. Are you sure you want to marry him?"

The first time the question was asked, Yancey had answered flippantly. This time she answered from the deepest place of her heart. "I have never been surer of any decision I've ever made."

Papa stepped beside Mama and put his hand around her waist. "There, my dear. Are you satisfied?"

"I am." Mama turned and patted her husband's cheek. "I felt the same way when I married you."

Yancey blinked to keep the tears at bay.

Carline pushed between them. "You will not make the bride cry."

Mama waved her hands at her face like she was trying to dry her cheeks. "I'm going." She hurried out of the room, leaving the door ajar.

Papa turned so he stood at Yancey's side and pushed out his elbow. "Shall we?"

Yancey placed her gloved hand in the crook of his arm. "I am."

"Not without this." Carline reached sideways to retrieve a bridal bouquet of pink and red roses interspersed with purple clematis and white Madonna lilies. She handed it to Yancey. "And there's one more thing." Carline turned her wrist and pulled a long blue ribbon from her sleeve. "Something told me to rescue this when you threw away your Hale treasures."

"My something blue," Yancey whispered as she took the satin ribbon into her hand. She'd forgone the final accessory of the tradition, rationalizing that the memory of her blue hair ribbon from the day she met Hale was enough. To hold it in her hands broke the tenuous hold on her emotions. She let go of her father's arm and pulled Carline into a hug while crying happy tears. "Thank you, my sweet friend."

"No, thank you. I have family still and a new family to look forward to because of you," Carline whispered. "But if you don't stop crying, I'm going to pinch you."

Yancey laughed and let go. She wiped her tears, then held up the ribbon. "Where am I going to put this?"

"If I may?" Papa took it from her, then lifted her left hand and tied the satin around her wrist. "Let this remind you that today you join your life to Hale. Love him well, teach him how to love you, and may the God who loves you both bind you close to each other and to Him."

"Amen," Luanne whispered.

"Oh Lord, hear our prayer," Carline added.

Yancey broke into tears again. True to her threat, Carline pinched Yancey's forearm. Not hard, but enough to make her stop crying. She brought her emotions under control with several deep breaths. When she was calmer, she took one last peek at herself in the mirror and wiped traces of her tears from her cheeks. "All right. I'm ready."

Papa offered his arm again. Yancey took it, and they followed Carline and Luanne out of the room, up the stairs, and down the aisle.

Hale stood still as a statue, only his hands moving as he clenched and released his fingers. He was dressed in a black suit, his blond hair freshly cut and brushed away from his high forehead. Behind his glasses, his eyes were solemn with a touch of—was it awe?

Ten-year-old Yancey resurfaced in a giggle which twenty-one-year-old Yancey ruthlessly suppressed. Still, she had to appreciate the irony. Every childish dream she'd ever imagined was coming true in this moment.

Mac and Isaak stood to Hale's right. Mac kept sneaking peeks at his wife and baby Finn. Isaak grinned and stood tall, his demeanor different now that his gentle bride had convinced him to relax and enjoy life a bit more.

Wishing to capture every moment of this perfect day, Yancey peered through her filmy veil to take in all the well-wishers crowded into the church pews.

Jakob and his new fiancée, Colette, were sitting next to her aunt, Mrs. Hollenbeck.

Mr. and Mrs. Pawlikowski smiled like they were the proud parents of the principals.

Antonia Archer and her mother smiled like they were responsible for the nuptials, which—to be fair—they were. Somewhat.

Roy held eight-month-old Grace, who had her chubby hands entangled in his beard.

Geddes stood next to Mama, both of them beaming.

The Earl and Countess of Devon stood on the other side of the church, Hale's mother pressing a handkerchief to the corners of each eye in turn. Their son, Edward, stood at attention beside his mother, though he kept looking around as if he was trying to find an escape.

Beside them were two empty places, one reserved in memory of Lily Forsythe and the other for the man Jonas Forsythe once was.

Next to the open seats, Hale's father stood alone. His second family had been invited, but he'd chosen to journey without them. He'd arrived two days ago and was heading back home tomorrow. The reunion between him and Hale had been stilted, but Yancey appreciated the effort both men were making to repair their bond.

In the next moment, she stepped beyond the pews and had eyes only for her groom. He moved to stand next to her father.

"Who gives this woman to be married to this man?" Pastor Neven recited the familiar opening question of the ceremony.

Papa cleared his throat and sniffed. "Her mother and I." He took Yancey's right hand, placed it in Hale's left, then stepped back to sit beside Mama and Geddes.

Hale squeezed Yancey's hand, and they stepped forward in unison.

The ceremony took on a dream-like quality. Yancey heard Hale vow to love, honor, and cherish her. She spoke her vows to him, repeating Pastor Neven's words verbatim. She handed her bouquet to her sister so Hale could slip the warm gold band on her ring finger. They prayed. And then were pronounced husband and wife.

She was *Mrs.* Hale Adams.

"You may now kiss the bride."

Hale lifted the veil between them. The look of awe was more pronounced than at the beginning of the ceremony. Yancey placed her hand on his chest, an instinctive gesture she didn't understand until she felt his heart beating under her palm. His heart was now hers. It beat for her and her alone.

He leaned closer. She lifted her face to welcome his kiss, shifting her hand from his chest to wrap it around his neck and draw him closer. "My precious Yancey," he whispered an instant before his lips claimed hers.

She melted into him, repeating her vows without words. For better or worse, this perfectly imperfect man was hers to love and cherish for the rest of her days. She wrapped her other hand around his neck so she could touch the blue ribbon tied around her wrist.

Oh, how she loved a happy ending.

Authors' Note

This was a difficult book to write. We did not take lightly the deaths of Carline's parents or Lily Forsythe. Sometimes terrible things happen which have no rhyme or reason, and sometimes they happen because of a choice we make or someone else makes that affects us. While we love our happily ever afters as much as the next person, we also know that real life includes painful events. We intentionally skimmed over much of the grieving process—this is a romance after all—to emphasize the point of taking the good and the bad in people and in situations. That theme ran through not only this book but the entire series in the characters of our warring judge and brothel madam.

Much of Jonas Forsythe's character was formed after a conversation Becca had with Dr. Ellen Baumler about real Montana politics and William Clark. He was a huge advocate of Anaconda as the capitol city and bought votes with five dollar bills, although not counterfeits to our knowledge. He did say, "I've never bought a man who wasn't for sale," which we paraphrased. He also owned a mine and used convicts for free labor. With such a wealth of chicanery, we didn't have to make up much.

As for Madame Lestraude, we patterned her after Josephine Airey (aka, "Mary Welch" and "Chicago Joe") who owned several businesses—both legitimate and illegitimate—in Helena. She was one of its wealthiest residents in her heyday. In his autobiography, *The Land of My Dreams,* Phil Weinard wrote: "She (Chicago Joe) used to say that she had no one she could trust . . . I would often find gold pieces under the sofa or behind a door, and other out-of-the-way places." That little tidbit showed up in *The Promise Bride* and accounts for "Mr. Green's" loyalty in this story. Joe was a shrewd businesswoman who figured out ways around the law. When charged with operating a "hurdy gurdy house" in 1886, her lawyer argued that the music in Joe's saloon was provided by a violin, a piano, and a cornet, and not by a hurdy gurdy—a boxed, stringed instrument played by turning a crank. The jury returned a verdict of "not guilty" (from *Montana: The Magazine of Western History*). Maison de Joie was a real brothel owned by Lillie McGraw. We chose to use it instead of one of Joe's houses because we liked the juxtaposition of a brothel called a House of Joy.

One final historical tidbit: The St. Peter's Hospital we described opened in 1887. An operating room was added in 1889. It was built by women who used their considerable wealth and influence to improve the lives of everyone around them. The hospital superintendent was a real person. Her full name was Miss Georgia C. Young. She graduated from the Nurse's Training School at Connecticut State Hospital and managed St. Peter's from 1886 until 1906.

We hope you have enjoyed this series, including the eBook novellas. We'd love to hear from you, so find us online at www.GinaWelborn.com or www.BeccaWhitham.com.

DON'T MISS

From the Montana Territory to the farthest railroad stops across the magnificent West, love has a way of finding those who need it the most . . .

ANYWHERE WITH YOU
A Montana Brides eNovella

Available everywhere eBooks are sold.

Enjoy the following excerpt from *Anywhere With You* . . .

Chapter One

Sometimes one is guided by what they say of themselves, and very frequently by what other people say of them, without giving oneself time to deliberate and judge.

—JANE AUSTEN, Sense and Sensibility

Denver, Colorado
Fitzroy estate
Thursday, August 9, 1888, approaching midnight

"Letty, what"—*sniff*—"what did you"—*sniff*—"say?"

At the sound of Beatrix's heartbroken voice, Colette Vanderpool-Vane grabbed a second novel off the shelf, then descended the library ladder. "There's more to life than this, and I have two books that will prove it to you."

"Jane Austen does *not* have the answer to everything."

"She was right when she wrote, 'Know your own happiness.'"

A pitiful groan reverberated from Beatrix. "You quote Jane Austen because, like her, your heart has never been ripped out of your chest by a mons—" Another round of wails drowned out the last syllable in *monster*.

Colette stepped off the ladder. Her heart ached as she stared down at her dearest friend crying prostrate on the

Persian rug, an uncorked bottle of wine in one hand, a corkscrew in the other. For all Beatrix's claim that she'd spend the rest of the evening at home drowning her sorrows away, neither of them had anything to drink or eat since leaving the opera. Of course, they'd had no choice but to flee at intermission after the callous Henderson Smyth abruptly announced his wish to end his and Beatrix's engagement.

Colette tossed the novels into Beatrix's favorite reading chair. Life was too short for Beatrix to waste another second bemoaning a lost future as Mrs. Henderson Smyth. His actions tonight proved him to be the cad Colette knew him to be, and what Bea had refused to see because of his ability to say what a person wanted to hear.

With determination and force, Colette pried the corkscrew then the wine bottle from her friend's grip. "Come on, get up. We're going downtown."

Beatrix turned her head toward Colette. "Why?"

"It's time you see how big the world really is." Colette wiped away Beatrix's tears. "Uncle Schelley's building has the best views in Denver."

"Do you have a key?"

"We can sneak up the fire escape."

"But that's"—Beatrix's voice lowered despite them being alone in the library—"trespassing."

"Uncle Schelley is my godfather. He won't mind." And Colette knew he wouldn't. For all practical purposes the Schellenberg building was hers, since she was the main inheritor of his estate, so she wouldn't really be trespassing.

"Letty, did you forget that Denver has a curfew?"

Of course she hadn't forgotten. She'd considered every potential hindrance to her cheer-up-Beatrix plan. "The curfew doesn't apply to us."

Beatrix's brow furrowed in thought. "I'm pretty sure the mayor said *anyone* under the age of twenty-five caught out between midnight and five a.m. would be arrested."

"No, only gang members and hooligans," Colette clarified. "And we are neither."

Besides, the curfew was wrong at best and discriminatory at worst—reasons enough to ignore the ordinance. She read the papers. She knew not all crime was committed in the evening or was done by those under the age of twenty-five. She also knew full well that some city officials and police earned graft from underworld bosses and brothel owners, like Soapy Smith and Mattie Silks.

"Come on." Colette nudged Beatrix into standing. "Trust me, Bea. We can sneak in and out and no one—not even your parents—will be the wiser. You need this. Your heart needs to experience something wonderful." Seeing the world—and Bea's romantic future—was far grander than one little man named Henderson Smyth.

Beatrix's eyes welled with tears. "You would do this for me?"

Colette touched her dear friend's tear-moistened cheek. "I would do anything to make you happy again." She paused, thought about what she'd committed herself to, then amended her pronouncement with: "Except murder." She grinned mischievously. "I have to draw a line somewhere."

The corners of Beatrix's lips eased up a fraction. Not a smile per se. Nor did her desolate expression change any, but for the first time since Henderson Smyth shattered his better-than-he-deserved fiancée's heart, Colette saw—and felt—a spark of hope. Today was the beginning of Beatrix Fitzroy's future, and a good future it would be . . . if Colette had any say about it.

Monday morning, August 20

Colette folded the quilt, then wedged it between the jail bars separating her cell from Nehemiah Foster's. "From one friend to another."

Mr. Foster's eyes grew watery. "Thank you." He stretched his mammoth hand out to her.

She clasped his hand between her equally grimy ones. "Please write that letter to your wife."

"Ruth won't forgive me."

"She may already have and is merely waiting for you to say you're sorry."

A throat cleared.

Mr. Foster's gaze flickered left, to the police officer standing outside the door to Colette's cell, and he withdrew his hand from her hold. "You do right, Miss Colette, and stay out of trouble, you hear?"

"I hear." And she fully intended to. Of course, what she should do and what she did didn't always match up. Which was why she'd spent the last ten days in jail. Eleven, if one wanted to count the night she and Beatrix were arrested.

She should've—

She halted the thought because, if her godfather taught her anything, it was that life was too short to live with re-grets and *should've*s.

Colette raised her chin. "If trouble finds me, Mr. Foster, I will do as Mr. Shakespeare advised—'The robbed that smiles, steals something from the thief.'" Pleased with her clever response, she strolled through the cell door that Sergeant John Phillips held open while wearing a look on his face as if he'd rather be anywhere but guarding the city jail today.

"You're not funny," John Phillips said—more like grumbled—as he walked next to her.

"That's mean of you to say."

"I don't get paid to be nice to you."

Colette winced. How could he say that? She'd been a dear friend to John Phillips since her father had hired his father to be the gardener of their estate. She'd helped him win the love of his life. She'd never been anything but sweet to him. Yet the moment he locked her in a jail cell, he'd been cold and distant. Maybe something else was bothering him.

Was that gray at his temple? Colette tilted her head to the side for a better look at John Phillips's close-cropped black hair. Twenty-two was too young to start graying. The poor dear seemed burdened. A wife and children did that to a man. Or so Papa claimed was the reason his ginger hair had been gray since Colette could remember, which meant a majority of Papa's burdens came during her siblings' maturation years and not hers.

She lowered her voice so no one else in the jail would hear. "Did you and Millie have a spat?"

He gave her a flat-eyed, don't-meddle-in-my-life stare.

Before she could respond, he impolitely nudged her into the main office. A trio of police officers standing next to a desk stopped talking. They all looked her way. Chief Lomery exited his office. The four men took turns shaking her hand and wishing her well, a surprise considering how uncordial Chief Lomery and half his police force had been to her after she'd insisted she could not in good conscience pay the fine for trespassing or the one for breaking curfew, nor would she pay any other fine they thought they could get away with charging her with. Nor would she accept anyone—not even her godfather—paying the fines.

"Under the circumstances," Chief Lomery finished saying.

Colette gave him a gracious smile. "Actually, sir, Uncle Schelley had wanted to dismiss the charges against—"

"She understands," John Phillips said, cutting off her defense, "and she won't make the same mistake again." He gripped her elbow, then rudely pulled her down a side corridor leading to an iron-covered, wooden door.

Colette raised her chin. "You certainly know how to make a girl feel welcome."

"You're still not funny."

"I wasn't trying—"

"Stop!" He jerked the door open. After they stepped outside, he slammed the door behind them. "You need to take life more seriously."

More seriously? Colette blinked as her eyes adjusted to the afternoon sunlight. "I lasted ten days in jail without my parents' financial aid or emotional assistance. I survived on two meals a day and slept on a tick cot with nothing but the quilt Beatrix was only allowed to give to me only after she paid a minor fee, which we all know was a bribe. To top it off, I endured a lack of toiletries and luxuries to which I am accustomed. Not once did I cry. Not once did I complain. Nor did I accept my godfather's willingness to come to my aid."

She paused to give John Phillips a moment to praise her fortitude, integrity, and good cheer.

He continued to glare.

Marriage to one of the sweetest girls in Denver had done nothing to improve his demeanor.

Leaving him to his sullenness, Colette turned to study the unmarked carriage parked in the alley. How strange. The gray-haired driver stayed on the driver's bench, his gaze forward as if he had no intention of jumping down to open the door for her. She understood not sending the mahogany carriage with the Vanderpool-Vane crest; no reason to risk ruining the family coach with her stench. Why not send their usual coachman? Why send someone she'd never met?

Understanding increased the hammering in her chest.

Uncle Schelley had warned her of this. Oh, she'd entertained—*feared*—the possibility that her parents wouldn't escort her home in light of no communication from them these last ten days, but reason and logic enabled her to discount the likelihood for the sole fact her parents loved her. Other than an occasional admonishment, she'd never experienced any great punishment from them like what her older siblings oft claimed they'd endured.

Colette stared at the door lever. Her feet were frozen, unable to move the final five steps toward what would confirm her heartbreak. "Give Millie my love," she said to John Phillips in a weak voice. Not weak. Tired. And grimy.

"I will." He sighed loudly. "Colette, I didn't think you had it in you to last a day in jail."

Colette winced. "You really didn't think I could last a day in jail?"

"Millie championed you. She insisted you would stick through it until the end because you are determined, brave, and resourceful."

Of course Millie would be supportive. She was a good and faithful friend . . . who, despite being married to a police officer, hadn't been allowed to give Colette food without paying a "minor fee," which Colette had insisted Millie not pay.

"I can't figure out why my wife adores you." John Phillips huffed a breath. "All I see is a girl who lives like not all rules apply to her."

"If a rule is foolish, why should anyone follow it?"

"I can think of myriad reasons. The biggest problem is when your disregard for the rules causes harm to others."

Colette winced. "I wasn't trying to cause anyone harm."

"You never try to. You do it because you don't think about the consequences first before you act." John Phillips sighed again. "I know you're going to do whatever you want. Just don't break the law again," he ordered.

"I won't." After giving him a hug, she eyed the hired carriage her parents had sent to usher her home. This empty carriage would not break her.

Yet her heart just ached. How could her parents do this to her?

Blinking away the tears she refused to shed, Colette crossed the alley. The door opened the moment she reached for the lever. She smiled. "You came for me!"

"Get in," Father said tersely.

She hurried inside.

Mother and Father sat on the bench. Neither smiled. Neither looked as happy to see her as she was to see them.

Colette sat opposite them.

Mother raised a hankie to her nose. "This is going to be a long drive home."

"Indeed," muttered Father. He tapped his cane on the carriage roof, and the carriage jerked forward. His hard gaze settled on Colette. "This will go better for you if you don't speak."

Chapter Two

I have not wanted syllables where actions have spoken so plainly.

      —JANE AUSTEN, Sense and Sensibility

The Vanderpool-Vane estate
That evening

Colette used her fork to flake the crust of her apple pie as her talkative parents sat at each end of the dining table while an equally chatty Robert sat opposite her in the middle. From the moment the unmarked carriage had arrived at the house, not another word had been spoken about Colette's ten days in jail, or her arrest for trespassing. Not a single maid or the housekeeper or even her ever-faithful beau Robert, once he'd arrived for supper, had mentioned Colette's absence. Everyone behaved as if she'd never been away.

Why hadn't anyone missed her? She'd missed them.

Colette's fork tinged the side of her plate. She waited for her parents or Robert to look her way; neither did. She'd chosen to wear her favorite emerald and sapphire silk gown because it made her feel like a beautiful peacock, despite her carrot-colored hair and freckled face. Not even her favorite gown could boost her mood, not when Father's lecture from the carriage continued to grate at her nerves.

Our parental duty was to let you suffer the consequences.

Let her? Colette released a soft *pffft* in response.

She *chose* to stay in jail instead of paying the fine. She *chose* not to contact her parents for help. She *chose* not to let Uncle Schelley come to her aid. She *chose* to accept responsibility for breaking curfew in order to climb to the roof of Uncle Schelley's building because she knew a viewing of the vast night sky from the tallest building in Denver would cheer up her dear and precious Beatrix after the crushing heartbreak her fiancé had inflicted.

The only begging Colette had ever done in her life was done asking Chief Lomery to release Beatrix because she was an unwitting accomplice.

That alone was enough to earn anyone's admiration.

Except William and Amity Vanderpool-Vane's.

Why can't you be sensible for once?

Mother's words haunted Colette. She stared absently at the pie she'd yet to eat. She was sensible. She was twenty-two years old, owned two farms, and was a patron to a handful of artists because she recognized their potential. Her leadership involvement in six charities should be enough to prove to her parents that she had maturity and good sense. And she had goals. She alone had the vision for an exclusive art studio in Denver to provide an avenue for local artists to showcase their works.

Her parents lacked vision because they didn't see beyond their own lives or social class. Besides their regular gifts to the church and occasional donations to social fund-raisers, her parents never did anything *unto the least of these* as Jesus commanded. They never gave aid at the orphanage or served meals to the impoverished. They never delivered food to the widows.

And yet she did all of that . . . and did it without expectation of praise for her actions.

Father finished the joke he was telling.

Mother and Robert laughed.

Colette sighed. If her parents could choose between her and Robert as their child, they'd choose him. Why not? He would never do anything to earn a lecture like the ones her parents had cruelly dispensed in the carriage.

Why can't you be sensible for once?

Mother would never say that to Robert. She would never have reason to.

Robert Moring, Esq. Reputable lawyer. Youngest deacon in the church. Admired by members of both political parties, he'd served on former Governor Eaton's staff and then on Governor Adams's until he accepted the position of campaign organizer for Job Cooper's gubernatorial bid. Her parents adored Robert, and not solely because he shared their political views. He never dominated a conversation. Never gave the impression he thought he was better than anyone. He was as comfortable with children as he was those his age or his parents' or grandparents' ages.

Robert was a true gentleman.

Colette tapped her fork against her pie. During their two years of courting, not once had they ever discussed love or marriage. Did he not think she would agree to marry him?

She would . . . wouldn't she?

She'd never thought about marrying him until now. She couldn't know what she would answer until he proposed. She did know what she wanted was a passionate, forgiving, and empowering love like the one her parents shared.

Colette studied Robert's comfortable face. Would she

want to wake up to that pleasantry for the rest of her life? Of course. If he was like his father and grandfather, he would age well, although unlike her father, Robert would likely bald. For all his virtues, Robert was too cautious. He never took risks. He never leaped before looking. Never did anything silly just for the fun of it. While no one would ever describe Robert as having a zest for life, she could do worse than him.

Why can't you be sensible for once?

"Oh, Mother," Colette said under her breath. She laid her fork on her dessert plate and looked at her father. "I've given your lecture some thought."

Her words brought a halt to the conversation in the room.

She continued with, "I apologize for bringing dishonor to the Vanderpool-Vane name. First thing in the morning, I will apologize to Uncle Schelley for trespassing on his property and apologize to Beatrix for enlisting her to join my"—she sought the exact descriptor her father had used—"*imprudent* action." She looked at her mother. "You're right about the purchase of my donkey farm being impetuous." Impetuous it was. Insensible it wasn't. "I will do the wise thing and hire a manager."

"Darling, I specifically said the wise thing was to *sell it*." Mother's chin lifted. "As I also told you to do with that llama farm you wasted money on. At the rate you spend money, your inheritance will be gone before you reach thirty. Will that be fair to your husband and to your children?"

Colette winced. She should say something to Mother about how hurtful her words were. But Mother continued to look so disappointed and so sure of her low opinion of Colette that she had to look away. This moment was about proving to her parents that she was a grown woman who made mature decisions.

"Father, I've only owned the donkey farm for two weeks,"

she said and hated how her voice trembled with emotion, "but I believe time will prove it, as with my llama farm, to be a wise investment. Would you advise me on how I go about hiring a manager?"

He tugged on the pointed edge of his orange-and-gray beard. "I will. Come to my office tomorrow after you pay your apologies to your godfather and to Beatrix."

"Thank you. I need you and Mother to realize that opening an art studio isn't a passing fancy." Colette noted the skeptical looks her parents exchanged. "I've dreamed of this studio since I was a child. I have the finances to support the artists who have the skills I wish I had. In the carriage, you said I needed to start having long-term goals. This studio and my eventual art museum *are* lifelong passions for me. I am committed to this and will do whatever necessary to prove to you both my commitment."

Mother shook her head. "You have no idea what a lifelong commitment requires."

Father's slight nod in agreement tore at Colette more than his harsh lecture in the carriage had. What would it take for them to realize she was a committed person? Become more like Robert would be a start.

Realizing the answer sat across from her, Colette turned a sweet smile upon Robert. "A girl could not ask for a more gentlemanly suitor. That is why I agree we should marry. Would you like to have the ceremony before or after the election?"

His unreadable expression stayed focused on her as he took his leisure in thinking. "You have no preference for *when* we marry?"

What an odd question. Not one she would've had, but it was one typical of Robert and his I'm-too-busy-planning-tomorrow-to-enjoy-the-moment-today way of thinking.

She shook her head. "No preference. I'm ready whenever you are."

His smile seemed strangely suspicious, totally unlike Robert. "Then how about this Sunday?"

Mother's face paled to match her ivory-and silver dinner dress. "A six-day engagement is unacceptable. People will talk about the marriage being a . . . necessity."

"It can be a small ceremony," Robert said in that serene voice of his, clearly unfazed by Mother's insinuation. "We could have a celebration ball at a later date."

"You may as well elope," Father remarked.

Elope? Colette forced a smile to cover her horror.

She couldn't elope. She had things to do, such as purchase train tickets for a forget-about-your-broken-engagement shopping trip to St. Louis with her dear, sweet Beatrix. Not to mention Colette's charity work. Someone needed to help Millie come up with ideas for the autumn fund-raiser to help Reverend Layfield start a mission to the natives living near Grand Junction. No one enjoyed brainstorming ideas like Colette did. She also needed to meet with the local artists whose work she was supporting.

She sipped her coffee as she sought for a way to explain why she and Robert needed to wait at least three months to marry. Or six. Robert needed time to focus on Mr. Cooper's gubernatorial campaign, and then came the holidays. Should Mr. Cooper win, like his processors, he would appoint Robert to his staff, and Robert would need time to adjust to a new job. Nine months would be better to wait to marry. No, a year because their friends needed time to grow used to seeing them as the future Mr. and Mrs. Robert Moring.

A year engagement minimum.

They should wait to marry until next summer.

But if she said that, in light of how she'd proclaimed

she was "ready whenever he was," she would look fickle. Fickle was another word for not taking life seriously.

Colette took another slow sip of her coffee.

"Mrs. Vanderpool-Vane," Robert said, breaking the uncomfortable silence, "what date would you recommend?"

Mother grinned in delight. "I've always loved Christmas weddings." She pushed her chair back and stood. "Robert, please join me in the parlor. We should consult my calendar for open dates."

He looked at Father.

"Go on, Rob. I'd like to have a few moments to speak to my daughter alone."

"Of course, sir." Robert dutifully followed Mother out of the dining room, without a backward glance at Colette. Mother's "I'm leaning toward mid-December" were the last words Colette heard before they disappeared from view.

She shifted in her chair to face her dour-faced father. "Why do you look displeased with me? I listened to your rebuke and am doing all you asked of me."

Father laid his napkin on the table. "Follow me."

Colette stood and obeyed, following him out the dining room, down the foyer, and outside onto the patio. He wrapped her arm around his before leading her into the garden. Colette steadied herself for a lecture on if she was sure she was making the right decision because her actions seemed hasty and ill-conceived, which was typical of her, although she knew that not to be true because many of her decisions came after long periods of inward reflection.

"Your mother and I are concerned that you're too unfocused with your compassion."

That was an abrupt change of topic. "I don't understand."

"Having wealth has allowed you to throw a little compassion here and a little compassion there without it doing much good . . . but also without it doing much harm."

Colette raised her chin in defiance. "The people who are helped by my charity work would disagree."

"They probably would," he conceded. "That compassionate heart of yours wanted to cheer up Beatrix, so you broke the law. You saw llamas being mistreated, so you bought a farm, and you did the same for a score of donkeys. The more you love, the more your capacity to love grows. How many local artists do you support so they can spend their day on creating future masterpieces?"

"Not enough."

His gaze flickered toward hers. "What will those llamas, donkeys, and artists do when you lose interest in helping them? Before you answer, think about all the projects you've started and resolutions you've made and never finished."

Colette trailed her fingers along a flowering hedge. Too many unfinished projects and resolutions littered her path. Why focus on them? That was yesterday. Today she was a new person. "Father, I can hire a manager *if* the task is beyond my abilities or *if* I lose interest. But think about how long I've been doing charity work."

"Even when you were a child, you gave your toys away."

"My interest in helping artists will never waver." She waited for Father to acknowledge he believed her, but he said nothing more as they strolled around the garden.

Colette breathed deep, inhaling the sweet pine and floral scent, listening to the sounds of insects chirping. She loved their family garden as much as she loved the Rocky Mountains. Oh, she enjoyed an occasional holiday in San Francisco. She'd had as much fun in Portland as she had during visits to Santa Fe, New Orleans, and New York City. Never did she want to live anywhere but here. Near her friends. Near family.

"Let's have a seat." Upon reaching an iron bench, Father waited to sit until after Colette did. He crossed one leg over the other and rested an arm on the back of the bench. "It's a beautiful night."

Colette studied the star-dotted sky. "It's so peaceful. Sitting here, I see trees and mansion rooftops. On the roof of Uncle Schelley's building, Beatrix and I saw nothing but open sky. The world is so much bigger when one's view isn't limited."

"Indeed it is." He shifted on the bench to face her. "The world is so much bigger once you see what real hurt and real poverty in life circumstances looks like. That's why I want to give you a glimpse of what a focused charity looks like. And when you return, if you still want to open an art studio and a museum, I will help finance them."

"What do you mean by a *focused* charity?"

His voice softened. "Several years ago, the two-week anniversary train trip that your mother and I take became more than a holiday for us. It's a cover."

Her parents doing something secretive? How intriguing . . . and yet unbelievable. Her parents were some of the least exciting people she knew.

Father, though, looked utterly serious.

Colette leaned forward. "A cover for what?"

Connect with U(s)

Visit us online at
KensingtonBooks.com
to read more from your favorite authors, see books
by series, view reading group guides, and more.

Join us on social media

for sneak peeks, chances to win books and prize packs,
and to share your thoughts with other readers.

facebook.com/kensingtonpublishing
twitter.com/kensingtonbooks

Tell us what you think!

To share your thoughts, submit a review,
or sign up for our eNewsletters, please visit:
KensingtonBooks.com/TellUs.